What they say about Kate Atkinson:

'An exceptionally **funny**, quirky and **bold** writer' *Independent on Sunday*

'One of the country's most **innovative**, **exciting** and **intelligent** authors' *Scotsman*

'Kate Atkinson is **brilliantly**, defiantly **playful** with the stuff of fiction' *New Statesman*

'A **brilliant** and **profoundly original** writer' *Daily Express*

'**Funny**, bracingly **intelligent** . . . a genuinely **surprising** novelist' *Guardian*

What the critics wrote about
Started Early, Took My Dog

'As ever, Kate Atkinson's prose is diamond-cut to twinkle and slice by turns. Her playful sense of humour dances round the darkness of her themes. She skips through the difficult steps required to balance the reader's need for satisfying (and surprising) resolution with a realist's view of human nature and the messiness of real-life criminality'
Daily Telegraph

'Kate Atkinson's finest novel to date. Indeed, it's one of the finest British novels, in any genre, to have emerged for years...sharp and dexterous, subtle and stylish, very funny and at times extraordinarily cutting...This is very much a state of the nation novel – far sharper and more observant and satirically understanding than anything else out there at the moment. And yet Kate Atkinson also gives us humanity, insight and entertainment...a story that deserves to be read for decades to come' **Mirror**

'The wonder of Kate Atkinson's novels has been their joie de vivre... An irrepressible exuberance shines throughout...extraordinary combination of wit, plain-speaking, tenderness and control' **Guardian**

'Accept Kate Atkinson's vision; enjoy, admire, laugh and be moved... Kate Atkinson is witty and satirical of modern mores; she is a virtuoso of dialogue' **The Times**

'Manages to sashay a fine line between comedy and tragedy... A stellar cast, the sophisticated plotting we've come to expect, and an incendiary denouement...hypnotic, compulsive reading' **Scotland on Sunday**

'*Started Early* builds into a state-of-the-nation novel that delicately balances bleak cynicism and affecting humour' **Metro**

By KATE ATKINSON

Behind the Scenes at the Museum

A surprising, tragicomic and subversive family saga
set in York, Kate Atkinson's prizewinning first novel,
like all her novels, has a mystery at its heart.

'Little short of a masterpiece'
Daily Mail

Human Croquet

A multilayered, moving novel about the forest
of Arden, a girl who drops in and out of time,
and the heartrending mystery of a lost mother.

'Brilliant and engrossing'
Penelope Fitzgerald

Emotionally Weird

Set in Dundee, this clever, comic novel depicts student life
in all its wild chaos, and a girl's poignant quest for her father.

'Achingly funny . . . executed with wit and mischief'
Meera Syal

Not the End of the World

Kate Atkinson's first collection of short
stories – playful and profound.

'Moving and funny, and crammed with incidental wisdom'
Sunday Times

Life After Life

What if you had the chance to live your life again
and again, until you finally got it right?

'Grips the reader's imagination on the first page and never
lets go. If you wish to be moved and astonished, read it'
Hilary Mantel

A God in Ruins

A masterful companion to *Life After Life*. For all Teddy – would-be poet,
RAF bomber pilot, husband and father – endures in battle, his greatest
challenge will be to face living in a future he never expected to have.

Featuring Jackson Brodie:

Case Histories

The first novel to feature Jackson Brodie, the
former police detective, who finds himself investigating
three separate cold murder cases in Cambridge,
while still haunted by a tragedy in his own past.

'The best mystery of the decade'
Stephen King

One Good Turn

Jackson Brodie, in Edinburgh during the Festival,
is drawn into a vortex of crimes and mysteries,
each containing a kernel of the next,
like a set of nesting Russian dolls.

'The most fun I've had with a novel this year'
Ian Rankin

When Will There Be Good News?

A six-year-old girl witnesses an appalling crime.
Thirty years later, Jackson Brodie is on a fatal journey
that will hurtle him into its aftermath.

'Genius . . . insightful, often funny, life-affirming'
Sunday Telegraph

Started Early, Took My Dog

Jackson Brodie returns to Yorkshire, in search of
someone else's roots, while shopping mall security chief
Tracy Waterhouse makes an impulse purchase that will
turn her life upside down.

'The best British crime novel of the year'
Heat

STARTED EARLY, TOOK MY DOG

Kate Atkinson

BLACK SWAN

TRANSWORLD PUBLISHERS
61–63 Uxbridge Road, London W5 5SA
www.transworldbooks.co.uk

Transworld is part of the Penguin Random House group of companies
whose addresses can be found at global.penguinrandomhouse.com

Penguin
Random House
UK

First published in Great Britain in 2010 by Doubleday
an imprint of Transworld Publishers
Black Swan edition published 2011
Black Swan edition reissued 2015

A CIP catalogue record for this book
is available from the British Library.

ISBN
9780552772464

Typeset in 11/15pt Giovanni Book by Falcon Oast Graphic Art Ltd.
Printed and bound in Great Britain by Clays Ltd, St Ives plc

Penguin Random House is committed to a sustainable
future for our business, our readers and our planet. This book
is made from Forest Stewardship Council® certified paper.

MIX
Paper from
responsible sources
FSC® C018179

For my father

All mistakes are mine, some deliberate. I have not necessarily kept to the truth.

My thanks are due to:

Russell Equi, as usual; Malcolm Graham, Detective Chief Superintendent, Lothian and Borders Police; Malcolm R. Dickson, former Assistant Inspector of Constabulary for Scotland; David Mattock and Maureen Lenehan, for revisiting Leeds and the seventies with me.

For want of a nail the shoe was lost.
For want of a shoe the horse was lost.
For want of a horse the rider was lost.
For want of a rider the battle was lost.
For want of a battle the kingdom was lost.
And all for the want of a horseshoe nail.

Traditional

'I was just cleaning up the place a bit.'

Peter Sutcliffe

Treasure

1975: 9 April

Leeds: 'Motorway City of the Seventies'. A proud slogan. No irony intended. Gaslight still flickering on some streets. Life in a northern town.

The Bay City Rollers at number one. IRA bombs all over the country. Margaret Thatcher is the new leader of the Conservative Party. At the beginning of the month, in Albuquerque, Bill Gates founds what will become Microsoft. At the end of the month Saigon falls to the North Vietnamese army. *The Black and White Minstrel Show* is still on television, John Poulson is still in jail. *Bye Bye Baby, Baby Goodbye.* In the middle of it all, Tracy Waterhouse was only concerned with the hole in one of the toes of her tights. It was growing bigger with every step she took. They were new on this morning as well.

They had been told that it was on the fifteenth floor of the flats in Lovell Park and - of course - the lifts were broken. The two PCs huffed and puffed their way up the stairs. By the time they neared the top they were resting at every turn of the stair. WPC Tracy Waterhouse, a big, graceless girl only just off probation, and PC Ken

Arkwright, a stout white Yorkshireman with a heart of lard. Climbing Everest.

They would both see the beginning of the Ripper's killing spree but Arkwright would be retired long before the end of it. Donald Neilson, the Black Panther from Bradford, hadn't been captured yet and Harold Shipman had probably already started killing patients unlucky enough to be under his care in Pontefract General Infirmary. West Yorkshire in 1975, awash with serial killers.

Tracy Waterhouse was still wet behind the ears, although she wouldn't admit to it. Ken Arkwright had seen more than most but remained avuncular and sanguine, a good copper for a green girl to be beneath the wing of. There were bad apples in the barrel – the dark cloud of David Oluwale's death still cast a long shadow on police in the West Riding, but Arkwright wasn't under it. He could be violent when necessary, sometimes when not, but he didn't discriminate on the grounds of colour when it came to reward and punishment. And women were often *slappers* and *scrubbers* but he'd helped out a few street girls with fags and cash, and he loved his wife and daughters.

Despite pleas from her teachers to stay on and 'make something of herself', Tracy had left school at fifteen to do a shorthand and typing course and went straight into Montague Burton's offices as a junior, eager to get on with her adult life. 'You're a bright girl,' the man in personnel said, offering her a cigarette. 'You could go far. You never know, PA to the MD one day.' She didn't know what 'MD' meant. Wasn't too sure about 'PA' either. The man's eyes were all over her.

Sixteen, never been kissed by a boy, never drunk wine, not even Blue Nun. Never eaten an avocado or seen an aubergine, never been on an aeroplane. It was different in those days.

She bought a tweed maxi coat from Etam and a new umbrella. Ready for anything. Or as ready as she would ever be. Two years later she was in the police. Nothing could have prepared her for that. *Bye Bye, Baby.*

Tracy was worried that she might never leave home. She spent her nights in front of the television with her mother while her father drank – modestly – in the local Conservative club. Together, Tracy and her mother, Dorothy, watched *The Dick Emery Show* or *Steptoe and Son* or Mike Yarwood doing an impression of Steptoe and his son. Or Edward Heath, his shoulders heaving up and down. Must have been a sad day for Mike Yarwood when Margaret Thatcher took over the leadership. Sad day for everyone. Tracy had never understood the attraction of impressionists.

Her stomach rumbled like a train. She'd been on the cottage cheese and grapefruit diet for a week. Wondered if you could starve to death while you were still overweight.

'Jesus H. Christ,' Arkwright gasped, bending over and resting his hands on his knees when they finally achieved the fifteenth floor. 'I used to be a rugby wing forward, believe it or not.'

'Ay, well, you're just an old, fat bloke now,' Tracy said. 'What number?'

'Twenty-five. It's at the end.'

A neighbour had phoned in anonymously about a bad smell ('a right stink') coming from the flat.

'Dead rats, probably,' Arkwright said. 'Or a cat. Remember those two dogs in that house in Chapeltown? Oh no, before your time, lass.'

'I heard about it. Bloke went off and left them without any food. They ate each other in the end.'

'They didn't eat each other,' Arkwright said. '*One* of them ate the other one.'

'You're a bloody pedant, Arkwright.'

'A what? Cheeky so-and-so. Ey up, here we go. Fuck a duck, Trace, you can smell it from here.'

Tracy Waterhouse pressed her thumb on the doorbell and kept it there. Glanced down at her ugly police-issue regulation black lace-ups and wiggled her toes inside her ugly police-issue regulation black tights. Her big toe had gone right through the hole in the tights now and a ladder was climbing up towards one of her big footballer's knees. 'It'll be some old bloke who's been lying here for weeks,' she said. 'I bloody hate them.'

'I hate train jumpers.'

'Dead kiddies.'

'Yeah. They're the worst,' Arkwright agreed. Dead children were trumps, every time.

Tracy took her thumb off the doorbell and tried turning the door handle. Locked. 'Ah, Jesus, Arkwright, it's humming in there. Something that's not about to get up and walk away, that's for sure.'

Arkwright banged on the door and shouted, 'Hello,

it's the police here, is anyone in there? Shit, Tracy, can you hear that?'

'Flies?'

Ken Arkwright bent down and looked through the letterbox. 'Oh, Christ—' He recoiled from the letterbox so quickly that Tracy's first thought was that someone had squirted something into his eyes. It had happened to a sergeant a few weeks ago, a nutter with a Squeezy washing-up bottle full of bleach. It had put everyone off looking through letterboxes. Arkwright, however, immediately squatted down and pushed open the letterbox again and started talking soothingly, the way you would to a nervy dog. 'It's OK, it's OK, everything's OK now. Is Mummy there? Or your daddy? We're going to help you. It's OK.' He stood and got ready to shoulder the door. Pawed the ground, blew air out of his mouth and said to Tracy, 'Prepare yourself, lass, it's not going to be pretty.'

Six months ago

The suburban outskirts of Munich on a cold afternoon. Large, lazy flakes of snow fluttering down like white confetti, falling on the bonnet of their anonymous-looking German-made car.

'Nice house,' Steve said. He was a cocky little sod who talked too much. It was doubtful that Steve was his real name. 'Big house,' he added.

'Yeah, nice big house,' he agreed, more to shut Steve up than anything else. Nice and big and surrounded, unfortunately, by other nice big houses, on the kind of street that had vigilant neighbours and burglar alarms dotted like bright carbuncles on the walls. A couple of the very nicest, biggest houses had security gates and cameras attached to their walls.

The first time you recce, the second time you pay attention to detail, the third time you do the job. This was the third time. 'Bit Germanic for my liking, of course,' Steve said, as if the entire portfolio of European real estate was at his disposal.

'Maybe that's something to do with the fact that we're in Germany,' he said.

Steve said, 'I've got nothing against the Germans. Had a couple in the Deuxième. Good lads. Good beer,' he added after several seconds' contemplation. 'Good sausages too.'

Steve said he'd been in the Paras, came out and found he couldn't handle civilian life, joined the French Foreign Legion. *You think you're hard and then you find out what hard really means.*

Right. How many times had he heard that? He'd met a few guys from the legion in his time – ex-military guys escaping the flatline of civilian life, deserters from divorces and paternity suits, fugitives from boredom. All of them were running from something, none of them quite the outlaws they imagined themselves to be. Certainly not Steve. This was the first time they'd done a job together. The guy was a bit of a gung-ho wanker but he was OK, he paid attention. He didn't smoke in the car, he didn't want to listen to crap radio stations.

Some of these places reminded him of gingerbread houses, right down to the icing-sugar snow that rimmed their roofs and gutters. He had seen a gingerbread house for sale in the Christkindl market where they had spent the previous evening, strolling around the Marienplatz, drinking *Glühwein* out of Christmas mugs, for all the world like regular tourists. They'd had to pay a deposit on the mugs and on that basis he had taken his back to the Platzl, where they were staying. A present for his daughter Marlee when he got home, even though she would probably turn her nose up at it, or, worse, thank him indifferently and never look at it again.

'Did you do that job in Dubai?' Steve asked.

'Yeah.'

'I heard everything went tits up?'

'Yeah.'

A car rounded the corner and they both instinctively checked their watches. It glided past. Wrong car. 'It's not them,' Steve said, unnecessarily.

On the plus side, they had a long driveway that curved away from the gate so that you couldn't see the house from the road. And the driveway was bordered by a lot of bushes. No security lights, no motion-sensor lights. Darkness was the friend of covert ops. Not today, they were doing this in daylight. Neither broad nor bright, the fag end of the afternoon. The dimming of the day.

Another car came round the corner, the right one this

time. 'Here comes the kid,' Steve said softly. She was five years old, straight black hair, big brown eyes. She had no idea what was about to happen to her. *The Paki kid*, Steve called her.

'Egyptian. Half,' he corrected Steve. 'She's called Jennifer.'

'I'm not racist.'

But.

The snow was still fluttering down, sticking to the windscreen for a second before melting. He had a sudden, unexpected memory of his sister coming into the house, laughing and shaking blossom off her clothes, out of her hair. He thought of the town they were brought up in as a place devoid of trees and yet here she was in his memory like a bride, a shower of petals like pink thumbprints on the dark veil of her hair.

The car pulled into the driveway and disappeared from view. He turned to look at Steve. 'Ready?'

'Lock and load,' Steve said, starting the engine.

'Remember, don't hurt the nanny.'

'Unless I have to.'

Wednesday

'Watch out, the dragon's about.'

'Where?'

'There. Just passing Greggs.' Grant pointed at Tracy

Waterhouse's image on one of the monitors. The air in the security control room was always stale. Outside, it was beautiful May weather but in here the atmosphere was like that of a submarine that had been under too long. They were coming up to lunchtime, the busiest time of the day for shoplifters. The police were in and out all day, every day. A pair of them out there now, all tooled up, bulky waist-belts, knife-proof vests, short-sleeved shirts, 'escorting' a woman out of Peacocks, her bags stuffed with clothes she hadn't paid for. Leslie got sleepy from peering at the monitors. Sometimes she turned a blind eye. Not everyone was, strictly speaking, a criminal. 'What a week,' Grant said, making a gurning face. 'School half-term and a bank holiday. We'll be going over the top. It'll be carnage.'

Grant was chewing Nicorette as if his life depended on it. He had a stain of something on his tie. Leslie considered telling him about the stain. Decided not to. It looked like blood but it seemed more likely that it was ketchup. He had such bad acne that he looked radioactive. Leslie was pretty and petite and had a degree in chemical engineering from Queen's University in Kingston, Ontario, and working in security in the Merrion Centre in Leeds was a short, not entirely unpleasurable dogleg in her life's journey. She was on what her family called her 'World Tour'. She'd done Athens, Rome, Florence, Nice, Paris. Not quite the world. She'd stopped off in Leeds to visit relatives, decided to stay for the summer after she hooked up with a philosophy post-grad called Dominic who worked in a bar. She had met his parents, been to their house for a meal. Dominic's mother heated up an individual 'Vegetarian Lasagne' from Sainsbury's for her while the rest of them ate chicken. His mother was defensive, worried that Leslie would carry her son off to a faraway continent and all her grandchildren would have accents and be vegetarians. Leslie wanted to reassure her, say, It's only a holiday romance, but that probably wouldn't go down well either.

'Leslie with an "ie",' she had to tell everyone in England because they spelt it with a 'y'. 'Really?' Dominic's mother said, as if Leslie was herself a spelling mistake. Leslie tried to imagine taking Dominic home to her own family, introducing him to her parents, how unimpressed they'd be. She missed home, the Mason and Risch piano in the corner, her brother, Lloyd, her old golden retriever, Holly, and her cat, Mitten. Not necessarily in that order. Her family took a cottage on Lake Huron in the summer. She couldn't even begin to explain this other life to Grant. Not that she would want to. Grant stared at her all the time when he thought she wasn't looking. He was desperate to have sex with her. It was kind of funny really. She would rather stick knives in her eyes.

'She's passing Workout World,' Grant said.

'Tracy's OK,' Leslie said.

'She's a Nazi.'

'No she's not.' Leslie had her eye on a group of hoodies lurching past Rayners' Opticians. One of them was wearing some kind of Halloween fright mask. He leered at an old woman who flinched at the sight of him. 'We always prosecute,' Leslie murmured, as if it was a private joke.

'Ey up,' Grant said. 'Tracy's going into Thornton's. Must need her daily rations topping up.'

Leslie liked Tracy, you knew where you were with her. No bullshit.

'She's a right fat pig,' Grant said.

'She's not fat, just big.'

'Yeah, that's what they all say.'

Leslie was small and delicate. A cracking bird if ever there was one, in Grant's opinion. Special. Not like some of the slags you got round here. 'Sure you don't want to go for a drink after work?' he asked, ever hopeful. 'Cocktail bar in town. Sophisticated place for a sophisticated laydee.'

'Ey up,' Leslie said. 'There's some dodgy kids going into City Cyber.'

Tracy Waterhouse came out of Thornton's, stuffing her forage into the big, ugly shoulder bag that she wore strapped, like a bandolier, across her substantial chest. Viennese truffles, her midweek treat. Pathetic really. Other people went to the cinema on an evening, to restaurants, pubs and clubs, visited friends, had sex, but Tracy was looking forward to curling up on her sofa with *Britain's Got Talent* and a bag of Thornton's Viennese truffles. And a chicken bhuna that she was going to pick up on the way home and wash down with one or two cans of Beck's. Or three or four, even though it was a Wednesday. A school night. More than forty years since Tracy left school. When had she last eaten a meal with someone in a restaurant? That bloke from the dating agency, a couple of years ago, in Dino's in Bishopsgate? She could remember what she'd eaten – garlic bread, spaghetti and meatballs, followed by a crème caramel – yet she couldn't recall the bloke's name. 'You're a big girl,' he said when she met him for a drink beforehand in Whitelock's.

'Yeah,' she said. 'Want to make something of it?' Downhill from there on really.

She ducked into Superdrug to pick up some Advil for the Beck's headache she would wake up with tomorrow. The girl behind the till didn't even look at her. Service with a scowl. Very easy to steal from Superdrug, lots of handy little things to slip into a bag or a pocket – lipsticks, toothpaste, shampoo, Tampax – you could hardly blame people for thieving, it was as if you were inviting them. Tracy glanced around at the security cameras. She knew there was a blind spot right on Nailcare. You could have taken everything you needed for a year's worth of manicures and no one would be any the wiser. She placed a protective hand on her bag. It contained two envelopes stuffed with twenties – five thousand pounds in all – that she'd just removed from her account at the Yorkshire Bank. She would like to see someone trying to snatch it from her – she was looking forward to beating them to a pulp with her bare hands. No point in having weight, Tracy reasoned, if you weren't prepared to throw it around.

The money was a payment for Janek, the workman who was extending the kitchen in the terraced house in Headingley that she'd bought with the proceeds of the sale of her parents' bungalow in Bramley. It was such a relief that they were finally dead, dying within a few weeks of each other, minds and bodies long past their sell-by date. They had both reached ninety and Tracy had begun to think that they were trying to outlive her. They had always been competitive people.

Janek started at eight in the morning, finished at six, worked on a Saturday – Polish, what else. It was embarrassing how much Tracy was attracted to Janek, despite the fact that he was twenty years younger and at least three inches shorter than she was. He was so careful and had such good manners. Every morning Tracy left out tea and coffee for him and a plate of biscuits wrapped in cling-film. When she returned home the biscuits were all eaten. It made her feel wanted. She was starting a week's holiday on Friday and Janek promised everything would be finished by the time she returned. Tracy didn't want it to be finished, well, she did, she was sick to death of it, but she didn't want *him* to be finished.

She wondered if he would stay on if she asked him to do her bathroom. He was champing at the bit to go home. All the Poles were going back now. They didn't want to stay in a bankrupt country. Before the Berlin Wall came down you felt sorry for them, now you envied them.

When Tracy was on the force her fellow officers – male and female – all assumed she was a dyke. She was over fifty now and way back when she had joined the West Yorkshire Police as a raw cadet you had to be one of the boys to get along. Unfortunately, once you'd established yourself as a hard-nosed bitch it was difficult to admit to the soft and fluffy woman you were hiding inside. And why would you want to admit to that anyway?

Tracy had retired with a shell so thick that there was hardly any room left inside. Vice, sexual offences, human trafficking – the underbelly of Drugs and Major Crime – she'd seen it all and more. Witnessing the worst of human behaviour was a pretty good way of killing off anything soft and fluffy.

She'd been around so long that she had been a humble foot soldier when Peter Sutcliffe was still patrolling the streets of West Yorkshire. She remembered the fear, she'd been afraid herself. That was in the days before computers, when the sheer weight of paperwork was enough to swamp the investigation. 'There were days before computers?' one of her younger, cheekier colleagues said. 'Wow, Jurassic.'

He was right, she was from another era. She should have gone sooner, only hanging on because she couldn't think how to fill the long empty days of retirement. Sleep, eat, protect, repeat, that was the life she knew. Everyone was fixated on the thirty years, get out, get another job, enjoy the pension. Anyone who stayed on longer was seen as a fool.

Tracy would have preferred to have dropped in harness but she knew it was time to go. She had been a detective superintendent, now she was a 'police pensioner'. Sounded Dickensian, as if she should be sitting in the corner of a workhouse, wrapped in a dirty shawl. She'd thought about volunteering with one of those organizations that helped mop up after disasters and wars. After all, it was something she felt she'd been doing all her life, but in the end she took the job in the Merrion Centre.

At her farewell piss-up they had given her a laptop and two hundred quid's worth of spa vouchers for the Waterfall Spa on Brewery Wharf. She was pleasantly surprised, even flattered, that they imagined she was the kind of woman who would use a spa. She already had a laptop and she knew the one they gave her was one of those that Carphone Warehouse gave away for free, but it was the thought that counted.

When she took the job as head of security in the Merrion Centre Tracy thought 'fresh start' and made some changes, not just moving house but getting her moustache waxed, growing her hair into a softer style, shopping for blouses with bows and pearl buttons and shoes with kitten heels to wear with the ubiquitous black suit. It didn't work, of course. She could tell that, spa vouchers or no spa vouchers, people still thought she was a butch old battleaxe.

* * *

Tracy liked getting up close and personal with the punters. She strolled past Morrisons, the gap where Woolworths used to be, Poundstretcher – the retail preferences of the lumpenproletariat. Was there anyone in the entire soulless place who was happy? Leslie perhaps, although she kept her cards close to her chest. Like Janek, she had a life somewhere else. Tracy imagined Canada was a good place to live. Or Poland. Perhaps she should emigrate.

It was warm today. Tracy hoped the weather would last for her holiday. A week in a National Trust cottage, lovely setting. She was a member. That was what happened when you grew older and had nothing fulfilling in your life – you joined the National Trust or English Heritage and spent your weekends meandering around gardens and houses that didn't belong to you or gazing in boredom at ruins, trying to reconstruct them in your mind – long-gone monks cooking, pissing, praying inside walls of cold stone. And you spent your holidays on your own, of course. She'd joined a 'singles social club' a couple of years ago. Middle-aged, middle-class people who didn't have any friends. Rambling, art classes, museum visits, all very sedate. She joined thinking it might be nice to go on holiday with other people but it hadn't worked out. Spent all her time trying to get away from them.

The world was going to hell in a handcart. The Watch Hospital, Costa Coffee, Wilkinson's Hardware, Walmsley's, Herbert Brown's ('Lend and Spend' a fancy rhyme for a pawnbroker, eternal friend of the under-class). All human life was here. Britain – shoplifting capital of Europe, over two billion quid lost every year to 'retail shrinkage', a ridiculous term for what was, after all, straightforward thieving. And double that figure if you added the amount of stuff that the staff nicked. Unbelievable.

Think how many starving kids you could feed and educate with all that missing money. But then it wasn't money, was it, not real money. There was no such thing as real money any more, it was just an act of the collective imagination. Now if we all just clap our hands and believe . . . Of course, the five thousand pounds in her bag wasn't going to benefit the Inland Revenue either but modest tax evasion was a citizen's right, not a crime. There was crime and then there was crime. Tracy had seen a lot of the other sort, all the p's – paedophilia, prostitution, pornography. Trafficking. Buying and sell-ing, that's all people did. You could buy women, you could buy kids, you could buy anything. Western civilization had had a good run but now it had pretty much shopped itself out of existence. All cultures had a built-in obsolescence, didn't they? Nothing was for ever. Except diamonds maybe, if the song was right. And cockroaches probably. Tracy had never owned a diamond, probably never would. Her mother's engage-ment ring had been sapphires, never off her finger, put on by Tracy's father when he proposed, taken off by the undertaker before he put her in her coffin. Tracy had it valued – two thousand quid, not as much as she'd hoped for. Tracy had tried to squeeze it on to her little finger but it didn't fit. It was somewhere at the back of a drawer now. She bought a doughnut in Ainsleys, put it in her bag for later.

She clocked a woman coming out of Rayners' who had a familiar look about her. Resembled that madam who used to run a brothel out of a house in Cookridge. Tracy had raided it when she was still in uniform, long before she was exposed to the full horrors of Vice. All home comforts, the madam offered her 'gentlemen' a glass of sherry, little dishes of nuts, before they went upstairs and committed degrading acts behind the lace curtains. She had a dungeon in what used to be her coal cellar. Made Tracy feel squeamish, the stuff that was down there. The girls were indifferent, nothing could surprise them. Still, they were better off in that house, behind the lace curtains, than they would have been on the streets. Used to be poverty that drove women on the game, now it was drugs. These days there was hardly a girl on the streets who wasn't an addict. Shopmobility, Claire's Accessories. In Greggs she bought a sausage roll for her lunch.

The madam was dead a long time ago, had a stroke at the City Varieties when they were filming *The Good Old Days*. All dressed in her Edwardian finery and dead in her seat. No one noticed until the end. Tracy had wondered if they'd caught it on camera. They wouldn't have shown a corpse on TV in those days, these days they probably would.

No, not the ghost of the dead madam, it was that

actress from *Collier*. That was why the face looked familiar. The one who played Vince Collier's mother. Tracy didn't like *Collier*, it was a load of crap. She preferred *Law and Order: SVU*. The actress who resembled the Cookridge madam looked older than she did on screen. Her make-up was a mess, as if she'd put it on without a mirror. It gave her a slightly unhinged air. The woman was obviously wearing a wig. Perhaps she had cancer. Tracy's mother, Dorothy Waterhouse, died of cancer. You get to over ninety and you'd think you would die of old age. They talked about treating it with chemo and Tracy had objected to wasting resources on someone so old. She had wondered if she could sneak a DNR bracelet on to her mother's wrist without anyone noticing but then her mother had surprised them all by actually dying. Tracy had waited so long for that moment that it felt like an anticlimax.

Dorothy Waterhouse used to boast that Tracy's father had never seen her without make-up, Tracy didn't know why as she gave the impression of never having liked him. She put a lot of effort into being Dorothy Waterhouse. Tracy instructed the undertaker to leave her mother *au naturel*.

'Not even a bit of lippie?' he said.

Electricity everywhere. All the bright shiny surfaces. Long time since everything was made from wood and lit by firelight and stars. Tracy caught sight of herself in the plate glass of Ryman's, saw the wild-eyed look of a woman falling over the edge. Someone who had started out the day carefully put together and was slowly un-ravelling during the course of it. Her skirt was creased over her hips, her highlights looked brassy and her bulging beer belly stuck out in a mockery of pregnancy. Survival of the fattest.

Tracy felt defeated. She glanced down and picked some lint off her jacket. Things could only get worse. Photo Me, Priceless, Sheila's Sandwiches. She could hear a child crying somewhere – part of the soundtrack of shopping malls the world over. It was a sound that was still capable of piercing the shell like a red-hot needle. A group of listless teenage hoodies were hanging around the entrance to City Cyber, jostling and shoving each other in a way that passed for wit amongst them. One of them was wearing a Halloween fright mask, a plastic skull where his face should be. It unnerved her for a moment.

Tracy might have followed the youths into the shop but the screaming child was moving closer, distracting her. She could hear the child but she couldn't see it. Its distress was startling. It was doing her head in.

Regrets, she had a few. Quite a lot actually. Wished she'd found someone who appreciated her, wished she'd had kids and learned how to dress better. Wished she'd stayed on at school, maybe gone on and done a degree. Medicine, geography, art history. It was the usual stuff. Really she was just like everyone else, she wanted to love someone. Even better if they loved you in return. She was considering getting a cat. She didn't really like cats though. That might be a bit of a problem. Quite liked dogs – sensible, clever dogs, not stupid little lapdogs that fitted in a handbag. A good big German shepherd perhaps, woman's best friend. No burglar alarm could better it.

Oh yeah – Kelly Cross. Kelly Cross was the reason for the screaming child. No surprise there. Kelly Cross. Prostitute, druggie, thief, all-round pikey. A scrag-end of a woman. Tracy knew her. Everyone knew her. Kelly had several kids, most of them in care and they were the lucky ones, which was saying something. She was storming along the main drag of the Merrion Centre, a woman possessed, anger coming off her like knives. It was surprising how much power she radiated, given how small and thin she was. She was wearing a sleeveless vest that revealed some tasteful trailer-trash bruises and a set of prison tats. On her forearm, a crudely drawn heart with an arrow through it and the initials 'K' and 'S'. Tracy wondered who the unlucky 'S' was. She was talking on her phone, mouthing off to someone. She had almost certainly nicked something. The chances of that woman walking out of a shop with a valid till receipt were almost zero.

She was pulling the kid by the hand, wrenching her along because there was no way that the child could keep up with Kelly's furious pace. Imagine, you've not long learned to walk and now you're expected to run like an adult. Occasionally, Kelly jerked her off the ground so that for a second the kid seemed to fly. Screaming. Non-stop. Red-hot needle through the shell. Through the eardrum. Into the brain.

Kelly Cross parted the throng of shoppers like an unholy Moses striding through the Red Sea. Many of the onlookers were clearly horrified but no one had the nerve to tackle a berserker like Kelly. You couldn't blame them.

Kelly stopped so suddenly that the kid kept running forward as if she was on elastic. Kelly thumped her hard on the backside, sending her into the air as if she was on a swing and then, without a word, she set off running again. Tracy heard a surprisingly loud middle-class voice, a woman's, say, 'Someone should do something.'

Too late. Kelly had already stomped her way past Morrisons and out on to Woodhouse Lane. Tracy followed her, cantering to keep up, her lungs ready to collapse by the time she caught her at a bus stop. Jesus, when did she get so unfit? About twenty years ago probably. She should haul her old Rosemary Conley tapes out of the boxes in the spare room.

'Kelly,' she wheezed.

Kelly spun round, snarling, 'What the fuck do you want?' A faint glimmer of recognition on her venomous face as she glared at Tracy. Tracy could see the wheels ticking round until they came up with 'copper'. It made Kelly even more enraged, if that was possible.

She looked worse close up – flat hair, grey corpse-skin, bloodshot vampire eyes and a junkie edginess to her that made Tracy want to step back but she held her ground. The kid, tear-stained and mucky, had stopped crying and was staring slack-mouthed at Tracy. Made her seem gormless but Tracy guessed adenoidal. Her appearance wasn't helped by the green caterpillar of snot crawling out of her nose. Three years old? Four? Tracy wasn't sure how you told the age of a kid. Maybe it was from their teeth, like horses. They were small. Some were bigger than others. That was about as far as she was willing to go in the guessing stakes.

The kid was dressed in various shades of pink, with the addition of a little pink rucksack stuck on her back like a barnacle, so that the general impression was of a misshapen marshmallow. Someone – surely not Kelly – had attempted to plait the kid's stringy hair. The pink and the plaits signalled her gender, something not immediately obvious from her podgy, androgynous features.

She was a small lumpy kind of kid but there was a spark of something in her eyes. Life perhaps. Cracked but not broken. Yet. What chance did this kid have with Kelly as her mother? Realistically? Kelly was still holding the kid's hand, not so much holding it as gripping it in a vice as if the kid was about to fly up into the air.

A bus was approaching, indicating, slowing down.

Something gave inside Tracy. A small floodgate letting out a race of despair and frustration as she contemplated the blank but already soiled canvas of the kid's future. Tracy didn't know how it happened. One moment she was standing at a bus stop on Woodhouse Lane, contemplating the human wreckage that was Kelly Cross, the next she was saying to her, 'How much?'

'How much what?'

'How much for the kid?' Tracy said, delving into her handbag and unearthing one of the envelopes that contained Janek's money. She opened it and showed it to Kelly. 'There's three thousand here. You can have it all in exchange for the kid.' She kept the second envelope with the remaining two thousand out of sight in case she needed to up the ante. She didn't need to, however, as Kelly suddenly meerkatted to attention. Her brain seemed to disassociate for a second, her eyes flicking rapidly from side to side, and then, with unexpected speed, her hand shot out and she grabbed the envelope. In the same second she dropped the kid's hand. Then she laughed with genuine glee as the bus drew to a halt behind her. 'Ta very much,' she said as she jumped aboard.

While Kelly stood on the platform fumbling for change, Tracy raised her voice and said, 'What's her name? What's your daughter's name, Kelly?' Kelly pulled her ticket out of the machine and said, 'Courtney.'

'Courtney?' Typical chav name – Chantelle, Shannon, Tiffany. Courtney.

Kelly turned round, ticket clutched in her hand. 'Yeah,' she said. 'Courtney.' Then she gave her a puzzled look, as if Tracy was a Polo short of a packet. Started to say something, 'But she's not—' but the bus doors closed on her words. The bus drove off. Tracy stared after it. Gormless, not adenoidal. She registered a sudden spike of anxiety. She had just bought a kid. She didn't move until a small, warm, sticky hand found its way into hers.

'Where did Tracy go?' Grant asked, scanning the bank of monitors. 'She just disappeared.'

Leslie shrugged. 'I don't know. Keep an eye on that drunk outside Boots, will you?'

'Someone should do something.' Tilly was surprised to find herself speaking out loud. And *so* loud too. Resolutely middle-class. *Resonate!* She could hear her old voice coach at drama college exclaiming, *Resonate! Your chest is a bell, Matilda!* Franny Anderson. *Miss Anderson,* you would never call her anything more familiar. Spine like a ramrod, spoke Morningside English. Tilly still did the voice exercises Miss Anderson had taught them – *ar-aw-oo-ar-ay-ee-ar* – every morning, first thing, before she even had a cup of tea. The flat she lived in, in Fulham, had walls like paper, the neighbours must think she was mad. Over half a century since Tilly was a drama student. Everyone thought life began in the sixties but London in the fifties had been thrilling for a naïve eighteen-year-old girl from Hull, straight out of grammar school. Eighteen then was younger than it was now.

Tilly had shared a little place in Soho with Phoebe March, *Dame* Phoebe now of course – hell to pay if you forget the title. She'd been Helena to Phoebe's Hermia at Stratford, oh God, decades ago now. Started off on an equal footing, you see, and now Phoebe was forever playing English queens and wearing frocks and tiaras. She had Oscars (supporting) and Baftas coming out of her ears, while Tilly was stuffed into a pinafore apron and slippers pretending to be Vince Collier's mother. Hey-ho.

Not really an equal footing. Tilly's father had owned a wet fish shop in the Land of Green Ginger – a street more romantic in name than in reality – whilst Phoebe, although she *called* herself a 'northern girl', was really from the landowning classes – house designed by John Carr of York near Malton – and she was the niece of a cousin of the old king, huge house on Eaton Square that she could repair to if things got tricky in Soho. The stories Tilly could tell about Phoebe – *Dame* Phoebe – would make your hair curl.

Miss Anderson would be long dead now, of course. She wasn't the kind to rot messily in the grave either. Tilly imagined she would have become a parched mummy, eyeless and shrivelled, and as weightless as dead bracken. But still with perfect diction.

Tilly knew her outrage was impotent, she wasn't going to be the one to tackle the fearsome tattooed woman. Too old, too fat, too slow. Too frightened. But someone should, someone braver. A *man*. Men weren't what they used to be. If they ever had been. Agitated, she glanced around the shopping centre. Dear God, this was an awful place. She would never have come back but she had to pick up her new specs from Rayners'. She wouldn't have come here at all but a production assistant, nice girl, Padma – Indian, all the nice girls were Asian now – had made the appointment for her. *There you go, Miss Squires, anything else I can do to help?* What a sweetheart. Tilly had sat on her old specs. Easy thing to do. Blind as a bat without them. Difficult driving the old jalopy when you couldn't see a thing.

And after all this time buried in the country she had fancied being in a city. But perhaps not this one. Guildford or Henley perhaps, somewhere civilized.

They had her holed up in the middle of nowhere for the duration of her filming. Guest appearance on *Collier*, twelve-month contract, her character killed off at the end of it, not that she knew that when she took it on. *Oh, darling, you must,* all her theatre friends said. *It'll be amusing – and think of the money!* You bet she was thinking of the money! She was more or less living hand-to-mouth these days. Nothing in the theatre for three years now. Scripts were tricky, the old memory not what it was. She had awful trouble learning her lines. Never used to have a problem, started off in rep when she was eighteen. The ingénue. (Rote learning at school, of course, out of fashion now.) Different play every week, knew all her lines and everyone else's as well. She had once, long ago, just to prove she could, learned the whole of *The Three Sisters* by heart, and she was only playing Natasha!

'Senile old bat,' she heard someone say yesterday. It was true everything was dimming. *The lights are going out all over Europe. Suffer the little children.* Should she find a policeman? Or phone 999? It seemed an awfully dramatic thing to do.

The last thing she'd done for the telly was a *Casualty* where she'd played an old dear who had manned an ack-ack gun in the war and who'd died of hypothermia in a high-rise flat, which led to a lot of hand-wringing from the characters (*How can this happen in this day and age? This woman defended her country in the war.* Et cetera). Of course she wasn't really old enough to play the role. She was still a child during the war, could only remember certain awful things about it, Mother harrying her into the shelter in the middle of the night, the smell of damp earth inside. Hull took a terrible beating.

Flat-footed Father was given a desk job in the Army Catering Corps. Not much fish to sell during the war anyway, trawlers requisitioned by the navy. The ones that kept on fishing were blown out of the water, fishermen's bodies coiling down into the cold, icy depths. *Those are pearls that were his eyes.* She had played Miranda at school. *Have you thought about the stage, Matilda?* Her headmistress didn't think she was much good for anything else. *Not exactly academically inclined, are you, Matilda?*

Tilly wished she had been old enough to fight in the war, to be a bold girl on an ack-ack gun.

The producers of *Collier* had seduced her in the Club at the Ivy over a cocktail called the Twinkle, rather disturbing nomenclature for Tilly as that was the name her prudish mother assigned to female genitalia. Tilly had always rather liked the word 'vagina', it sounded like a swotty girl or a new found land.

When she had first spotted her, the little girl was skipping along, singing, 'Twinkle, Twinkle, Little Star'. The anthem of children everywhere. Made Tilly think of her mother again. The little girl made fists of her hands (so tiny!) and every time she sang the word 'twinkle' she opened them out, like little starfish. The girl was in tune, perfect pitch, someone should have told her mother that the little thing had a gift. Someone should have said something.

When Tilly saw them again, ten minutes later, the poor child was no longer singing. The mother – a brutal woman with crude tattoos and a mobile phone clamped to her ear – was yelling at her, 'Would you just shut the fuck up, Courtney, you're getting on my tits!' She was furious, pulling her along and shouting at her. You knew what happened to children like that when they got home. Behind closed doors. Child cruelty. Snipping off all the little buds so that they could never blossom.

A little black thing among the snow. That was Blake, wasn't it? Not that the 'Twinkle, Twinkle' little girl was black. Quite the opposite, as if she never saw the sun. *Crying 'weep! weep!' in notes of woe.* It was surprising more children didn't have rickets. Perhaps they did. Tilly's grandmother had had rickets, there was a photograph of her as a child, the only photograph of her, taken in a studio in some bleak, flat part of the East

Riding. *I by the tide of Humber would complain.* Her grandmother, three years old if she was a day, had little bowed legs in boots, your heart wept for the past. You can't change the past, only the future, and the only place you could change the future was in the present. That's what they said. Tilly didn't think she'd ever changed anything. Except her mind. Ha, ha. *Very droll, Matilda.*

Collier had turned out not to be so 'amusing', after all. Certainly nothing amusing about hanging around on set (basically, a big aircraft hangar in the middle of nowhere) at six thirty in the morning, freezing your cockles off. The set had been built in the grounds of a stately home belonging to Earl or Duke somebody-or-other. Bizarre, but then the aristocracy were always looking for money these days. 'Purpose-built set,' the producers said to her. 'Cost millions, shows a commitment to longevity.' *Collier* used to be on once a week, now it was three times and they were talking about four. Actors like donkeys, turning a wheel.

They'd brought Tilly in to play Vince Collier's mother because they wanted to make the character 'more human', more vulnerable. Tilly had worked before with the actor who played Vince Collier, when he was a teenager, and she kept calling him by his real name – Simon – instead of Vince. Seven takes today just to say goodbye to him on a doorstep. *Goodbye, Simon* six times, the seventh take she just said *Goodbye, dear.* 'Thank fuck,' she heard the director say (a little too loudly). The name ('Vince, *Vince,*' the director muttered, 'how hard can it

46

be?') just kept eluding her. It was in her brain but she couldn't find it.

Nice boy, Simon. Ran her lines with her all the time, told her not to worry. Gay as a goose. Everyone knew, worst-kept secret in television. You couldn't say anything because Vince Collier was supposed to be very macho. Simon's boyfriend, Marcello, was staying with him, rented cottage, nicer than Tilly's. They'd had Tilly over to dinner, lots of gin and Marcello had cooked a chicken, 'Sicilian style'. Afterwards they drank some lovely rum that the boys had brought back from holiday on Mauritius and played cribbage. All three of them gloriously tiddly. (She wasn't a lush like Dame you-know-who.) Lovely old-fashioned evening.

She thought she'd signed up for the duration ('My pension,' she murmured happily over her third Twinkle) and then last week they told her that her contract wasn't being renewed and she was going to die at the end of her run. She had only a few weeks to go. They hadn't told her how. It was beginning to worry her in some curiously existential way as if Death was going to jump out at her from round a corner, swinging his sickle and shouting, 'Boo!' Well, perhaps not boo. She hoped that Death had a little more gravitas than that.

Tilly herself was beginning to feel a lack of commitment to longevity. Some days the old ticker felt like a hard little knot in her chest, other days it was like a soft, fluttering bird trying to escape from its ribbed cage. She suspected that her alter ego, poor old Marjorie Collier, was going to meet a sticky end rather than expire gracefully in her bed. And then! Just as she was coming out of Rayners' she encountered Death, exactly as she'd feared. Thought she was going to drop dead on the spot but it was just some silly boy in a skull mask. Sneering at her, jumping up and down like a skeleton on strings. Shouldn't be allowed.

Bluebell Cottage. That was the name of the place she was staying in. A made-up name obviously. Used to be a farm worker's cottage. Poor peasants, all mud and blood and up at dawn with the beasts in the field. She'd done a Hardy, oh years ago, for the BBC, learned a lot about agricultural labourers in the course of it.

We've got you a lovely cottage, they said, *usually rented out to holidaymakers*. They had cast and crew stashed everywhere – B and Bs, cheap hotels in Leeds, Halifax, Bradford, rental houses, even caravans. They would have been better off just building a Travelodge on set. Tilly would have liked a nice hotel, three-star would have done her. What they didn't tell her was that she would be sharing the cottage with Saskia. Didn't tell Saskia either by the look on her face. Not that she had anything against Saskia per se. All skin and bone, far too thin, lived on fresh air and fags – the Dame Phoebe March diet. 'You don't mind, do you?' she said to Tilly the first time she produced a packet of Silk Cut. 'I mean I'll only smoke in my own room, or outside.'

'Oh, go ahead, dear,' Tilly said, 'I've been around smokers all my life.' (It was a miracle she wasn't dead.)

She wouldn't want to fall out with her. Tilly hated falling out with people. It was funny because Saskia was such a clean girl (obsessively so, obviously had a problem, conducting germ warfare single-handedly) and smoking was such a filthy habit. Ballet dancers were the worst, of course, lighting up like chimneys the second they came out of class. Lungs like lampblack. Tilly used to live with a ballet dancer. That was after Phoebe left the Soho flat (1960 – turned out to be quite a decade for both of them), moving on and up to live with a director in Kensington. Douglas. He had belonged to Tilly first but Phoebe couldn't abide Tilly having something that she didn't. Very handsome man. Batted for the other side as well, of course. Nowt so queer as folk, as they said in the north. Phoebe used him up and left him behind after a year or so. Tilly and Douglas had remained fond of each other to the end. His end anyway.

Saskia played Vince Collier's sidekick, DS Charlotte ('Charlie') Lambert. Keep it under your hat but she wasn't the world's greatest actress. She only seemed to have two expressions. One was 'worried' (with the variation 'very worried') and the other was 'grumpy'. Very limited range, poor girl, although, like a lot of them, she looked good on the telly. Tilly had seen her in a play at the National. She was awful, just awful, but no one seemed to notice. Emperor's new clothes. (Shades of Dame Phoebe again.)

Now that she had her new specs and could actually *see*, it was terrifying. Wednesday used to be half-day closing. Her father pulled the shutters down on the shop in the Land of Green Ginger and went off to live his mysterious other life with his fellow Rotarians. He spent a lot of time on the allotment as well, although there were never many vegetables to show for it. No more half-day closing, everything open all the time now, getting and spending we lay waste our powers. And where had all the money gone? You go to sleep living in a prosperous country and you wake up in a poor one, how did that happen? Where had the money gone, and why couldn't they just get it back?

She had to get out of this God-forsaken place, make her way to the car park. *Should you still be driving?* an AD had asked her after she'd failed several times to reverse into her allotted parking space in the car park on set and he'd had to take over from her. Ruddy cheek! And anyway *parking* wasn't the same as *driving*. She was still in her seventies, plenty of life left in the old bird yet.

Up above the world so high! She was a coward. How could anyone be so horrible to a child? A little scrap of a thing. Poor little mite. It broke Tilly's wheezy old heart. If Tilly had had a child she would have wrapped it in lamb's wool and treated it like an egg, fragile and perfect. She'd lost a baby, back in the Soho days. A miscarriage but she never told anyone. Well, Phoebe. Phoebe who had tried to persuade her to get rid of it, said she knew a man in Harley Street. It would be like going to the dentist, she said. Tilly wouldn't have dreamed of doing that. The baby had lived for nearly five months inside her, a dormouse nesting, before she lost it. It was a proper baby. Nowadays they might have been able to save it. 'It was for the best,' Phoebe said.

It never happened again and Tilly supposed that she had avoided it. Perhaps if she had married or found the right man, if she hadn't been so concerned with her career. She might have a family around her skirts now, a strapping son or a friendly daughter, grandchildren. She would have a *life*, instead of being stranded in the middle of nowhere. Although Tilly was from the north (such a long time ago) the place scared her now, both town and country. *From the north*, like a wind, like a winter queen.

Tilly could understand why the first people had trekked out of Africa but why they continued on, north of the Home Counties, was beyond her. She was an idiot, she should have gone to Harrogate instead. A little tootle around the dress shops and lunch in Betty's. Should have known better. No sign now of the tattooed woman and the poor child. You didn't like to think what kind of home life she had. She should have done something, she really should. Weep, weep, Tilly.

In a newsagent she bought a *Telegraph*, a packet of Halls Mentho-Lyptus throat tablets (to keep the old pipes going) and a bar of Cadbury's Fruit and Nut for a treat. Days off meant no set catering. Tilly loved set catering – big fried breakfasts, proper puddings with custard. She was a terrible cook herself, lived off cheese on toast at home.

She didn't have enough coins so she gave the girl

behind the counter a twenty-pound note but the girl gave her the change on ten.

'Excuse me,' Tilly said hesitantly, because she hated this kind of thing, 'but I gave you a twenty.' The girl looked at her indifferently and said, 'It was a ten.'

'No, no, I'm sorry, it wasn't,' Tilly said. Confrontation tied her up in knots inside. That came from Dad, all those years ago. *He* was never wrong. A big, blustery man, slapping cod fillets down on his marble counter as if he was teaching them a lesson. Tilly had had to learn a few lessons from him. Ran away in the end, never went back to the Land of Green Ginger, reinvented herself in Soho, like many a girl before her. 'It *was* a twenty,' Tilly persisted gently. She could feel herself getting upset. Calm, calm, she said to herself. *Breathe, Matilda!*

The girl behind the counter held up a ten-pound note that she'd taken from the till as if it was incontrovertible proof. But it could have been any ten-pound note! Tilly's heart was thudding uncomfortably in her chest. 'It was a twenty,' Tilly said again. She could hear herself sounding less certain. She'd been to the cashline and it had given her twenties. She'd had nothing else in her purse, that was why she had given the girl the twenty in the first place. She could hear a mutter of discontent behind her in the queue, heard a gruff voice say, 'Get a move on.' You would think that after all these years in the profession she would be able to slip into a role, she was, after all, most comfortable in someone else's skin. An imperious, commanding character, Lady Bracknell, Lady Macbeth, would know how to deal with the girl but when Tilly searched inside all she could find was herself.

The girl was staring at her as if she was nobody, nothing. Invisible.

'You're a thief,' Tilly heard herself suddenly say, too shrilly. 'A common thief.'

'Get lost, you stupid cow,' the girl said, 'or I'll call security.'

She would need money to pay her way out of the multi-storey. Where did she put her purse? Tilly looked through her bag. No purse. She looked again. Still no purse. Plenty of other things that didn't belong there. Recently she'd noticed all these objects suddenly appearing in her bag – key rings, pencil sharpeners, knives and forks, coasters. She had no idea how they got there. Yesterday she had found a cup *and* a saucer! The emphasis on cutlery and cups suggested she was trying to put together a complete place-setting. 'Turning into a bit of a klepto, Tilly?' Vince Collier had laughed at her the other day in the canteen. 'What do you mean, dear?' she said. Vince wasn't his real name. His real name was . . . hm.

Mother kept a long-handled brass toasting fork hung with the fire-irons on the hearth. Always polishing the fire-irons. Always polishing everything. Father liked things clean, would have got on well with Saskia. The toasting fork had three wise monkeys on the top of the handle. *See no evil.* Plenty of evil to see in that house. Tilly used to sit by the fire and toast teacakes, Mother would butter them. The teacakes used to get stuck on the prongs of the fork. Father threw the toasting fork at Mother once. Like a spear. Got stuck in her leg. Mother howled like an animal. A poor bare forked animal.

She emptied the contents of her handbag on to the passenger seat. A mysterious tablespoon and a packet of crisps – cheese and onion. She hadn't bought those, she didn't like crisps, how had they got there? Definitely no purse. Fear squeezed her heart. Where was it? She'd had it in the newsagent. Had that horrible girl taken it, but how? What was she going to do now? She was trapped in the car park. Trapped! Could she phone someone? Who? No point in phoning anyone in London, not much they could do. The nice production assistant who had made her appointment at the optician's, what was her name? Tilly drew a blank. Something Indian and therefore more difficult to remember. She went through the alphabet – A-B-D-C-E – a method that often helped to prompt her memory. She went through the whole alphabet and came up with nothing. *Silly Tilly.*

Perhaps she was just being highly strung. That's what they said about her when she was a child. Family doctor prescribed an iron tonic – thick green stuff like mucus that made her gag although not as bad as castor oil or syrup of figs, gawd, the things they used to give the poor suffering child. Highly strung indeed. Artistic temperament, that's how Tilly preferred to think of it. As if an iron tonic could cure that.

Think about something else and then it'll come. Hopefully. She checked herself in the rear-view mirror, adjusted her wig. Who would have thought it would come to this? At least it was a very good wig, made by one of the best, cost a fortune. No one could tell. Made her look younger (well, one lived in hope), not like the awful rug she had to wear to be Vince Collier's mother. Looked like a Brillo pad. She wasn't completely bald, not like Mother had been at this age (like a billiard ball), just rather thin on top. Nothing more laughable than a bald woman.

Padma! That was the girl's name. Of course. Tilly fumbled for her phone, she wasn't very good with mobiles, the buttons were so small. She put on her new spectacles and peered at the phone. Wrong ones, she needed her reading specs but when she found them she realized that she couldn't remember how to use the phone, not the foggiest. She took her specs off and looked through the car windscreen, gazed out at the other parked cars. Everything a blur. She didn't have the faintest idea where she was.

She put the phone down on the passenger seat. *Breathe, Matilda.* She looked at her hands in her lap. Now what was she going to do?

When you were lost you needed a map. Ariadne and her thread, Tilly the *Leeds A–Z* that she found in a newsagent. Somehow or other she had wound her way back from the car park to the shopping centre. It was very brightly lit, brighter than the sun. Tilly could have sworn that she felt the hum of electricity passing through her bones. She had been disconcerted by hearing her mother's voice on the tannoy system, echoing down the years from her childhood, saying, 'If you get lost, go up to a policeman.' Tilly knew she must be mad because the last time her mother said that to her was well over sixty years ago, not to mention the fact that her mother had been dead for three decades and even if she had been alive it seemed unlikely that she would be making public announcements in a shopping centre in Leeds.

Anyway there wasn't a policeman to be seen anywhere.

The newsagent was familiar, she had definitely been here before. She put her spectacles on and opened up the *A–Z*. Why? What was she looking for? A way out of the ninth circle of hell. That was where traitors went, wasn't it? Where Phoebe belonged, not Tilly. As she walked out of the shop, face buried in the *A–Z*, a mean-faced, gum-chewing girl behind the counter shouted, 'Oi!' at her. Tilly thought it best to ignore her, you never knew what girls like that wanted.

She reached the foot of an escalator. The *A–Z* flapped uselessly in her hand. It was very hot in here, it must be the heat that was affecting her brain. She fanned herself with the *A–Z*. A youth, face raw with acne, like the inside of a pomegranate, loomed in front of her.

'Have you paid for that, madam?' he asked, pointing at the *A–Z*. Tilly's heart began to pound, a steam hammer threatening the end. Her mouth was dry, there was a buzzing in her ears as if an insect was trying to escape from her brain. A curtain descended before her eyes, waving and undulating, how she imagined the aurora borealis would be, although she'd never seen it. She would like to, she had always wanted to go to the North Pole – such a romantic destination. The Northern Lights. She was so hot, feverish. *Be not afeard.* Think of something cold. Tilly remembered shivering on the dockside with her father in the winter, watching the trawlers sailing into harbour after fishing the Arctic waters. Mysterious places – Iceland, Greenland, Murmansk. Ice still slick on the decks of the boats. Her father buying fish in the market, great trays of cod, bedded on crushed ice. Big fish, pure muscle. Poor things, Tilly used to think, swimming in the deep, cold waters of the north and then ending up on her father's slab. *From the north.* Like the wind, like winter monarchs. King Cod.

'Do you have a receipt for that, madam?' The spotted youth's voice boomed and receded. The curtain of Northern Lights vibrated and shrank, disappearing to a pinpoint of black. 'Please, excuse me,' Tilly murmured. Going down, she thought but then a pair of strong arms had her and a voice was saying, 'Steady the Buffs. Hold on there. Are you OK, do you need some help?'

'Oh, thank you, I'm all right really, you know.' She could hear herself panting. Like a hart. Her heart pulsing like a fleeing hart. *If a hart do lack a hind, / Let him seek out Rosalinde*. She had done *As You Like It* twice when she was younger. Nice play. The white hart was a harbinger of doom for the Celts. Douglas told her that. He knew so much! Wonderful memory. The White Hart in Drury Lane, used to go there sometimes with Douglas and drink pink gins. No one drank pink gins any more, did they? Oh God, make it all stop.

'I was looking for a policeman,' she said to the man who had asked her if she needed help.

'Well, I used to be one,' he said.

The nice man who used to be a policeman steered her into a room. The spotted youth led the way. Bleak little room, painted in several different shades of institutional beige. Reminded her of the sick room at school. There was a Formica-topped metal table and two stiff plastic chairs. Was she going to be interrogated? Tortured? There was a girl there now instead of the spotted youth, she pulled out one of the chairs from the table and said to Tilly, 'Stay here, I'll be back in a minute,' and was as good as her word, returning with a cup of hot sweet tea and a plate of Rich Tea biscuits.

'My name's Leslie,' the girl said, 'with an "ie". Do you want one?' she said to the man who used to be a policeman.

'No, you're all right,' he said.

'Are you American?' Tilly asked the girl, making an effort to enter into polite conversation. Tea, biscuits, chat. One should keep one's end up.

'Canadian.'

'Oh, of course, so sorry.' Tilly usually had a good ear for accents. 'I lost my purse, you see,' she said.

'She's not going to be arrested for shoplifting, is she?' the man who used to be a policeman said.

Shoplifting! Tilly moaned with horror. She was not a

thief. Never knowingly stolen so much as a pencil. (All those knives and forks and key rings and packets of crisps couldn't be stolen because she didn't *want* them. Quite the opposite.) Not like Phoebe. Phoebe was always 'borrowing' bracelets and shoes and frocks. Borrowed Douglas, never gave him back.

'Are you going to be OK?' the man asked, crouching down next to her.

'Yes, yes, thank you very much,' she said. So nice to encounter a proper gentleman these days.

'Right, I'll be off then,' she heard him say to the girl.

'Feel better now?' the girl called Leslie said when the man had gone.

'Are you going to prosecute me?' Tilly asked. She could hear the wobble in her voice. Tilly supposed the girl thought she was doolally. Not that Tilly blamed her. She was a stupid old woman who couldn't find her way home. *Silly Tilly.*

'No,' the girl said. 'You're not a criminal.'

The tea was wonderful. Tilly could have cried when she took her first sip. It restored her in every way. 'Silly me,' she said. 'I don't know why, I just went blank, you know? No, of course you don't,' she added, smiling at the girl. 'You're young.'

'It must have been the shock of losing your purse,' the girl, Leslie, said sympathetically.

'There was a woman,' Tilly said, 'she was being horrible to a child. Poor little thing, I wanted to find someone who would do something about it. But I didn't. You're really not going to arrest me?'

'No,' Leslie said. 'You forgot yourself, that's all.'

'I did!' Tilly said, immensely cheered by this idea. 'That's exactly it, I forgot myself. And now I've remembered myself. And everything will be all right. It really will.'

⁓

He thought of Leeds as a place where it always rained but the weather today was perfect. Roundhay Park was full of people who were anxious to wring a good day out of the English climate. Hordes everywhere, didn't anyone have a job to go to? He supposed he could ask himself the same question.

He came across an unexpected picture of happiness. A dog, a small scruffy one, was racing around the park as if it had just been released from prison. It disturbed a flock of pigeons intent on an abandoned sandwich and the birds rose up in a flutter of annoyance when it yapped excitedly at them. It started off again, running at full tilt and skidding to a halt, a second too late, next to a woman lying on a rug. She yelled and threw a flip-flop at it. The dog caught the flip-flop mid-air, shook it as if it were a rat, and then dropped it and ran off towards a small girl who screamed as it jumped up, trying to lick the ice cream in her hand. When the child's mother threatened it with blue murder the dog ran off and barked for a long time at something imaginary before finding a broken branch that it dragged round in circles until its attention was caught by the scent of something more interesting. It truffled around until it found the source – the dried turd of another dog. The dog sniffed it with the delight of a connoisseur before growing bored and trotting off towards a tree where it lifted its leg. 'Bugger off,' a man nearby shouted.

It seemed as if the dog didn't belong to anyone but then a man lumbered up, bearing down on the dog, barking orders at it, 'Youfuckinglittleshityoucomewhen Icallyou!' He was a big guy, with a mean expression on his face, barrel-chested like a Rottweiler. Add to that the shaved head, the weight-lifting muscles and a St George's flag tattooed on his left bicep, twinned with a half-naked woman inked into his right forearm, and, *voilà*, the perfect English gentleman.

The dog was wearing a collar but instead of a lead the man was carrying a rope, thin like a washing-line, with a noose at one end and without warning he grabbed the dog by the scruff and lassoed it. Then he hitched the dog up in the air so that it started to choke, its small legs paddling helplessly. Just as suddenly the dog was dropped to the ground and the man aimed a kick that connected with the dog's delicate-looking haunch. The dog cringed and started to tremble in a way that made his heart go out to it. The man yanked on the rope leash and pulled the dog along, shouting, 'Going to put you down, should have done it the minute that bitch left.' Dogs and mad Englishmen out in the midday sun.

A commotion was growing quickly, agitated people

protesting loudly at the man's behaviour, a jumble and hum of angry-sounding words – *innocent creature* – *pick on someone your own size* – *watch it, mate*. Mobile phones came out and people started to photograph the man. He took out his own iPhone. He had resisted the temptations of the Apple for a long time but now he had fallen. It was a lovely bit of kit. Until he was eight years old when his family bought a second-hand television that looked as if it was transmitting from Mars, they had only the radio for entertainment and information. In the half-century of his life, a tick on the Doomsday clock, he had borne witness to the most unbelievable technological advances. He had started off listening to an old Bush valve radio in the corner of the living room and now he had a phone in his hand on which he could pretend to throw a scrunched-up piece of paper into a waste bin. The world had waited a long time for that.

He shot off a couple of pictures of the man hitting the dog. Photographic evidence, you never knew when you were going to need it.

A woman's voice rose shrilly above the others, 'I'm calling the police,' and the man snarled, 'Mind your own fucking business,' and he continued to drag the dog along the path. He was pulling it so fast that a couple of times it tumbled head over heels and scraped and bounced along the hard surface of the path.

Cruel and unusual punishment, he thought. He had been around violence in one form or another all his life, not always on the receiving end of it, but you had to draw the line somewhere. A small, helpless dog seemed like a good place to draw that line.

He followed the man out of the park. The man's car was parked nearby and he opened the boot and plucked up the dog and flung it inside where it cowered, shivering and whimpering.

'You just wait, you little bastard,' the man said. He already had his mobile phone open, holding it to one ear as he raised a warning finger to the dog in case it made a move to escape. 'Hey, babe, it's Colin,' he said, his voice turning oily, a cage-fighting Romeo.

He frowned, imagining what would happen to the dog when the man got it home. Colin. It seemed unlikely it would be good. He stepped forward, tapped 'Colin' on the shoulder, said, 'Excuse me?' When Testosterone Man turned round, he said, 'On guard.'

'What the fuck are you talking about?' Colin said and he said, 'I'm being ironic,' and delivered a vicious and satisfying uppercut to Colin's diaphragm. Now that he was no longer subject to institutional rules governing brutality he felt free to hit people at will. He might have been around violence all his life but it was only recently that he was beginning to see the point of it. It used to be that his bark was worse than his bite, now it was the other way round.

His philosophy where fighting was concerned was to keep clear of anything fancy. One good, well-placed blow was usually enough to lay a man down. The punch was driven by a flash of black anger. There were days when he knew who he was. He was his father's son.

Right enough, Colin's legs went from beneath him

and he dropped to the ground, making a face like a suffocating fish. Strange squeaking and squealing noises came from his lungs as he fought for breath.

He squatted down next to Colin and said, 'Do that to anyone or anything again – man, woman, child, dog, even a fucking tree – and you're dead. And you'll never know whether or not I'm watching you. Understand?' The man nodded in acknowledgement even though he still hadn't managed to take a breath, looked in fact like he might never take another one. Bullies were always cowards at heart. His phone had clattered to the pavement and he could hear a woman's voice saying, 'Colin? Col – are you still there?'

He stood up and stepped on the phone and ground it into the pavement. Unnecessary and ridiculous but somehow satisfying.

The dog was still cowering in the boot. He could hardly leave it there so he picked it up and was surprised to find that it was warm even though it was shivering all over as if it was frozen. He cradled it against his chest and stroked its head in an effort to reassure it that he wasn't another big man about to beat it up.

He walked away, the dog still in his arms, glancing back once to make sure that Colin was still alive. It wouldn't have bothered him too much if he was dead but he didn't want to find himself on a murder charge.

He could feel the dog's frightened little heartbeat, a pulse, against his chest. *Tic-tic-tic.* 'It's OK,' he said, using the tone of voice he had used to soothe his own daughter when she was small. 'Everything's OK now.' It was a long time since he had spoken to a dog. He tried to loosen the rope around the dog's neck but the knot was too tight. He turned round the tag on the dog's collar so that he could read it. 'Let's see if you've got a name,' he said.

'The Ambassador?' Jackson said, looking doubtfully at the small dog. 'What kind of a name is that?'

He was drifting, a tourist in his own country, not so much a holiday as an exploration. A holiday was lying on a warm beach in a peaceful country with a woman by your side. Jackson had tended to take his women wherever he found them. He didn't usually go looking.

He had been living in London for the last couple of years, taking over the rent on the little Covent Garden flat in which he had briefly shared a counterfeit marital bliss with his fake wife, Tessa. A man called Andrew Decker had killed himself (somewhat messily) in the living room of the flat and Jackson was surprised how little this bothered him. A specialist trauma-scene cleaning company had come in (now there was a profession you wouldn't want) and by the time Jackson had changed the carpet and disposed of the chair that Andrew Decker had shot himself in you would never have known that anything untoward had happened. It had been a righteous death and Jackson supposed that made a difference.

Jackson's official identity was all in the past – army, police, gumshoe. He had been 'retired' for a while but that had made him feel as if he was redundant to the world's needs. Now he called himself 'semi-retired' because it was a term that covered a lot of bases, not all of them strictly legal. He was off the grid a lot these days, picking up work here and there. His specialist subject on *Mastermind* would be looking for people. Not necessarily finding them, but half the equation was better than none. 'Really you're looking for your sister,' Julia said. 'Your own dear grail. You're never going to find her, Jackson. She's gone. She's never coming back.'

'I know that.' Didn't make any difference, he would go on looking for all the lost girls, the Olivias, the Joannas, the Lauras. And his sister, Niamh, the first lost girl (the last lost girl). Even though he knew exactly where Niamh was, thirty miles away from where he was at the moment, mouldering in cold, damp clay.

Lowering his expectations of cars, Jackson had been pleasantly surprised by the third-hand Saab he bought in a dodgy auction in Ilford. There were a few unhelpful clues to the Saab's previous ownership – a light-up Virgin Mary on the dashboard, a creased postcard from Cheltenham (*Looking good here, all the best, N.*) and an Everton mint, covered in fluff, in the glove compartment. The only thing Jackson did to improve the Saab was to fit a CD player. He discovered it was easy to live on the road. He had his phone and his car and his music – what more did a man need?

Before Tessa, Jackson had enjoyed expensive cars. The money his second wife stole from him had been an unlooked-for legacy – two million pounds left to him by a batty old woman who had been his client. It had seemed an immense sum at the time, diminished now in comparison to the trillions lost by the masters of the universe, although two million would still probably buy you Iceland.

'Well,' his first wife, Josie, said, 'as usual, you were the architect of your own downfall.' He hadn't exactly been left destitute. The proceeds of the sale of his house in France hit his bank account the day after Tessa emptied it. 'Jackson lives to ride another day,' Julia said.

Of course, he had never really felt entitled to the money and Tessa's theft of it felt more like a turn in the wheel of fortune than outright robbery. Not a proper wife but a trickster, a grifter. Tessa wasn't her real name, of course. She had taken him for the longest of cons – seduced, courted, married and robbed him blind. It seemed the perfect irony that the policeman had married the criminal. He imagined her lying on a beach somewhere in the Indian Ocean, a cocktail in hand, the classic movie ending for a heist. ('Well, women were deceivers ever, Jackson,' Julia said, as if she were complimenting her sex rather than condemning it.) Finding people was his forte, ironic therefore that his errant wife had so far completely eluded him. He had followed clues, a trail of breadcrumbs that so far had taken him everywhere and led him nowhere. He was good but Tessa was oh-so-much better. He almost admired her for it. Almost.

He was still looking for her, his search unfurling across the country, tracking her like a lazy hunter following spoor. It wasn't so much that he wanted his money back – a lot of it was in shares that had fallen into the financial basement – he just didn't like being taken for a fool. ('Why not, when you are one?' Josie said.)

In the company of the Saab, he had been to Bath, Bristol, Brighton, the Devon coast, down to the toe of Cornwall, up to the Peak District, the Lakes. He had avoided Scotland, the savage country where both his heart and his life had been in danger twice now. (The best of times, the worst of times.) Third time even unluckier, he suspected. But he had ventured into Wales which he was surprised to like, before driving through the suffocating rural peace of Herefordshire, Wiltshire, Shropshire, the fatlands of Gloucestershire, the post-industrial blight of the Midlands. He had zigzagged across the Pennines to take in the bleak victims of Thatcherism. The coal gone, the steel gone, the ships gone. Like most countries, he discovered, the puzzling jigsaw that was his native land seemed to be at odds with itself. A disunited kingdom.

Since disengaging from the rat race Jackson had found himself increasingly drawn to the less direct ways. He had become a dawdler on the back roads, following the thread veins on the map. A traveller on the scenic route, idly put-putting around the green and leafy byways, searching for the lost pastoral England that was lodged in his head and his heart. A golden, pre-industrial age. Unfortunately that Arcadian past was no more than a dream.

'Arcadia' was a word that Julia had taught him one

lost weekend in Paris that felt like a lifetime ago now. They were visiting the Louvre and she had pointed out Poussin's painting of *Les Bergers d'Arcadie* and the tomb it depicted with the words '*Et in Arcadia ego*'. 'Open to interpretation, of course,' she said. 'Does it mean death is here, even in this simple paradise, i.e. there's no escaping it, chum – a *memento mori*, if you will, "As you are now so once was I" kind of thing – or does it mean the person who is dead also once enjoyed the good life, which is the same message really. Either way, we're all doomed. Only of course – irritatingly – it got all mixed up in that *Da Vinci Code* piffle.'

Julia might have been instinctively attracted to all kinds of nonsense but at heart she was a classicist. She was also very *wordy* and Jackson had stopped listening to her long before she finished explaining. Nonetheless, he had been struck by the poignancy of the inscription.

And now he was looking for his own Arcadian bower. What had begun as a rather vague search for Tessa had morphed into a quite different purpose. He was a man on a real-estate mission. He was looking for a peg to hang his hat on, an old dog looking for a new kennel, one untainted by the past. A fresh start. Somewhere there was a place for him. All he had to do was find it.

He had saved the best to last. North Yorkshire, God's own county, the gyre he had been circling around all this time. None of his other stops on his peregrinations could exert the same pull on the lodestone of his heart as North Yorkshire did. Of course, Jackson was a West Riding man himself, made from soot and rugby league and beef dripping, but that didn't mean he was about to go and live there. The last place he intended to end up in was the place he had started from, the place where his entire family lay restlessly in the earth.

He set the SatNav for the heart of the sun, or, to be more accurate, York. The voice on Jackson's SatNav was 'Jane', with whom he had been in a contentious relationship for a long time now. 'Why not just mute her?' Julia said reasonably. 'In fact, why do you need her at all, you're always going on about what a good sense of direction you've got.' He *did* have a good sense of direction, he said defensively. He just liked the company.

'Get a life, sweetie.'

'Go east, old man,' he had muttered to himself as he tapped his coordinates into Jane and prepared to cross the spine of the Pennines again and return to the cradle of civilization.

Slightly south-east, Jane corrected him silently.

He had been trying to visit all of the Betty's Tea Rooms – Ilkley, Northallerton, two in Harrogate, two in York. A genteel itinerary that would have done a coachload of elderly ladies proud. Jackson was a big fan of Betty's. You could guarantee a decent cup of coffee in Betty's, but it went beyond the decent coffee and the respectable food and the fact that the waitresses all looked as if they were nice girls (and women) who had been parcelled up some time in the 1930s and freshly unwrapped this morning. It was the way that everything was exactly right and fitting. And clean.

'The older you get, the more like a woman you become,' Julia said.

'Really?'

'No.' Long after their relationship had ended, after Julia had herself married and had the child which for a long time she had denied was Jackson's, she was still chattering away in his brain.

If Britain had been run by Betty's it would never have succumbed to economic Armageddon. Over a pot of house blend and a plate of scrambled eggs and smoked salmon in the café in St Helen's Square in York, Jackson fantasized about being governed by a Betty's oligarchy – Cabinet ministers in spotless white aprons and cinnamon toast all round. Even Jackson in his most aggrandizingly masculine moments would have to agree that the world would be a better place if it was run by women. 'God created Man,' his daughter Marlee said to him a few weeks ago, and for a moment Jackson thought that her adolescent pessimism had made her turn to some kind of fundamentalist Christian religion. She registered the look of alarm on his face and laughed. 'God created Man,' she repeated. 'And then he had a better idea.'

Ha, ha. Or LOL, as his daughter would have said.

In York he had spent many hours in the great cathedral train shed of the National Railway Museum where he paid tribute to the *Mallard*, Yorkshire-built and the fastest steam train in the world, a record that could never be taken away from her. Jackson's heart had swelled with pride at the sight of the beautiful shining blue flanks of the engine. Not a day went by that he didn't mourn the loss of engineering and industry. This was no country for old men.

As well as teashops Jackson had also discovered an unlooked-for delight in bagging the ruined abbeys of Yorkshire on his journey – Jervaulx, Rievaulx, Roche, Byland, Kirkstall. Jackson's new pastime. Trains, coins, stamps, Cistercian abbeys, Betty's – all part of the semi-autistic male impulse to collect – a need for order or a desire to possess, or both.

He still needed to collar Fountains, the mother of all abbeys. Years ago (decades ago now) Jackson had been on a school trip to Fountains Abbey, a rare thing, Jackson hadn't gone to the kind of school that had out-ings. All he could remember was playing football amongst the ruins, until a teacher put a stop to it. Oh yes, and trying to kiss a girl called Daphne Wood on the back seat of the coach on the way home. And receiving a thumping for his pains. Daphne Wood had a tremendous right hook. It was Daphne Wood who had taught him the value of getting in there with one swift, mean blow rather than prancing around with a duellist's finesse. Jackson wondered where she was now.

Rievaulx was sublime but his favourite abbey so far was Jervaulx. Privately owned, with an honesty box at the gate and no English Heritage branding, the ruins had touched his soul in some inarticulate and melancholy place, the nearest thing to holiness for an atheistic Jackson. He missed God. But then who didn't? As far as Jackson was concerned, God slipped out of the building a long time ago and he wasn't coming back, but, like any good architect, he had left his work behind as his legacy. North Yorkshire had been designed when God was in his pomp and each time that Jackson came here he was struck anew by the power that landscape and beauty had over him these days.

'It's your age,' Julia said.

Of course, these were the very same rich and powerful abbeys that in the Middle Ages farmed the sheep, the golden fleeces which provided the foundation of the wool trade and England's wealth and which led in turn to the Satanic mills of the West Riding, and thence to poverty, overcrowding, disease, child exploitation on levels beyond belief and the death and destruction of the dream of Arcadia. For want of a nail. Those mills were museums and galleries now, the abbeys in ruins. The world turns.

The day that Jackson visited Jervaulx it had been deserted apart from the everlasting sheep (nature's lawnmowers) and their fat lambs and he had wandered amongst the peaceful stones where wild flowers sprang from between the cracks and wished that his sister was laid to rest in a place like this instead of the mundane municipal cemetery that had been her last stop on earth. He had unfinished business there, a promise never given to a dead sister to avenge her senseless death. He supposed Niamh would always be calling him home, the siren song of the dead, for the rest of his life.

'All roads lead home,' Julia said.

'All roads lead away from home,' Jackson said.

Josie, his first wife, had once said to him that if he ran far enough he would end up back where he started but Jackson didn't think that the place he had started from existed any more. He had returned a few years ago, taken Marlee to meet her dead relatives, and he had found that it wasn't the town he remembered. The slag heaps were levelled, the mine's machinery long gone, only the pit-head wheel remained, cut in two and planted on a roundabout on the outskirts of town, more like an ornament than a memorial. There was not much evidence to show that it had ever been a place where his father had spent his life toiling in the velvet dark.

Niamh herself had been underground nearly forty years – too late to track down clues, sniff out DNA, interview witnesses. The coffin was closed, the case as cold as that clay she was buried in. When she was murdered his sister was just three years older than his daughter was now. Marlee was fourteen. A dangerous age, although, let's face it, Jackson thought, every age was a dangerous age for a woman.

Seventeen, Niamh's life hardly begun when it was halted. His sister couldn't stop for death, so he had, very kindly, stopped for her. Emily Dickinson. Poetry? Jackson? Believe it or not.

Poetry had started to get under his skin a couple of years ago, round about the time he had almost died in a train crash. (In synopsis, Jackson's life always sounded more dramatic than the mild ennui of living it every day.) He didn't think the two things necessarily had anything to do with each other, but in his resurrected life he had decided to catch up, rather late in the day, with some of the things he had missed out on in his impoverished education. Like culture, for example. While living in London he had committed himself to a programme of self-improvement, feasting from the liberal banquet on offer in the capital – art galleries, exhibitions, museums, even the occasional classical concert. He developed a bit of a taste for Beethoven, the symphonies at any rate. Lush and tuneful, they seemed designed to address the soul. He caught the Fifth at the Proms. He'd never been to the Proms before, put off by all those jingoistic Last Night shenanigans, and, indeed, the self-important Promenaders proved to be over-privileged smug wankers but Beethoven hadn't written the music for them. He had written it for Everyman, in the guise of a middle-aged trooper who was surprised to find himself moved to tears by the triumphant blossoming swell of brass and horsehair.

Not a lot of theatre, Julia and her actor friends had killed off any hope for him in that arena. He had made the mistake of taking Marlee to three hours of bum-numbing Brecht, by the end of which he wanted to shout out, 'Yes! You're right, the earth revolves around the sun, you said that when you first came on stage, you've been saying it ever since, you don't need to keep saying it. I get it!' Marlee slept through most of it. He loved her for that.

This attempt at betterment had extended beyond paintings and piano recitals and museum artefacts, he had also been grimly working his way through the world's classics. Fiction had never been Jackson's thing. Facts seemed challenging enough without making stuff up. What he discovered was that the great novels of the world were about three things – death, money and sex. Occasionally a whale. But poetry had wormed its way in, uninvited. *A Toad, can die of Light!* Crazy. So that here he was, thinking of his long-dead, long-lost sister, bolstered by a woman who felt a funeral in her brain.

As he left Jervaulx, Jackson had placed a twenty-pound note in the honesty box – more than any English Heritage fee but it was worth the money. And besides, he liked the fact that even in these days and times there was someone willing to trust to a man's honesty.

When he was thirteen Jackson had spent one of the better summers of his life staying on a farm called Howdale on the edge of the Yorkshire Dales. He was never sure how this rural idyll had come about, church or state, one of them was probably involved somewhere along the line – the parish priest or his social worker must have organized it, he supposed. The social worker had been a temporary acquisition, appearing out of the blue one day in the middle of the worst year of his life and disappearing just as mysteriously a few months later, even though it was still the worst year of his life. The social worker was there (apparently) to help guide him through that terrible year of bereavement which began with his mother dying of cancer and ended with his brother killing himself after their sister was murdered. ('Top that if you can,' he occasionally found himself thinking grouchily when he was a policeman and listening to some stranger's less impressive lament.)

The holiday at Howdale had been a reprieve from the bleak afterlife he was sharing with his father, an angry man with a heart of coal. At the time, Jackson didn't analyse his feelings of grief, nor did he wonder why a pleasant, elderly man he had never met before ('I'm what they call a volunteer, lad') drove him from his small, soot-encrusted terraced home to the green out-back of the Dales, dropping him in a farmyard where a herd of black-and-white cows were in the act of shouldering their way into a milking parlour. Jackson had never been close up to a cow before.

The farm was run by a couple called Reg and Joan Atwell. They had a grown-up son and daughter. The son worked for an insurance company in York and the daughter was a nurse at St James's Infirmary in Leeds and neither of them was interested in running the Atwells' fifth-generation farm. The wolf child that Jackson had become must have been a severe trial for the Atwells' patience, but they had been unusually tolerant and kind people and Jackson hoped he hadn't disappointed them, and if he had he was certainly sorry now.

He could still see the farmhouse kitchen with the Rayburn that was always hot and was home to a big brown teapot containing tea the colour of old oak leaves. He could still smell the huge breakfasts, porridge with cream and brown sugar, fried eggs, ham, bread and home-made marmalade that Mrs Atwell served up. Two farm workers joined them at breakfast, men who had already put in half a day's work by the time they sat down to breakfast.

There was an ancient sofa in the kitchen, covered with a scratchy crocheted throw, where they sat in the evenings. The Atwells more or less lived in the kitchen. The sheepdog, a Border collie, Jess, would lie on the rag rug in front of the Rayburn. Mr Atwell would say, 'Make room on the sofa for the boy, Mother,' but Jackson often as not sat on the rag rug with Jess. It was the only time before or since that Jackson could recollect feeling close to a dog. His family never had a pet and, when he had his own family, his wife, Josie, had restricted their pet ownership to the small end of Creation – hamsters, guinea pigs, mice. When she was little his daughter, Marlee, used to have a pet rabbit, Muffin, a big brute of a thing with floppy ears that used to square up to Jackson as if he was in the ring with it and prepared to go the distance. 'Pet' wouldn't have been the word Jackson would have used to describe it.

He had given a Border collie to Louise. A puppy. It had been an unconscious choice. He had fled from Scotland, and DCI Louise Monroe, and in his place he had – unconsciously – left a creature close to his emotional heart. She was better off with the dog than with him. He could never be with Louise now. She was within the law, he was outside it.

There had been some talk of him staying on at Howdale at the end of the summer but unfortunately he had been returned, by the same mysterious, elderly gentleman, to the grim comforts of home. Jackson wrote to the Atwells (the first letter he had ever written), thanking them for their hospitality, but heard nothing back until several months later their daughter wrote to him (the first letter Jackson had ever received) to 'inform' him that her parents had died within a month of each other, her father first, of an unhealthy heart, and then his wife of a broken one. Jackson, having imbibed guilt in his Catholic mother's milk, felt the unspoken accusation that he had somehow contributed to their untimely deaths.

He sometimes wondered, if the Atwells had been in possession of stronger hearts, would they have kept him? Would he have become a farm boy, would he even now be driving a tractor up on the hills with a sheepdog riding shotgun? (For want of a nail.)

For a while, after his *annus horribilis* (the Queen had helpfully taught him the phrase), Jackson had fantasized that he had another family somewhere, Irish diaspora that his mother had carelessly omitted to mention. He imagined her coming back from the dead to tell him about them (*Ah, for sure, the McGurks in Pontefract, they'll look after you, Jackson*). Perfectly ordinary people, the kind he saw on television and read about in comics and (occasionally) in books – cousins who worked in offices and shops, drove taxis, delivered babies. Uncles who hung their own wallpaper and kept allotments, aunts who baked cakes and knew the value of love and money – they all existed somewhere, inhabitants of his personal soap opera, waiting for him to find them and be crushed to their collective, comforting bosom. But these people never manifested themselves and for the next three years Jackson inhabited an emotional void, just himself and his father locked together in mute disregard.

When he was sixteen Jackson joined the army. He embraced his new austere existence with the zeal of a warrior monk discovering the profit of discipline. He was broken down and then built up again, his one and only allegiance to his new, brutal family. The army was tough but it was nothing compared to the life before. Jackson was just relieved to have a future at last. Any future.

If his mother had gone to a doctor sooner with her cancer instead of suffering the archetypal ancient martyrdom of the Irish mother, then perhaps she would have hit his brother about the head with a rolled-up newspaper (a common form of communication in their family) and told him to get off his backside (he was nursing a foul hangover) and get out into the rain and meet his sister off the bus. Then Niamh wouldn't have been attacked by her unknown assailant who raped her and strangled her and then threw her body into the canal. For want of a nail.

After his visit to Jervaulx, Jackson had gone on a pilgrimage to find Howdale again. Working on instinct, with a little help and some hindrance from SatNav Jane, he made his way down back roads until he came to a sign that announced *Howdale Farm Holiday Homes*. He turned down the drive, once a muddy track but now weed-free and fresh with tarmac, and saw the farmhouse still sitting squarely at the end. The adjacent dairy and a scattering of farm workers' cottages that he had forgotten about were now all done up in matching white-and-green-painted livery. No sign of cows or sheep, no smell of manure and silage, none of the usual rusting litter of old farm machinery. The place had been transformed into a sanitized, story-book kind of farm. Once upon a time Jackson had erased his past, now his past had erased him.

Jackson climbed out of the car and looked around. There was a small children's play area where Joan Atwell had hung her washing, a large gravelled turning circle where a run-down old barn had once stood. A group of people of all ages (they called that a family, Jackson reminded himself) was hanging out, drinks in hand, on a lawn that had once been the farmyard. He caught the primitive smell of searing meat. At the sight of Jackson, the adults in the group looked uneasy and one of the men raised his voice, ready for belligerence, a pair of barbecue tongs clutched in his hand like a weapon, and said, 'Can I help you?'

Jackson had no taste for hostility in these surroundings and so he shrugged and said, 'No,' a response which seemed to unsettle the group further.

He climbed back in the Saab and caught a glimpse of himself in the rear-view mirror. Someone slightly feral looked back. He hadn't shaved for several days and his hair flopped dirtily in his eyes. There was a lean and hungry look about him that he didn't recognize. At least he still *had* his own hair. Every guy you saw these days had shaved away his male-pattern baldness in a futile attempt to look hard rather than merely hairless. Jackson had recently turned fifty, a fact he still hadn't entirely come to terms with. *The golden years.* (Yeah, right.) 'A milestone,' Josie laughed as if it were a huge joke. He had avoided the birthday altogether, spending the weekend miserably on his own in Prague, side-stepping drunken English stag and hen parties. On his return he had set off on this journey.

His definition of elderly had changed as he himself had moved nearer to the event horizon of death. When he was twenty, old people were forty. Now he was over the hill of his half-century the definition began to stretch towards something more yielding, but nonetheless once you hit fifty there was no escaping the fact that you had a one-way ticket on a non-stop service to the terminus.

He drove off, aware that the barbecuing family were watching him all the way down the drive. He understood, he would have been wary of himself as well.

In Knaresborough Jackson had sought out Old Mother Shipton's Cave, a destination that had once been a stopover on that school trip to Fountains. The schoolboy Jackson had gazed in surprise at the petrified items in Old Mother Shipton's Cave – umbrella, boots, teddy bears – hanging beneath the well. The alchemy of the Dropping Well was due simply to the high mineral content of the water and yet even now the adult Jackson still found something strangely affecting in its preservation of mundane objects. His younger self had thought that 'petrified' meant 'terrified' and had wondered if he were to become too frightened by something, or someone, would he end up like those inert, everyday objects? It didn't work like that, he knew now. It wasn't being frightened that turned you into stone, it was being the one who did the frightening.

After Jackson had almost died in the train crash he was grateful to have survived but there was a part of him that had feared that being saved would turn him soft and he would become one of those grateful evangelists of positive living (*Every day is a gift, I'm going to make my time on earth count*, et cetera). However, somewhat to his surprise, the new version of Jackson that emerged from this harrowing was a colder and harder one than he had expected. 'The leaner, meaner Jackson,' Julia laughed. 'Ooh, I'm scared.' Perhaps she should be.

He would never be free of her now that they were united through their son. Two become one. As the Spice Girls might say.

He had met Julia at Rievaulx. He tended to meet her on neutral territory these days. There had been an unfortunate incident a couple of years ago when a tired and emotional Jackson had turned up on the doorstep of the Dales cottage she was sharing with her arty, über-bourgeois husband, Jonathan Carr, and bluntly 'explained' to him that Nathan was not, as Jonathan thought, his child. And he had the evidence to prove it,

Jackson said, triumphantly waving the results of a DNA test in his face.

There was, naturally, some violence but it hardly mattered. Jackson had threatened a custody suit but he was aware that he was blustering and Julia knew it too. (Jonathan Carr's opinion didn't count, not to Jackson anyway.) Jackson didn't want to bring up another child, with or without Julia, he just wanted to establish the fundamental principle of ownership.

Now there was an unstated delicacy in their triangular relationship. The man who fathered the boy, the man who was raising him and the treacherous woman at the apex. *My Son Calls Another Man Daddy.* Trust Hank to tell it how it is.

He had met Julia and Nathan not at Rievaulx itself but on the Terraces above, from where there was a panoramic vista of breathtaking beauty. It brought out the Romantic soul in Jackson, once hidden in a dark, deep mineshaft but lately peeking its head, unabashedly, into the daylight. He might have become a harder version of himself on the outside but on the inside the spirit could still soar. Rievaulx, Beethoven's Fifth, a mother and child reunion.

They had strolled between the two Grecian temples – follies, built to amuse eighteenth-century aristocrats, now in the custody of the National Trust. 'Crikey, fancy having all this as your private picnic ground,' Julia said. 'Imagine.' She sounded even more husky than usual. 'High pollen count,' she said, shaking a packet of Zyrtec at him. Jackson was relieved that Nathan showed no sign of having inherited his mother's lungs (or, indeed, her histrionic disposition).

'No one should be allowed to own a view like this,' Jackson said.

'Ah, you can take the boy out of his collectivist past, but you can't take the collectivist past out of the boy.'

'That's nonsense,' Jackson said.

'Is it?'

Nathan skipped ahead of them on the grass. 'The boy', Julia called him, bonhomous with love. The only boy. Men were a continual presence in Julia's life but always of peripheral importance, including, Jackson suspected, her arty-farty husband (hats off to the man who managed to stay married to inconstant Julia). But not the boy, the boy beamed hotly at the centre of her universe.

'Does Jonathan know you're here?' he asked.

'Why should he?' Julia said.

'Why shouldn't he?' Jackson said.

She ignored the question. There was nothing you could do with her, she was impossible. (In that, at least, she was constant.)

'Bare ruined choirs and all that,' Julia said, changing the subject. 'Shakespeare, the dissolution of the monasteries,' she added instructively, having over the years realized the great black holes in Jackson's general knowledge.

'I know,' he said. 'I know that. I'm not entirely ignorant.'

'Really?' she said, absent-mindedly rather than ironically. Her attention was all on the boy, none on the man. Jackson had, in fact, learned a great deal about the shock and awe of the Reformation in the course of his wanderings around the abbeys of Yorkshire but there was no point in being didactic with Julia, she was always going to know more about everything than him. She was the product of a sound education and a good memory, while, let's face it, Jackson was in possession of neither.

Jackson ignored Julia in turn, gazing meditatively (some – mostly women – might say mindlessly) at the amphitheatre, nature's heavenly bowl, that contained Rievaulx. Even in ruins the abbey was matchless, celestial. Awesome. *Awesome*, his daughter Marlee's blasé teenage voice sounded in his head. By the time Nathan was a teenager Jackson would be into his sixties. His diamond years.

'Cheer up, sweetie,' Julia said, 'it may never happen.'

'It already has,' Jackson said gloomily.

Jackson had occasionally to remind himself that there was a third purpose to his leisurely Byzantine progress around the country. Everything came (and went) in threes, as far as he could see. Three Fates, three Furies, three Graces, three Kings, three monkeys, a three-personed God.

'Three-headed dogs,' Julia added. 'To the Pythagoreans, three was the first real number, because they saw it as having a beginning, a middle and an end.'

Jackson was working on behalf of a client. Despite the fact that he was no longer a private detective, despite the fact that he no longer *had* clients, that he no longer dabbled in the soul-destroying tedium of divorce cases and debt chasing and missing pets, despite all that, he had somehow acquired a woman called Hope McMaster who lived as far away from Yorkshire as you could get without getting closer again. New Zealand, in other words.

He should have said no, in fact, he was pretty sure he did say no when Hope McMaster sent him a long email (too long, a life story) out of the blue at the end of the previous year. *I was adopted and I wondered if you could find out some information about my biological parents?* How uncomplicated that sounded to his ears now.

Exactly how Hope McMaster had got hold of a contact address for him was unclear but somewhere along the line – as was so often the case – it seemed to involve Julia ('a friend of a friend of a friend'). Nowhere in the world was safe. Julia probably had friends on the moon (or friends of friends of friends, ad infinitum). And somehow six degrees of separation from Julia always ended up at Jackson.

In the course of his lackadaisical odyssey around the country Jackson had been able to dovetail neatly the stalking of his thieving false wife with the pursuit of Hope McMaster's case. Cornwall, Gwynedd, Doncaster, Harrogate were all locations where he had tried unsuccessfully to hunt down Hope McMaster's mysterious identity. 'So,' Julia said, as they left Rievaulx Terraces behind them and headed towards the comforting arms of the Black Swan in Helmsley, 'you're basically looking for two women, your wife and Hope McMaster, and you have no idea who either of them really are.'

'Yes,' Jackson said. 'Exactly so.'

On the outskirts of Leeds, he had netted Kirkstall Abbey. It was the first abbey he had come across whose stones were incongruously blackened with industrial soot from the days when all the golden fleeces were turned into bolts of cloth. Tomorrow he had an appointment with a woman called Linda Pallister, an adoption counsellor with Social Services who Hope McMaster had already been in contact with. Hope's lawyer in Christchurch had drawn up a power of attorney, instructing Jackson to act on her behalf. Jackson had hopes for Leeds. Leeds was the place where it had all started for Hope McMaster and he very much hoped it would be the place where it would all finish.

Linda Pallister failed to keep the appointment. 'Linda's had to go home, I'm afraid. A family emergency,' a woman on reception at Social Services told him. 'But she said to reschedule for tomorrow.'

After Linda Pallister had failed to keep her appointment with him, Jackson had spent what was left of the afternoon wandering around – a *boulevardier* – in Briggate, the Calls, the Arcades. The Corn Exchange, the town hall (that great monument to municipal clout), the Merrion Centre, Roundhay Park – all constituted a city that seemed both familiar and at the same time utterly strange. He felt as though he was looking for something that he would only recognize when he found it. His lost youth, perhaps. Or the lost youth that he himself had been. The dirty old town he remembered had been overlaid by something new and shiny. It didn't mean the dirty old town wasn't still there, of course.

He reckoned that the last time he was in Leeds must have been more than thirty years ago. He used to come here as a boy when it represented the height of metropolitan sophistication, not that 'metropolitan' was a word in his vocabulary in those days and 'sophistication' didn't rise much above buying a packet of ten Embassy and sneaking into an X-rated film. Jackson remembered shoplifting in Woolworths in Leeds. Petty things – sweets, key rings, batteries. His father would have flayed him alive if he had found out but it had never really seemed like stealing, just a cheeky flouting of authority. Now Woolworths didn't even exist any more. Who would have thought it? Perhaps it would still be going if kids hadn't kept on nicking the sweets and key rings and batteries. Over the years all that ill-gotten loot probably added up to a fortune.

In the Merrion Centre he had come to the aid of a confused old woman that a security numpty was trying to haul away. 'Are you OK?' he had asked her. 'Do you want some help?' Jackson voiced his personal mantra, 'I used to be a policeman,' which seemed to act as a reassurance. There had been something familiar about her but he couldn't put his finger on it. She was wearing a wig which had slipped to an unfortunately jaunty angle. Jackson hoped someone would put him down before he got to that stage. He supposed he would end up having to put himself down. He planned to go out on the ice (*I may be some time*), lie down with a bottle of something as old as himself and drift off into the big sleep. He hoped global warming didn't scupper this plan.

His final stop had been Roundhay, a leisurely stroll, he thought, some sunshine and fresh air away from the urban crowds. He had not expected to walk away as a dog owner. The interrupted journey, the unexpected gift, the unforeseen encounter. Life had its plots.

Later, looking back, Jackson could see that his failed appointment with Linda Pallister was the moment when it all started to go wrong. If she had kept their rendezvous he would have spent a constructive hour or so, would have felt satisfied and purposeful, and might quite possibly have undergone another evening in a hotel, eating a room-service meal and watching a bad pay-for-view movie, instead of spending a restless time, blacking out for large portions of it and having meaningless, promiscuous sex. For want of a nail. Blame Linda Pallister. In the end everyone else would.

Tracy phoned in sick to cover her tracks. 'Bit of a tummy bug, I think, I'm just going to go home early,' and Leslie said, 'No problem, I hope you feel better soon.' Then Tracy sneaked back into the car park to pick up her Audi A4 and drive with Courtney to a Mamas and Papas store in Birstall Shopping Park where she bought a car seat that cost an arm and a leg. She spent the entire drive to the retail park waiting to be arrested for lack of the said car seat and in a fit of paranoia had got the kid to lie down on the back seat, just like a proper kidnap victim. Tracy felt as if there were a neon sign on the roof of the car that screamed, 'This isn't the mother!' She gave the kid the Greggs sausage roll to keep her occupied. There was a plaid blanket in the boot and Tracy wondered if the kid would freak out if she covered her with it. Probably. She decided against it.

An uneasy tour of the Mamas and Papas store revealed what Tracy had always suspected – children were mind-blowingly expensive. She should know, she'd just bought one, even if it was at a bargain price. Kids were all about retail. If you weren't buying and sell-ing the kids themselves, you were buying and selling on their behalf. Tracy felt a sudden twitch of anxiety. The two thousand pounds that remained in her bag weighed heavy. She should have handed over the full five thousand pounds to Kelly Cross. Buying the kid cheap felt like a mistake now.

Tracy left the car seat in the shop while she walked towards Gap, Courtney plodding along beside her like a doped-up dog. The kid had been pretty vocal in the

Merrion Centre, yelling her head off, but now she was taking her cues from Helen Keller.

Tracy was acutely aware of all the security cameras. She imagined the pair of them on *Crimewatch*, Courtney's face a blanked-out blur and her own magnified for a viewing public. *Have you seen this woman? She abducted a child from outside a shopping centre in Leeds.* She had stepped over the thin blue line, from the hunter to the hunted in one easy move.

What would she say if she was stopped – 'It's OK, I bought the kid fair and square'? Yeah, that would go down well when they hauled her off to the nick. She was the Childcatcher, the Bogeywoman, every mother's nightmare. But not Kelly's. Kelly probably saw her as her saviour. Kelly certainly wasn't the first mother to sell her own kid. But what if . . . what if Kelly wasn't actually the kid's mother? Tracy had lost track of how many kids Kelly had spawned. Were they all in care? What if she was minding Courtney for someone else? In that case, Tracy reasoned to herself – already working up arguments for the social workers, the police, the courts – whoever her mother was, she hadn't cared enough about Courtney to put her in a safe pair of hands. Handing your kid over to Kelly Cross was like handing her over to a pit bull. Bottom line – the kid was at risk.

She remembered Kelly Cross standing on the bus platform before the doors closed, the puzzled look on her face as she said, *But she's not—* Not what? Not my kid? Tracy closed the bus doors in her mind. Put big metal security shutters down. She hadn't heard anything. Thought instead about that little warm hand slipping into hers.

She knew someone who could find out more for her. Linda Pallister. She was still in fostering and adoption, wasn't she? If she hadn't retired yet, she could find out the status of Kelly Cross's kids.

Tracy couldn't remember when she had last seen Linda Pallister. It must have been at Barry Crawford's daughter's wedding, three years ago. Detective Superintendent Barry Crawford, Tracy's ex-colleague. Linda's daughter, Chloe, was best friends with Barry's daughter, Amy, and was the chief bridesmaid, a fright in burnt-orange satin. 'I had "bronze" in my head for their dresses, you know,' Amy Crawford said ruefully to Tracy. Nothing in the poor girl's head but mush now that she inhabited the land of the living dead. Her own dress had been the usual overblown white garment, her bouquet made up of raffish orange and yellow flowers. The men's buttonholes were a single orange gerbera, like something a clown would squirt water out of. ('I wanted something a little bit different,' Amy said.)

'Very cheerful,' Barbara Crawford, mother of the bride, had commented, wincing at the gaudiness of it all. Barbara herself tastefully overdressed in turquoise silk ('Paule Vasseur,' she murmured to Tracy as if it were a secret). It had been no parish tea affair for Barry and Barbara's one and only, but a lavish case of overspend. Politely, no one mentioned that the bride's belly was already straining at her wedding dress.

The bridesmaids' shoes were burnt orange too, their

pointy feet poking out from beneath jaundiced dresses that looked like the sunset at the end of the world. Their bouquets hung from their arms on ribbon-like handbags, big pomanders or perhaps colourful cannonballs. 'I tried to suggest something different, I really did,' Barbara Crawford said in the loudest *sotto voce* that Tracy had ever heard. 'Amy was always so headstrong.'

Amy's husband was called Ivan. *Ivan the Terrible*, Barry always called him, naturally. 'Ivan? What kind of a name is that?' he said to Tracy after Amy's engagement was announced. 'Bloody Russian.'

'Actually, I think it's because he had a Norwegian grandfather,' Tracy said.

'Norwegian?' Barry said incredulously, as if she'd just announced that Ivan's family came from the moon. Ivan was a financial adviser, Tracy had consulted him when she was wondering where to stash her annual ISA. 'Pop in and have a chat, no charge for a friend of Barry's,' he said to her at the wedding. He seemed a nice enough chap, pretty harmless on the whole, which was about the best you could hope for from a human being, in Tracy's opinion. Unfortunately, he went bankrupt shortly afterwards and lost the business. No one wanted financial advice from a man who couldn't even keep his hands on his own money. Barry implied there was fraud involved but when Tracy went to see Ivan to retrieve some paperwork he explained that he had lost a flash drive with all his clients' details on it. 'Must have slipped out of my pocket,' Ivan said miserably to Tracy. Most of his clients took away their business after that. 'I would have done the same,' Ivan said.

'Not even a traditional fruit cake,' Barbara fretted, coming across Tracy forking up the chocolate sponge and butter cream wedding cake.

'Well, at least it's not orange,' Tracy said.

Of course, Tracy was in no position to make style notes about anything. Uncomfortable in a powder blue, polyester-mix two-piece that was giving off so much static she worried she would spontaneously combust before they got to the cutting of the cake. She'd bought a hat but didn't wear it because it made her look like a man in drag. Tracy could count the number of weddings she'd been invited to on the fingers of one hand, whereas the funerals she had attended in her time were stacked to the rafters. Murder victims mostly. Never been to a christening. Said something about your life, didn't it?

The burnt orange had been a particularly unfortunate choice for Amy's friend Chloe Pallister with her mousy hair and tallow complexion. 'Mother of the bridesmaid, never mother of the bride,' Linda Pallister said, sidling up to Tracy, smiling hopefully. She didn't have anyone else to talk to. Linda Pallister's own wedding clothes, a black velvet T-shirt and a skirt that seemed to have been made out of tie-dyed cobwebs, couldn't have been more out of place. Linda was also sporting a large assortment of silver rings and bracelets as well as an enormous crucifix on a leather shoestring. The crucifix looked more like penance than religion. Linda had become a Christian in the eighties, an unfashionable decade for evangelism, although Linda had gone, uncharacteristically, for straight-down-the-middle C of E. No sign at the wedding of Linda's eldest, Jacob. Tracy had heard a rumour that he was a bank manager.

'Your Chloe looks lovely,' Tracy lied.

If Tracy phoned Linda Pallister and started asking about Kelly Cross's kids she'd be flagging herself up, wouldn't she? *What, one of Kelly Cross's children missing? Why only the other day Tracy Waterhouse was asking me to count them!* Tracy had nicked a kid. Didn't matter how much you paid, didn't matter how much you dressed it up with righteousness, it didn't make it legal.

She took the kid for lunch in Bella Italia. Kid worked her way through her own weight in penne and Tracy nibbled on some garlic bread. She had lost her appetite. The kidnapper diet. Tracy had done them all in her time – grapefruit, F-Plan, cabbage, Atkins. Self-inflicted torture. She'd been a big baby, a big child, a big teenager, it seemed unlikely that she would suddenly become a small, post-menopausal woman.

In Gap, Tracy bought clothes for Courtney, holding them up against her to gauge their fit, rather than going by the labels which didn't seem to relate to the kid's actual size. 'How old are you, Courtney?'

'Four,' Courtney said, more of a question than an answer. She fitted the '2–3 year' clothes easily. 'You're small for your age,' Tracy said.

'You're big,' Courtney said.

'Can't argue with that,' Tracy said. Unsure of the rules

of engagement with a small child, Tracy had decided it worked best if they both pretended they were grown-up and conversed accordingly.

She bought more clothes for Courtney than she had intended, but they were so nice and pretty, the kind of clothes Tracy never had when she was a little girl. Half a century ago her mother had dressed her in limp pinafore dresses and nylon jumpers with brown lace-up Clarks shoes, a look which even a cute kid, let alone Tracy, would have had trouble pulling off. Her parents had been over forty when Tracy was born, already old before their time. 'We'd given up,' her mother said, as if it had been a relief to do so. 'And then you came along.'

Her parents had been too much at war with each other to bother with their child. They had battled passively, locked together in silent hostility while Tracy lived in the solitary confinement of the only child. Tracy thought of herself as a war baby even though the war was long over when she was born.

Courtney wiped her ever-present trail of snot on the sleeve of her grubby pink top. Tracy would have to buy tissues, tissues were the kind of thing that people who looked after kids carried in their bags at all times. There must be a caravan of kid-related supplies that she needed but Tracy had no idea what they might be. It would be helpful if kids came with instructions and a list of requirements.

Tracy's final purchase for Courtney was a red duffel coat in the sale, a garment that a younger Tracy, dreary in brown gabardine, had always coveted. The duffle coat had a soft plaid lining and real wooden toggles. It was an article of clothing that said someone cared. If it hadn't been so warm in the shop she would have suggested the kid wear it straight away but Tracy could feel the sweat trickling uncomfortably down her back and the kid looked positively overcooked.

Tracy was flagging. She had read somewhere that shops and museums were the most tiring places for people. The kid looked dog-weary. 'Do you want a carry?' Tracy said.

Her knees almost buckled under the weight. Who knew a tiny kid could be so heavy? She had the gravity of a small, dense planet. Tracy staggered back to Mamas and Papas with Courtney in her arms and retrieved the car seat and fixed it in the Audi. She'd had the kid less than three hours and she felt mangled by exhaustion, no wonder the parents she saw in the Merrion Centre walked around like zombies.

She helped Courtney into the car seat, was surprised when the kid strapped herself in. Should they be able to do that? If you could fasten a buckle it meant you could unfasten one as well. 'Don't undo that,' she advised the kid. 'There are a lot of bad drivers on the road.' The kid murmured a kind of assent. Her eyelids were blue with tiredness and she had the stunned look that Tracy had seen on abused kids. You had to wonder. It would hardly be a surprise, more likely than not, in fact. The things people did to kids could make your brain hurt. Hot needle, et cetera. Or maybe, like Tracy, the kid was just worn out with the turn the day had taken. It was four o'clock in the afternoon but time had become elastic, stretching out the day to infinity.

She glanced in the rear-view mirror and saw that Courtney was already asleep, making little buzzing sounds, like a large bee.

⁓

Jackson wondered what a dog might need. Food and a bowl to eat it out of, he supposed. He found both in a shop called Paws for Thought. He sensed he was entering deep into unknown territory. He had a new role. He knew who he was, he was a dog owner. He found it hard enough coping with having a son, the dog felt like even more of a stretch.

'Lovely Border terrier you've got yourself there,' the woman behind the counter said.

'Is it?' Jackson said, studying the dog. He had assumed it was some kind of mongrel, not a breed. It certainly looked like a mongrel, and not a particularly prepossessing one either. There were traces of blood on the dog's snout and on his fur and the woman said, 'Oh dear, has he been in a fight?'

'Sort of,' Jackson said.

The woman gave the rope around the dog's neck a disapproving glance and said, 'What's the poor little chap's name?'

Jackson ran through a mental list of names that might

be more suitable than the one the dog already had and came up with nothing, apart from Jess, but that name was owned for ever by the Atwells' sheepdog.

'The Ambassador,' he finally owned up. 'He's called The Ambassador.' The dog's ears perked up attentively. Jackson wondered where the dog had got its name from. He tried to imagine its big, ugly owner – ex-owner – shouting 'Ambassador!' into the depths of a field. In Roundhay it had been a torrent of expletives that had flowed from Colin's mouth. He supposed it was a joke, imagined someone saying, 'The Ambassador needs brushing' or 'The Ambassador's asleep in his basket.'

The pet-shop woman raised sceptical eyebrows and said, 'The Ambassador? I would have thought that was a name for a bigger dog.'

'He's big inside,' Jackson said defensively.

The woman swept her hand around the shop and said, 'Anything else? How about a coat? For the dog,' she added when Jackson looked at her blankly. It seemed to Jackson that nature had given the dog a perfectly good coat so he said no but bought a leather lead and left before he got carried away by, say, the small four-legged sailor uniform that was hanging behind the counter, complete with jaunty little hat.

Jackson took out his Swiss Army knife and, showing it to the dog, said, 'Man's best friend.' The dog sat passively while Jackson cut through the tightly knotted rope around its neck. 'Good dog,' Jackson said.

When Jackson first encountered the dog it had

seemed unruly but now seemed merely full of spirit, walking nicely on the lead, no pulling or messing about, and appeared delighted to be in Jackson's company. He wondered if he looked foolish striding along the streets with a small dog on a lead trotting purposefully by his side. He wondered how women felt about men with small dogs. Would they think he was gay? Would they find him more trustworthy than a man without a dog? (Hitler liked dogs, he reminded himself.)

He found himself pausing at traffic lights. He would normally have made a heroic dash across the road (or a lunatic dash, depending whose side you were on – Jackson's or most of the women in his life) but now he was waiting stoically for the green man, suddenly transformed into a parent again by being in charge of something smaller than himself.

Back in the vicinity of the Merrion Centre (he wondered how the confused old woman had got on, he had trusted the Canadian girl not to call the police) he checked into a somewhat unsightly Best Western and asked for a double room because he didn't like to think of himself as a single man in a single room. ('You seem to be living the life of a travelling salesman,' Josie said.

'Let's hope you don't turn into a giant insect,' Julia laughed.

'Eh?' Jackson said.)

The hotel gave him a twin-bedded room, which seemed worse, the unoccupied bed like a reproach somehow.

Jackson was a naturally frugal traveller. 'Tight as a tic's arse' is what his brother would have said. He had been brought up on prudence and thrift – or to put it another way, in poverty – and the older he got the more he found himself reverting to parsimony. That didn't mean that he was beyond the occasional startling largesse, to Betty's waitresses, for example.

Jackson had stayed in some of the best hotels in the world but now he found himself quite content to sleep within the bland budget walls of the Travelodges and Premier Inns that he encountered along his nomadic route. They were places where you paused and moved on and nothing stuck to you. Waking in the middle of the night there was something comforting to be found in the drone of the engine of the hotel as it sailed on into the morning. He knew who he was in a hotel, he was a guest.

After his six months on the road he was beginning to wonder if he even wanted to stop. Jackson Brodie, the rambling man. A vagabond. Hotels were becoming boring, but what about a caravan? Josie's parents had been in possession of a small Sprite that they had loaned to Jackson and Josie in the early days of their marriage when they still qualified as newly-weds and Jackson, just back from the Gulf and out of the army, had thought of enlisting in the French Foreign Legion if this was what his life was to be from then on – caravanning holidays in the company of Little Englanders. Now, though, he could see a certain charm in his ex-in-laws' obsession with loading up the wagons and moving on, pioneers of the open road.

He could fit out a caravan (he imagined Romany rather than Sprite) as neatly as a little boat and a ship-shape Jackson could boil up water on an open fire, catch rabbits with little wire traps, sleep with the smell of woodsmoke in his hair. Apart from the odd accidental roadkill or the mercy killing of a victim of myxomatosis, he had never knowingly dispatched a rabbit but supposed he could if it was a necessity. Especially if it was a big rabbit called Muffin.

On reflection he wasn't a caravan man. And, truth be told, he was growing tired of his vagrant life. He wanted a home. He would like a woman in that home. Not all the time, he had grown too used to his own company. There was a time when he had been a man who only felt fulfilled when facing life shoulder to shoulder with a woman. He had enjoyed being married, perhaps more than his wife had. His real wife, not the crooked trickery which had been his second wife. ('A Fata Morgana,' Julia said. 'A mirage.')

Julia had once told him that the ideal partner was one that you could keep in a cupboard and take out when you felt like it. Jackson thought it unlikely that there were women out there who would acquiesce to being kept in a cupboard. Didn't stop men trying to find them though.

Sensing animals would not be welcome in the Best Western he had sneaked the dog in, concealed in his rucksack. Beforehand, in the car park, Jackson had tipped out half the bag's contents and invited a not entirely compliant dog to enter into the bespoke space. With some encouragement from Jackson, the dog had eventually settled into the innards of the bag. There was something to admire in the dog's character. 'Good dog,' he said, because praise seemed to be called for.

Once he was in the room he released the dog from its prison. He opened a can of dog food and dumped it in the bowl he had bought and the dog ate as if famished. There was a 'hospitality tray' in the room with tea, coffee, a kettle and cups and saucers. Jackson took one of the saucers and filled it with water from the bathroom. The dog drank as if it had been in a drought.

He had dropped into a chemist on the way to the hotel and picked up an ad hoc first-aid kit and now used the TCP and cotton wool to clean up the dog's scratches. The dog stood stoically while it was prodded and poked and only flinched slightly when the antiseptic touched broken skin or Jackson found a bruise. 'Good dog,' Jackson said again.

Jackson flicked the switch on the kettle and made a mug of tea, dividing the little packet of biscuits between himself and the dog. When he had finished, the dog jumped up on to one of the twin beds, circled round and round until it appeared satisfied, and then curled up and fell asleep immediately. It was the bed Jackson would have chosen for himself, being nearest to the door (a room for Jackson was all about exits) but the dog, despite its size, had a remarkably unmovable look about it.

Jackson's phone vibrated in his pocket like a hefty trapped wasp. Two messages. The first was a text from Marlee asking him if she could have her birthday money early. Her birthday wasn't for another six months, which seemed to Jackson to give 'early' a new meaning. It was a blatantly mercenary message with a perfunctory 'love you' added at the end. He thought he would sit on it and make her sweat for a few days. He had never imagined, when his daughter was small and infinitely, eternally lovable, that he would ever develop a combative relationship with her.

The second message was more benign – an email from Hope McMaster. *How's it going?* it said. *Haven't heard from you in a while.* He tried to work out what time it would be in New Zealand. Were they twelve hours ahead? Early morning there. Hope McMaster was living in tomorrow – a concept that baffled Jackson's brain. She struck him as the kind of person who might be up early to email. Or was she an insomniac, growing more anxious as Jackson came nearer to the black hole at the beginning of her life? ('It's a void,' she said.)

Jackson sighed and tapped out a message. *Am in Leeds. Seeing Linda Pallister tomorrow.*

There was an immediate response from Hope McMaster. *Fantastic!* she replied. *Let's hope she comes up with some answers.*

'Yeah, whatever,' Jackson said to the phone, sounding to his own ears disconcertingly like his mulish daughter. 'No,' he had told her the last time they were together, 'you cannot have a tattoo, no matter how "pretty", or a ring in your belly button, a blue streak in your hair, a boyfriend. Especially not a boyfriend.'

Yes, he tapped out to Hope McMaster, *let's hope so*.

Hope McMaster's case had turned out to be a slow-burn affair. For months now Jackson had been reporting back to her, occasional, laconic emails that elicited an immediate chirpy response about the weather in Christchurch (*Snow!*) or 'little Aaron's' first day at nursery school (*I don't mind telling you I went home and sobbed my heart out*). Hope McMaster shared with Julia a (misplaced) faith in exclamation marks. Jauntiness never conveyed itself well in the written word, in Jackson's opinion.

He had always thought of New Zealanders as a rather gloomy race – the Scots abroad – but Hope seemed as happy-clappy as you could get. Of course, much of Jackson's information about New Zealanders came from watching *The Piano*. At the cinema, in the early days of his (true) marriage, before they had a baby, before it all started to go wrong. After Marlee was born they rented videos and fell asleep in front of them. Now, like so much else in Jackson's world, videos were obsolete.

Nonetheless he was intrigued by New Zealand, although not so much because of Hope McMaster as the fact that last year he had read Captain Cook's journals and had been impressed by the heroism of his navigation and leadership. First man to sail round the world in both directions. Like the *Mallard*, a record never to be broken. The *Endeavour* and the *Mallard*, consummate examples of the female form.

Cook was a Yorkshireman, naturally. You could but be in awe of the first voyage, the magnificent voyage, to observe the transit of Venus, to find the mythical southern continent, that took him to Tahiti, Australia, New Zealand. Heart of oak. Sometimes Jackson regretted that he would never make his mark on history, that he would never map a new country, that he would never fight in a just war. 'Be grateful for an ordinary life,' Julia said, Julia who had always wanted to be extraordinary in some way.

'I am,' Jackson said. 'I really am.'

But.

Imagine sailing into Poverty Bay for the first time, imagine captaining a heroic little three-masted barque to the other side of the world. A new-found land where the sun rises first. *Well, Christchurch is really quite* English, *in many ways, you know*, Hope McMaster wrote to him. *I wouldn't want you to be disappointed. You should visit! You would love New Zealand!* Would he?

She was two years old when she last saw England. How much could she remember about it? Nothing. How much could she remember about her life before she was adopted? Nothing.

The next planned stop on Jackson's itinerary after Leeds was Whitby, Cook's old stamping ground. He rather fancied living by the sea, could see himself in an old fisherman's cottage built from ancient ship's timbers. Hearts of oak. He could take a bracing walk along the beach every day in the company of the dog and sink a pint in the evening with old sailors. Jackson, the fisherman's friend.

Whitby was where Cook had served his apprentice-ship and where the *Endeavour* had started her life as a big-bellied barque, plying the coal trade up and down the east coast. A collier. Jackson groaned at the word. He hated *Collier*. TV detective. Vince Collier, not a man but a construct, a hybrid of all that was bad, put together by a committee and approved by a focus group.

Mum said I was born Sharon Costello, Hope wrote. Her adoptive parents had been a childless couple from Harrogate – Dr Ian Winfield, a paediatrician at St James's Infirmary in Leeds and his wife, Kitty, a former model. The Winfields renamed Sharon 'Hope'.

Now that Mum's dead – lung cancer, not a great way to go – I feel I can ask these questions about my 'origins', Hope McMaster had written. ('She does like details, doesn't she?' Julia said.) It seemed to Jackson that the best time to find answers to Hope McMaster's questions might have been *before* her mother died but he didn't say that.

Hope Winfield married Dave McMaster (*runs a successful real-estate office*) five years ago and had given up teaching geography at a secondary school to bring up little Aaron and her as yet unborn second child ('*the squid' – as we call her!*). In the beginning it had been a mere matter of *curiosity*, she said. She would like to be able *to tell the kids* more about their genealogy. *When you have a child you start to wonder about their genetic inheritance and although my 'real' parents will always be Mum and Dad I can't help but be curious . . . you know how it is, you feel as if you've lost something but you just don't know what it is.*

Jackson's own bad genes had been modified in Marlee (he hoped) by Josie's more temperate birthright. But what hope was there for Nathan? It wasn't just Julia's lungs that were compromised. Her whole family had been riotously dysfunctional in a way that went beyond the Gothic. Betrayed emotionally by her parents, Julia had lost a clutch of sisters, the eldest, Sylvia, to suicide, Amelia to cancer and the baby of the family, Olivia, to murder – by Sylvia. There had been another baby, too, Annabelle, who had lived for only a handful of hours, joined in the grave shortly afterwards by the girls' mother.

Julia was the only person Jackson knew who could outplay him in the game of personal misery. It was what had drawn them to each other in the beginning, it was what had pulled them apart in the end.

'One by one all those little birds fell out of the nest,' Julia said. She claimed there was 'comfort to be had in metaphors'. Jackson didn't see it himself. He didn't point out to her that Amelia had been more like a ponderous bustard and suicidal, murderous Sylvia was worse than a cuckoo.

'Christ robs the Nest – / Robin after Robin / Smuggled to Rest,' Julia said and Jackson said, 'Emily Dickinson,' just to see the look of astonishment on her face.

'You're not ill, are you?' she asked. 'Or mad?'

'Much Madness is divinest Sense,' he said cheerfully.

'Murder and suicide aren't *genetic*,' Julia said, scoffing sandwiches in the Black Swan in Helmsley after their visit to Rievaulx Terraces. 'Nathan isn't *predisposed* to tragedy.' Jackson wasn't so sure about that but he kept that thought to himself.

According to Hope, John and Angela Costello, from Doncaster, were killed when a drunken lorry driver ploughed into the back of their car. Their two-year-old daughter, Sharon, wasn't with them at the time, which seemed rather to beg the question, 'Where was she?' Newly orphaned, she was adopted by the Winfields, renamed Hope and shortly afterwards they emigrated to New Zealand.

They'd given up hope of having children, Hope said, *then I came along, like a gift*. Some people donated organs when they died. John and Angela Costello donated their child.

'So it wasn't the Winfields who had given up hope,' Julia said. 'It was the Costellos.'

Looking back, Jackson could see that even as he was reading Hope's introductory missive from the ether (some novels were shorter and less detailed than Hope McMaster's emails) his intuitive antennae had been twitching. No relatives? The past obliterated? A name changed? A child too young to remember anything? A sudden removal to a faraway land?

'Kidnapped,' Julia had said decisively, buttering a scone, but then she always had a flair for the dramatic.

Before he had taken on the task of investigating her past he had felt obliged to remind Hope McMaster how curiosity had worked out for the cat.

'Pandora's box,' Julia said, already reaching for a

second scone before finishing the first. 'Although the word *pithos* actually translates as "large jar". Pandora released evil into the world and—'

'I know,' Jackson interrupted. 'I know what she did.'

'People have a need to find the truth,' Julia said. 'Human nature can't abide a mystery.'

In Jackson's experience, finding the truth – whatever that was – only deepened the mystery of what had really happened in the past. And perhaps Hope's little Aaron and the squid would discover a family history that they would rather had stayed securely locked away, well out of pesky Pandora's reach.

'Yes, but it's not about *liking* what you find out, it's about *knowing*,' Julia said.

Any time he spent with Julia always degenerated in the end into a mixture of comforting familiarity and irritable argument. Rather like marriage but without the divorce. Or the wedding for that matter.

Nathan had run himself into oblivion on the Terraces and one sandwich and a dish of ice cream later he was asleep in Jackson's arms, leaving Julia free to tackle her afternoon tea untrammelled. The soft, sandbag weight of his boy in his arms was disturbing. Jackson wasn't sure that he wanted his heart stirred by unbreakable, sacrificial bonds.

He had been surprised to find himself daunted rather than happy when Nathan proved to be his son. It just went to show, you never knew what you were going to feel until you felt it.

Recently, Julia had begun to imply that Jackson should

be 'more of a father' to Nathan and they should spend time 'as a family'. 'But we're not,' Jackson protested. 'You're married to someone else.' When Jackson had been forced into deciding which of his offspring to spend Christmas Day with he had opted for his moody daughter (a disastrous decision). Julia saw it, perhaps rightly, as a clear case of favouritism.

'Jackson's choice,' she said.

'I can't be in two places at once,' Jackson complained.

'An atom can be in several places at once, according to quantum physics,' Julia said.

'I'm not an atom.'

'You're nothing *but* atoms, Jackson.'

'Maybe, but I still can't be in two places at once. There's only one Jackson.'

'How true. Well, have a very Merry Christmas. God so loved the world he gave his only begotten son, et cetera. Jackson couldn't even manage to give his a present on Christmas Day.'

'Bah, humbug,' Jackson said.

In the Black Swan, Julia licked cream off her fingers in a way that would have once looked provocative to Jackson. She used to wear scarlet lipstick but these days her lips were unpainted. In the same way, her unruly hair was scraped back and bundled into a restraining clip. Motherhood had in some ways made her into a paler version of the woman she used to be. Jackson was surprised at how much he sometimes missed the old Julia. Or maybe she was the same Julia and what he missed was being with her. He hoped not. There wasn't room in his heart anyway. The (rather small) space available these days for a woman in the cupboard of Jackson's heart was almost entirely occupied by the candle burning for his Scottish nemesis, Detective Chief Inspector Louise Monroe. An old flame flickering weakly rather than burning brightly, denied oxygen by their absence from each other. They had never had sex, he hadn't seen her for two years, she was married to someone else and had a child by him. It was not what most people thought of as a relationship. Someone should put out the light.

'The heart is infinite,' Julia said. 'Plenty of room.' In Julia's heart maybe, not Jackson's, contracted and growing smaller with every blow it suffered. *A poor torn heart, a tattered heart.*

'Poppycock,' Julia said.

The thing was, John and Angela Costello, the purported parents of little Sharon, soon to be transformed into Hope Winfield, had never become dust. Never been totalled in a car crash, never walked the dark streets of Donny. They hadn't died, because they had never lived.

No car crash, no death certificates, no record of a couple by that name ever having lived in Doncaster. There was no birth certificate for a 'Sharon Costello' with parents of that name. Just to be sure Jackson had chased up another Sharon Costello, born on Hope McMaster's birthday – 15 October 1972 – who lived in

Truro. She turned out to be a wild goose, puzzled by his interest in her.

Of course the Winfields might have changed Hope's birth date as well as her name. Jackson would have done if he'd been trying to disguise a child.

The Winfields themselves checked out. They had definitely lived in Harrogate, home of the Betty's mother ship, and an excuse – not that he needed one – for Jackson to spend a pleasant twenty-four hours in that town, possibly one of the most civilized places he had ever visited. But then, of course, everyone knew, Jackson in particular, that civilization was a thin veneer.

Ian Winfield was definitely a paediatrician at St James's from 1969 to 1975, when he left to take up a post in Christchurch. And he was certainly married to Kitty, who really had been a model. Hope McMaster had emailed some of her professional photographs – Kitty Gillespie, all sixties fringe and eye make-up, a type Jackson felt a strangely instinctive attraction to. Jackson had a vague recollection in his head – 'Kitty Gillespie, the poor man's Jean Shrimpton'. Not such a poor man by the look of her. The sixties didn't look like history to Jackson, maybe they never would.

Mum was quite the thing, wasn't she? Hope McMaster wrote. *Nothing like dumpy little me – proof positive I was adopted!* Hope had emailed him many little thumbnails of her family – of herself, of Dave, of Aaron, of their dog (a golden retriever, what else), of the Winfields and of Hope as a child (*Dave has scanned everything!*).

The Winfields seemed indeed to have gone out of

their way to adopt a child who looked nothing like them. They had been tall, dark and elegant, Hope was a blonde, sturdy, old-fashioned-looking child who had turned into a blonde, sturdy, old-fashioned-looking woman, if her photographs were anything to go by. *First known photograph of me!* she had tagged a picture taken on the Winfields' arrival in New Zealand. The newly formed family were at some kind of tourist attraction, and Hope – freckled podgy face and a spiky urchin cut – was grinning for the camera, the epitome of happiness. The camera can lie, Jackson reminded himself. All those abused kids who only got noticed when they died. The papers always ran a photograph of them, smiling happily. Some kids automatically turned it on for the camera. *Smile!*

What had started off as an innocuous request (*I wondered if you could find out some information about my biological parents?*) had taken Jackson into a maze that had led to dead ends at every turn. Hope McMaster was an existential conundrum. She might exist in the antipodean here and now, wife to Dave, mother to little Aaron. She might be attending ante-natal classes in the invisible company of the squid (*and Pilates – it's a miracle!*) but any previous incarnation of her seemed to be a figment of the imagination. Although just whose imagination, Jackson wasn't sure.

Pandora advanced towards the box, the curious cat looked to be in mortal danger. 'Perhaps there's a cat *in* the box,' Julia mused, 'like Schrödinger's.'

'Who?' Jackson asked before he could prevent himself.

'You know, Schrödinger's cat. In the box. Both alive and dead at the same time.'

'That's a ridiculous idea.'

'In practice maybe, but theoretically . . .'

'Is this related to atoms by chance?'

'*Verschränkung,*' Julia said with relish. Luckily the arrival of a fresh pot of tea at that moment distracted her from these mysteries.

After some mandatory adoption counselling in New Zealand, Hope McMaster had applied to Leeds Crown Court for her original birth certificate. Last week she received the news that there wasn't one. Nor was there any record of her adoption ever having taken place.

'See – kidnapped. Shall I be mother? Seeing as I am one and you're not.'

The phone was ringing when they came in the house. Tracy picked up the receiver and said, 'Hello?' but found only silence on the other end. There was someone there, she was sure, and she exchanged a mute dialogue with the caller, like a battle of wills. The caller gave up first and she heard the click of a receiver. 'Good riddance,' Tracy said. She had more important things on her agenda. Like a kidnapped kid.

They hadn't done any food shopping – not that Tracy had enough energy to cook – and she had picked up pizza on the way home. Play it safe, all kids liked pizza, it might not be the healthiest thing in the world but right now Tracy didn't care, as long as Courtney didn't throw it back up again. Plenty of time for green vegetables and fruit in the future. The future was suddenly a place that you might want to be, rather than a place where you were going to have to slog it out with tedium on a day-by-day basis. A really, really terrifying place that you might want to be.

The cupboard was bare, not a bone for a dog, not a tin of beans for a kidnapped kid, just some blackening bananas sitting accusingly in a fruit bowl. Tracy hadn't really cooked anything since Janek started on the kitchen, she'd been living off takeaways and micro-waved ready meals (nothing new there, of course), but when she looked around now she realized that the kitchen was nearly finished, just decorating and the lino to go down, a few tweaks here and there. The bag with Janek's tools sat neatly in a corner. She would have to go back to the bank and get more money for him. Only this morning the idea that he would soon be gone had been profoundly depressing to her, now it hardly seemed to matter at all. She had embarked on an un-expected and perilous adventure and it was possible that she would fall off the edge of the world.

'Another slice?' Tracy asked and Courtney looked at her blankly, her mouth hanging open. Would Tracy have to get the kid's adenoids removed, did they even do that any more? She wasn't a bonny kid but Tracy could relate to that. It took a few seconds for

Tracy's words to reach Courtney's brain (probably be a good idea to get her a hearing test as well) and then she nodded her head, up and down, and kept on nodding until Tracy advised her to stop. Was she the full shilling? *Backward* – but you weren't allowed to say that any more. What did it matter, a kid was a kid.

Tracy was too wound up to eat. Only alcohol could address the state of mind she was in but she didn't want the kid to see her drinking, she had probably been around drunks all her short life, so instead Tracy made a sober cup of Typhoo and watched Courtney eating, imagining private tutoring to bring her up to speed, a lot of visits to the ENT department, an eye test (she had a bit of a squint going on), a good haircut, followed by a thoughtful, child-centred school, perhaps one of those hippy-dippy ones – Linda Pallister might know about those. After that, who knows, kid might manage to get a place at the kind of university that was a polytechnic by another name, and Tracy would be there when she graduated in cap and gown, drinking cheap white wine afterwards with other proud parents.

Part of Tracy's brain was still on the beat in the Merrion Centre and hadn't caught up with the bizarre turn the day's events had taken. This lagging part of the brain seemed to suddenly sit up and take notice. What the hell is going on? it asked. You're making long-term plans to live outside the law! Yes, Tracy said, to the recalcitrant bit of brain. That's exactly what I'm doing. She was a kidnapper. She had napped a kid. She had never thought about where the word came from before.

How *was* she going to explain the sudden appearance of a child in her life? It would be easier if they both vanished, started again somewhere else where nobody knew them (*I'm Mrs Waterhouse, and this is my little girl, Courtney*). Change Courtney's name to something more middle-class – Emily or Lucy. Put down new roots in the country perhaps – the Dales or the Lakes – they could easily live on Tracy's police pension. The kid could go to a little village primary and Tracy could get a few chickens, grow some veg, cook nourishing meals. She imagined herself at the annual village fête, doing face-painting, baking cupcakes (*Oh, Tracy's a wonderful mum, isn't she?*). Of course, she had never baked a cupcake in her life but everyone started somewhere.

Run for the hills. Or the Dales or the Lakes. Bloody good job she had that National Trust holiday cottage booked for Friday, couldn't have timed it better even if she'd known ahead that her life was going to turn upside down. A breathing space. Time to think. Foxes in a hole, hiding from the hounds. Just in case someone came looking for them before they could make their final escape. Someone like Kelly Cross, changing her mind about the recent sale. *Caveat emptor.* What after that – stay or run? Fight or flight. Start a new life (*Imogen Brown and her little girl, Lucy*) or try and carry on with the old one (butch Tracy and the kidnapped kid) and risk discovery and its consequences?

She would have to change her own name as well, she'd never liked Tracy. Imogen or Isobel, something feminine and romantic. She supposed she didn't look like an Imogen. Imogens were middle-class Home Counties girls with long blonde hair and vaguely Bohemian mothers. Her surname would have to change too, something plain, unremarkable perhaps. *Imogen Brown and her little girl, Lucy,* walking hand in hand with the kid into a clean, untarnished, white future. She would make up for all the other lost kids. One fallen fledgling popped back into the nest.

Was she too old to pass as a mother? IVF, followed by sudden, early widowhood would take care of a lot of questions. New names, new identities, it would be like being in witness protection. The one thing that was odd was that Courtney hadn't mentioned her mother. No 'Where's Mummy?' or 'I want my mummy.' No sign at all that she was missing someone. Was she a throwaway, or something precious that had been stolen?

'Courtney,' she said hesitantly, 'where do you think Mummy is just now?' Courtney shrugged extravagantly and worked her way through another slice before volunteering, 'I don't have a mummy.' (Really? This was very good news. For Tracy anyway.)

'Well, you do now,' Tracy said. The kid snapped her head up and stared at Tracy before glancing warily round the kitchen.

'Where?'

Tracy put her hand on her chest and said, rather heroically, 'Here. I'm going to be your mummy.'

'Are you?' Courtney said, looking doubtful. As well she might, Tracy thought. Who was she kidding? (That word again.)

'Last slice?' Courtney gave her a thumbs-down, a small emperor in the Colosseum. She yawned. 'Time for bed,' Tracy said, trying to sound as if she knew what she was doing.

She gave the napped kid a bath. A lot of grime but no bruises, no obvious sign of damage. Skinny little legs and arms, thin shoulder blades that were like wing nubs. A noticeable birthmark, tattooed by some tiny misreading of the genetic code on to the kid's forearm. The birthmark was the shape of India, or was it Africa? Geography had never been Tracy's strong point. *Any distinguishing marks?* A seal of ownership stamped on the skin for ever. A stigma. Maybe there was a way of removing it. Laser treatment perhaps.

Courtney sat passively while Tracy soaped and rinsed her, untangled the scrawny plaits, carefully washed her hair and then wrapped her in a towel and lifted her out of the water. Tracy hadn't appreciated just how small a kid really was. Small and vulnerable. And heavy. It was like being put in charge of a Ming vase, terrifying and exhilarating at the same time. Thank God Courtney wasn't a tiny baby, Tracy didn't think she would have been able to cope with the nerves.

Tracy's newly acquired house had last been re-furbished some time in the early eighties – hardly the pinnacle of style in décor – and the bathroom suite was a sludgy avocado, the colour of Shrek. Tracy had watched all three *Shrek* DVDs on her own. If you had a kid you could watch cartoons, go to the pantomime, visit Disneyland, without feeling like a pathetic loser. Just the sight of the small, naked body sitting in her own snot-coloured bath had almost moved her to tears. She was surprised to find (let alone explain) such deep wells of primal, untapped emotions inside the calcified shell.

'Just a sec, pet,' she said, perching a towel-swaddled Courtney on the bathroom stool. She raked through the bathroom cabinet and found a pair of nail scissors. 'Just tidy you up a bit,' she said, taking a lock of the kid's limp hair and snipping it off. Felt like a violation, but it was just hair, she told herself.

She helped Courtney into the new Gap pyjamas and said, 'Just pop into bed, pet,' and felt her heart moved all over again when Courtney obediently scrambled into bed, lay on her back and pulled the covers up to her chin. Christ, you could get a little kid to do anything, you just told them and they did it. Horrifying.

Tracy looked around with new eyes and realized that the small spare room with its mean little bed seemed hopelessly barren and inhospitable. There was a third bedroom but it was still full of cardboard boxes from her own move as well as all the junk from her parents' house that Tracy hadn't had the energy or the interest to look into – a jumble of embroidered tray-cloths, chipped plates and old photographs of unidentifiable relatives. Why unpack the stuff, she could just take the whole lot and dump it on the pavement outside an Oxfam shop.

She should have done something about the bedrooms before she started on the downstairs. Tracy had
been pleased when she decorated the living room,
having toiled her way through *The World of Interiors* and
House & Garden for weeks, but when it was finished and
she looked around she realized it looked more like a
public space in a corporate hotel than a comfortable
nest. Her own bedroom had been decorated by the
previous owner with a wallpaper patterned with big
purple flowers that had a vaguely obscene look to them.

The little spare room, papered in boring woodchip,
seemed to have been used as a study. Flimsy plastic
Venetian blinds hung at the window and the floor was
covered in cheap beige contract carpeting. Tracy wished
that she had thought ahead, bought cheerful curtains
and a nice soft rug and painted the room in pleasant
pastel colours. Or white. Pure and unsullied, the colour
of swans and birthday cake icing. A woman with fore-
sight would have anticipated kidnapping a kid.

Hot milk? Or cocoa? Tracy was trying to invent a childhood she had never had herself, her own self-absorbed
parents having expected Tracy to bring herself up somehow. They had never taken much interest in her and it
was only when they died that she realized they never
would. Better parents (loving parents) and she might
have turned out differently – confident and popular,
with the ability to charm the opposite sex into bed and
into love so that now she would have a child of her own
rather than a second-hand one.

Hot chocolate, she decided, her own idea of a treat. When she came back with a mug for each of them she found Courtney sitting up in bed with the contents of her little pink backpack spread out on the thin Ikea duvet. It seemed she had a collection of totemic objects, their significance known only to their small owner:

a tarnished silver thimble
a Chinese coin with a hole in the middle
a purse with a smiling monkey's face on it
a snow globe containing a crude plastic model of
    the Houses of Parliament
a shell shaped like a cream horn
a shell shaped like a coolie hat
a whole nutmeg

'Quite a treasure trove,' Tracy said. The kid looked up from her wampum and stared inscrutably at her and then, for the first time since Tracy bought her, Courtney smiled. A beatific sunbeam of a smile. Tracy beamed back, a bubble-burst of mixed emotion – ecstasy and agony in equal, confusing measure inside her – rising in her chest. Jesus. How did parents manage with this kind of stuff on a daily basis? She found herself blinking back tears. 'I haven't got a bedtime book, I'm afraid,' she said quickly.

Tracy herself liked to read big fat Jackie Collins books. She would never have told anyone, they were like a secret vice, an unspeakable pleasure like pornography (or Disney). Hardly suitable for a kid so instead she made up a bespoke fairy tale about a poor little princess called Courtney who had a wicked mother and was rescued by a very good stepmother. She threw in a lot of mythic paraphernalia – spinning wheels and dwarves – and by the time the glass slipper was being tried for size on Princess Courtney's little foot, the kid was asleep.

Tracy kissed her tentatively on the cheek. The kid smelled of soap and new cotton. Tracy didn't remember ever kissing a child before and a small, primitive part of her felt as if she had trespassed, broken some natural law. She half expected something momentous to happen – for the sky to crack open like an egg or an angel to appear – and when neither of these things occurred Tracy breathed a sigh of relief. She felt as if she'd achieved something, although she wasn't sure what.

When she came back downstairs the answer machine was blinking even though she hadn't heard the phone ringing. She played the message back, worried that it might be announcing her downfall. *Can you confirm that you are harbouring a child who belongs to someone else?* Children were possessions, people didn't like it when you stole their stuff. For years it had been her job to see that they didn't. Sleep, eat, protect, repeat.

She was relieved that it was only Linda Pallister, although why Linda should be getting in touch out of the blue was a puzzle. There was something spooky about the way Tracy had been thinking about contacting Linda and now Linda was contacting her. When had

Linda Pallister ever phoned her at home? Never, as far as Tracy could remember. Her message was even more puzzling. *Tracy? Tracy? I didn't know who to call. I have to talk to you. I think I'm in . . . trouble.* How could Linda Pallister be in trouble? And what was it to do with Tracy? There was a long silence and then Linda started up again, hardly more than a mumble. *It's about Carol Braithwaite. Do you remember Carol Braithwaite, Tracy? Someone's been asking me about her. Phone me back when you get this message, will you? Please.*

Carol Braithwaite? Tracy puzzled. After all these years? Linda Pallister was phoning her about *Carol Braithwaite?* Tracy had put Carol Braithwaite away in a box, put the box on a shelf at the back of a cupboard, shut the door of the cupboard and hadn't opened it for more than thirty years. And now here was Linda Pallister wanting to talk about her. Linda Pallister, the whited sepulchre. Linda Pallister who had made a small child disappear into thin air. *Poof.*

The past was the past, Tracy counselled herself, and the past was dead or lost but the present was alive and well and asleep in the back bedroom. On the other hand . . . if she returned Linda's call she could casually slip something into the conversation, *Kelly Cross, Linda, are all her kids in care, do you know?* But when she dialled Linda's number it rang out. Tracy was relieved, she had enough problems of her own without having to shoulder Linda Pallister's burdens. But still . . . Carol Braithwaite. Tracy hadn't gone there in a long time. That awful day. That poor little kid.

She retrieved a can of Beck's from the fridge. She popped the top and dialled her former colleague Barry Crawford's number. He sounded tetchy but then that was his default mode.

'Just wondered if you'd run into Kelly Cross recently, Barry?'

'What, the original good-time girl? Nah, I'm too far up the food chain to come across a bottom-feeder like her. Why? Missing the streets, are you?'

'No, no, it's nothing. There've been no kids reported going astray, have there?'

'Kids? I can ask about. I don't know if you're too ga-ga to remember but you retired a few months back.'

'Yeah, yeah.'

Barry called her back almost straight away. Nada, nothing, no chicks fallen out of any nests. She caught the sound of a siren in the background, lots of semi-audible police chatter. Bloody hell but she missed it. 'Where are you?'

'In the incident van. Dead woman in a skip in Mabgate,' Barry said. 'Working girl.'

'We're all working girls, Barry. What are you doing there?'

'Just having a shufti. I happened to be on call and caught it.'

'Who's the SIO?'

'I've put Andy Miller on it,' Barry said. 'New to you. Fast-track graduate. Very shiny.' Nothing shiny about Barry at all. *Jurassic.* Like Tracy. Educated in the school of hard knocks before graduating from the university of life. 'I've got a new girl, one of yours methinks,' he said. 'Come over from Drugs and Organized Crime. Gemma something.'

'Gemma Holroyd. She made inspector a couple of months ago. Why don't you make her the SIO? It would be her first.'

'A virgin, no thanks.'

'She's good and she's not a girl, Barry. They're called women.'

'Thought she was a lezzy?'

'Yeah, they're women too.' Why even bother? Barry was as unreconstructed as they got and was going to retire and die that way, completely out of step with the way things were these days. You could have popped him back into the seventies and he would have fitted in perfectly. Gene Hunt without the charisma, Jack Regan without the hard moral centre.

'So, who are you thinking for it?' Tracy asked. 'A punter, I presume?'

'Who else?' Barry probably thought prostitutes had it coming to them. In fact she knew he did. 'Whores,' Barry always said, couldn't get him out of the habit no matter what you said to him. ('Political correctness? About whores? Do me a favour.')

Tracy had a sudden, unexpected memory of the endless, thankless task of indexing cards during the Ripper investigation. The police had people out taking down registrations of cars in the red-light district, spotting ones that turned up regularly, triple sightings in Bradford, Leeds and Manchester. Sutcliffe was one of those, of course – interviewed nine times, exonerated.

So many mistakes. Tracy was still naïve, no idea how many men used prostitutes, thousands from all walks of life. She could hardly believe it. Gambling, drinking, whoring – the three pillars of western civilization.

Tracy could still remember the first time she saw a prostitute. She was twelve years old, in Leeds town centre on a Saturday with a schoolfriend, Pauline Barratt. A burger in Wimpy was the height of sophistication for them and the surreptitious application of Miners eyeliner in the toilets in Schofields felt downright audacious. They got into a matinee of *What Ever Happened to Baby Jane?* in the old Leeds Odeon and afterwards in a side street somewhere near the station, looming out of the drab fog of a winter twilight, there had been a startling woman. She was lounging in a doorway, Myra Hindley hair and a short skirt that revealed her dimpled thighs, blue with cold and bruises. Her glittering green eye-shadow made Tracy think of a snake. 'Prozzie,' Pauline hissed, and they ran away in terror.

She was the least attractive woman Tracy had ever seen, deepening even further the mystery of what boys wanted from girls. If she thought about her mother, repressed and conventional, or her own unprepossessing twelve-year-old self, Tracy understood that there was no competition with the green-eyed woman of the night.

'I won't miss all this,' Barry said. 'Standing around in the cold looking at dead whores.'

'Standing around? I thought you were in the incident van.'

Barry sighed heavily and said, apropos of nothing as far as Tracy could tell, 'It's a different world now, Trace.'

'Yeah. It's a better one, Barry. What's going on, suffering from existential dread for the first time in your life?' Probably the wrong thing to say to a man who'd lost a grandson, whose daughter was a vegetable. ('Persistent vegetative state,' Barbara corrected.) Some mornings Tracy woke up, especially if she'd been on the Beck's, and wondered if she was in a persistent vegetative state herself. Stagnant.

'I miss the good old days.'

'They weren't good, Barry. They were rubbish.' *The Good Old Days*. She had a sudden vision of the Cookridge madam, dead in her plush velvet seat at the City Varieties. Barry might remember her name, she wouldn't give him the satisfaction though. 'How long now before you're retired, Barry?' Barry had stayed in the force even longer than Tracy had.

'Two weeks. Going on a cruise. The Caribbean. Barbara's idea. God knows why. I bet you were glad to get out, weren't you, Trace?'

'Is the Pope a Nazi?' Tracy forced a laugh. 'Would have got out years ago if I'd known.' Liar, she thought to herself.

'You heard about Rex Marshall?' Barry asked.

'Dropped dead on the golf course. Good riddance to bad rubbish.'

'Yes, well, he wasn't a bad boss,' Barry said defensively.

'To you maybe,' Tracy said.

'You won't be going to the funeral on Saturday then?'

'Not unless you pay me . . . Barry? There's something else.'

'There's always something else, Trace. And then you die and there's nothing else. Of course it turns out you don't even need to be dead for that,' he said glumly.

'Linda Pallister left a message on my answer machine,' Tracy said.

'Linda Pallister? That mad bat?' Barry couldn't stop the snort of laughter that escaped him. The laugh turned into a tremendous sigh of dissatisfaction. Tracy knew how it went for Barry – Linda Pallister made him think of Chloe Pallister, Chloe Pallister made him think of Amy, thinking of Amy pulled him down into a dark place.

'What about?' he asked. 'What was the message about?'

'She said she was in trouble. She mentioned Carol Braithwaite's name.'

'Carol Braithwaite?' Barry said, as if he'd never heard the name before. Barry was a bad liar, always had been.

'Yeah, Barry, Carol Braithwaite. The Lovell Park murder. You remember, don't pretend you don't.'

'Oh, *that* Carol Braithwaite,' he said, all studied nonchalance. 'What about her?'

'I don't know,' Tracy said. 'Linda didn't say. I tried to phone her back but there was no answer. Has she been in touch with you?'

'Carol Braithwaite?'

'No, Barry,' Tracy said patiently, 'not unless she's risen from the grave. Linda *Pallister*, has Linda phoned you?'

'No.'

'Well, if she does, try and find out what she was on about, will you? Maybe she's going to come clean.'

'Come clean?' he said.

'About what happened to the kid.'

Tracy didn't know why she was bothering. She had bigger fish to fry. And it was nothing to do with her any more. She was starting a new life. *She's leaving home.* 'Well, anyway, cheers for the info, Barry,' she said, suddenly brisk. 'See you around.'

'Not if I see you first, you old mare.'

'I'm on holiday actually, from Friday.'

'Well, make sure you're back in time for my leaving do.'

'What leaving do?'

'Ha, ha. Piss off.'

Would this day never end? Apparently not.

Just before midnight the phone rang. Who called at this time? Trouble, that was who. A spasm of fear grabbed Tracy's heart. She'd been found out, someone wanted the kid back. She thought of that helpless little thing upstairs in the spare bedroom and her heart cramped further.

She took a deep breath and picked up the receiver, let it just be mad-as-a-bag-of-cats Linda Pallister, she prayed. Tracy was relieved that it was just the mystery caller. They listened to each other for a minute or so. The silence was almost soothing.

❧

'Not if I see you first, you old mare.' Nearest he could get to affection. What was all that about? *There've been no kids reported going astray, have there?* It had always been the kids that got to Tracy. Well, they got to everyone, but Tracy had this thing about kids. Started with Lovell Park.

Carol Braithwaite wasn't a name that Barry had ever expected to hear again and then that mad cow Linda Pallister phoned earlier, babbling on about being in trouble. He hadn't spoken to her since Sam's funeral. Chloe had been Amy's chief bridesmaid. He couldn't go to that place, couldn't think about that day, walking her down the aisle. He shouldn't have given her away, he should have kept her. Safe.

'Mr Crawford,' Linda had said, 'Barry? Do you remember Lovell Park?'

'No, Linda,' Barry said. 'I don't remember anything.'

'Someone's asking questions,' she said.

'Someone's always asking questions,' Barry said. 'That's because there's never enough answers to go round.'

'A private detective called Jackson came to see me this morning,' Linda Pallister said. 'He was asking questions about Carol Braithwaite. I didn't know what to say.'

'I'd keep on keeping my mouth shut if I were you,' Barry said. 'You've managed it for thirty-five years.'

And now here was Tracy phoning him, asking if Linda

had been in touch about Carol Braithwaite. He had lied, of course. What was that, Barry thought, a cock crowing? *Risen from the grave*, Tracy had said. A bloody great rooster. One, two, three.

Tracy used to bang on about Linda Pallister and Carol Braithwaite, claiming Linda had made the kid 'disappear'. At the time he'd told her she was talking through her hat. But of course she was right, everyone had known more about Lovell Park than they let on, everyone except Tracy. She'd been like a bloodhound, trying to find out. It was a long time ago. All those blokes, DCS Walter Eastman, Ray Strickland, Rex Marshall, Len Lomax, one law for themselves, one law for everyone else. Eastman long dead and now Rex Marshall had played his last round of golf too, lying in an undertaker's somewhere with his arteries furred up like old lead pipes. Falling like skittles. Only Strickland and Lomax left. And Barry. Who'd be the last man standing?

Barry should have said something, done something, but at the time one dead prostitute hadn't seemed very important in the greater scheme of things. When you got older you realized that every single thing counted. Especially the dead.

He turned his collar up against the cold. All the warmth of the day had disappeared. Why didn't men his age wear hats any more? When did that stop? His father used to wear a flat cap. Tweed. He quite fancied one himself but Barbara wouldn't allow it. She controlled his wardrobe. He would rather be out here in the cold looking at the body of a dead whore in a skip than at home with his wife. Barbara would be sitting on the sofa, all prim and proper, not a hair out of place, watching some shit on the telly, quietly seething beneath the make-up. She'd spent thirty years trying to change him, she wasn't going to give up on the challenge now. It was a woman's job to try and improve a man. It was a man's job to resist improvement. That was the way the world worked, always had, always would.

Before, before his grandson died, before Amy, his lovely daughter, was reduced to an empty shell, he hadn't minded what state his relationship with her was in. It was a traditional, old-fashioned marriage, all the trimmings – he went out to work, Barbara stayed home and nagged. He spent half his life in the doghouse for one domestic misdemeanour or another. Didn't bother him, he just went down the pub.

After the accident there was no point to anything. All hope gone. But still he shuffled on, one foot in front of the other. Mr Plod the Policeman. Doing his job. Because when he stopped he was going to have to stay at home with Barbara every day. Face up to the futility of everything. Bloody Caribbean cruise, as if that would make things better.

'Boss?'

'Yep?'

'The SOCOs say we can move the body.'

'Not my case, lad, talk to DI Miller. I'm just an innocent bystander.'

❧

Ten o'clock. A long, lonely night stretched ahead of him.

Jackson thought about phoning Julia, last resort of the insomniac, a woman who abhorred the vacuum of a silence. She could talk anyone to sleep, could give a flock of sheep a run for their money any day, leave a donkey completely legless. Then he remembered how annoyed she had been last time he had called her late at night ('I have to be on set at six. Is this important?') and he decided not to risk her indignation.

Boredom drove him to read the folder of hotel information from cover to cover, the fire escape plans on the back of the door, a copy of *Yorkshire Life*, anything that wasn't nailed down. He considered, and rejected, the idea of playing a mindless game on his phone and was eventually driven to look for a Gideon Bible in the bedside drawers but when he found one he realized he wasn't that desperate yet. A yellow Post-it note fluttered out of the Bible. In pencil, someone had written, 'The treasure here is you.' Jackson stuck the Post-it note on his forehead and died of boredom.

He came back from the dead after ten minutes, a Lazarus licked to life by a canine redeemer. The dog looked worried. Could a dog look worried? Jackson yawned. The dog yawned. There had to be more to life than this. He folded the Post-it note and put it in his wallet in case he pitched up dead and the people who found him doubted his true worth.

'Well, the sun's long past the yardarm,' he said. 'Time to raid the minibar.' Did he used to speak out loud? Before he had the dog? He was pretty sure that he hadn't. *Ergo,* as Julia would have said, he was talking to the dog. Was that a bad sign? The dog looked at him as if it was interested in what he was saying. Jackson suspected that he was assigning emotions to the dog that it wasn't actually experiencing.

He drank down a doll's house-sized bottle of whisky and chased it with another. Leeds was famed for its nightlife, Jackson thought, why not go out and sample some of it? Just because he was in his golden years didn't mean he couldn't kick up his heels a little, make contact with his inner shining silver youth. Better surely than sitting in a hotel room, talking to a dog.

His sister used to go dancing in Leeds on Saturday nights with her friends. He could still conjure up Saturday evenings – Francis bolting his tea so he could get out and drink and pick up girls and Niamh in a cloud of hairspray and perfume, fretting about missing the bus. She always came home on the last bus. Until the day she never came home at all.

Later, before Peter Sutcliffe was caught and confessed, when he was still the nameless Ripper and had a large back catalogue of murders to his name, Jackson sometimes wondered if it wasn't possible that Niamh had fallen within his evil ken. His first victim wasn't until 1975 but he had started attacking women before that, as early as 1969 he had been found with a hammer and charged with 'going equipped for stealing' and only with hindsight could you see what the hammer was for. Manchester, Keighley, Huddersfield, Halifax, Leeds, Bradford his hunting ground, only a short drive from Jackson's home town. Niamh was strangled, Sutcliffe's victims were hit on the head and then stabbed as a rule. But who knew what mistakes a man committed when he was still new to the job.

Why did men kill women? After all these years Jackson still didn't know the answer to that question. He wasn't sure that he wanted to.

He had a quick shower and attempted to spruce himself up before taking the dog out to perform its evening toilette, going through the whole palaver with the rucksack again. He wondered about buying something smaller, a terrier-sized bag, he was pretty sure that Paws for Thought would sell them. He had tried zipping the dog inside his jacket but it made him look as if he was pregnant. Never a good look. Not on a man anyway.

Jackson felt bad about the steaming brown coil the dog left behind and he had to retrieve an old newspaper from a bin to wrap it in. This was not a problem he had considered before, now he realized that he would have to buy something to pick up crap with. It was the first real drawback he'd encountered to having the dog.

He took the dog back to the room and left it lying Sphinx-like on the bed, watching him sadly. He felt its tragic abandoned eyes on him all the way down in the lift, through reception, and into the street. Perhaps he should have left the television on for it.

When he hit the street he realized that he was starving. He'd had nothing since a coffee and sandwich in the café at Kirkstall Abbey much earlier in the day. He went in search of food and ended up in an Italian restaurant that felt like a garden centre where he drank a half-carafe of Chianti and ate an indifferent bowl of pasta before heading off to look for the bright lights. After that it was all a bit of a blur. Unfortunately.

She woke in the dark, no idea how long she'd been asleep. Thought she was back at home in her own bed. Took her a long time to remember she was in Bluebell Cottage. Tilly missed the noise of London, she needed it to sleep. It was dark here. Too dark. Dark and quiet. Unnatural.

Tilly sat up in bed and listened but the silence was profound. Sometimes when she listened in the middle of the night she could hear all kinds of tiny rustlings and squeaks and squeals as if mysterious wildlife was cavorting around the cottage. She was occasionally woken by a dreadful high-pitched keening which she suspected was some small creature having its life snuffed out by a fox. She always imagined foxes dressed in checked waistcoats and breeches, a hat with a feather. A legacy, she supposed, of some book from her childhood. As a child she had seen a diorama somewhere of stuffed rabbits dressed up as humans. Does in frocks and pelisses, bucks dressed like dandies and squires, a musical quartet, complete with miniature instruments. Rabbits posing as servants in mob caps, in aprons. A heartbreaking row of tiny baby rabbits tucked up in bed, fast asleep for ever. It was repellent and fascinating at the same time and it haunted Tilly's imagination for years afterwards.

But tonight there were no rabbit hoedowns or mice quadrilles, cunning Mr Fox wasn't seducing the hen-house, there was just a silence so deep and dark that it was like the sounds of a different dimension rather than the absence of noise.

Tilly clambered awkwardly out of bed, went over to the open window. When she drew back the curtains she was surprised to see a candle burning steadily in a bedroom window in the cottage across the way. *Jesus bids us shine with a pure, clear light.* Someone keeping a vigil or sending a signal? Late to bed or early to rise? The candle seemed to have a meaning beyond itself but she couldn't imagine what it might be. *Like a little candle burning in the night.*

And then an invisible hand lifted the candlestick and moved it away from the window. Shadows flared and loomed on the wall and then the room fell back into darkness.

Suddenly she was awake again. She had been running

after a little girl, running and running, down endless corridors, up and down staircases, but she couldn't catch up with her. And then *she* was the little girl and she was holding the paw of a small rabbit. They were running for their lives, hand in paw, while being chased by a giant cod. The cod was swimming through the air, sinuous and powerful, whipping its silver body around corners. Ridiculous, it really made you wonder where dreams came from. The rabbit let out a terrible cry as the big ugly lips of the cod closed on its tail. The rabbit was her baby, she understood. The one she had lost all those years ago. She woke up when she heard a voice say, *Someone should do something, Matilda.* Was it the cod who spoke? It was a very posh accent, you didn't think of cod speaking with a posh accent. Well, of course, you didn't think of them speaking at all. It was only when she was drifting off to sleep again that Tilly realized it was the voice of her old drama teacher, Franny Anderson.

Tracy retrieved the Viennese truffles from her bag. It was in another life that she had bought them in Thornton's. A different life. Before Courtney. BC.

She switched on the TV. The truffles had melted and fused together. Tasted the same though, if you didn't look at them. *Britain's Got Talent* was long finished. She looked for a film on cable and all she could find that was watchable was an unseasonable *Elf*. She recorded it on Sky Plus for Courtney. Pressing the red record button felt like a commitment to the future. Not that they were going to hang around here to watch it but it was the thought that counted.

If Carol Braithwaite's life hadn't been interrupted so abruptly she might be sitting down on her sofa now, feet up, glass and fag in hand, searching through six hundred channels and finding nothing worth watching. In the intervening years she probably wouldn't have lived a life of much consequence but then who did? But she was long gone. You would think she had disappeared for ever but her name remained, it seemed. The cupboard door was open, the box was off the shelf, the lid was up. Why did Linda Pallister want to talk to her about Carol Braithwaite?

Linda had worked in Child Services all her life, she must have seen the worst that people could offer. Tracy had seen the worst and then some. She felt soiled by everything she had witnessed. Filth, pure and simple. Massage parlours and lap-dancing clubs at the soft end and at the other end the hardcore DVDs of people doing repugnant things to each other. The unclassified stuff that scrambled your synapses with its depravity. The young girls trading their souls along with their bodies, the bargain-basement brothels and saunas, sleaziness beyond belief, girls on crack who would do anything for a tenner. Anything. Arresting girls for soliciting and seeing them go straight back on the streets; foreign girls who thought they were coming to work as waitresses and nannies and found themselves locked in sordid rooms, servicing one man after another all day; students working in 'gentlemen's clubs' (ha!) to pay their fees. Free speech, liberal do-gooders, the rights of the individual – *as long as it's not harming anyone else.* Blah, blah, blah. This was where it got you. Rome under Nero.

No end to evil really. What could you do? You could start with one small kid.

1974: *New Year's Eve*

A black-tie dinner-dance in the Metropole. It was in aid of some charity for kiddies – the sick or the deaf or the blind. Ray Strickland hadn't taken much notice, just knew it was expensive. 'Charity begins at home,' his wife, Margaret, said. Ray wasn't entirely sure he knew what that meant. His wife was a kind person. 'Daughter of the manse,' she said. 'I was brought up to believe that you have a duty to help the less fortunate.' 'That would be me then,' Ray joked.

Margaret was from Aberdeen originally. They had met one night ten years ago, in the A and E, when Ray was still in uniform, interviewing a drunk who'd been in a fight. She had come down to do her nurse's training at St James's, wanting 'to see England'. Ray told her that there was more to England than Leeds although at the time he hadn't been further afield than Manchester. Before she met him Margaret had had plans to become a missionary in some far-flung dark corner of the world. Then they became engaged and that was it, he became her mission, her own dark corner of the world.

When they were courting, he used to meet her off her shift and they would pop across the road to the old Cemetery Tavern and have a drink. Long time now since that was pulled down. Half of Tetley's mild for Ray, lemonade shandy for Margaret, daring for her at the time – she'd been raised in abstinence. So had Ray, of course, a West Yorkshire Wesleyan, signed the pledge and everything when he was younger. The pledge broken long ago.

In another life Margaret would have been a saint or a martyr. Not in a bad way, not in the way that other men he knew said of their wives, 'Thinks she's a bloody saint, she does.' Or, 'She's a martyr to the housework.' Ray valued her goodness. Hoped in some way it would rub off on him. He came to the end of every day feeling as if he had failed somehow. 'Don't be silly,' Margaret said. 'You make the world a better place, even if it's only in a small way.' Her faith in him was faulty. He lived his life in a state of guilt, every day waiting to be found out. He wasn't even sure what it was he had done.

He looked around the room for Margaret and couldn't see her anywhere.

Bigwigs. Magistrates, businessmen, solicitors, councillors, doctors, police, lots of police. The great and the good out in force to say farewell to the old year. The air was soupy – cigars, cigarettes, alcohol, perfume, all mixed with the smell of the remains of the buffet. Seafood cocktail, plates of ham and chicken and curried eggs, potato salad, bowls of trifle. It was making him feel sick. His chief superintendent, Walter Eastman, had been plying him with malts. They were all hard drinkers – Eastman, Rex Marshall, Len Lomax. 'You're one of us, lad,' Eastman said, 'so ruddy well drink like one of us.' Ray wasn't sure who 'us' was. Freemasons, police, members of the golf club? Perhaps he just meant men as opposed to women.

'You're on the up, Strickland,' Eastman said. 'DC now but you'll be an inspector before you know it.'

Lots of bigwigs here in the room, of course. That was why Ray – self-conscious in the penguin suit that he'd had to hire from Moss Bros – was here. Eastman had persuaded him to buy the tickets. 'It'll be good for you, lad, t'rub shoulders with your elders and betters.' Eastman, he was Eastman's protégé. 'That's good,' Margaret said. 'Isn't it?'

The women were all dressed up to the nines, satin and rhinestones – cajoling husbands and fiancés out on to the dance floor, where they grumbled their way around, doing inept foxtrots and stumbling quicksteps, desperate to get back to their fags and pints. Eastman was proud of his waltz, he was light on his feet for such a heavy bloke. He had insisted on taking Margaret 'for a turn' round the dance floor.

'Your wife's a nice woman,' he said.

'I know.' Ray followed Eastman's gaze and caught a

glimpse of Margaret at the far side of the room. She was wearing her midnight-blue lace and her soft hair was freshly set in concrete curls. She was thirty but the sixties had never happened for her. She looked very demure compared to some of the flesh on show, mutton dressed as lamb. Margaret was the other way round, lamb dressed as mutton. Ray admired modesty in a woman. His mother was his ideal wife but she would never have married someone as movable as Ray. No fixed foot, that was his trouble. 'Stop doing yourself down, Ray,' Margaret said, spooning his cold, worried back in the barren acreage of the marriage bed.

She was sitting at a table with Kitty Winfield, their heads close together as if they were sharing secrets. They made an odd pair. Kitty Winfield in black velvet, pearls around her neck, long hair sculpted up into a sophisticated do. The only woman in the room who knew that less was more. Everyone aware she used to be a model. Kitty Gillespie, as she had been in those days. They all presumed she had a racy past, she had dated famous people, she had been in the papers, she was one of the first to wear a miniskirt, but now she was pure class. Women wanted to be her friend, men held her in awe, beyond reproach, almost beyond lust. If Margaret was a saint, Kitty Winfield was a goddess. *'She walks in beauty,'* Eastman murmured at Ray's side. Eastman was a big golfing pal of Kitty Winfield's husband, Ian. Margaret worked alongside Ian Winfield at the hospital. Margaret looked like a different species sitting next to Kitty. A dowdy pigeon next to a swan. 'Kitty,' Eastman said. 'So fragile.' Ray understood that was a polite word for neurotic.

Ray knew what bonded Margaret and Kitty Winfield. Fertility. Or lack of it. Kitty Winfield couldn't conceive a baby, Margaret couldn't keep one inside. Margaret had endured three miscarriages, one premature stillbirth. Last year the doctors told her that she couldn't try for any more, something wrong inside her. Sobbing all the way home from the hospital.

She had spent years doing all this knitting, little lacy things in pastel colours. 'Have to have something on the needles,' she said. Cupboards full of baby clothes. Sad. Now she knitted for 'babies in Africa'. Ray wasn't sure that African kiddies would appreciate wearing wool but didn't say anything.

'We can adopt,' he had said on that last dreadful car journey home from the hospital. That made her cry even more.

He excused himself to Eastman and made his way round the dance floor to where Margaret and Kitty Winfield were sitting. Tragedy of it was, of course, that Margaret was a nurse on the kiddies' ward, spent all day with other women's children. And – an irony this as well – Kitty Winfield's husband was a kiddy doctor. Paediatrician at St James's.

Until recently they hadn't mixed in the same social circles. The Winfields were part of a cocktail crowd, big house in Harrogate. 'Cosmopolitan,' Margaret said. 'Big word,' Ray said. Now it was all different. Margaret always 'popping over' to see Kitty Winfield. 'She understands what it feels like not to be able to have a baby,' Margaret said.

'*I* understand,' Ray said.

'Do you?'

'Why don't we adopt?' Ray tried again. Margaret was more amenable to the idea this time. A nurse and a policeman, churchgoers, fit as fleas, surely they would be the ideal couple in an adoption agency's eyes?

'Maybe,' Margaret said.

'Not African kiddies, mind,' Ray said. 'No need to go that far.'

Before Christmas they had been invited to a party at the Winfields' Harrogate house. Margaret had fussed about what to wear, in the end decided on the midnight-blue lace again. 'For God's sake,' Ray said, 'buy yourself something new.'

'But this is perfectly good,' she said, so he was surprised when she came downstairs wearing a black sleeveless dress. 'Little black dress,' she said. 'Kitty gave it to me. We're the same size.' You would never have thought that to look at them, not in a million years.

'Do I look all right?' she asked doubtfully. He'd never seen her wearing anything that suited her less than Kitty Winfield's cocktail dress.

'Lovely,' he said. 'You look lovely.'

Ray felt out of his depth with the Winfields. Ian Winfield was all jovial friendship, 'Detective Constable, come to arrest us?' he said when he opened his holly-wreathed front door, full glass in hand.

'Why? Up to something, are you?' Ray said. Hardly witty repartee, was it? Kitty Winfield had caught him beneath the mistletoe in the hallway and he had felt himself blush when she kissed him. It was delicate, on the cheek, not like some of the women when it felt like you were being snogged by a salmon, all lips and tongues – any opportunity to get their hands on a man who wasn't their husband. Kitty Winfield smelled like Ray imagined French women smelled. And she was drinking champagne. Ray had never met anyone who drank champagne. 'Won't you have a glass?' she said, but he nursed a small whisky all evening. The Winfields' Harrogate house wasn't the kind of venue where you got drunk and disorderly. Margaret liked a Dubonnet and gin these days. 'Just a small one.'

The band in the Metropole finished up a clumsily danced cha-cha and a singer came on, looked like he'd been left over from the war. If they weren't careful he'd start on 'Danny Boy' but he surprised Ray by launching into 'Seasons in the Sun', leading to some rebellion on the dance floor. 'Give us something bloody cheerful,' Len Lomax muttered. Detective Sergeant Len Lomax, a womanizing hard drinker. A rugby player. A bastard. Ray's friend. His wife, Alma, was a hard-nosed bitch, worked as a buyer for a clothes factory. No kids, by choice, liked their 'lifestyle' too much. Alma was the only person Ray could think of that Margaret disliked. If Ray thought about his own 'lifestyle' (whatever that was) he felt an iron band tighten around his forehead.

'Ray!' Kitty Winfield said when he advanced upon her and Margaret. She smiled at him as if he were a camera. 'I'm sorry, I'm monopolizing your wife.'

'No, you're all right,' Ray said awkwardly. He lit her cigarette for her, she was close enough for him to smell that French perfume again. Wondered what it was. Margaret smelled of nothing more than soap.

They had been on the same table, the Winfields, the Eastmans, Len and Alma Lomax and some councillor called Hargreaves who was on the transport committee. Len Lomax had leaned across Margaret and in an undertone had said to Ray, 'You know that the woman with Hargreaves isn't his wife?' Margaret made a point of pretending he was invisible. The woman in question – more grey than scarlet – was self-consciously staring at her empty plate.

'He's very rude, your friend,' Kitty Winfield said reprovingly to Ray, inhaling deeply on her cigarette. 'I felt for that poor woman. So what if they're not married? It's 1975 for heaven's sake, not the Dark Ages.'

'Well, technically it's still 1974,' Ray said, looking at his watch. Oh God, Ray, he thought to himself. Lighten up. Kitty Winfield made him into a dullard.

Everything a mess now at the table, the cloth stained with food and wine, dirty plates that the waitresses were still clearing. A lone pink prawn curled like an embryo on the cloth. It turned his stomach again.

'Are you all right?' Margaret asked. 'You look pale.'

'Call a doctor,' Kitty Winfield laughed. 'You haven't seen him, have you?' she asked Ray.

'Who?' He had no idea what she was talking about.

'My husband. I haven't seen him for yonks. I think I'll go look-see. You two should dance,' she said, rising gracefully from the ruins of the table.

'Should we?' Margaret said when Kitty Winfield had disappeared into the mêlée. 'Dance?'

'I'm feeling a bit queasy, to be honest,' he admitted. 'Too much of the old firewater.'

Then Eastman came over again and said, 'Ray, there's some people I want to introduce you to.' Turning to Margaret, he said, 'You don't mind if I borrow your husband, do you?' and she said, 'As long as you bring him back in one piece.'

He went to the Gents and then got lost in a corridor somewhere. He hadn't realized how drunk he was. He kept bouncing off the walls as if he was in a ship ploughing a choppy sea. He had to stop a couple of times and lean on the wall, once he found himself slumped on the floor, just trying to concentrate on breathing. Buzzing, everything buzzing, he wondered if someone had slipped him a Mickey Finn. Waiting staff going up and down the corridor ignored him. When he finally got back to the ballroom Margaret grabbed hold of him and said, 'There you are, I thought you'd been kidnapped. You're just in time for the bells.'

The singer from earlier was counting down, '. . . five, four, three, two, one – Happy New Year, everyone!' The room erupted. Margaret kissed and hugged him and said, 'Happy New Year, Ray.' The band broke into 'Auld

Lang Syne', no one knew the words beyond the first two lines, except for Margaret and a couple of drunk, mouthy Scots. Then Eastman and some of his pals came over and pumped his hand up and down.

'Here's to 1975,' Rex Marshall said. 'May all your troubles be little ones,' and out of the corner of his eye Ray caught Margaret flinching. Stupid bugger.

The men all kissed Margaret and he could see her trying not to shrink away from their stinking breath. The Winfields reappeared, Kitty had managed to find her husband apparently, although he looked even more the worse for wear than Ray felt. There was more shaking of hands and kissing, Kitty offering her lovely pale cheek in a way that made them all want to behave better. But not for long.

'Gentlemen, to the bar!' Len Lomax shouted, holding his arm out in front of him as if he were about to lead them in the charge of the Light Brigade.

Both Ray and Ian Winfield demurred but Kitty Winfield laughed and said, 'Oh, shoo, go on, shoo,' pushing her husband away. She hooked her arm through Margaret's and said, 'Come on, Maggie, these men are here for the duration. I'm calling a taxi, I'll give you a lift.'

'Good idea,' Margaret said affably. 'You have a good time,' she said to Ray, patting him affectionately on the cheek.

'Boys will be boys,' he heard Kitty Winfield murmur as the two women walked away.

Men didn't deserve women.

'We don't deserve them,' he said to Ian Winfield as they rolled their way to the bar.

'Oh God, no,' he said. 'They're far superior to us. Wouldn't want to be one though.'

Ray had to dodge and weave his way back to the Gents where he threw up every last bit of prawn, chicken and trifle. Eastman came bustling in like a man in a hurry and took up a stance at a urinal. He unzipped himself in an expansive manner as if he was about to release something that would be admired.

'Pissing like a horse,' he said proudly. He zipped up again, ignored sink, soap and water and, patting Ray on the back, said, 'Good to go again, lad?'

God knows how much later. 1975 already eaten into, lost time never to be found again. Back in the Gents, leaning against a stall, trying to remain conscious. Wondered if he was going to end up in the hospital with alcoholic poisoning. He imagined how disappointed his mother would be if she could see him now.

Somehow he found himself in the kitchen. The kitchen staff were having their own kind of celebration. They were all foreign, he could hear Spanish, he'd taken Margaret to Benidorm last year. They hadn't liked it much.

A man in chef's whites set fire to a bowl of alcohol and the whole bowl became one great blue flame, ethereal, like a sacrifice to ancient gods. Then the man took a ladle and started lifting it from the bowl, leaving a trail of blue flame behind. He kept doing it again and again, higher and higher. It was hypnotic. Stairway to heaven.

He'd fallen. He'd had an affair with a girl in clerical – Anthea, a snappy modern sort, always going on about women's rights. She knew her own mind, he would give her that. She didn't really want anything from him but sex and it was a relief to be with someone who wasn't in permanent mourning for an empty womb. 'Fun,' she said, 'life's supposed to be fun, Ray.' He'd never thought of life like that before.

They went at it anywhere and everywhere, cars, woods, back alleys, the thin-walled bedroom in the flat she shared with a friend. It had nothing in common with what he and Margaret did in bed, where he always felt he was imposing an indignity on her and she was trying to pretend he wasn't. Anthea did things that Ray had never even heard of. It was certainly an education. Len Lomax covered for him all the time. Lying came to Len as easily as breathing. The education was over now, Anthea said she didn't believe in long-term relationships, was worried that he would 'become emotionally dependent' on her. Part of him was relieved beyond measure, he'd lived in terror that Margaret would find out, but another part of him ached for the simplicity of it all. 'Ah, the uncomplicated fuck,' Len said appreciatively. 'Right,' Ray said, although he hated the crudity of such a word being applied to his own life. 'You're an old woman, really, Ray,' Len laughed.

Ray thought maybe he'd passed out on his feet

because the next moment the kitchen staff were all fighting, yelling God knows what at each other. One of them threw a huge cooking pot across the kitchen that made a terrific clatter when it landed.

Staggered out, back into the bar. Bumped into Rex Marshall. 'Fucking hell, Strickland,' Marshall said, 'you look far gone. Have a drink.'

If he put a match to himself he would catch fire. Burn with a blue flame. He put his head down on the bar. He wondered where Len Lomax was.

'Have to go home,' he whispered when Walter Eastman came over to him. 'Before I die. Get me a taxi, will you?' Eastman said, 'Don't waste money on a fucking taxi. Call the police!' Raucous laughter from the bar. Eastman used the phone on the bar top to make a call and some time later – it could have been ten minutes, it could have been ten years, Ray had no relationship to the normal world any more – a young constable entered the bar and said, 'Sir?' to Eastman.

Those were the days.

'What are *you* doing here?' Tracy said.

'Chauffeur for the night,' Barry Crawford said. 'Eastman asked me to pick up a legless DC, take him home.'

155

'You're a real brown-nose.'

'Yeah, well, beats staying in with me mam and watching New Year crap on TV.' He was leaning casually on the car, smoking. It was freezing out here. She should have put a thermal vest on. Every time someone came out of the Metropole they brought a wash of noise and light out with them. 'It's like a Roman orgy in there,' Barry said.

'You think?' Tracy wondered what Barry knew about either Romans or orgies. Precious little, she suspected. They'd been through police training college together and from that she'd gathered that he was both ambitious and lazy so he would probably do well. He 'fancied' a girl called Barbara, a nippy girl who teased her hair into a big old-fashioned beehive and worked on a cosmetics counter in Schofields, but he was too scared to ask her out.

'What about you?' Barry said to Tracy.

'On shift. Obviously,' she said, indicating her uniform. 'Been called to a disturbance. Some kind of brawl in the kitchen. I think they just found out they weren't getting overtime for working after midnight or something.' How had Barry got his hands on a panda car? Tracy had applied to do the driver's course and heard nothing.

'You on your own?' he asked her.

'I'm with Ken Arkwright. He's off to the toilets. Who's this DC you're driving then?'

'Strickland.'

'Speak of the devil, Barry, here comes your fare for the

night. Jesus, look at the state of him. You're going to be spending the first day of 1975 cleaning up vomit.' Ray Strickland was being manhandled out of the Metropole, supported by a couple of burly CID blokes.

'Fuck off,' Barry said amiably to Tracy, dropping his cigarette and grinding it out with his foot.

Ken Arkwright shambled up. 'Ey up,' he said to Tracy, 'Third World War's breaking out in there. These Mediterranean types, they don't half know how to get worked up. We'd better get in there and call a truce before they kill each other.'

'Well,' Tracy said to Barry, 'you carry on being a taxi service, Barry, and we'll get on with some real policing.'

'Sod off.'

'Same to you,' she said cheerfully. 'Happy New Year.'

'Yes, Happy New Year, lad,' Arkwright said.

When Tracy looked back over her shoulder she saw DCS Eastman lean in to the driver's window and heard him give Strickland's address to Barry. Then he slipped him something else, Tracy couldn't see what, money or drink probably.

'What a twat,' Arkwright said.

'Barry Crawford?'

'No. Ray Strickland.'

'Home then, boss?' Barry said.

'No,' Ray said.

'No?'

'No.' Strickland leaned forward and slurred an address in Lovell Park and Barry said, 'Are you sure?'

'Of course I'm fucking sure.' Strickland fell back against the seat and closed his eyes.

When they arrived in Lovell Park he almost fell out of the car. Barry watched him weave his way unsteadily towards the front doors. You had to hope for the poor bastard's sake that the lifts were working.

Halfway there, Strickland turned and held a half-bottle of Scotch aloft as if in triumph. 'Happy New Year!' he shouted. He stumbled on another few yards and then turned again and shouted, louder this time, 'What was your name?'

'Crawford,' Barry shouted back. 'PC Barry Crawford. Happy New Year, sir.'

Jeopardy

Thursday

Tracy was woken by a cry, an inchoate sound in the dark. Half comatose, she thought it was the foxes who visited the garden most nights and who made mating sound like murder. She heard the cry again and it took several seconds before she remembered that she was not alone in the house.

Courtney!

Clambering out of bed, she stumbled drowsily to the spare bedroom where she found the kid sound asleep on her back, breathing heavily, her mouth slack. As Tracy turned to go Courtney cried out again, a cawing noise that seemed to indicate distress. She flailed an arm suddenly as if she was trying to ward off an attack but the next second she was so deeply asleep that she could have been a corpse. Tracy felt compelled to give her a little poke and was relieved when she twitched, making a whimpering noise, like a dog dreaming.

Tracy sat on the bed, waiting to see if the kid was going to wake again. No wonder Courtney's sleep was disturbed – she didn't know where she was, who she was with. Tracy felt a pang of guilt at having

161

subtracted her from her natural habitat, but then she recalled the murderous expression on Kelly Cross's face as she dragged Courtney through the Merrion Centre. Tracy had seen enough bashed-up, beat-up kids that social workers had kept in families you wouldn't give a dog to. Families weren't always such great places to be, especially for kids.

She must have fallen asleep because the next time she woke up Tracy found herself sprawled uncomfortably across the foot of the narrow bed while daylight washed the ugly woodchip. Of Courtney, there was no sign and Tracy experienced an unexpected moment of panic as if a giant hand had clutched at her heart. Perhaps the kid's rightful mother had appeared under the cloak of night and stolen her back. Or perhaps a stranger had climbed in through the window and spirited her away. Although what were the odds against a kid being abducted twice in twenty-four hours? Probably not as long as you imagined.

When a bleary-eyed Tracy blundered into the kitchen, however, she found the kid sitting at the table spooning her way stoically through a bowl of dry cereal.

'You're here,' Tracy said.

Courtney glanced at her briefly. 'I am,' she said. 'I am here.' She returned to spooning in cereal.

'Do you want milk with that?' Tracy said, pointing at the cereal bowl. The kid nodded extravagantly and kept on nodding until Tracy advised her to stop.

Tracy wasn't sure which was more disturbing, losing the kid or finding her.

* * *

Tracy had slept in a washed-out Winnie-the-Pooh night-shirt from British Home Stores that barely reached the top of her thunderous thighs and her hair was sticking out in all the wrong places. She had hastily pulled on a pair of old tracksuit bottoms to complete the ensemble. She looked dismal, probably not a million miles from how Kelly Cross looked first thing in the morning, just a lot bigger. Still, she could have been wearing a bin-liner and Courtney wouldn't have noticed. Kids weren't interested in what you were like on the outside. There was something definitely cheering about being with a small, non-judgemental person.

Courtney, on the other hand, had made more of an effort, dressing herself from a selection of yesterday's new clothes. Some of them were on backwards but she had got the general idea right. Tracy's efforts at hair-dressing the previous evening weren't entirely successful. In the cruel light of day the kid looked hand-made. She had finished her cereal and was staring, Oliver Twist-like, at the empty bowl.

'Toast?' Tracy offered. The kid gave her a thumbs-up.

Tracy cut the toast into triangles and arranged them on the plate. If it had just been for her she would have slapped a doorstep on to a piece of kitchen roll and been done with it. It was different having someone to do things for. Made you more careful. 'Mindful', a Buddhist would have said. She only knew that because a long time ago she had dated a Buddhist for a few weeks. He was a wimpy bloke from Wrexham who ran a second-hand bookshop. She was hoping for enlightenment, ended up with glandular fever. Put her off spirituality for life.

Tracy parked Courtney on the sofa in front of the television, where she sat mesmerized by a noisily incomprehensible cartoon, weird and Japanese. Obviously the kid should be doing something more mentally stimulating – playing with Lego or learning the alphabet or whatever it was that four-, maybe three-year-olds were supposed to do.

Tracy switched on her laptop and waited for it to get up a head of steam before beginning to scroll through the wares being offered by several estate agents. Everything nice in a pleasant location – the Dales, the Lakes – cost more than twice as much as she would get for her house in Leeds. Abroad seemed a better option for all kinds of reasons. They could lose themselves in rural France or hectic urban Barcelona, somewhere where no one would think twice about their relocation.

Spain, you couldn't give away property in Spain these days, Brits leaving in droves. Bring the kid up in the sun. Costa del Gangster. Enough career criminals did it, why not the people who'd failed to catch them? *Mi casa es mi casa*. Not the kind of property you could buy online. They'd have to fly out there. Not come back. Once she'd got a passport for the kid, of course. Somewhere further? New Zealand, Australia, Canada. Leslie could give her some gen on Canada. Plenty of wilderness there to get lost in. How far did you have to run before you couldn't be caught? Siberia? The moon?

When the cartoon finished Tracy switched over to GMTV, looking for the news. Nothing on the national or the local, still nobody missing a kid. You would notice straight away if you lost one. (Wouldn't you?) Kelly Cross was Courtney's mother. Had to be. No doubt about it. None at all.

They had another day to kill until Tracy could get the key to the holiday place. She wondered what they should do. There was a kids' film showing at the Cottage Road Cinema in Headingley. Or there was a Wacky Warehouse in Leeds – a play area attached to a pub, the ultimate dream of the Useless Parenting classes, and she had often passed something called Diggerland near Castleford where, apparently, kids got to drive construction machinery. Bob the Builder had a lot to answer for.

Tracy fired off an email to Leslie at the Merrion Centre (not Grant, a police cadet reject. Somewhere there was a village missing an idiot) saying that she would see them after her holiday and that she wouldn't be in today, 'still got a bit of a bug, wouldn't want to hand it on to you'. That would surprise them, Tracy was as fit as a butcher's dog normally. Constitution of an ox. She was a Taurean, born under the sign of the bull. Not that she believed in any of that stuff. Didn't believe in anything that she couldn't touch. 'Ah, an empiricist,' a man she had met at the singles social club said. He was a prof at the university, full of hot air and cold calculation. Took her to the Grand to see *Seven Brides for Seven Brothers* 'based on the – largely legendary –

incident of the "Rape of the Sabine Women",' he said. 'Although, as in the musical itself, "rape", *raptio*, is really abduction or kidnapping. The interior of the theatre, of course, is said to be based on La Scala in Milan.' And so on, and so on. And so on.

The following week he took her to see *Dial M for Murder*. 'That should be right up your street,' he said.

Courtney turned to look at Tracy and said plaintively, 'I'm hungry.'

'Again?'

'Yes.'

The kid was an eater, there was no doubt about that. Maybe she was making up for something.

'Courtney?' Tracy said tentatively. 'You know how you're called Courtney?' The kid nodded. She seemed bored, although her expressions tended to be unreadable at the best of times. 'Well, I was thinking, now that you've got a new home –' she saw Courtney's eyes skim the anodyne living room – 'how about a new name to go with that?' Courtney gazed at her indifferently. Tracy wondered if the kid had been given a new identity before, that Courtney wasn't even her name. Was that the reason no one was looking for her, were they looking for a completely different kind of kid – a Grace, a Lily, a Poppy? (A Lucy, perhaps.) Something like acid bile rose in Tracy's gorge. It came, she supposed, from the well of terror that had opened up in her stomach. What had she done? She closed her eyes in an effort to blank out the guilt – futile – and when she opened them the kid was standing in front of her, looking interested. 'What name?' she asked.

She should get some fresh air into the kid, Tracy thought. She looked peaky, as if she'd been grown in a cellar all her life. 'Come on,' Tracy said when more toast had been eaten – turned out the kid liked Marmite – 'why don't we go out, get some fresh air? I'll change.' Courtney looked at her with interest and Tracy added, 'Into different clothes.'

Tracy slipped into something less comfortable and when she returned to the living room the kid had got down from the table and fetched her pink backpack. She was as biddable as a dog although without a dog's tail-wagging enthusiasm.

Before they could leave the house they heard a key turning in the front-door lock. Tracy had a mental blank, couldn't think of any reason why someone would have her front-door key, why anyone would be coming into her house. For a mad moment she thought it might be her anonymous phone caller. For an even madder moment she thought it might be Kelly Cross and did a quick recce of the hallway to see what she could use as a weapon. The door opened.

Janek! Tracy had forgotten all about him.

He looked bemused by her surprise and then he spotted Courtney lingering in the doorway of the kitchen and he smiled in delight.

'Hello,' he said. Courtney stared blankly back at him. 'My niece,' Tracy said. 'My sister's much younger than me,' she added, embarrassed suddenly by how old she must seem to Janek. Of course he had kids of his own, didn't he? Poles probably really liked kids. Most foreigners liked kids more than the British did.

'We're on our way out,' she said hastily before she got involved in anything more complicated about the kid's origins.

'Help yourself to biscuits,' she added. What a difference a day made.

❦

He woke up with no idea where he was or how he had got there. That was alcohol for you.

Jackson wasn't alone. There was a woman lying next to him, her face pressed into the pillow, her features partly hidden by a messed-up nest of hair. He never ceased to be amazed by how many round-heeled women there were in the world. In a sudden moment of paranoia he reached over and checked the woman's breathing and was relieved to find it sour and regular. Her skin had the bruised and waxy look of a corpse but, on inspection, Jackson realized that it was just her make-up from the previous evening, smeared and blotchy. Close up, even in the street-lit gloom of the bedroom, he could see that she was older than he had first thought. Early forties, Jackson reckoned, maybe a little younger. Maybe a little older. She was that kind of woman.

A digital clock by the bed told him it was five thirty. In the morning, he assumed. Winter or summer it was the time he woke at, thanks to his body's own internal alarm clock, set a long time ago by the army. Up with the lark. Jackson didn't think that he'd ever seen a lark. Or heard one for that matter. *Split the Lark – and you'll find the Music, / Bulb after Bulb, in Silver rolled.* What kind of a woman came up with an image like that? Jackson felt pretty sure that Emily Dickinson didn't wake up hungover, with a strange man in her bed.

Dawn was just cracking open the sky. It was good to get a march on the day. Time was a thief and Jackson felt he gained a small triumph by stealing back some of the early hours. He had a feeling it was Thursday but he wouldn't have sworn to it.

The nameless woman lying next to him muttered something unintelligible in her sleep. She turned her head and opened her eyes, they had the same blank quality as the dead. When she saw Jackson her eyes came to life a little and she murmured, 'Christ, I bet I look rough.'

She did look a bit of a dog's breakfast but Jackson bit down on his unfortunate compulsion for honesty and, smiling, said, 'Not really.' Jackson didn't often smile these days (had he ever?) and it tended to take women by surprise. The woman in the bed (surely she must have told him her name at some point?) squirmed with pleasure and giggled and said, 'Gonna make me a cuppa tea then, lover boy?'

He said, 'Go back to sleep. It's still early.' Strangely

obedient, the woman closed her eyes and within minutes was snoring gently. Jackson suspected that he might be punching below his weight.

He had a memory – vague at first but growing unfortunately clearer now – of dropping into a bar in the town centre, intent on casting off his golden years. He seemed to recollect that he had been looking for a *pastis*, a warm billet in a cold city, but the place turned out to be some kind of cocktail joint containing a job lot of clapped-out men who were easily outnumbered by the hordes of brash women. A gang of them had descended on him, feverish with alcohol and eager to pick him off from the herd of homely suits. The women seemed to have started drinking some time last century.

They were celebrating the divorce of one of their pack. Jackson thought that divorce was possibly an occasion for a wake rather than a knees-up but what did he know, he had a particularly poor track record where marriage was concerned. It surprised him to discover that the women all seemed to be teachers or social workers. Nothing more frightening than a middle-class woman when she lets her hair down. Who were those Greek women who tore men to pieces? Julia would know.

Despite it being midweek, the women were all drinking shooters with ridiculous names – Flaming Lamborghini, Squashed Frog, Red-Headed Slut – and Jackson felt faintly disturbed by the sickly contents of their glasses. God only knew what kind of faces they would have on them when they turned up for work the next morning.

'I'm Mandy,' one of the women said brightly.

'Go on, love – fly her,' another one said, her throat filthy with years of smoking.

'This is how it goes,' Mandy said, ignoring her friend. 'I say, "My name is Mandy," and you say . . . ?'

'Jackson,' Jackson said, reluctantly.

'What's "Jackson"?' one of them asked. 'A first name or a last name?'

'Take your pick,' Jackson said.

He liked to keep conversations simple. There wasn't much you couldn't convey with 'Yes', 'No', 'Do' and 'Don't', anything else was pretty much ornamental, although throwing in the occasional 'please' could get you a surprisingly long way and 'thank you' even further. His first wife had deplored his lack of small talk ('Jesus, Jackson, would it kill you to have a meaningless conversation?'). This was the same wife who, at the beginning of their courtship, had admired him for being 'the strong, silent type'.

Perhaps he should have found more words to give Josie. Then she might not have left him, and if she hadn't left him he wouldn't have taken up with Julia who drove him to distraction and then he certainly wouldn't have met the false second wife, Tessa, who had fleeced him and robbed him blind. For want of a nail. 'Good wife, bad wife,' Julia said. 'You know in your heart which one you really prefer, Jackson.' Did he? Which? No one, not even Tessa, had ever messed with his mind the way Julia did. 'The Black Widow,' she said with relish. 'You were lucky that she didn't eat you.'

Women were often drawn to Jackson – to begin with, at any rate – but he didn't set much store by looks any more, either his own or (it seemed) those of the opposite sex, having witnessed too often the havoc wrought by beauty without truth. Although there was a time when, no matter how drunk, he would not have been attracted to someone like the woman he had woken up to this morning. Or perhaps standards simply fell as you grew older. Of course, Jackson, as faithful as a dog at heart, had spent a lot of his adult life in monogamous relationships where these problems had been merely hypothetical.

He had not thought of himself as priapic. Since Tessa he had been in an ascetic, almost monkish place, appreciating the lack of necessity in his life. A Cistercian. And then suddenly all the untaken vows had been broken by a muster of the monstrous regiment.

'What brings you to this neck of the woods?' one of the more sober of the coven asked. ('My name's Abi, I'm the designated grown-up,' a fact that seemed to make her bitter.)

Jackson wasn't big on questions and if faced with a choice he would rather be asking than answering them. Teachers and social workers, he remembered. 'I don't suppose any of you know Linda Pallister, by any chance?' he asked. A couple of the women howled like hyenas. 'You wouldn't catch Linda dead in a place like this. She'll be recycling cats or worshipping trees somewhere.'

'No, she's not a pagan, she's a Christian,' someone said. This fact seemed to take them to a new level of hilarity.

'What do you want her for anyway?' the rather petulant Abi asked.

'I had an appointment with her this afternoon but she was a no-show.'

'She's in adoption counselling. Were you adopted?' one of them said, reaching out and holding his hand. 'Poor baby. Were you an orphan? Abandoned? Unwanted? Come to Mummy, pet.' Another one said, 'She's *ancient*. You don't want her. You want *us*.'

One of the women moved so close to him that he could feel the heat of her face next to his. She was drunk enough to think that she was being seductive when in a breathy voice she said to him, 'Would you like a Slippery Nipple?'

'Or a Blowjob?' another woman shrieked.

'They're having you on,' yet another one said, sidling close to him, 'they're the names of drinks.'

'To you maybe,' the first woman laughed.

'Go on, love, give her a shag,' someone else said. 'She's gagging for it, put her out of her misery.'

What had happened to women? Jackson wondered. They made him feel almost prudish. (Obviously not prudish enough to have resisted the dubious charms of one of them.) More and more these days, he had noticed, he felt like a visitor from another planet. Or the past. Sometimes Jackson thought that the past wasn't just another country, it was a lost continent somewhere at the bottom of an unknown ocean.

'You're scowling,' Abi said.

'That's just the way I look,' Jackson said.

'Don't worry, we don't bite.'

'Not yet,' one of them laughed.

Jackson smiled and the temperature around him went up a degree. The treasure here was clearly Jackson. The atmosphere in the bar was so charged that there was a very real danger that these wild women might simply explode with excitement.

Well, Jackson thought, what happens in Leeds stays in Leeds. Isn't that what they said?

'I'm not worried,' he said. 'But if you're buying, ladies, I'll have a Pernod.'

Time to get the hell out of Dodge. Jackson slipped quietly out of the bed and found his clothes where he must have shucked them on to the floor a few hours earlier. He moved with a certain delicacy. His head felt leaden, as if the weight of it was too much for the fragile stem of his neck. He crept along a narrow hall-way and was thankful that he guessed correctly which door led to the bathroom. Treating the house as a recce in hostile territory seemed as sensible an approach as any. It was a better version of the house he had been brought up in, a fact which unnerved him, the way some dreams did.

The bathroom was warm and clean and had matching bath and pedestal mats in strawberry pink. The suite was also pink. Jackson couldn't remember urinating into a pink toilet before. First time for everything. The bath tiles had flowers on them, the supermarket toiletries were lined up neatly at the end of the bath. Jackson wondered about the woman who lived here and why she would sleep with a complete stranger. He could ask himself the same question, of course, but it seemed less relevant. Two toothbrushes stood in a mug on a shelf above the sink. Jackson considered what that meant.

He washed his hands (he was house-trained, by a line of women that stretched back to the Stone Age) and caught sight of himself in the mirror. He looked about as debauched as he felt. He had fallen. Like Lucifer.

He was desperate for a shower but more desperate to get out of this claustrophobic house. He went downstairs, keeping to the edge of the steep, carpeted staircase where the boards wouldn't creak so much. The woman lived with someone who had left a bike parked in the hallway. Probably the same person had carelessly tossed a pair of muddy football boots down by the front door. A skateboard was propped up against the wall. The sight of the skateboard (where was the owner?) made Jackson feel depressed.

Somehow he would have preferred it if the second toothbrush had belonged to a partner or a lover rather than a teenage son. He felt suddenly unexpectedly grateful that his first wife had remarried, not because she was (apparently) happy, he didn't give a toss for her happiness, but because it meant that she wasn't picking up strange men (like himself) for the night. Strange men who were free to prowl around the house where his daughter was in the throes of an intense and brooding adolescence.

Jackson didn't breathe until he had shut the front door behind him and stepped out into the misty early morning air. The day looked as though it could go either way and he wasn't just thinking about the weather.

He set his internal compass to 'Town Centre' and jogged back into town at a more sedate pace than normal, hoping to outdistance a heroic hangover. Jackson had recently taken up running again. With any luck, if his knees held up, he planned to keep on running right through his golden years and into his diamond ones.

('Why?' Julia asked. 'Why running?'

'Stops the thinking,' he said cheerfully.

'That's a good thing?'

'Definitely.')

As a bonus, on his tour of England and Wales he had discovered that running was a good way of seeing a place. You could go from town to countryside before breakfast and move from urban decay to bourgeois suburb without breaking stride. A great way to evaluate the real estate on offer. And no one took any notice of you, you were just the madman out at dawn trying to prove he was still young.

Jackson finally reached the Best Western, where he had fully intended to spend the night rather than in the arms of a stranger. It was a long time since Jackson had had a one-night stand. 'Will You Still Love Me Tomorrow?' Hopefully not.

He took the lift up to his floor and thought he might make up some of the sleep he had lost. His appointment with Linda Pallister was at ten o'clock, a stone's throw from the hotel. Plenty of time for forty winks, a shower and a shave and some breakfast, he thought as he entered the room. A decent cup of coffee. Even an indecent cup would do at this juncture.

He had completely forgotten about the dog.

It was waiting anxiously on the other side of the door as if it was unsure who was going to come through it. When it saw that it wasn't the erstwhile Colin it went wild with tail-wagging. Jackson dropped to a crouch and indulged its happiness for a minute. He felt bad about leaving the dog locked in solitary all night. If he had taken the dog with him last night perhaps it could have monitored his antics, guarded his morals – a friendly paw on the shoulder at some point, advice to think twice, *Go home, Jackson. Don't do it. Just say no.*

He looked around the hotel room to check if any little brown gifts had been deposited and when he found nothing said, 'Good dog,' and, although it was possibly the last thing in the world that he wanted to do at that moment, he fetched the lead and said, 'Come on then,' and unzipped the rucksack for the dog.

She had done nothing to help that poor mite. Suffer the little children. She thought of the little girl who had been singing her song of innocence, 'Twinkle, Twinkle, Little Star', in the Merrion Centre and her horrible bully of a mother. Courtney. *Shut the fuck up will you, Courtney.* What was wrong with people that they could behave like that? An echo of Father, *Children should be seen and not heard, Matilda.* He thought they should be neither heard nor seen. There had been another child, a brother, already dead when Tilly was born, his shadow walking ahead of her all of her childhood. All those graveyards in the past, full of little children, their headstones like small broken teeth. Modern medicine would have saved most of them, would have saved her brother. It would take more than medicine to save the little Courtneys of this world though.

Funny how she could remember the name of a child she didn't know and had trouble recalling what simple everyday objects were called. Kettle. This morning it had taken her ten minutes to dredge up the word 'kettle'. 'The thing for boiling water,' she said helplessly to Saskia. 'Billabong. Billy. Billy boiled. You know.'

'Billabong?' Saskia repeated doubtfully. You could see she had no idea what that was. ' "Waltzing Matilda",' Tilly said. 'Which is my name, of course. Matilda.' She sang a few helpful bars, *'Once a jolly swagman camped by a billabong,'* and Saskia said, 'Oh, um, yes. Of course.' At least 'billy' was in the right area. The first word she had trawled and brought up from the deeps was 'chicken'. 'I'll just pop the what's-it – chicken – on for a cup of tea, shall I?' Saskia looking at her as if she'd grown two heads. Silly Tilly. Silly billy Tilly. Yesterday it had been lilies for lamps, *Oh, it's dark, will I turn the lilies on?* They toil not, neither do they spin. The lamps are going out all over Europe. And nonsense words for everyday objects, curtains, drawers, cups transformed into *pockle, gip, rottle.* All her words turning into mush, language disappearing until there would be nothing left except sounds, *ar-aw-oo-ar-ay-ee-ar* – and eventually just silence.

Tilly frightened the girl. The madness of Lear. Poor Ophelia drifting downstream with a handbag of knives and forks – and – just this morning – a spool of red ribbon and a knitting needle, as if she had wandered through a haberdashery department in her sleep. She had played Ophelia in rep. The actor playing Hamlet had been on the short side. The audience had been restless. Tilly had understood, one expected Hamlet to have a little height. *Row, row, row your boat, gently down the stream.* 'Have you ever done the classics?' she asked Saskia the other day. 'Shakespeare and so on?'

'Oh God, no,' Saskia said, as if Tilly had suggested something distasteful.

Saskia was nothing like Padma, Padma was kind, always asking if she could do anything for Tilly. Sometimes Tilly felt like an invalid the way the girl treated her. *Invalid. Invalid.* Depended where you put the emphasis, didn't it? Sick or without validity. She was becoming both. Better to be dead than mad. Ophelia knew.

The little 'Twinkle, Twinkle' girl was mixed up now with all the other poor mites in the world. Some stuffed baby rabbits in there too. Her own lost baby. All conflated into one small, helpless infant howling in the wind. The name of the 'Twinkle, Twinkle' girl had slipped away, she'd had it a minute ago and now . . . gone, the way of all kettles. Oh, lord.

She had wanted to tell the man who said he used to be a policeman about the 'Twinkle, Twinkle' girl. Had she said something to the nice girl in the whatever centre? Muckle, mickle, metric, Merrion Centre. She had been so taken up with her own troubles that she had probably said nothing. Evil will prevail when good women do nothing. She still hadn't found her purse, of course. Julia and Padma had loaned her some money. And even Saskia had given her a five-pound note and said, 'This'll tide you over.' She was sure the girl had a good heart really even though Tilly had heard her complaining to someone on the production team. *That old toad. Filthy habits. I need to live on my own.* You'll be lucky, ducky, they're a tight-fisted bunch.

She should have stepped in. She imagined herself snatching the child in her arms and running out of the Merrion Centre with her. She could have put her in the car (if she could have remembered how to start it) and driven off to Bluebell Cottage where she would have fed the poor little mite on coddled eggs and some of those nice Beurre d'Anjou pears that Padma had bought for her. Didn't know how to coddle an egg, of course. Mother used to make them for her in a little china egg-coddler. Pretty thing. Coddle was a lovely word, like cuddle. If Tilly had a little girl to look after she would coddle her. Or a rabbit, a poor little velvety rabbit running from the fox or the gun. *Run, rabbit, run.*

Her thoughts were rudely interrupted by an urgent knocking at the door.

She couldn't imagine who it could be at this hour. She opened the door cautiously. A young woman who looked familiar was standing there. She was out of breath, her insubstantial bosom heaving. She was wearing an awful lot of make-up. Beneath the make-up Tilly eventually recognized Saskia. She pushed her way rudely into the house, asking, 'Is Vince here?' as if her life depended on it.

'Vince?' Tilly said. 'There's no one here called Vince, dear.'

Tilly supposed that Bluebell Cottage, being a holiday let, had been occupied by lots of different people. Although why Saskia should be looking for any of them she didn't know. She suddenly noticed the gun in Saskia's hand. 'Oh, my dear,' Tilly said, 'what on earth are you going to do with that?'

'Cut!' someone bellowed.

Cut? Cut what? Tilly wondered.

181

Tracy decided to stop off at a supermarket to pick up supplies. First she loaded up the trolley with bananas, convenience food for small children. As they trawled the aisles, Tracy's mind had been divided between worrying about the security cameras and wondering if Courtney was going to get stuck in the shopping-trolley seat – and what she would do about it if she did – when she saw a familiar face coming towards them.

Barry Crawford's wife. Barbara. Shit. She would want to know who Courtney was. Of all the supermarkets in all the world . . .

Barbara Crawford was advancing along the canned-vegetable aisle as if she was walking on pins, treating her shopping trolley like a Silver Cross pram. A zombie in full slap and heels. It didn't matter what was happening on the inside, Barbara was always rigged out ready for an impromptu invitation to lunch with the Queen. Immaculate nails and make-up. Wool dress, gilt chain-belt, fine-denier stockings, her black hair as patent as her shoes. Tracy reckoned if she was grief-stricken she would dress herself in rags, smear coal and mud on her face, let her hair turn into dreadlocks. Each to their own, she supposed. After she married Barry, Barbara spent years as an Avon lady. Ding-dong. *Have you thought about blusher, Tracy? It could do wonders for you.* It would take more than blusher.

Barbara was wearing a rigid smile on her face that looked as if she'd put it on this morning and would be damned if she would take it off for anyone. She was the kind of wife you were glad to leave at home. The strict rules-and-duties kind, a creature of routine, married to someone whose job was anything but routine. Drove her crazy. Drove Barry to the pubs and the prostitutes. 'What any man who loved his wife would do,' he said. 'Wives for the missionary position, showed you respected them, and whores for the funny stuff.' All whores wanted was money, Barry 'explained' to Tracy. Wives made you pay with your lifeblood. Made Tracy glad she was no one's wife. Most days she was grateful for her single state, relieved not to be growing old in the company of someone who looked at her indifferently over the toast and marmalade while she wondered what he was really thinking.

Those days were over for Barry now though. Lots of things ended the day little Sam died.

'Oh shit,' Tracy muttered as Barbara drew nearer. It was the anniversary any day now, wasn't it? Two years. 'Shit, shit, shit.'

Courtney looked at her anxiously, her face suddenly pinched. 'S'all right, sweetheart,' Tracy said, 'I just remembered something, that's all – Barbara! Hello.' Tracy modified her voice to a more sensitive and com-passionate one, suited to the bereaved. 'How are you?' Tracy had been with Barry when he took the call, his hand had started to shake so much that he'd dropped the phone. Tracy had picked it up, said, 'Hello,' into the receiver, got someone else's bad news at first hand.

Barry Crawford was born a miserable old git but they rubbed along. Tracy remembered when Amy was born, remembered wetting the baby's head in a pub full of coppers. Barry a DC by then, Tracy still in uniform. (Of course.) Not long after the Ripper was caught. 'Women are safe again,' an inspector said to her over the congratulatory beers and Tracy was so drunk that she had laughed in his face. As if taking one mad, bad bloke off the streets made women safe.

'To my new daughter,' Barry said, raising his glass of double malt high to the room in general. Must have been about his sixth that night. 'Better luck next time,' some joker at the back of the room said.

When Amy's own baby, Sam, was born, Amy's husband, Ivan, was in the delivery room with her, sweating out every minute of the labour. 'Times have changed,' Barry said sardonically to Tracy. 'Now you have to be *supportive*. Men have to be like women these days, God help us.'

'Some of us are becoming the men we wanted to marry,' Tracy said.

'Eh?'

'Gloria Steinem. Early feminist.'

'Heck, Tracy.'

'Quote of the day on my quote-a-day calendar. Just saying.'

Barry sighed and raised his glass. 'To my grandson. Sam.' They were in a pub in Bingley. Birthplace of the Ripper. They should put up a plaque. Ancient history now. There were just the two of them toasting the baby this time, dinosaurs left over from prehistoric times. 'If you don't evolve you get left behind,' Barry said.

'If you don't evolve you die,' Tracy said.

Amy wasn't christened when she was a baby. 'We're not really religious,' Barry said. They had her christened after the accident though, while she lay on life support. 'Just in case,' Barry said. Clutching at straws. Amy came off life support, Sam didn't. Ivan himself was on another ward, strung up in traction like a fly in a web. Barry and Barbara only went to visit him once, when they had to talk to him about turning off all those nice shiny machines and consigning Sam to eternity.

'You can't understand,' Barbara Crawford had said when Tracy had offered her condolences at the crematorium. 'You don't have children, grandchildren. If only it could have been me instead.'

Tracy wondered if her own parents would have been willing to sacrifice themselves to save her. Her mother had lingered on after Tracy's father died and in her final days gave the impression that she wasn't going unless she could take Tracy down with her. Her mother had the DNA of a scorpion, built to outlast a nuclear winter. The cancer got her in the end though. Nobody lasted for ever, not even Dorothy Waterhouse. The diamonds and the cockroaches were free to inherit the earth now she was gone.

Barbara Crawford was right, of course. Tracy had never experienced that feeling. Overwhelming, gut-wrenching, lay-down-your-life kind of love. Except perhaps for that one time before with Carol Braithwaite's kid in that hellish flat in Lovell Park. And now – with this scrap of a human being sitting in a supermarket trolley. Tracy wasn't even sure that love was the right word for this feeling, but whatever it was it made you want to weep, whether your kids were alive or dead.

Barbara and Barry's daughter, Amy, was neither alive nor dead but floating somewhere in between. In a 'facility'. Tracy wondered how often Barbara visited Amy. Every day? Every week? Did it become less and less frequent as time went on?

Tracy had been to see her once. Could only think of Disney – Snow White, Sleeping Beauty. Seemed a rubbish frame of reference. Tracy wanted to end it for her, do Barry and Barbara the favour they couldn't do for themselves. Tracy never went back for a second visit. She could still see Amy, dancing with her father on her wedding day, the huge skirt of her white dress crushed against his dark suit, the comedy flower in his button-hole. Now Amy was suspended for ever, a sleeping fairytale princess without an ending, happy or other-wise. What had Barry said? *And then you die and there's nothing else. Of course it turns out you don't even need to be dead for that.*

Sam was dead though. Torn up in a car crash, the car driven by his own father, Ivan. Nearly three times over the limit, 'driving like a maniac', according to a witness. He'd turned out to be Ivan the Terrible, after all. Why had Amy got in the car with him, with a child? No saying, now, too late. Ivan was given a short custodial sentence, judge considered that he had 'already paid a heavy price for a day he would regret for the rest of his life'. 'Bollocks,' Barry said.

Tracy could hardly bear the sight of Barry Crawford walking up the aisle of the church, staggering under the weight of the small white coffin. 'Heavy,' he said afterwards to Tracy, 'for such a little thing inside.' Red eyes washed with whisky. Poor bugger. Same aisle that he had taken his daughter up a year before. Ivan would be getting out some time soon. Tracy wondered if Barry would kill him as he stepped into the free daylight. Sometimes Tracy wondered about doing it for him, something covert. She was pretty sure she could pull off the perfect murder if she had to. Everyone had a killer inside them just waiting to get out, some more patient than others.

'How am I?' Barbara Crawford said as if it was a question that needed serious consideration rather than a polite greeting. 'Oh, you know,' she said vaguely, picking up a can of peas and scrutinizing it as if an alien had just handed it to her and told her, *This is what we eat on our planet*. She was drugged up to the eyeballs, of course. Well, why wouldn't you be? She didn't even remark on Courtney's presence in the shopping trolley, didn't even seem to notice her. Tracy had been all ready with some patter – *Foster kid, thought I'd do something useful now that I'm in an easier job* – but it wasn't called for.

Barbara put the can back on the shelf and wafted her hand in the air as if she was trying to say something but couldn't think of the words. 'Well,' Tracy said, breaking away, 'good to see you, Barbara. Give my best to Barry.' She didn't say, *I talked to Barry on the phone last night. He was with a dead woman.* He had said to Tracy once that he preferred them dead, they couldn't talk back. 'Joking, Tracy,' he said. 'Jesus, what's wrong with women? Don't you have a sense of humour?'

'Apparently not,' Tracy said.

'Well, anyway,' she said to Barbara, 'must be getting along.'

'Yes,' Barbara murmured. Her gaze suddenly fixed on Courtney and she recoiled slightly.

'Babysitting,' Tracy said, doing a three-point turn with the shopping trolley and accelerating down the dairy aisle, plucking cartons of milk and yoghurts as if cows were about to go out of fashion.

The kid, meanwhile, was quietly demolishing a packet of Jaffa cakes that she had managed to filch from somewhere. 'Shoplifting's a crime,' Tracy said. Courtney offered her the packet. Tracy took two Jaffa cakes and crammed them in her mouth.

'Thanks,' she mumbled.

'You're welcome,' Courtney said. Tracy's heart plummeted. Where had the kid learned manners? It hardly seemed likely that it was from Kelly Cross.

'What would you like to do now?' she asked Courtney. She looked like a kid who never got to make a choice, Tracy thought she'd give her one. Give the kid a choice. Give the kid a chance. Give them all a chance.

⁂

1975: 21 March

Eight o'clock in the evening. Kitty was cold and had gone upstairs to fetch a cardigan. It was draughty, the wind was trying to get in the house through any gap it could. *The wind has such a rainy sound / Moaning through the town*. Who wrote that? Kitty had never been one for literature. She had been the 'muse' of a writer for a while. You hardly heard his name any more. He was quite famous at the time, although possibly more famous for his lifestyle than his works. He was unfaithful and drank from breakfast to bedtime. Boozing and whoring, he said, the Rights of Man. She had been one of his trophies, 'muse' a fancy word for mistress. He lived in Chelsea but had a wife and three small children tucked away in the country somewhere.

She had been very young, it was right at the beginning of her career, had been terribly shocked by some of the things he wanted her to do. Never talked to Ian about that part of her life. She shivered. It was chillier in the bedrooms than anywhere else in the house. They kept the radiators off upstairs, Ian thought it was unhealthy to sleep in a warm room. He was always opening the windows wide, Kitty was always closing them. It wasn't a dispute, just a difference of opinion. After all it wasn't a subject you could come to a compromise on. A window was either open or closed.

From a drawer she took out a camel-coloured cashmere cardigan that she draped gracefully over her shoulders. Those were the words in her head, *Kitty Winfield draped the cashmere gracefully over her shoulders.*

Ever since she was a child she had done that. Commented on herself. Stepped outside and watched herself, almost like an out-of-body experience. All that ballet, tap, elocution, deportment, her mother told her she was destined for something. A part in the local pantomime every Christmas, there was a sense of promise. Brought up in Solihull, she spent a lot of time losing her accent. When she was seventeen she decided it was time to seek her fortune in London. What 'promising' girl would want to stay in the West Midlands in 1962? *Newcomer Kathryn Gillespie is destined for great things.*

She came down to the capital, to attend a dance academy as a full-time student, fees paid for her by her mother, and had only been there a week when a man came up to her in the street and said, 'Did anyone tell you that you could be a model?' She thought it was a joke, or dodgy, her mother had spent a lifetime warning her about men like this, but it turned out to be kosher, he really was a scout for an agency. And overnight she was no longer Kathryn, she was Kitty. They tried to make it one word, like Twiggy, but it never took off.

Her mother had died at the beginning of this year. *Kitty Winfield stood beside her mother's grave and wept silently.* Lung cancer, awful. Kitty went back to Solihull and nursed her. Didn't know which was worse, watching her mother die or revisiting her own promising past. She was finding it awfully difficult to get over her mother's death. Silly really because she hardly ever saw her.

Modelling was much easier than dancing. All you needed were good bones and a certain stoic temperament. She was never asked to do anything tacky, no nudity. Lots of lovely black-and-white portraits by famous photographers. Big fashion shoots, all the magazines, and once on the cover of *Vogue*. People called her 'the face of the sixties' for a while. People still remembered her name. *Sixties' icon Kitty Gillespie, where is she now?* Only last week a Sunday supplement had chased her down, wanting to do an interview with her about her 'obscurity'. Ian politely fended off the caller.

It had all been over by '69. She met Ian and decided to forgo the bright lights for security. For steadfastness. She could honestly say, hand on heart, that she had never regretted the decision.

She had wanted to be a film star, of course, but, let's face it, she couldn't act for toffee. *Kitty Gillespie walked on to the set and illuminated it.* Unfortunately not. She looked the part but just couldn't say the words. Wooden, as a board. She'd had a tiny part in a film, one of those edgy, avant-garde jobs starring a controversial rock singer. All very Bohemian. Kitty had been lolling on a sofa, supposedly in some kind of sex-and-drugs haze. One line to say, 'Where are you going, babe?' Hardly anyone remembered the film now, and no one remembered Kitty's performance. Thank goodness.

The rock star laughed and said to her, 'Don't give up the day job, darling.' They slept together once, it was almost expected. *De rigueur*, the rock star said. Sometimes she thought that when she was very old and everyone else was dead she might write her autobiography. Of her life during those years anyway. The years after her marriage would make for a very dull book in other people's eyes.

She made the film the year after she left the writer. She was under his spell for nearly two years, it was rather like being held hostage. They were the years when she should have been larking around with her friends, enjoying all the things a girl of her age would normally enjoy. Instead she was pouring his drinks and nursing his ego and having to read his tedious manuscripts. People thought it was glamorous and grown-up but it wasn't. It was like being a nanny who occasionally had to perform sordid sex acts. He was nearly twenty years older than she was, used to get annoyed that most of the time she had no idea what he was talking about.

Kitty sat down at her dressing-table mirror and took a cigarette out of her silver case. It was engraved with her initials and inside the lid there was another engraving, a birthday message from Ian: *To Kitty, the woman I will always love most in the world.* The famous writer had once given her a lighter engraved with something obscene in Latin. 'Catullus,' he said, translating it for her. Embarrassing. She had never used it in case someone who understood Latin glimpsed the words. She was much more prudish than people imagined. She threw the lighter into the Thames from Victoria Embankment the morning she walked out of his house. *Kitty Gillespie was tied naked to a bedpost and degraded.* There were limits. And anyway he had grown tired of her, and her place in his bed and at his side had been usurped by a Swedish poet, 'intelligent woman,' he said, as if Kitty wasn't. He suffered a great tragedy not long afterwards and Kitty couldn't but feel sorry for someone who was so imperfectly equipped to deal with any drama that they weren't themselves the centre of.

How much better it was now to be a lovely doctor's wife and live in a lovely house in lovely Harrogate and look in your bedroom mirror and see your lovely white neck, lovely, lovely pearls glowing against your skin. *Kitty Winfield tucked a strand of hair behind one of her neatly shaped ears.* She sighed. There were times when she just wanted to curl into a ball on the floor and pretend nothing existed. *Kitty Winfield opened the bottle of sleeping pills prescribed for her by her husband.*

She stubbed out her cigarette, freshened her lipstick, sprayed a little shot of Shalimar on the delicate, veiny skin on the inside of her wrists. The faintest scars, thready bracelets like white cotton where she had tried to slice through them, a long time ago now.

Ian was downstairs reading a medical journal, listening to Tchaikovsky. Soon he would go into the kitchen and make them both a cup of something milky. 'We're a real old Darby and Joan,' he laughed.

Such a great emptiness inside where a baby should be. 'You can never conceive,' a consultant obstetrician had told her in London, not long before she and Ian had married. Ian was at Great Ormond Street in those days, Kitty had met him in Fortnum and Mason's. He was buying chocolates for his mother's birthday, she was sheltering from the rain and he had invited her to have tea and scones in the Fountain restaurant and she thought, why not?

'Do you want me to have a chat with your fiancé?' the obstetrician asked. 'He's a medical man, isn't he? Or shall I leave it up to you?' They were speaking a polite code. Did she want him to explain to Ian how 'a medical procedure she had undergone when younger had resulted in her being unable to conceive a baby'? But Ian, a doctor, would want to know more and he was sure to understand what that 'medical procedure' had been. *Kitty Gillespie lay beneath the white sheet and opened her legs.*

After she left the writer, after she threw the obscene cigarette lighter in the Thames, she had realized that she was pregnant. She ignored it, thinking it might go away, but it didn't. She knew the writer wouldn't be the slightest bit interested in her predicament, and neither did she want him to be. She was five months gone before she had an abortion. Phoebe March had given her the name of a doctor. 'He'll fix you up,' she said. 'All the girls go to him, it's nothing, it's like going to the dentist.'

And it wasn't some knitting-needle job in a grubby flat up an alleyway. He had rooms in Harley Street, a receptionist, flowers on the desk. Little man, tiny feet, you always notice their feet. *Now* Miss *Gillespie, if you could just open your legs.* Made her shiver even now just to think about it. She had expected it to be clinical, painless, but it had been a brutal affair. He nicked an artery and she almost bled to death. He drove her to the nearest hospital, told her to get out of the car outside the A and E department.

Phoebe came to visit her in hospital, bearing cheerful daffodils. 'You were unlucky,' she said, 'but at least you got rid of it. We're working girls, sweetie, we have to make tough decisions. It's all for the best.'

Phoebe was currently playing Cleopatra at Stratford. They had been down, they often did, made a weekend of it, stayed in a nice pub. She didn't mention to Ian that she used to know Phoebe. Kitty still thought about that little man in Harley Street. His small feet. Seemed to Kitty that he must have despised women. He messed up her insides for ever.

A gruff Scottish consultant was called in from his game of golf in Surrey to try and stitch her up. 'You've been a very silly lassie,' he said. 'And I'm afraid you're going to pay for it for the rest of your life.' He didn't tell the police though, he might have been dour but he had a heart.

She had told Ian she could never conceive, it seemed only fair. She told him that it was 'a plumbing problem', a defect, and he said, 'Which doctors have you seen, which consultants?' and she said, 'The best. In Switzerland,' and when he said, 'We'll consult more,' she said, 'Please don't push me to see any more, darling, I can't bear it.' He was older than her by quite a bit, said he always thought he would have a son, teach him cricket and so on. 'You should marry someone else,' she told him on the eve of the wedding, and he said, 'No.'

He was willing to sacrifice everything for her, even children.

'Are you all right up there?'

'Sorry, darling, got distracted, started tidying the drawers. Just coming.' *Kitty Winfield rose from her dressing table and rejoined her husband.* Before she did so, the doorbell rang. She checked her watch, lovely delicate gold one that was her Christmas present from Ian. (No engraving.) Nearly nine o'clock. They never had visitors at this hour. She looked over the banister on the landing as he opened the door, letting in a huge draught of icy March air.

'Good God,' she heard Ian say. 'What's happened, Ray?'

Kitty Winfield tripped lightly down the stairs. Ray Strickland was standing on the doorstep, holding a little child in his arms.

Walking the dog swallowed up more time than Jackson had expected. By the time they returned to the hotel and he had showered off the previous night's evidence he found himself running late and had to leave the hotel again in haste. He realized that he would have to take the dog with him, he could hardly leave it to be discovered by someone coming in to clean the room. A 'maid'. An old-fashioned word. A servant, a virgin. His sister had been a maid. A young maid. She belonged to another time when girls kept their maidenhood like a treasure.

He unzipped the rucksack and said, 'Come on, get in,' to the dog. Jackson hadn't realized that dogs could frown.

Jackson's mouth felt as if a mouse had nested in it overnight. Several mice possibly. There was a mirror in the lift and on the way down to the lobby Jackson contemplated his somewhat dissipated reflection for the second time that morning. He couldn't imagine that it would make a good impression on Linda Pallister. ('When did *you* worry about making a good impression?' he heard Julia say. The one who lived in his head.) It was only quarter to ten in the morning and yet the day already felt as if it had been going on too long. The woman in a management suit on duty at the concierge's desk gave him a suspicious look as he exited the lift. He gave her a little Queen Mother wave. She frowned at him.

A takeaway bacon roll from a greasy spoon on the short walk from the Best Western helped to perk him up a little. He tore off a piece and posted it into the rucksack for the dog.

Hope McMaster had been silent through his Greenwich mean time night, which was her New Zealand day. If Linda Pallister couldn't enlighten him about Hope McMaster's origins then he had no idea what path to take next. A family tree was a fractal, its branches dividing endlessly. Julia, being from middle-class stock, could trace her family back to the Ark but for Hope McMaster there weren't even bare roots.

A young woman, a secretary maybe, her function was unclear, appeared and said, 'Mr Brodie? My name's Eleanor, I'll show you to Linda's office.' This was an improvement. He hadn't got past reception yesterday before being told that Linda Pallister wasn't available to see him. Eleanor had a plain face and limp hair that looked as if it resisted styling. And a fantastic pair of legs that seemed wasted on her. Just observing, not judging, Jackson said silently in his defence against the monstrous regiment.

He was carrying a folder. He had bought it yesterday in a pound shop. Way back in his days as a military policeman Jackson had learned that carrying a folder could convey a certain official authority, even, occasionally, menace. In interrogations it implied you had a cache of knowledge about a suspect, knowledge that you were about to use against them. Not that Linda Pallister was a suspect, he reminded himself. And they definitely weren't in the army any more, he thought as he followed Eleanor's shapely pins down a corridor. The folder was plastic, a lurid pink neon not found in nature that detracted somewhat from any authority invested in it. It contained nothing even vaguely official, only a flimsy National Trust guide to Sissinghurst and an estate agent's details for a thatched cottage in Shropshire that had briefly, very briefly, tickled his fancy.

Eleanor was the chatty sort, Jackson noticed rather wearily – lack of coffee was beginning to take its toll on him. She stopped outside a door and knocked on it. When there was no answer she said loudly, 'Linda? Mr Brodie's here to see you.'

Absence of Linda left Eleanor at a loss as to what to do with him and Jackson said, reassuringly, 'Don't worry about me, I'll wait outside her office.'

'I'll try and find Linda,' she said, scurrying off.

Twenty minutes later and there was no sign of either Linda or Eleanor. Jackson thought there would be no harm in having a quick look inside the mysteriously absent Linda Pallister's office. He carried the authority of the folder, after all.

It was a mess. Her desk was home to a jumble of things – clumsy ornaments that seemed to have been made by children, pens, paperclips, books, paperwork, a Marks & Spencer sandwich, as yet unopened, although the date on it was yesterday's. There were haphazard stacks of paperwork and folders everywhere. She didn't seem like the tidiest of people.

The sandwich was sitting next to an open appointments diary. All Linda Pallister's meetings for today, including his own, were crossed out, which didn't seem like a good sign. He flipped back through the diary, idly, not looking for anything ('Stop snooping through my stuff!' Marlee had yelled at him when she caught him looking through her diary).

Yesterday, the two o'clock appointment that she had cancelled with him ('J. Brodie') was duly crossed out, as was every appointment after 'B. Jackson' at ten o'clock. It seemed an odd coincidence of names. The two Jacksons. Was she confused or had this other, earlier Jackson upset her so much that she started cancelling everything?

When Jackson made the first appointment with Linda Pallister he had spoken with her on the phone. He didn't say he was a private detective, because he wasn't, he insisted to himself. It was just this one case. ('A specious argument,' he imagined Julia saying.)

At first, Linda Pallister sounded perfectly normal, pleasantly efficient – a demeanour at odds with the state of her office. The mention of Hope McMaster's name didn't change things – Hope had already been in email contact with her over her missing birth certificate – nor the names John and Angela Costello, but when he mentioned Dr Ian Winfield she seemed to be thrown completely off balance.

'Who?'

'Ian and Kitty Winfield,' Jackson said. 'He was a consultant at St James's. She was a model, Kitty Gillespie. They were Hope McMaster's adoptive parents.'

'They—' she began to say and then clammed up. Jackson had been intrigued but assumed whatever the confusion was it would be cleared up when he met Linda Pallister. He was hoping, for example, that she was going to be able to explain why John and Angela Costello didn't exist.

Hope McMaster had pulled a thread and everything she had believed about the fabric of her life had started to unravel. *But I must have come from somewhere,* she wrote. *Everyone comes from somewhere!* Jackson thought that perhaps it was time to ditch the exclamation marks, they were beginning to sound like notes of panic. Despite her breeziness it seemed that she had begun to struggle with existentialist musings about the nature of identity – *Who are we, after all?* A nugget of suspicion, that was all it took, until it had nibbled quietly away at everything you believed in.

A lot of those old adoption societies have lost their records, he wrote soothingly. Maybe, he thought to himself, but not a Crown Court, surely. Hope hadn't suddenly appeared on the earth, fully formed, at the age of two. A woman had given birth to her.

It's as if I don't really exist! I'm baffled!

You and me both, Jackson thought. Hope McMaster's past was all echoes and shadows, like looking into a box of fog.

The dog was sound asleep in the rucksack on the floor. Either that or it was dead. Jackson gave it a gentle prod and the rucksack squirmed. He thought of the woman he had woken up next to. He didn't usually have to check that his inamoratas were alive the morning after. He unfastened the rucksack and the dog opened one weary eye and looked at him with the resignation of a pessimistic hostage. 'Sorry,' Jackson said. 'We'll go for a walk after this.'

The sandwich was egg and watercress. Not Jackson's favourite, although he was so hungry that it was beginning to look attractive. The bowl of pasta yesterday evening on the Headrow had provided an inadequate cushion for the alcohol and dissolution that had followed. The bacon roll from earlier had disappeared into the maw of his hangover. He heard a clock strike eleven. It sounded like a church clock, incongruous somehow in this area. It seemed he had been forgotten about.

Jackson gave up and wrote a note of the 'I was here' variety on the back of one of his cards. The card – *Jackson Brodie – Private Investigator* – was one of many he'd had made when he set up on his own several years ago. A print run of a thousand. Such optimism. He had probably handed out no more than a hundred of the things, usually because he forgot he had them.

He placed the card on top of the sandwich, where hopefully Linda Pallister would notice it. Yesterday's egg and cress was in turn sitting on top of a photograph, almost entirely obscured by the sandwich's triangular box. The photograph was jumping up and down shouting at him, asking to see the light of day. It almost leaped into his hands when he uncovered it. Unframed, dog-eared, an old snap. He hadn't seen it before but he had definitely seen the subject recently. Snub nose, freckles, an old-fashioned caste to the plump features – the spit of Hope McMaster in the photograph taken on her arrival in New Zealand. On the top edge of the photograph there was the mark where a rusty paperclip had attached it to something.

The photograph from Linda Pallister's desk had been taken on a beach. A British beach, judging by the way the child was bundled in outdoor clothes. Despite the fact that she looked freezing she had a big grin on her face. Her hair was worn in cock-eyed bunches. First thing you would do with an illicit child would be to cut that long hair, adopt a disguise with a new haircut. Spiky, urchin. New hair, new clothes, new name, new country.

He would have sworn on oath that he was holding in his hand a photograph of Hope McMaster. He turned it over. Nothing. No helpful name or date, unfortunately, nonetheless Jackson experienced a visceral feeling, something that he recognized from his days in law enforcement. It was the reaction of a dog to a bone, a detective to a great big fat clue. He didn't know what the photograph meant, he just knew that it meant something tremendously important. He thought about the ethics of taking the photo for all of two seconds before placing it in his wallet. Photographic evidence, you never knew when you were going to need it.

Enthused by his discovery and working on the theory that one clue generally led to another, he started to rake through the debris of paperwork on Linda Pallister's desk. Nothing. No references to Winfields or Costellos. He tried the drawers in the desk. More confusion and chaos. But there in the last drawer – it was always the last drawer, the last door, the last box – was another object trying to claw its way out of the darkness. 'Eureka,' Jackson murmured to himself.

It was a folder, an old manila one, and there on the front of it was a small rusty paperclip, just the same size as the after-image on the photograph of the girl with the cock-eyed bunches. Jackson, in an instinctive sleight of hand, slipped the folder inside his own neon-pink plastic one. He felt like a spy who had just discovered a dossier of secrets. In the nick of time too, as Eleanor, she of the great legs and not so great face, finally put in a return appearance. He caught the look on her face, a mixture of distaste and confusion which eventually resolved into something more cryptic. Women usually needed to be acquainted with him a little longer before he saw that expression on their faces.

'Oh,' she said. 'You're still here. In fact, you're *in* here.'

'Ms Pallister hasn't turned up,' he said, spreading his arms wide, a conjuror demonstrating innocence, as if he might have been hiding Linda Pallister on his person. Eleanor frowned.

'Have you actually seen her this morning?' Jackson queried mildly.

Eleanor's frown grew deeper. She had the sort of face that should be kept in neutral. 'I don't know,' she said.

'Maybe she's ill,' Jackson suggested. 'Maybe it was the sandwich she didn't eat.'

The frown developed into something threatening. Jackson left before he was turned to stone.

He retreated to the nearest café, a little Italian place where he wasn't disappointed in his assumption that they would know how to make coffee. He took a corner table and over a double espresso examined his stolen trophies.

The thin card of the manila folder was soft and felted with age. This was what folders used to be like before they became pink neon plastic. He had dealt with enough of them in his time. Of course, even the pink neon was an anachronism now in the days of the paperless office. Not something Linda Pallister had heard of, he thought, remembering the Dickensian piles of papers and files in her messy office. You could hide a small child – or a dog – in there and not notice it for days.

He opened the folder expecting to find something surprising – a clue, a secret, even a piece of bureaucratic tedium – but the surprise was that there was nothing at all. Jackson turned the manila folder upside down and shook it, just to be sure.

Nonetheless, despite being empty, the worn beige folder did have something it wanted to say. There was a small typed label affixed to the top left-hand corner. No one used typewriters any more, it was like seeing a message from a primitive culture, a lost time. 'Carol Braithwaite,' Jackson read. 'Case worker: Linda Pallister' and a date, 2 February 1975. Linda Pallister must have been very young at the time. Jackson would have been fifteen in 1975, a year older than his daughter was now. Getting up to no good, bunking off school, petty thieving, minor vandalism, sinking the good ship Woolworths. It was a long time ago.

And across the front of the folder was written the name 'WPC Tracy Waterhouse' again, this one in faded black biro, and another date, 10 April 1975. There was a phone number too, dating from before the national codes were changed. The year was the same year that Hope McMaster was adopted. April was the month that was on her adoption certificate, the one that didn't exist officially. She had scanned it and emailed it to him, along with her birth certificate, which also didn't exist officially. If they were forgeries they looked pretty genuine, although he supposed a scan wasn't the best way of telling. His own forgery of a wife had been in possession of a pretty genuine-looking birth certificate, not such a hard thing to create.

In her appointments diary, Linda Pallister had written, 'Phone Tracy Waterhouse,' and here was Tracy Waterhouse's name thirty-five years ago. Jackson took the photograph out of his wallet and looked at the stocky, wholesome little girl, with cock-eyed bunches. As he always knew it would, the paperclip on the folder fitted exactly over the rusted impression on the photograph.

Schrödinger, whoever he was, and his cat, and anyone else that felt like it, had all climbed inside Pandora's box and were dining on a can of worms. Jackson felt the beginnings of a headache, another one, on top of the one he already had.

⁂

Tracy was surprised that more kids weren't killed on so-called play equipment. People (parents) seemed blithely oblivious to the peril of small bodies arcing high into the sky on swings they weren't strapped into, or of the same small bodies launching themselves from the top of a slide when they were knee-high to a gnat. Courtney was astonishingly reckless, a kid without reck was a dangerous thing.

Other children in the play park yelled and screamed and laughed but Courtney was merely determined to test everything, including herself, to the limits, like a dogged little crash-test dummy. There didn't seem to be much in the way of pleasure involved. Abused kids – and there were many forms of abuse – were frequently shut down and closed off to enjoyment.

It was a beautiful day again and the crowds in Roundhay were already out in force, half-naked white bodies lying like corpses on the green grass, people desperate to get some rays and some fresh air. That's what parks had always been, breathing spaces for the poor who lived six long days a week in factories. All those little kids, slaves to the machines, their tiny help-less lungs full of damp wool fibres.

Perhaps it was insanity to be out like this, they were exposed to the world and his wife, but then – what better place to hide a child than in plain sight, in a play park surrounded by parents and little kids? People took kids *from* parks, they didn't take them *to* them. And as a bonus Roundhay was not the kind of place that Kelly Cross came to in daylight hours. Plus, Tracy reasoned against reason, it was good for her to practise being a parent in public. Sooner or later she was going to have to come out to the world (and his wife) as a mother, so here she was, Imogen Brown, pushing her little girl Lucy on swings, twirling her on roundabouts and helping her negotiate a variety of apparatus that Tracy couldn't even give a name to, most of it unrecognizable from the uninspired parks of her own childhood.

Tracy was relieved when Courtney clambered off a giant chicken on springs and announced, 'I'm hungry.' Tracy checked her watch, they had been in the play park barely fifteen minutes. It felt like hours. She handed over a banana.

'OK?' she asked when it was finished and Courtney gave her a solemn silent thumbs-up sign. She was economical with language, and why not? Perhaps when you were little you thought you might use up all your words at the beginning and not have any left for the end.

Tracy wiped away the green maggot of snot emerging from one of Courtney's nostrils and congratulated herself on remembering to buy tissues in the supermarket. From her bottomless bag Tracy scavenged the corpse of the doughnut she'd bought in Ainsleys a million years ago, tore it in half and shared it with the kid, sitting on the grass. ('Cake? Before lunch?' she heard her mother's voice say and Tracy answered silently, 'Yes. What are you going to do about it, you old cow?')

When Courtney had finished her half of the dough-nut she licked each finger religiously before giving another silent thumbs-up to Tracy, and then she took out the contents of the little pink backpack and laid each item, one by one, on the grass for perusal:

the tarnished silver thimble
the Chinese coin with a hole in the middle
the purse with a smiling monkey's face on it
the snow globe containing a crude plastic model of
    the Houses of Parliament
the shell shaped like a cream horn
the shell shaped like a coolie hat
the whole nutmeg
a pine cone

The pine cone, Tracy noted, was new. She wondered where it had come from. It was like that game they used to play at children's parties where you had to remember the objects on a tea-tray. They probably didn't have parties like that any more. Pin the tail on the donkey, pass the parcel – someone's dad standing by the record player and lifting the needle on 'The Runaway Train' or 'They're Changing Guard At Buckingham Palace'. Nowadays they all went to 'indoor soft play areas' – Rascals and Funsters – and ran amok. Tracy had been called to one of those places in Bradford once. They thought a kid had disappeared, turned out it was at the bottom of a ball pool and nobody could see it. It was fine, alive and kicking, literally. Paedophile heaven.

Tracy picked out the cream horn-shaped shell and rolled it in her palm. When she was a child her father used to pick up a box of three cream horns from Thomson's cake shop in Bramley every Friday evening on his way home from work in the town hall. Tracy couldn't remember when she had last eaten a cream horn, couldn't remember the last time she had stuck a shell to her own shell-like and listened to the sea. Tracy realized that at some point in this reverie Courtney had surreptitiously retrieved the shell and was packing her treasure away again.

'Yeah, you're right,' Tracy sighed. 'How about we have our picnic? Heaven forfend that we should go more than ten minutes without eating.'

Tracy had lugged with her an old plaid blanket from the boot of the car. She rolled it out and spread out the picnic fodder they'd bought in the supermarket – tuna rolls, cartons of apple and orange juice, packets of crisps and a bar of Cadbury's chocolate, the latter neutralized – in Tracy's mind anyway – by a small bag of carrot sticks. It was the kind of picnic (possibly minus the carrot sticks) that she would have liked when she herself was a child, instead of the cold hard-boiled eggs that her mother used to pack, alongside flabby white-bread sandwiches that had been spread thinly with meat paste before being wrapped – for some arcane reason – in damp lettuce leaves. They had taken these meagre provisions with them on Sunday drives in the family Ford Consul – to Harewood House, to Brimham Rocks or to 'Brontë country' – as her mother always familiarly called it, even though she had never read a book by a Brontë, or indeed any book unless it had been helpfully condensed first by the *Reader's Digest*. The nearest they ever got to the parsonage was when they once stopped in Haworth village so her father could buy a pack of cigarettes.

Tracy couldn't think of these Sunday outings without remembering what it felt like to craze a boiled-egg shell and peel away the membrane from the solid greyish white beneath. Sick-making. She suddenly remembered how her father would sometimes pop an egg whole into his mouth, like a conjuror, and part of the young Tracy had expected a dove or a row of flags to emerge in place of the egg. They had seen something similar once in a summer show in Bridlington. Top of the bill was Ronnie Hilton, long past his heyday but nonetheless a Yorkshireman and therefore someone to be proud of.

Tracy's father was a war veteran, the Green Howards, landed on Gold beach on D-Day. He must have seen things but if he had he never said. Sometimes a war was wasted on people. He was born in Dewsbury. Shoddy capital of the world. It said something about a mill town that it couldn't aspire to even second-rate cloth, weaving instead the lowest quality from rags and shreds. A filthy trade, shoddy. A town where now women drugged and kidnapped their own kids for money. The Ripper was questioned in Dewsbury after being caught in Sheffield. Routine patrol, his luck running out, theirs running back in, late in the day. Tracy remembered being in a corner shop when she heard the news, buying crisps and chocolate for her and her partner. On the beat. The bloke behind the counter had the radio on and when the news came on he yelled, 'They've caught him, they've caught your Ripper!' He was second-generation Bangladeshi and Tracy didn't blame him for denying ownership of Sutcliffe. She couldn't remember where she was for all those other newsworthy world events (probably in front of the box, getting the news on the telly), although she was in a TV repair shop buying a new scart lead for her DVD player when she saw the second of the World Trade Center buildings fall. You usually expected *Countdown*.

On the day of Charles and Diana's wedding, an event that Tracy would have liked to watch (although she would never have admitted to it), she was co-ordinating house-to-house after the so-called honour killing of a woman in Bradford. Fairytale wedding.

Had the kid ever been to the seaside? 'Have you ever been to the seaside, Courtney?'

Courtney, mouth stuffed with tuna roll, shook her head and then nodded it.

'Yes *and* no?'

'Yes,' Courtney mumbled.

'Yes?'

'No.'

It was an unfathomable exchange. They would go to the seaside. And pantomimes and circuses and Disneyland Paris. They would go to the seaside and paddle in the waves. Cautiously. Before the kid, Tracy would have thought, *sea, sand, beach*. Now she thought of little kids being swept away like corks by the tsunami. And let's not forget that on an average British beach, you could expect a hefty percentage of paedophiles to be out and about enjoying themselves. Beware lone men at the seaside, the swimming baths, the school gates. Play parks, funfairs, beaches – the playgrounds of the paedos. Everything that should be innocent. If people only knew. Did the kid know? Did Tracy need to add a therapist to the list of specialists she'd already mentally lined up for Courtney? Or could fresh air, green veg and Tracy's love (however amateurish and transgressive) do the trick? Good question. What had Kelly been doing with the kid if she wasn't her mother? Minding her on behalf of something or someone sinister. Was the kid used to being handed around? Trafficked? Tracy shuddered at the thought.

She should buy a camera, state-of-the-art digital, so she could start preserving the kid's new life in inkjet. It would look better if there was evidence of her existence in Tracy's own life. She had an old camera somewhere, nothing as slick as the ones you got nowadays. There hadn't been much point in using it, she hadn't encountered much of anything worth photographing. She mostly went on solitary outings and there was no pleasure to be had from views of landscapes with no people in them. Might as well just buy a postcard.

Tracy's father – wore the trousers, wielded the camera – had documented their lives for years. He had been in the habit of taking a photograph of the Christmas tree every year. There were other photographs of the family, opening presents, drinking a decorous sherry, even pulling a cracker, in which parts of the tree, a swoop of tinsel, a drooping branch, might feature but not *The tree, the whole tree and nothing but the tree*. Not a joke, not even a witticism.

Most of those photographs were jumbled with others in a box in Tracy's back bedroom, no way of knowing which Christmas a tree belonged to, only the same uninspiring baubles every year in slightly different arrangements, the tinsel star on top, more like a ragged starfish than a star to guide wise men by, and the exhausted pipe-cleaner gnomes perching drunkenly at the ends of the branches, the tips of matches for noses and eyes. When Tracy's parents reached seventy her father ceased buying a tree. 'Why bother?' her mother said when Tracy came round on Christmas Day. Cheer and merriment, something lovely, Tracy thought, but too late for any of that.

If she sifted through the box with an archaeologist's vigilance, Tracy wondered, would she find some clue as to why her parents had embraced their drab lives with what could only be called enthusiasm?

Would she find her younger self in that box and be surprised at how far she had come, or be depressed by the distance between? Ronnie Hilton at the Spa Theatre and a lifetime ahead of her. 'A Windmill in Old Amsterdam'. Pass the parcel. It was funny, Tracy had spent a lot of time trying to put her lacklustre childhood behind her (where it belonged) but ever since she'd come into possession of the kid she kept being reminded of it, shards and chips of memory. The mirror cracked.

* * *

'Time to move. Why don't we go to the lake and feed the ducks?' There were some crusts left from their picnic, the kid had polished off everything else. Perhaps Tracy had kidnapped a cuckoo, a giant's child. She would pay for that, imagined the kid growing bigger and bigger, puffing up until she filled the car, the spare room, the whole house, eating up everything in sight, including Tracy. Kidnap what looks like a kid and find out too late that it's going to be the death of you. Like Greek tragedy. She had been to a production of *Medea* at the West Yorkshire Playhouse a few years ago. An African production, 'Nigerian, Yoruba, actually,' her theatre companion said knowledgeably. The academic from the singles social club again. You had to wonder about the educated classes. He tried to grope her on her doorstep. She felt insulted that he thought she was so desperate she would have even considered it. She kneed him in the balls, showed him the kind of empiricist she was. That was it for the club as far as Tracy was concerned.

Of course with Medea it was the other way round, she killed her kids, she wasn't killed by them. As a plot, Tracy didn't find it shocking, it happened all the time.

The ducks had no appetite, half of Leeds already seemed to be out, tossing the remains of their sliced whites to the indifferent wildfowl. The rats would be out later to mop up the soggy leavings. Courtney, clearly not one to waste food, ate the crusts herself.

* * *

Courtney was drooping. Kids should come with wheels attached.

'How about an ice cream?' Tracy said. Courtney gave her the thumbs-up. Tracy wanted to give the kid everything, but all the ice creams in the world weren't going to make up for Kelly Cross and whatever horrors she represented. *Ice cream, ice cream, I scream for ice cream.*

They walked back across Soldier's Field, both of them clutching a cornet, strawberry for Courtney, mint choc chip for Tracy. The Ripper had attacked two victims in Roundhay, one lived, one died. Luck of the draw. '76 and '77. Two years after the Lovell Park murder. They never connected that to the Ripper, but it made you wonder. Wilma McCann, his first victim, was murdered only six months after Arkwright had broken down that door in Lovell Park, and before that Sutcliffe had been practising. Arkwright told Tracy that he had heard that someone had confessed to Carol Braithwaite's murder in prison and then had died. Seemed a convenient sort of way of clearing up a crime.

'Tracy?' A little voice interrupted her thoughts. It was the first time Courtney had addressed her as anything. It made her want to cry. Could she get her to call her 'Mum'? What would that feel like? Like flying. Wendy in *Peter Pan*, Tinker Bell at her heels. Lost girls together.

'Come on,' Tracy said. 'There's a Toys "R" Us in Batley. We'll have a bit of a drive.' Because going back to her house in Headingley was disturbing. Alone with a kid in her house. Like a proper parent. How did you do that? Tracy had no idea. She suddenly remembered Janek.

No, of course she couldn't go home while he was there. Looking at Courtney with his sad Polish eyes, questioning who she was, where she had come from.

‰

Next on his list of tasks was the purchase of a sizeable stock of plastic nappy sacks for the onslaught of dog shit that was inevitably coming his way. Jackson felt more of an upstanding citizen once he was fully equipped. He supposed he should have looked to see if the plastic sacks were biodegradable before planning to weigh the planet down with even more debris, but some days there was only so much a man could do.

This was followed by a visit to an old-fashioned barber's that he had spotted earlier, near the Best Western, in order to effect a transformation, courtesy of a number one haircut and hot shave with a straight-bladed razor, from which Jackson emerged half an hour later feeling as shorn as a new-born lamb (or a convict). A *boule à zero*, the Foreign Legion boys would have called it. He just hoped that no one thought it was anything to do with male pattern baldness. Jackson was relieved to see that the reflection that looked back at him in the mirror looked more like himself than previously.

The dog had been allowed to accompany him into the barber's shop and sat watching the proceedings intently, as if storing up an experience that it might need to explain later. The barber turned out to be a dog lover, said he 'showed pugs', a statement which Jackson took a little time deciphering.

He also demonstrated that the dog knew how to shake hands, 'or shake paws, I should say', he laughed.

'Right,' Jackson said.

'We share eighty-five per cent of our genes with dogs,' the barber said.

'Well, we share fifty per cent of our DNA with bananas,' Jackson said, 'so I don't think that really means anything.'

Smuggling a dog in and out of places was proving easier than Jackson would have imagined, not that it was a topic he had ever given much attention to before now. He couldn't believe the number of places that dogs weren't allowed. Kids – not that he had anything against kids obviously – kids were allowed everywhere and dogs were much better behaved on the whole.

Next on his list was the Central Library, where he combed the archives of the *Yorkshire Post* for April 1975. In the paper for the 10th, he finally found what he was looking for, tucked away on an inside page. 'Police were called to a flat in Lovell Park yesterday afternoon where they discovered the body of a woman, identified as Carol Braithwaite. Miss Braithwaite had been the subject of a brutal attack. Her body had been lying in the flat for some time, a police spokesman said.' A byline, 'Marilyn Nettles'. And that was it, no update on a murder investigation in subsequent weeks, no report of an inquest that he could find. Just one more woman thrown away like rubbish. A woman killed, the murderer never brought to justice, the very echo of Jackson's own life.

His rucksack, currently resting on the floor, started wriggling as if it was about to produce an alien life form. A small, muffled bark came from inside and a snout struggled through the opening in the zip. Probably time to go, Jackson thought.

Even with an updated code the phone number for Tracy Waterhouse had proved a dud when Jackson tried it, long fallen into disuse. Was Tracy Waterhouse a warhorse, still on the force after all this time? Extremely doubtful.

It seemed to Jackson that if Tracy Waterhouse had been a member of the West Yorkshire Police Force in 1975 then there would be records. And if not records then someone who might recall her, although the chances of someone remembering a humble WPC from the seventies seemed remote. Policewomen in the seventies were still regarded as tea-makers and hand-holders. *Life on Mars* was only the tip of a sexist iceberg. That world had gone, never to return. (*How many men does it take to wallpaper a room?* Marlee asked. Jackson waited for the scornful punchline. *Four if you slice them thinly. LOL.*)

The dog was restless, despite sharing a ham sandwich with Jackson and having lifted its leg against several walls and the odd scrubby urban tree. It had spent a lot of the day so far confined to prison and Jackson supposed it wanted a good walk. There were very few places for dogs and men to exercise in Leeds, the town centre seemed to be almost devoid of green spaces.

He decided it might be best not to take it into the police station, so he tethered it to a hitching-post outside Millgarth Police HQ, positioning the dog in the line of fire of a CCTV camera at the entrance. That way if someone stole the dog at least there would be a record of it. 'Call me paranoid,' he said to the dog, 'but you can't trust anyone these days.' Millgarth was possibly one of the ugliest buildings he had ever seen, built like a Crusader fortress, some time in the seventies, to keep the enemy at bay.

Jackson explained to the sergeant on the duty desk that he was a private detective working for a solicitor. An aunt of Tracy Waterhouse had left a small legacy in a will but the family had lost touch ('You know how it is with families'), all they knew was that she had been a constable with the West Yorkshire Police in 1975. Lies were best kept simple (*It wasn't me*) and this one was complicated so he was half expecting to be found wanting, but the desk sergeant simply said, '1975? God, you're going back a long way.'

A man who looked like a washed-up boxer came out of a room at the back and, dropping a file on the desk, said, 'What's that?'

The desk sergeant said, 'This bloke's looking for a WPC Tracy – what was it?' he said, turning to Jackson.

'Waterhouse.'

'Waterhouse,' the desk sergeant repeated to the beat-up boxer, as if he was translating from a foreign language. 'Uniformed constable with us in . . . ?'

'1975,' Jackson supplied.

'1975.'

'Tracy Waterhouse?' the beat-up boxer said and laughed. 'Trace? You know Big Tracy, Bill,' he said. 'Detective Superintendent Waterhouse, recently of this parish.'

'Does that mean she's dead?' Jackson puzzled.

'God, no, Tracy's indestructible. Detective Inspector Craig Peters, by the way,' he said, holding out his hand to Jackson.

'Jackson Brodie,' Jackson said, returning the handshake. He didn't recollect the West Yorkshire Police Force being so affable during his misspent teenage years.

'Tracy retired at the back end of last year,' the inspector said. 'Went to the Merrion Centre as head of security.'

'Oh, Tracy *Waterhouse*,' the desk sergeant said as if he'd finally managed to interpret the language.

A door further down the corridor burst open and a grizzled old copper came barrelling out. They didn't make them like that any more, which was probably a good thing. He glared around the reception area and Peters said to Jackson, 'DS Crawford and Tracy go way back.' To Crawford himself, stomping towards them, he raised his voice and said, 'Barry – this bloke's asking after Tracy.'

'Tracy?' Crawford echoed, coming to a stop and glaring suspiciously at Jackson. Jackson supposed after a lifetime in the force you began to look at everyone suspiciously. Although he had his regrets, Jackson was glad he had got out when he had. 'Jackson Brodie,' he said, holding out his hand. Crawford shook it reluctantly. Jackson repeated the story about the will and long-lost cousin Tracy. He sensed he might be on shaky ground, he couldn't know for sure that Tracy actually had any cousins, but Crawford said, 'Oh yeah, I seem to remember her mother had a sister in Salford. They weren't close, I seem to recollect.'

'That's right, Salford,' Jackson said, relieved that he'd mined the correct seam.

DI Peters said, 'I was saying to him, Tracy works at the Merrion Centre now,' and it was his turn to be glared at by Crawford.

'What?' Peters shrugged. 'It's not a state secret.'

'Yes, well,' Crawford said to Jackson, all bluff and bluster, 'don't go bothering her at work. And I'm not giving you a home address so don't even ask. She's going on holiday, in fact she might already have gone. I'll give her a ring and tell her you were asking for her.'

'Well, thanks,' Jackson said. 'Tell her I'm staying at the Best Western. Hang on, I'll give you my card.' He handed over one of his *Jackson Brodie – Private Investigator* cards to Crawford, who thrust it carelessly into his pocket and said, 'Unlike you, I'm a proper detective so if you don't mind you can bugger off, pleasure to meet you, et cetera.'

Charmed I'm sure, Jackson thought. What an old curmudgeon. As Julia would have said. An old curmudgeon who had been around for a long time. Jackson wondered if there was a way of introducing Carol Braithwaite's name without it seeming odd. He decided there wasn't but went for it anyway.

'Oh, by the way,' he said casually. Crawford was already halfway along the corridor. He stopped and turned, hackles raised. 'Yes?' he said. 'What?'

'I just wondered – does the name Carol Braithwaite ring any bells with you?'

Crawford stared at him. 'Who?'

'Carol Braithwaite,' Jackson repeated.

'Never heard of her.'

The dog looked uneasy, when Jackson collected it outside Millgarth. It was very small in the grand order of things and must, he supposed, feel vulnerable most of the time. 'Sorry about that,' Jackson said. They were turning into Wallace and Gromit, he could feel it. Soon he'd be calling the dog 'lad' and sharing cheese and crackers with it. There were worse things, he supposed.

'I'm looking for Tracy Waterhouse,' Jackson said to the man, more youth than man, who eventually appeared from behind a nondescript grey door in the Merrion Centre. Ravaged by acne, if you knew Braille you could probably have read his face, he had a name badge that announced him to be Grant Leyburn. He looked like he was swimming in a very small gene pool. Jackson felt a twitch of disappointment that the pleasant Canadian girl wasn't available.

'Tracy Waterhouse. Is she here?' Jackson asked.

'No,' Grant Leyburn said sullenly. 'She isn't.'

'Do you know where I might find her?' Jackson persisted.

'She's on holiday from tomorrow. Not back for a week.'

'What about today?'

'Sick.'

'You can't give me a phone number, I don't suppose?' Jackson said. 'Or any other contact details?' he added hopefully.

Grant raised an overgrown eyebrow and said, 'What do you think?'

'I'm guessing no?'

'Got it in one.'

Jackson fished out a card and handed it over. 'Maybe you could give this to her when she's back?'

'A private detective?' he said with a sneer. 'Another one. She's very popular.'

'Another one?' Jackson puzzled.

'Yeah, someone here earlier.' He glanced up suddenly at a big round security camera suspended from a ceiling. It looked like a small spaceship. He frowned and said, 'Someone's always watching.'

'Tell me about it,' Jackson said.

He placed the photograph of the girl with the cock-eyed bunches on a chair near the bedroom window where the best light was. He took a photograph of it with his phone. It had a slight ghostly aura, the photograph of a photograph, twice removed from life. Virtual reality.

He flicked through the photographs on his phone's camera roll until he came across the one taken on Hope McMaster's arrival in New Zealand. If not the same child as the one shivering on a British beach then an identical twin. In both photographs the little girl was grinning from ear to ear, already a child with exclamation marks in her brain. If it was a photo of Hope McMaster then it confirmed one thing, she had not appeared fully formed out of nowhere. She had a past. She had once stood, shivering and grinning, on a windswept beach and someone had taken a photo of her. Who?

It would be the middle of the night in the topsy-turvy world that Hope McMaster inhabited. *Do you think this is you?* he wrote and then thought that sounded prejudicial and erased the sentence and retyped, *Do you recognize the girl in this photograph?* She would wake up in her tomorrow to either surprise or disappointment.

Jackson googled 'Carol Braithwaite' on his phone and came up with nothing. Any combination of Carol Braithwaite/murder/ Leeds/1975, plus any other word he could throw in the mix, came up with nothing. Carol Braithwaite was an adult in 1975 so she couldn't be Hope McMaster, but she could be Hope's mother. He had found no mention in the newspaper report of any children but that didn't mean there weren't any. Was the girl in the photograph Carol Braithwaite's daughter? Linda Pallister dealt with children nobody wanted, had she dealt with Carol Braithwaite's? Finessed an under-the-counter adoption? An act of goodwill perhaps, giving a small child a good home and saving it from festering in the system.

The only record he could find online of any girl being abducted in 1975 was the Black Panther's victim Lesley Whittle. The kidnapping of a small girl would have been news headlines and if she was never found it would reverberate through the media for years. In his time Jackson had looked for plenty of children who were missing, he had never looked for a child who *wasn't* missing. Even the most careless parent was unlikely to lose a child and not mention it, unless they had intended to misplace it, of course.

It was more likely that Hope McMaster had been unwanted and simply been given away. That would explain why there was no record. When Jackson was a child a lot of unofficial 'adoptions' took place, leaving no paper trail behind them. Illegitimate kids taken in by their grandparents, growing up thinking their mother was their sister. Barren sisters taking in a surplus nephew or niece, raising them as a prized only child. Jackson's own mother had an elder brother she had never met. He had been given away to a childless aunt and uncle in Dublin before Jackson's mother was born and he was 'spoilt', according to Jackson's jealous mother. 'Spoilt', in his mother's vocabulary, meant that he had an education, went to Trinity College, became a barrister, married well and died in bourgeois comfort many years later.

Linda Pallister was the key, all he had to do was talk to her, something she seemed to be going out of her way to avoid.

Neither Tracy Waterhouse nor Linda Pallister were in the phone book but that was no surprise. Police and social workers kept a low profile in public otherwise every nutter and ex-con would be hammering on their door at midnight. Jackson went on to 192.com, friend of snoops and investigators who had no access to official records.

There he found one 'Linda Pallister' and four 'T. Waterhouse's, one of those a 'Tracy'. He had plenty of credits with 192.com and was able to get addresses for both women. They knew enough to go ex-directory but weren't savvy enough to remove themselves from the electoral register, which was how 192.com had got hold of their details. It shouldn't be allowed, but it was, thank goodness.

Jackson retrieved the Saab from the multi-storey car park at the Merrion Centre where it had been corralled since he arrived in Leeds yesterday. He wasn't sure of the protocol of dogs in cars. You saw them all the time staring out of the back or hanging out of the passenger window, their ears fluttering in the slipstream, but an unsecured dog was an accident waiting to happen. When he was in the force there had been a woman killed in a traffic accident. She braked suddenly at a red light, and her Dalmatian in the seat behind her carried on travelling. Broke her neck. Stupid way to die.

The dog had hopped on to the back seat as if this were its accustomed place but Alpha Dog, Jackson, said, 'No,' sternly. The dog was unsure but eager to please, studying Jackson's face for a clue. 'There,' Jackson said, pointing at the front seat passenger footwell, and the dog jumped in and settled down. 'OK,' he said when he was finally satisfied that the dog wasn't going to be hurled through the car like a missile. 'Let's go and find us some women.' He put Kendel Carson's 'Cowboy Boots' on the car stereo, a song that wasn't as redneck as the title suggested.

He started the engine and adjusted the rear-view mirror. Catching sight of himself in it he was surprised anew by his military buzz-cut.

Linda Pallister lived in a traditional semi near Roundhay Park. The curtains were drawn even though it was the afternoon. It had the air of a house in mourning. Jackson rang the bell and knocked hard but there was no answer. He tried the back door with the same result. The mysteriously absent Linda Pallister remained just that, mysteriously absent.

Jackson knocked on the door of the neighbouring house. He struck lucky with the woman ('Mrs Potter') who answered the door. He knew the type – they were usually watching reruns of *Midsomer Murders* or *Poirot* behind the net curtains in the middle of the afternoon, pot of tea and a plate of chocolate digestives to hand. They made invaluable witnesses because they were always on watch.

'She had a visitor last night,' Mrs Potter duly reported. 'A man,' she added with relish.

'Have you seen her today?'

'I don't know, I don't spend all my time watching the neighbourhood goings-on, I don't know why people would think that.'

'Of course not, Mrs Potter,' Jackson said, feigning empathy. It was never a tactic that worked well for him (especially with women) but that didn't stop him trying. 'Look,' he took one of his cards out of his wallet and handed it to the woman, 'if she comes back, could you give her this and ask her to give me a ring.'

'Private detective?' she said, reading the card. He needn't have bothered with empathy, the idea of a private detective was intriguing enough for her to say, 'Call me Janice.' She dropped her voice as if Linda Pallister might be eavesdropping on them. 'Can you tell me why you're interested in Linda?'

'I could but then I'd have to kill you,' Jackson said. For a moment, the woman looked as if she believed him. Jackson smiled. Yep, willing to give a woman a cheap thrill at the drop of a hat these days.

There was more life inside Tracy Waterhouse's house down the road in Headingley, although unfortunately not coming from Tracy herself. The front door was open and a man was packing tools away in a van. Tracy, he informed Jackson in an East European accent (your classic Polish builder, Jackson supposed), had gone out this morning and he didn't know when she would be back. 'But I hope she will be,' he said and laughed. 'She owes me money.'

Despite Jackson's claim to be Tracy's long-lost cousin the workman wouldn't give him Tracy's mobile number. 'She's a very private person,' he said.

Instead of collecting Cistercian abbeys, now it seemed Jackson was collecting women who were missing in action.

He sat in his car in the car park and dialled Tracy's mobile. It went to voicemail and he left a message. Barry's car smelled of freesias, Amy's favourite flower. Why hadn't she had them in her wedding bouquet instead of those stupid orange daisy things? There was no flower that meant anything to her now. All Ivan's fault. Blame him for everything. He was coming out on Saturday, a pal of Barry's in the prison service had given him the date and time. Barry would be there to greet him.

He was taking the freesias to Sam's small grave. He went more often than he ever told Barbara. They visited the grave separately. Barbara left things that turned his stomach – teddy bears and toy trucks. He always left freesias.

Barry raked through his pocket for the card that the Jackson bloke had given him but couldn't find it anywhere. He phoned Tracy's number in the Merrion Centre and a prize pillock answered and said she was off sick. He phoned her home number and there was just a generic answer-machine message. Finally he phoned her mobile and left a message. Phoned again and left a second message. Remembered something else, left a third message.

Something was up, but what exactly? Tracy didn't have any cousins. Didn't have any family at all, she was the only child of only children. She had nobody in Salford, that was for sure. He had to warn her if someone dodgy was after her. Linda Pallister had mentioned a private detective named 'Jackson' snooping around and now here was this clot turning up at Millgarth looking for Tracy. *Does the name Carol Braithwaite ring any bells?* he said. One bloody great bell tolling for the dead, waking the living. Ring out the bells, bring out the dead.

Before Amy's accident he used to feel sorry for Tracy, one of those women who'd sacrificed motherhood to the job. They reached the menopause and realized that they hadn't had kids, that their DNA was going to die with them and nobody was ever going to love them the way a kid would. Sad, really. But after Amy's accident Barry envied Tracy. She didn't have to feel unbearable pain every living second of every living day.

He started the engine and drove to the cemetery, breathing in the scent of freesias all the way.

~

'Are we going home?' Courtney asked when Tracy strapped her back in the car seat outside Toys 'R' Us. The boot was full of stuff, most of it plastic. All those tiny ancient marine life forms falling to the ocean floor to come back to life one day as a Disney Fairies Tea Set.

At Courtney's request Tracy had also bought a dressing-up costume, a pink fairy outfit, complete with wings, wand and tiara. Courtney had insisted on getting changed into it in the car and she was now sitting stiffly in the back of the car in a pose that reminded Tracy of the Queen at her coronation.

'Are we going home?' Tracy repeated thoughtfully as if it wasn't so much a question as a philosophical conundrum. What did Courtney mean by 'home'? Tracy wondered. Where was it? Kelly's undoubtedly squalid pad, or somewhere else?

There was stuff you did with kids and stuff you didn't. For all of her working life Tracy had witnessed the stuff you weren't supposed to do with them. Building sandcastles on a beach, feeding bread to ducks, eating a picnic sitting on a plaid blanket in the park – these were things you did with kids. Stealing them was one of the things you didn't do. Bottom line. She had taken a child that wasn't hers.

'Actually,' Tracy said, 'we're not. Not going home just yet. Couple of errands to run.'

It took half an hour in the bank to empty her account

of its savings. Kid got through a banana and an apple. Tracy had brought her passport with her, knew the drill on fraud prevention, didn't stop the teller behaving as if she were robbing the place. Security cameras everywhere and thirty thousand in cash in her handbag. Hard not to look guilty.

After that they went to see her solicitor and Tracy gave him instructions to sell her house. Solicitors were slow-moving animals, you couldn't get out of their offices in under two bananas. Could you overdose on bananas? She could hear her mother's voice, 'You'll turn into a cheese and onion crisp if you carry on eating them like that.' (She hadn't.) And the bananas were small, 'fun-sized', according to the supermarket label. Tracy ate one in the car, wondered what people did before bananas. She didn't understand what 'fun-sized' meant in the context of a banana. She'd arrested a guy once peddling kiddy porn, *Fun-sized Treats* one of the videos was called. Nothing innocent. Anywhere.

'Are we going home *now*?' Courtney asked when they were back in the car. Kid was used to being moved around like a billiard ball. Kids had no power over where they went, who they went with.

'Soon. First we're going to see a man.' In the rear-view mirror she caught the frown pinching Courtney's face and added, 'A nice man.'

Nice-ish, anyway, if her memory served her. On the surface. He was also a conman, a thief and a fixer but Tracy didn't mention that to the kid. He lived in an impressive house in Alwoodley, bought, no doubt, with the proceeds of a life in crime, and was commendably poker-faced when he opened his front door to find Tracy and a small pink fairy standing in front of him.

'Superintendent,' he said genially, 'and a friend. What a pleasant surprise.'

'I'm retired,' Tracy said.

'Me too,' Harry Reynolds murmured. 'Do come in.'

He was a dapper little bloke – cravat, crease in his beige twill trousers, the kind of smart slippers that could pass for shoes – and had picked up his bus pass quite some time ago, although Tracy doubted somehow that Harry Reynolds travelled on public transport, especially as there was a Bentley parked on his driveway.

He led them into a knocked-through living room – high-quality patio doors and a koi carp pond almost directly outside, as if Harry Reynolds wanted to view the expensive fish without having to leave the airlock of his house.

Inside, the walls were covered with framed school photographs of two children, a boy and a girl. Tracy recognized the uniform of a fee-paying prep school with a name she never knew how to pronounce.

'The grandkids,' Harry Reynolds said proudly. 'Brett's ten, Ashley's eight.' Tracy presumed that Brett was the boy and Ashley the girl but you could never be sure any more. The rest of the décor was hideous, big glass vases that might have been regarded as 'art' in the seventies, sentimental china ornaments of clowns with balloons or sad-faced children with dogs. A big brass sunburst clock adorned one wall and on another a football match was being played out on the biggest TV screen that Tracy had ever seen. Crime pays. There was a surprising smell of baking wafting through the house.

'Don't want to interrupt the game,' Tracy said politely, although years in uniform policing dirty Leeds United home matches meant that she would have happily put a sledgehammer into the screen.

'No, no,' Harry Reynolds said. 'It's a shit game, excuse my French, pet,' he added in Courtney's direction. 'Anyway, it's on Sky Plus, not live, I can catch up later.' He had the kind of Yorkshire accent that Tracy thought of as 'aspirational'. Dorothy Waterhouse's accent.

Harry Reynolds switched the TV off and settled the pair of them on puffy sofas, as big as barges, that were upholstered in an outmoded mauve leather. It seemed an undignified end for a cow. He excused himself and went to fetch 'refreshments'. The sun was shining hotly on the garden but the windows and doors were all closed, the whole house hermetically sealed against the outside world. Tracy felt her blouse sticking to her back. The waistband of her big pants was cutting her in half. She always swelled during the course of the day. How did that happen? she wondered.

Courtney sat silently, staring out of the window. Maybe Kelly had drugged her. Nothing new there, think of the gallons of laudanum mothers used to ply their kids with to keep them quiet. These days more kids were being slipped tranquillizers and sleeping pills than people realized. If it had been up to Tracy she would have sterilized a lot of parents. You couldn't say that, of course, made you sound like a Nazi. Didn't take away from the truth of it though.

Tracy's phone rang. *Für Elise*. She raked it out of her bag, expecting it to be her silent caller. She frowned at the screen. 'Barry', it said. Fear washed through her, had he found out something about Courtney? She let it go to voicemail.

Harry Reynolds came back into the room, carrying a tea-tray. *Für Elise* again. Barry again. Voicemail again.

'Problem?'

'Nuisance call,' Tracy said dismissively.

Für Elise yet again. For God's sake, she thought, go away, Barry.

'Want me to do something about it?'

Tracy wondered what 'doing something' would be for someone like Harry Reynolds.

'No,' she said. 'It's probably one of those computer-generated calls. From India or Argentina or somewhere.'

'Bloody blacks,' Harry Reynolds said. 'Taking over everywhere. It's a different world these days.' He set the tray down. Teapot, cups and saucers – nice china – orange juice and a plate of scones. Butter, a little dash of jam. He pushed the plate of scones towards Tracy. 'Fresh batch from the oven, made them myself,' he said. 'You've got to keep yourself busy, haven't you?'

'Yeah,' Tracy said. 'Busy, busy.' She was going to pass on the scones but she couldn't resist. She'd been motoring all day on nothing more than two Weetabix and half a stale doughnut. Oh yeah, and two Jaffa cakes. And a tuna roll from the picnic. A packet of salt and vinegar crisps. A handful of carrot sticks, although they hardly counted. It was surprising how it all added up. She joined Slimming World last year and had to keep a 'food diary'. After a while she started making the diary up. *Ryvita, cottage cheese, celery sticks, two apples, a banana, tuna salad at lunchtime, grilled chicken, green beans for dinner.* She couldn't own up to the crap she grazed on all day. Put on weight the first week, didn't go back.

'Made the raspberry jam as well,' Harry Reynolds said. 'There's a pick-your-own place off the A65, just past Guiseley. Do you know it?'

'No, don't think I do.' As if. Tracy had never picked anything in her life apart from scabs and daisies and the latter was more of an assumption than an actual memory. She nibbled on a scone. It was warm and buttery in her mouth and the jam was both sweet and tart at the same time. She ate the rest of it, trying not to look greedy.

'Naughty but nice,' Harry Reynolds laughed, biting into one of the scones.

The scones made Tracy aware of a lot of things she might have missed out on in life. Like taking a turn off the A65 to a pick-your-own-fruit place. She'd been called out to a murder there once, just south of Otley. A prostitute who'd been taken for her last ride and dumped in a ditch. She'd heard rumours that Harry Reynolds had had his fingers in that particular pie, running girls and porn in the sixties, but he didn't seem the type to Tracy. Naughty but nice. She thought of the madam in her house in Cookridge handing out sherry and shelled nuts. That was the seventies, of course. Nothing innocent. Norah, that was her name. Norah Kendall.

'Did you know Norah Kendall?' she asked Harry Reynolds.

'Oh, Norah,' he laughed. 'She was some woman. Good business head,' he added admiringly. 'It used to be a different world, didn't it, Superintendent? Mucky books round the back and men in macs flashing the occasional schoolgirl. Innocence.' He sighed nostalgically.

Tracy bit down on her response. She didn't remember the innocence.

'You can't tell a good girl from a prostitute these days,' Harry Reynolds said. 'They all dress like they're on the game, act like it too.'

'I know,' Tracy said, surprised to find herself agreeing with someone like Harry Reynolds. But it was true, you looked at young girls, crippled in heels, dressed like hookers, stumbling around pissed out of their brains on a Saturday night in Leeds town centre and you thought, did we throw ourselves under horses for this, gag on forced feeding tubes, suffer ridicule, humiliation and punishment, just so that women could behave worse than men?

'They're worse than the blokes these days,' Harry Reynolds said.

'It's biological,' Tracy said, 'they can't help it, they've

got to attract a mate and breed and die. They're like mayfly.'

'*O tempora o mores,*' he said.

'Didn't think of you as a classicist, Harry.'

'I'm like an iceberg, Superintendent. I go deep.' He bit into a scone with his shiny false teeth and ruminated. 'Too many people on the planet,' he said. 'You cull deer, but you're not allowed to cull people.' It was an unfortunate echo of what Tracy had been thinking a moment ago. It sounded more fascist coming from his mouth than it had in her mind.

Had Harry Reynolds had people murdered? Tracy wondered. Possibly. Did that bother her? Not as much as it should have done.

'I see our friend Rex Marshall finally found the eighteenth hole,' Harry Reynolds said.

'Not my friend,' Tracy muttered, her mouth full of carbohydrate. 'Not yours either, I wouldn't have thought.'

'Members of the same golf club,' he said. 'It's like being in the Masons. Lomax, Strickland, Marshall, they all enjoyed having a round with yours truly. Even Walter Eastman in his day.'

'I don't know why I'm surprised.' Tracy swallowed the last of the scone and said, 'Harry?'

'Superintendent?'

'Remember 1975?'

'Cricket World Cup came to Headingley in the June. Australians against us. England all out for ninety-three. West Indies beat them in the final. Say what you like about the blacks, they can play cricket.'

'Yeah, well, apart from that. Do you remember the murder of a woman called Carol Braithwaite?'

'No,' he said, gazing out at his fish. 'I'm afraid I don't. Why?'

'Nothing. Just wondering.'

The kid had already hoovered up her juice and two scones and was looking slightly more animated. Her silver tiara had tilted and her mouth was smeared with raspberry jam. The wand was resting on the sofa next to her. She made fists with her hands and then opened them up into stars. This seemed to be the ultimate sign of approval. She picked up the wand again, returned to duty.

'Careful with that,' Harry Reynolds said, smiling indulgently. 'Don't want you casting any spells.'

Courtney stared at him.

'She's a right chatterbox, isn't she?' Harry Reynolds said. 'She's all there, is she?'

'Of course she is,' Tracy said crossly. She dabbed at the raspberry jam on Courtney's face with a tissue, to no effect. There were also archaeological remnants of tuna roll, doughnut and chocolate. Tracy realized that when she was in the supermarket again she would have to take it to the next level. Wet Wipes.

'So ... long time no see, Superintendent,' Harry Reynolds said. 'Both civilians now, eh? Another scone?'

'No, thanks. Well, maybe. Go on then. Are you really out of the game, Harry?'

'I'm over seventy,' Harry Reynolds said. 'My wife died since I last saw you. Cancer. I nursed her to the end, died in my arms. But I can't complain, I've got a wonderful daughter, Susan, and the grandkids stay over all the time. I spoil them rotten, but why not? Used to be different in my day, a clip round the ear and bread and dripping for your tea if you were lucky . . .'

Tracy could feel herself nodding off. Wondered if Harry Reynolds would mind – wondered if he'd even notice – if she were to lie down on his bigger-than-a-cow sofa and have a little snooze.

'. . . and, of course, they come every Sunday for a big roast, all the trimmings. I like to make a proper pudding – fruit pie, steamed sponge, jam roly-poly. Hardly anyone does that any more, do they? Yorkshire puddings – who makes them any more?'

Tracy could almost smell the scent of fatty roasting meat and overcooked vegetables. For a second she was back in the bungalow in Bramley, the dead air of Sunday mornings, her mother 'partaking' of a small schooner of sherry.

'You used to think of Sunday lunch as an immovable feast,' Harry carried on. 'Time immemorial, you didn't think it would be replaced by a pizza or takeaway from the Chinky. No wonder this country's going to the dogs.'

Tracy bit into another scone to keep herself awake. She felt as if she'd accidentally wandered into the middle of a Werther's Original advert. Did all criminals turn soft if they survived to old age? (Did police detectives? Probably not.) Maybe they could just move in with Harry Reynolds now that he'd transformed from career criminal into twinkly – albeit fascist and racist – granddad. How many bedrooms in this house? Four at least. Plenty. They could make themselves scarce at the weekends, or Courtney could stay and play with Brett and Ashley.

'Is this your kiddy?' Harry Reynolds asked. The tone was off-hand, pleasant, but suddenly there was less of the whole twinkling thing going on.

'I'm here on business,' Tracy said.

'I thought you said you were retired, Superintendent.'

'Different kind of business,' Tracy said.

The shopping they had bought this morning in the supermarket was still in the boot of the Audi. Tracy imagined anything fresh in there slowly rotting, turning to mush in the plastic bags. It was mostly stuff to take with them to the holiday cottage. Self-catering – you always bought five times what you needed. No way was she cooking tonight.

'Let's go out for our tea,' she said to Courtney once they were both strapped in the Audi. Courtney nodded, kept on nodding. A nodding dog. 'You can stop now,' Tracy advised her. The nodding slowed down. Stopped.

Before setting off Tracy listened to her voicemail, dreading bad news from Barry. Message one. *It's Barry, Tracy. There's been a bloke down the station looking for you. Says you've been left money in a will by an aunt in Salford. I know you don't have an aunt in Salford or anywhere else so I don't know what his game is.* Message two. Barry again. *Says his name's Jackson something or other. Mean anything to you? Give us a call.* Message three. *Claims he's a private detective. Think he's lying. He's staying at the Best*

Western, the one next to the Merrion Centre. He gave me his
card but I've lost it.

Nobody could invest the words 'private detective'
with as much scorn as Barry. Jackson? Name meant
nothing at all to her. Was he after the kid? Had he been
sent to get her back? She was going to give him a wide
berth whoever he was.

There was a grey Avensis flitting in and out of the rear-
view mirror. Tracy was sure it was the same car that had
been parked near them in the supermarket. She'd
noticed it because of the pink rabbit hanging from the
rear-view mirror. 'Air-freshener bunny'. Bloody stupid
thing, she'd been given one by her 'secret Santa' last
year. Secret Santas and vice didn't go together somehow.
The Avensis disappeared from view. Could it be the
Jackson bloke?

'Keep an eye out for a grey car,' she said to Courtney.
Did kids her age know all the colours? Could the kid
sing the whole rainbow? 'Do you know what colour
grey is?'

'It's the colour of the sky,' Courtney offered.

Tracy sighed. Therapist would have a field day with
this kid.

They ate supper in the local Chinese. The kid peered
closely at the menu and Tracy said, 'Can you read,
Courtney?'

'No.' Courtney shook her head and continued to
examine the menu.

She proceeded to dig her way through a plate of

Singapore noodles. 'I think there's a fat kid inside you trying to get out,' Tracy said. Courtney paused between mouthfuls and stared at Tracy. A few stray noodles hung out of her mouth, like a walrus's moustache. 'Not literally,' Tracy said. She sighed and dished out more steamed jasmine rice. 'My fat kid escaped a long time ago.'

When they finished, not before Courtney had packed a plate of banana fritters with ice cream into her hollow legs, Tracy paid the bill with two twenties peeled off her roll of thirty thousand but raking in vain through her purse for some change, said to Courtney, 'I haven't got enough for a tip.'

Courtney stared at her, doing her imitation of a sphinx, and then delved into the depths of her pink backpack and retrieved the purse with the monkey's face on it and took out four one-pence pieces that she placed carefully on the saucer, muttering, 'One, two, three, four,' under her breath.

'How high can you count, Courtney?'

'A million,' Courtney said promptly.

'Really?'

Courtney held up her left hand and slowly counted off four fingers and a thumb, 'One–two–three–four–a million.'

'That's it?'

Courtney stared steadfastly at her. Tracy could see a noodle lodged between her front teeth. Eventually she held up the index finger on her right hand and said, 'A million and one.' She hadn't finished with her generous tip. She was peering in the backpack, finally coming up with the nutmeg, which she placed with the coins. The waiter removed the saucer with waiter-like inscrutability and like a magician produced a fortune cookie and handed it ceremoniously to Courtney. She placed it carefully in her backpack without cracking it open.

'Let's go home,' Tracy said.

Before they got anywhere near the house in Headingley, Tracy's phone rang. Her heart sank the moment she heard the strident rant at the other end. Kelly Cross wanting a pound of flesh that Tracy didn't even realize she was owing. She could take it. She could take whatever she wanted. Sometimes you just had to step up. Sleep, eat, protect. Especially the protect bit.

1975: 9 April

The stench inside was unbelievable. Decomposition. Tracy wouldn't be able to get it out of her nostrils for days. It was on her skin, her uniform, her hair. Years later she just had to think about the flat in Lovell Park and she could smell it. Kiddy was just standing there in the hallway when they broke in. Filthy, nothing but skin and bone, looked like a famine victim.

Still knackered from climbing fifteen flights and putting in an unexpectedly resistant door, Ken Arkwright moved his beefy body with surprising speed along the hallway and snatched the kiddy up, passed the emaciated little thing to Tracy and started searching in the other rooms.

Tracy held the weightless little body and stroked the dirty hair and murmured, 'Everything's all right now.' Couldn't think what else to say, what else to do.

Arkwright reappeared and said, 'No more kiddies, but . . .' With an inclination of his head he indicated a door he had opened further up the hallway.

'What?' Tracy said.

'In the bedroom.'

'What?'

Arkwright dropped his voice to a whisper and said, 'The mum.'

'Shit. How long?'

'Couple of weeks by the look of it,' Arkwright said. Tracy felt her stomach heave. Told herself to hold on, to think about Dad's roses, Mum's Izal, anything that didn't smell of rotting flesh.

She carried the kiddy through to the living room, glanced in the bedroom as she passed, shielding the kiddy's eyes, even though they were already closed. She had a glimpse of something on the floor, couldn't make out what it was but she knew it was bad.

Detective Constable Ray Strickland and Detective Sergeant Len Lomax, first officers from CID on the scene in Lovell Park. They certainly took their time. Tracy looked out of the living-room window, all those dizzying flights down, and saw them finally arriving in a flurry of macho brakes but instead of rushing into the building they got out of the car and stood next to it, deep in conversation – or argument, it was hard to say from this height. There was something conspiratorial in their stance.

'What the fuck are they doing?' Arkwright said and Tracy replied, 'Dunno. Where's the ambulance? Why is it taking so long?' What if the kiddy pegged out now? It was a miracle that the kiddy had managed to stay alive all this time – must have grubbed around in cupboards for food. 'Don't die, please,' Tracy murmured, more prayer than request.

Tracy and Arkwright had walked all over the place. The contamination of evidence must have been phenomenal. You didn't think so much about that then. Now they would have scarpered the second they saw the body, not gone back in until the SOCOs had combed every inch.

Tracy watched as a bicycle rolled up. A girl dismounted and the two detectives pulled apart from each other. The girl was wearing a long smock that looked like a nightdress and her two curtains of hair hung limply on either side of her pale face. Arkwright said, 'Ey up, the hippies are here.'

'But where's the fucking ambulance?' Tracy said. Before she joined the police she had never said so much as 'damn', now she cursed like the best of them. She watched as the girl said something to Lomax and Strickland, all three of them wheeled round and came into the building.

'Listen,' Arkwright said, cocking his head to one side. 'That ruddy lift's working now, would you believe it? It's like the universe has got one rule for them and one rule for us peasants.'

When Lomax and Strickland arrived at Carol Braithwaite's door, the besmocked girl was trailing on their heels. 'Linda Pallister,' she said with a curt nod in the direction of Ken Arkwright, Tracy invisible apparently. 'I'm the social worker on call.' With her scrubbed face and robust cyclist's calves, she looked more like a fifth-former than a grown woman with a job.

'We don't need a fucking social worker, we need a fucking ambulance,' Tracy hissed at her. Strickland suddenly ran out of the room and they all listened to the sound of him throwing up in the bathroom.

'Sensitive lad, our Ray,' Len Lomax said.

'No sign of the pathologist,' Len Lomax said, 'but the ambulance is here.'

'Right,' Linda Pallister said, when the ambulance men arrived at the door of the flat. She took the kiddy off Tracy, Tracy holding on just a second longer than necessary. 'It's OK, I know what I'm doing,' Linda Pallister said and Tracy nodded mutely, suddenly afraid that she might cry.

When they'd gone, Tracy said to Len Lomax, 'I asked the kiddy who did it, who did this to Mummy.'

'And?'

'Said "Daddy".'

Lomax laughed, a brutal sound in the dead quiet. 'It's

a wise child that knows its own father. And as for that bint,' he said, jerking his thumb in the direction of the bedroom where the woman's decaying body was still lying, 'I'd bet a hundred to one that she couldn't name the father.' He took out his notebook with a strangely theatrical flourish and looked around as if he was going to conjure clues out of the walls.

'Did you know her?' Tracy asked. Lomax looked at her as if she'd just grown another head. 'Of course I didn't fucking know her,' he said.

Tracy glanced at Ray Strickland. He looked shaky and green as if he was about to throw up again. He hadn't even gone through to look at the body yet. When they first entered the flat Tracy heard them all talking in the hallway, heard Lomax say to Linda Pallister, 'That's the bedroom on the left, where the body is.'

'How did he know that?' she asked Arkwright in the pub when they came off shift.

'Psychic,' Arkwright said. 'He does table-knocking and spirit readings in the Horse and Trumpet's snug on Thursday evenings.' Arkwright had a way of saying things so dead-pan that Tracy took him seriously for a second.

'Think the next round's yours, lass,' he laughed.

Neither Lomax nor Strickland bothered with a statement from Tracy.

'What could you have to say that he hasn't said?' Lomax said, jabbing a finger in Arkwright's direction.

Barry, of all people, pitched up, said, 'Sir?' to Strickland.

'Getting to be Ray's bum-boy, isn't he?' Arkwright murmured to Tracy. Strickland said something inaudible to Barry and then Barry looked as sick as Strickland. They disappeared into the small, cold kitchen, where empty packets of cereal and anything else the kiddy had been able to find were strewn across the floor. It was a miracle that the kiddy hadn't died of hypothermia, let alone starvation.

Lomax said, 'Bugger off,' to Arkwright, 'and get knocking on a few doors. And take her with you,' he said, nodding his head in Tracy's direction. Arkwright retained an admirable poker face. 'Let's get going, lass,' he said.

Carol Braithwaite, the neighbours said. Blankly. Nobody seemed to know her. 'Only moved in at Christmas,' one of them said. 'Bit raucous, heard a few fights.' Hear anything else? 'Kid crying.' 'She brought men back,' another one said. The classic 'Kept herself to herself,' from another one. Nobody knew her. Never would now.

Of course, everything was subjective. No true fixed point in the world. Tracy was beginning to understand that.

Tracy and Arkwright, knocking on door after door in Lovell Park. Thin walls, Tracy said, you would think someone would have heard something.

Carol Braithwaite. Three 'O' Levels and two convictions for soliciting.

'A good-time girl,' Arkwright said. *A good-time girl*. Police-speak. It didn't help an investigation if you said the word 'prostitute'. They got what they deserved, deserved what they got.

'Doesn't look like she had much of a good time to me,' Tracy said.

One of those three 'O' Levels had been in needlework, another in cookery, the third in typing. Information courtesy of flower-child Linda Pallister. Carol would have made a good wife but somehow that wasn't the path she'd taken. At school Tracy had always been wary of the domestic science crowd – methodical girls with neat handwriting and neither flaws nor eccentricities. For some reason they were usually good at netball as well, as if the gene that enabled them to jump for the hoop contained the information necessary for turning out a cheese and onion flan or creaming a Victoria sponge-sandwich mix. Their career paths didn't usually lead to prostitution. Of course, if you said 'gene' in the seventies people thought Levi's or Wranglers. They weren't the hot topic they were now. Tracy wondered if Carol Braithwaite had ever played netball.

Even at school Tracy had already suspected that she would make no one a good wife. Couldn't sew a straight seam, couldn't even cook a simple macaroni cheese or do hospital corners. She had a knock-out right jab though. Something that she'd discovered one hectic Saturday night of catfights and drunken brawls when a leery pair of young blokes nearly had her cornered on Boar Lane. Did her reputation as a copper a bit of good but hadn't exactly enhanced her status as a woman. ('Built like a brick shithouse, that Tracy Waterhouse.')

When they eventually returned after knocking on doors everyone had gone and been replaced by Barry, a lone uniform, guarding the broken door of the flat.

'I was told not to let anyone in,' he said officiously. 'Sorry.'

'Fuck off, you big nit,' Arkwright said, pushing past him. 'I left my cigarettes in there.' Tracy laughed.

'Can you tell me what happened here?'

'Eh?' Arkwright said.

'Marilyn Nettles, *Yorkshire Post* crime reporter.' She flashed a card with her credentials on it. They were standing outside the entrance to the Lovell Park flats, in the cold, freezing their socks off, while Arkwright lit up. 'Colder than a witch's tit,' Arkwright said. Tracy caught sight of Linda Pallister's bike, leaning against a fence. She had travelled in the ambulance with the kiddy. It seemed unlikely that the bike would still be here when she returned for it. There was a kiddy seat on the back of it.

Tracy remembered Marilyn Nettles from somewhere but couldn't place her until Arkwright said later, 'She infiltrated Dick Hardwick's leaving do.'

'Infiltrated?' Tracy said. 'You mean she was in the same pub at the same time?'

'As I said, infiltrated. She's a nosy cow.'

'Aren't we all?'

Skinny, mid-thirties, dyed black hair left over from the previous decade, cut in a bob so sharp that it looked as if it would cut you if you got too close to her. She had a beaky nose that gave her a hungry look. She was the kind who would trample over the bodies of the fallen to get to the story.

''Fraid I can't comment on what happened here,' Arkwright said to her. 'Ongoing investigation. I expect there'll be a press conference, pet.'

Marilyn Nettles shrank from the word 'pet'. Tracy could see her wanting to say, 'Don't use condescending sexist language with me, you great big ignorant police oaf,' and having to bite down on it and say instead, 'Neighbours are saying it was a woman called Carol Braithwaite?'

'Couldn't comment on that.'

'I believe she was a known prostitute.'

'Wouldn't know about that either, I'm afraid.'

'Oh come on, Constable, can't you give me a *little* something?'

Marilyn Nettles did something funny with her mouth, followed up by something funny with her eyes. It took Tracy a second or two to realize that she was trying to flirt with Arkwright. She was deluded. It was like trying to flirt with a wardrobe.

'Have you got something in your eye?' Tracy asked her innocently.

Marilyn Nettles ignored Tracy, strangely fixated on Arkwright. 'Help a poor girl out,' she said. She pinched her thumb and forefinger together. 'Feed me just a little titbit? Give me something?'

With laboured slowness Arkwright delved into a pocket in his uniform and retrieved a ten-pence piece. It was over four years since Britain had gone decimal but Arkwright still referred to 'the new money'.

'Here, lass,' he said to Marilyn Nettles, handing over the coin. 'Go buy yourself a bag of chips. You need fattening up.'

She turned on her heel and stalked off in disgust towards a red Vauxhall Victor.

'Wouldn't like to have to get into bed with her,' Arkwright said. 'It would be like cuddling up to a skeleton.' He looked at the rejected coin and spun it high in the air. He caught it on the way down and slapped it on the back of his hand.

'Heads or tails?' he said to Tracy.

'You all right, lass?' Arkwright said, draining his bitter and looking around as if he was expecting another one to materialize from nowhere.

'Yeah,' Tracy said.

'Another one?'

Tracy sighed. 'No, I'll be off. My mum's making her lamb hotpot.'

At least he had learned his lesson, he was not going to be the foolish prey of boredom tonight. Instead he ordered something innocuous-sounding on room service, no alcohol to accompany it, and when the food arrived he stretched out on the bed with his plate and picked up the remote.

Collier. Of course. Jackson sighed. Just when you thought it was safe to switch on the TV.

Collier was a rugged but occasionally sensitive detective inspector who worked in both a gritty northern town ('Bradthorpe') and a green farming dale ('Hardale'). He frequently kicked against the traces of authority in the search for the truth and was invariably vindicated at the end. He was a maverick but (as someone said at least once in the course of every programme) 'a brilliant detective'. He was unreliable towards women but they were, nonetheless, continually charmed by him. In his own experience, Jackson had found the exact opposite to be true, the more unreliable he was (usually from no fault of his own, he would just like to point out) the less impressed women were with him.

Julia, of all people, Julia, who had 'given up acting to concentrate on being a mother and a wife' (a declaration that no one, particularly not Jackson, believed), had recently been cast in *Collier*. Jackson had presumed she would be a corpse, or, at best, a bit-part barmaid, but it turned out that she was playing a forensic pathologist. (*'A forensic pathologist?'* He had been unable to disguise the disbelief in his voice.

'Yes, Jackson,' she said, with exaggerated forbearance. 'I don't actually have to have a medical degree or conduct post-mortems. It's called *acting*.'

'Even so . . .' Jackson murmured.)

DS Charlie Lambert, an actress called Saskia Bligh,

was Vince Collier's glamorous (tough but fair, sexy but professional) sidekick. She argued, bullied, cajoled, sprinted and karate-kicked her way through the episode. She was a thin blonde with big, slightly weepy eyes and cheekbones that you could have hung washing on (as his mother would have said). Not Jackson's type. (He had a type? What? The woman from last night? Surely not.) Saskia Bligh looked as if she bruised easily. Jackson liked his women to be robust.

Collier and Lambert. There were just the two of them, Morse and Lewis, Holmes and Watson, a double-handed duo that could solve every murder in the district with only a smidgeon of background help from semi-anonymous techies and uniforms. Jackson would like to see the pair of them work a case in the real world. Julia, in the shape of her character, existed to provide 'a foil for their relationship'. 'It's not about crime, you have to understand,' Julia said. 'It's about them as *people*.'

'They're not real,' Jackson pointed out.

'I know that. Art *renders* reality.'

'Art?' Jackson repeated incredulously. 'You call *Collier* "art"? I thought *rendering* was what you did to dripping.'

'You know what I mean.'

Julia was replacing a previous pathologist, a man. The actor playing him had been caught with child pornography on his computer and had been quietly transformed into a nonce in a prison somewhere. Ironic justice, a form of jurisprudence that Jackson felt a particular fondness for. Cosmic justice was all well and good but generally its wheels took longer to grind.

Vince Collier had recently acquired a mother from nowhere (caring but nagging, sensible but anxious). One of those old actresses who had been around for ever. ('To humanize him,' Julia explained.) Jackson didn't think having a mother 'humanized' (whatever that meant) anyone. Everyone had a mother – murderers, rapists, Hitler, Pol Pot, Margaret Thatcher. ('Well, fiction's stranger than truth,' Julia said.)

The face of Vince Collier's mother was familiar. Jackson tried to remember why but the tiny people who resentfully ran his memory these days (fetching and carrying folders, checking the contents against index cards, filing them away in boxes that were then placed on endless rows of grey metal Dexion shelving never to be found again) had, in an all too frequent occurrence, mislaid that particular piece of information. This sketchy blueprint for the neurological workings of his brain had been laid down in Jackson's childhood by the Numskulls in his *Beezer* comic and he had never really developed a more sophisticated model.

Jackson supposed that other people's small brain-dwelling inhabitants ran their operations rather like air-traffic controllers, always aware of the location of everything they were responsible for, never sloping off for tea breaks or loitering in the shadowy recesses of rarely accessed shelves, where they smoked fly cigarettes and kvetched about their poor working conditions. One day they would simply lay down tools and walk off, of course.

Vince Collier's mother had apparently been misfiled somewhere on the endless Dexion.

Ten-take Tilly, Julia had called her. Jackson had visited her on set, dropped in unexpectedly when he realized he was driving past the place where they filmed *Collier*. 'Poor old thing, her memory's shot to pieces,' Julia said. 'They should have realized that before they took her on. She's going to be killed off soon.'

'Killed off?' Jackson said.

'In the programme.'

They were drinking coffee, sitting in what seemed to be a cowshed, a chilly adjunct to the catering truck, where trestle tables were set up.

'It's not a cowshed, it's a barn,' Julia said.

'Is it real or part of the set?'

'Everything is real,' Julia said. 'On the other hand, of course, you could argue that nothing is real.'

Jackson banged his head on the wooden table. But not in a real way.

Julia was dressed for her part, in blue scrubs, her hair strained into a bun. 'You've always been attracted to women in uniform,' she said.

'Maybe, but I've never had a thing for people who cut up corpses.'

'Never say never,' Julia said.

Jackson wondered where their son was. Neither of them had mentioned him. 'Is Jonathan looking after Nathan?' he asked eventually and Julia shrugged in a non-committal way.

'He either is or he isn't. And don't tell me that he could be doing both at the same time. We're not talking parallel universes here.'

She sighed heavily and said, 'Isn't. I've got a nanny, a local girl. And it's a bit late to worry about the welfare of your son.'

'Well, I haven't worried earlier because you told me he wasn't my son,' Jackson said reasonably.

'I have to go,' she said. 'I've got an autopsy at three o'clock.'

It came to him suddenly. 'Well I never,' Jackson said to the dog. The dog looked at him, waiting for the rest of the sentence. Vince Collier's mother was none other than the confused old woman in the Merrion Centre. 'I knew I'd seen her before. It was the wig that threw me.'

He watched *Collier* to the bitter end. Julia appeared twice ('Dr Beatrice Butler', maternal but savvy, sexy but intellectual – a sketchy version of Julia's own complexity). The first time she was on screen she was attending a murder scene where she estimated the time of death of a mutilated prostitute and then a short time later she was in the mortuary, where she was pretending to cut open the body of the victim. Jackson preferred nature programmes, even at their most blood-thirsty they were preferable to this crap. 'It's very popular,' Julia said. 'Great viewing figures.'

Real murder was disgusting. And smelly and messy and usually heartbreaking, invariably meaningless, occasionally tedious, but not this neat sanitized narrative. And the victims were often prostitutes, dispensable as tissues, both in reality and in fiction.

'Art, my arse,' Jackson muttered to the dog.

He waited for Vince Collier's mother's name to come up on the credits. Marjorie Collier, played by Matilda Squires. 'See, I was right,' he said to the dog. *Ten-take Tilly*. The dog sneezed suddenly, three times in a row, little *chew-chew-chew* sounds that Jackson found oddly (and inexplicably) touching.

He turned the television off and went back to his old friend Google, typing the name 'Marilyn Nettles' into the phone. All he ever did was search for women. He was about to give up when he found something on a site 'dedicated to Yorkshire writers'. *Marilyn Nettles writes under the pen name of Stephanie Dawson. Nettles is a former crime reporter with the* Yorkshire Post *and lives in the historic town of Whitby*. Jackson celebrated with a cup of tea from the hospitality tray. Since this morning everything had been replenished by the chambermaid and he broke open another packet of biscuits and rationed them out between himself and the dog.

'We're in luck,' he said to the dog, tossing it a custard cream. 'Marilyn Nettles, here I come.'

He was just thinking about taking the dog out for his last walk of the day and then turning in early when there was a knock at the door. The dog's ears went on to high alert. 'Room service,' a voice said loudly from the other side of the door.

'I haven't ordered anything on room service,' Jackson said to the dog. He might perhaps have recalled several scenes in films he had watched over the years where a waiter pushes a trolley, cloaked in white linen, into the room, a trolley which turns out to be hiding in its innards anything from a machine-gun to a voluptuous blonde. But Jackson didn't recall any of this, so he opened the door.

'Jesus,' he said when he saw what was on the trolley.

'For me? You shouldn't have.'

The trolley was laden with a silver ice-bucket containing a bottle of Bollinger that was sweating attractively with cold. It all seemed very upmarket for a Best Western. The trolley was in the room before Jackson had the chance to point out the unlikelihood of it being for him. Perhaps a woman was trying to woo him. Not any of the women he'd encountered recently, that was for sure. The waiter – thinning grey hair, crumpled grey skin – looked more like an old-fashioned, mild-mannered serial killer than your usual room-service staff. He spotted the dog on the bed and began to make a tremendous fuss of it. 'Had one of these myself when I was a lad,' he grinned at Jackson. 'Border terrier. Brilliant little dogs. Cheeky little chappies.'

The guy was scratching and tickling the dog to within an inch of its life. The dog looked surprised. It seemed to have a wide range of facial expressions. Its repertoire was probably greater than Jackson's own. He waited to see if the waiter would point out that dogs weren't allowed in the hotel but he didn't, eventually tearing himself away from the dog, saying, 'Would you like me to open this for you, Mr King?'

'Ah,' Jackson said. 'I'm not Mr King, think you've got

the wrong room. Nearly got away with that,' he said and laughed. Ha, ha.

'I wouldn't have said anything,' the waiter said. He grinned and tapped the side of his nose, a gesture that Jackson didn't think he had ever seen outside of an Ealing comedy. 'What you don't know can't hurt you.'

'I would be inclined to say the opposite was true,' Jackson said. 'What you *don't* know *can* hurt you.' They both laughed. Hardly enough space in the room for so much affability. LOL.

'Get you anything else, squire?' the waiter asked, backing the trolley out of the room.

'No. Thank you,' Jackson said. When he had gone Jackson looked at the dog. The dog looked at Jackson. Jackson sighed and sat on the bed next to it. The dog wagged its tail but Jackson said, 'Keep still, there's a good boy,' and ran his finger round the inside of the dog's collar until he found the tracking device. He showed it to the dog. 'Amateurs,' he explained.

One of the things that you definitely didn't do with kids was to drive with them in the back of a car through red-light districts at night, looking for a prostitute. In the badlands, near the junction of Water Lane and Bridge Road, an unmarked squad car from vice prowling for kerb-crawlers cruised past them in the opposite direction. Did they recognize her? Tracy drove sedately on, wondering if they had noticed the kid in the back.

Kelly Cross wanted more money. No surprise there then. The puzzle was how she had got hold of Tracy's mobile number. (*Listen, you fat fucking cow, you had no right to take that kiddy. If you want to keep her you're going to have to fork out a lot more.*) Well, there you go, Tracy thought, wasn't she paying the price of having bought the kid at a discount, as in her heart she'd always known she would have to? And how long would this kind of extortion go on for? Until Courtney was grown up and had kids of her own? Would Kelly last that long? She didn't really belong to a demographic that boasted of longevity. It would be much better if Kelly Cross died – a bad batch of heroin, a psycho punter – who would miss her, after all? *That kiddy*, Kelly Cross said. Not *my kiddy*. Although mothers like Kelly were pretty un-interested in their kids. Weren't they?

All the lovely places. Bridge End, Sweet Street West, Bath Road. A wasteland. Literally. No one to hear you scream. A couple of prostitutes on the swing shift, huddled up against a wall. Offhand, smoking fags like connoisseurs. One was raddled by life, the other one looked underage, shivering, glassy skin, coming down off something. *Pretty Woman* it ain't, Tracy thought. Tracy wondered if they were mother and daughter. They were on the job, she wasn't any more, she reminded herself.

As Tracy brought the car to a halt her phone rang.

Barry. Oh, for God's sake. The only way to stop him was to speak to him.

'Where *are* you?' he asked when she answered, sounding unnecessarily peeved, like a husband.

'Bath Road,' she said, watching as the younger of the two women began tottering towards her car. Thigh-high boots with hooker heels, short denim cut-offs, little strappy vest, nasty jacket.

'What are you doing there?' Barry puzzled.

'Looking for someone. What do you want?'

'Did you get my messages about this Jackson bloke?'

'Yes, I've got no idea who he is,' Tracy said.

'Want me to do something about it?' Barry asked. The echo of Harry Reynolds's words to her earlier. She rolled down the car window and the young prostitute, more child than woman, looked confused at the sight of her. 'You looking for business?' she asked doubtfully.

'Yeah,' Tracy said. She produced a twenty-pound note like a lure and said, 'Different kind of business.'

'Tracy?' Barry said. 'What are you up to?'

'Nothing.'

'I didn't say but this Jackson bloke, whoever he is, asked about Carol Braithwaite.'

'Carol Braithwaite? Look, I've got to go, Barry. I'll phone you later.' She snapped the phone shut and shouted, 'Hang on,' to the girl who had taken the money and was about to scarper. She returned reluctantly to the car and was joined by the older woman who, catching sight of Tracy, said, 'Trace, 'ow yer doing?'

'Bloody brilliant,' Tracy said. 'Quiet tonight, isn't it?'

'Recession. And we're being undercut all the time by crack-whores. There's girls offering full strip and sex for ten quid. It's a different world, Tracy.' It was what Barry had said, what Harry Reynolds had said. Tracy thought she must be missing something, it felt like the same world as ever to her. The rich getting richer, the poor getting poorer, kids everywhere falling through the cracks. The Victorians would have recognized it. People just watched a lot more TV and found celebrities interesting, that was all that was different.

'Yeah, terrible,' Tracy said. 'Everything discounted. I'm actually looking for Kelly Cross.'

'Me mam?' the younger one said.

Jesus, Tracy thought. Would the circle never be broken? She was acutely aware of Courtney in the back. Was this her half-sister? Was this the fate Courtney would have been destined for if Tracy hadn't rescued her? The older woman – Liz, if Tracy's memory served her – peered into the back of the car.

'Yours?' she asked Tracy, sucking thoughtfully on her cigarette.

'Not exactly,' Tracy said. Not much reason for dissembling with this pair, what were they going to do – stagger off to the nearest police officer and grass her up?

'Nice outfit, pet,' Liz said to Courtney, who in reply made a papal kind of gesture with her silver wand.

'Do you recognize her?' Tracy asked. All three of them scrutinized the kid in the back seat. She was halfway through an apple and paused mid-bite. Rosy red, eaten by Snow White. The apple and the wand, the orb and sceptre of her sovereign regalia.

'No, sorry,' Liz said.

'Nah,' the younger one said, to Tracy's relief.

'Have you got a name?' Tracy said to her.

'Nah.'

Tracy looked at the girl. A *fille de joie* who was forty times more likely to die a violent death than the fellow members of her sex. What could you do? Nothing.

'No, go on really,' Tracy said, 'what's your name?'

'Chevaunne. C-h-e-v-a-u-n-n-e, I have to spell it every time, it's a fucking pain. It's Irish.' At least the girl could spell, even if it was only her own misspelled name. Kelly Cross was so thick she couldn't even spell 'Siobhan'. Kelly's mother had been Irish. Fionnula. Tracy had been around so long that she'd seen three generations of prostitutes pass her by. 'A right Gyppo,' Barry used to say. Gypsies and Irish were interchangeable as far as Barry was concerned, both equally bad.

Tracy turned her attention to Liz. 'Can you give me an address for Kelly?'

'She *was* in Hunslet.'

'Harehills,' Chevaunne butted in. 'But it'll cost you.'

Tracy handed over another twenty-pound note in exchange for Kelly Cross's address. 'Now fuck off, the pair of you,' she said.

A grey Avensis turned into Bath Road, pulled off the road in front of them and parked on the forecourt of an abandoned warehouse of some kind, a blighted piece of real estate. Seemed a mite coincidental. Tracy looked for

the pink rabbit but the car was too far away for her to
see.

'Ey up,' Liz said and the *belles de jour* teetered off
again, towards the Avensis.

'*That*'s a grey car,' Courtney said helpfully.

'Yeah, I see it, pet.'

Tracy parked in the alley that ran along the back of the
street. Killed the engine, climbed out of the car and
unstrapped Courtney. The last place she wanted to take
the kid was Kelly Cross's house but what choice did she
have – she could hardly leave her alone in the back of a
car in a seedy alley. From the first moment she saw Kelly
Cross in the Merrion Centre yesterday it seemed Tracy
had done nothing but make choices, an endless series of
forks in the road. Sooner or later she was going to hit a
dead end. If she hadn't already.

Kelly was the only thing that linked Tracy to
Courtney. Get rid of Kelly and you broke the chain of
evidence leading back to Tracy. Then it would just be
Imogen and her little girl Lucy. No need for Tracy to
look over her shoulder for the rest of her life. Kill Kelly
Cross. Even the alliteration was alluring. Her heart
started to thud uncomfortably in her chest. Get rid of
the link between Kelly and the kid, between Kelly and
herself. Forge a new terrible bond but get rid of Kelly
Cross's claims on them. Who was better placed to
commit a murder properly than the police?

The door to Kelly's back yard was open. The yard was
small and claustrophobically full of rubbish – an old

washing machine, a filthy armchair, black bin bags containing God knows what. The windows of the house were filthy, cracked, full of powdery, fly-filled cobwebs. There was a piece of paper sellotaped on to the peeling paintwork of the back door that spelled out 'Cross' in a semi-literate hand. The door itself looked as if it had been kicked in a few times. Tracy sighed. She had spent a working lifetime knocking on doors like this.

And getting no answer.

She knocked again, louder this time, a police knock. Nothing. She gave the door a tentative push and it swung open. This was always an ominous moment in TV thrillers – nothing good was ever discovered behind the open door – but in Tracy's experience all it usually meant was that someone had forgotten to lock up.

The door opened straight into the kitchen. She took a cautious step inside and said, 'Kelly?' She was half expecting Kelly to fly out of nowhere screaming like a banshee. She took another couple of steps and realized that Courtney was on her heels as if they were playing a game of statues. 'Stay there, pet, OK?' Tracy said. Tracy took another couple of steps into the kitchen, the kid still following. Tracy pulled a chair out from the table and said, 'Sit down. Don't touch anything.'

Tracy put the light on. No one ever switched the light on either in TV crime thrillers. For the atmosphere, Tracy supposed. She could live without atmosphere. The whole kitchen was a health hazard. The flickering fluorescent light illuminated foil takeaway cartons, dirty pots and pans, rotten food, sour milk, a top note of alcohol and fags.

'Kelly?' Tracy said again, advancing into the hallway. Tracy switched on lights as she went. It was twilight outside but the house contained a deeper kind of dusk.

A small room at the back. Completely full of boxes, their insides spilling out, mostly clothes that looked only fit for shoddy. The second room was a living room, if you could call it that. About as bad as a room could get. Old fag packets, dirty plates and more takeaway cartons. Empty bottles and cans, a syringe poking out from beneath the sofa cushion, everything soiled and unsanitary. Tracy had read reports about Leeds from the nineteenth century, the poverty, the awful conditions of the industrial poor. Knee-deep in ordure. Not much different here.

No sign of a child in the house, Tracy noted, no clothes or toys or DVDs. Reluctantly, she made her way up the steep, narrow staircase. There were three doors to choose from, all of them closed. Like a fairy story. Or a nightmare. Tracy had a flashback to Lovell Park again, Ken Arkwright putting in the door with his shoulder. The smell that was released, the flies . . .

The bathroom was disgusting. Surely Kelly couldn't bring her clients back here? Even the least discerning of punters might jib at entering this den of iniquity.

The second door led to a small bedroom. Completely empty. Nothing, just fluff, dust, scraps of foil, stray polystyrene chips like albino Quavers on the bare boards.

Only one door remained. Tracy hesitated, recoiling

from the possibility of interrupting Kelly in the middle of providing services for one of her less selective patrons. She rapped loudly on the door and said, 'Kelly? Kelly, it's Tracy. Tracy Waterhouse.' When there was no answer she warily pushed the door open.

The offal and sewage smell of death was everywhere. Even Tracy's tough police ticker missed a beat. Kelly Cross was sprawled on the bed, her head mashed in, her belly slashed open. She looked as if she was in her work uniform, a tiny black skirt and a silver-sequinned halter top. Some of the sequins were scattered on the bed, glinting like fish scales in the harsh overhead light.

Tracy put two fingers against Kelly Cross's neck. No pulse. She didn't know why she was checking, as it was glaringly obvious that Kelly was dead. She was still warm. Tracy preferred her dead bodies to be cold.

Kelly Cross was dead. Tracy had got what she had wished for. It suggested a dark magic at work if Tracy's thoughts could be translated so fast. Tracy didn't believe in magic. She believed in darkness though.

She had seen worse in the past, although that didn't make the foul tableau in front of her eyes any less repugnant. No time to be shocked, however. Think like the police or think like a criminal? Tracy wondered. Turned out, as she had previously expected, that it was pretty much the same, but in reverse. She rooted in her bag for a tissue and wiped all the door handles and jambs. Shame she hadn't got round to buying the Wet Wipes yet. She had probably left trace evidence behind, a hair, a flake of skin, a scale of fish. A trace of Tracy.

Had the kid touched anything? Courtney was still waiting dutifully in the kitchen. Did she suspect anything? Her expression was, as usual, unreadable.

'Come on, pet,' Tracy said, her voice cracking with the effort of sounding inanely cheerful. 'Time to go home.'

The kid dipped the wand, a magisterial blessing on the house of the dead. She slipped off the chair and Tracy shepherded her out of the house. 'Let's get back in the car, Courtney.'

'It's Lucy,' the kid reminded her.

Courtney was asleep by the time Tracy pulled up in the lane at the back of her house. No tarmac, just a cinder-type covering, felt almost rural. It led to a row of rented lock-ups that served as handy garages for some of the car owners in the street. Tracy yanked open the door on her own lock-up and reversed into the empty space like a precision driver, killed the engine, rested her forehead on the steering wheel. She thought she might throw up.

Courtney woke with a start and said, 'What happened?'

'You fell asleep,' Tracy said. 'Nothing happened while you were asleep. We moved on a little in space and time, that's all. We're home. Have another apple.' Bananas were all gone now.

The kid gave the eating of the apple a lot of attention, as if she was studying to become a professional apple eater. The thought of ingesting anything made Tracy feel queasy. She couldn't wait to step in the shower and scrub off the smell of death that had followed her from Harehills and lingered like a foul aura.

'Come on then.' She sighed and opened the car door.

Courtney went to bed still wearing the pink fairy costume, refused to take it off. Tracy didn't care, she hadn't been in a maternal role long enough to have acquired any rules.

The kid's treasure was laid out on the bed and she began to pack it away. When she got to the fortune cookie she stared at it for a while as if it was going to crack open on its own.

'You have to break it,' Tracy said. The kid stared at her. 'Trust me,' Tracy said. The kid smashed it with her fist.

'Yeah, that'll do it,' Tracy said.

The kid removed the slip of paper from the debris of crumbs and handed it silently to Tracy to read.

'*The treasure here is you*,' Tracy read out loud.

The kid reached over and patted Tracy's hand. 'And you,' she said, sympathetic to Tracy's exclusion from good fortune.

'I don't think so somehow,' Tracy said.

'You have it,' Courtney said and Tracy tucked the slip of paper in her bra, a good luck charm. 'Hang on a minute,' she said and went downstairs. She came back with Dorothy Waterhouse's engagement ring which she'd shoved to the back of the dresser drawer. 'Real treasure,' she said, adding it to the contents of the backpack.

'Yes,' Courtney said. 'Real treasure.'

*   *   *

Princess Courtney went on another adventure, a rather dauntless one involving wolves and axes and porridge-eating bears. 'I don't like wolves,' Courtney said.

'Me neither,' Tracy said. 'But we're all right, they've been banned from Leeds.' If only.

Once Courtney was asleep, Tracy rummaged suitcases out of the hall cupboard, hauled them into her bedroom and stuffed them with Courtney's new Gap wardrobe and anything of her own that came to hand. Added another bag of toys. Took the supermarket bags out of the boot of the Audi and replaced them with the suitcases, put the supermarket bags in the back of the car. She'd sort them out when she got there. Everything probably inedible by now. 'There,' she said to herself. 'All ready for the off, first thing.' She sounded deranged. She sounded like her mother getting ready for the annual holiday in Bridlington.

Tracy checked on Courtney. The kid was fast asleep, snoring gently. A piglet, a kitten.

There was no Beck's left – how did that happen? So Tracy made do with half a bottle of Chardonnay she found in the fridge, left over from who knew when. The wine looked like urine and didn't taste much better. She could feel it roiling like acid in her stomach. Found half a packet of crisps hiding at the back of the cupboard and munched her way through them without tasting them.

When she turned on the TV the end credits for *Collier* were just scrolling.

❦

Dropped off in front of the telly. She had been watching *Britain's Got Talent* and then she must have fallen asleep because the next thing Tilly knew she'd woken herself up with her own snoring. *Pnorr, pnorrr, pnorrrgh!* She jerked awake, felt her heart trip. These little evening snoozes were going to be the death of her.

She was confused. What was on the box now seemed real, not television at all. There was Saskia aiming a gun at someone and shouting, 'Drop it or I'll shoot!' but she could hear Saskia moving about upstairs in the bathroom, the sound of running water. She was forever saying how dirty the cottage was and did Tilly actually know how to clean. 'Filth everywhere,' she said. For some reason Tilly imagined filth as a person, a man in an old-fashioned brown mackintosh, greasy and stained – a trilby shading his face. He lurked around a corner, waiting to jump out and flash her. Tilly had encountered a few like that in Soho in the old days, hanging round the back of the mucky bookshops and the strip joints. She had been propositioned a couple of times too. Tilly hadn't been tempted, even when she was hungry for a crust. She knew for a fact that Phoebe, Dame Phoebe, had gone off for a weekend on a yacht with some rich nabob. The man looked like a frog. She came back with diamonds. Draw your own conclusions.

Yesterday Saskia had silently presented Tilly with a mat of soapy hair from the bath plughole. Enough to make a wig from. She was holding the hair on a piece of loo roll as if it was a dangerous spider about to attack her. 'I don't know,' she said, 'maybe you could, um, clear up after yourself?'

It was just a bit of hair, for heaven's sake. People were funny about things like that. Phoebe couldn't abide toe-nails, her own or other people's. That woman went for a pedicure every single month, never cut her own toe-nails, not once! 'Nanny used to do it for me,' she said, when they were first living in Soho.

Tilly took the hair reluctantly from Saskia. 'Oh dear, I appear to be moulting,' she said, trying to muster some dignity.

And then suddenly Tilly was looking at herself, as if the television were a mirror. A cruel, distorting mirror. She looked terrible. Overweight, mad. That awful Brillo wig. Of course, she was watching *Collier*, she realized that. She hadn't entirely lost her marbles. Yet.

On screen, she was pottering around a kitchen, putting a roast dinner in front of Vince Collier, telling him he didn't eat properly, that he needed to settle down with a nice girl. Tilly had never made a roast dinner in her life. 'Don't nag, Mum,' Vince said. 'You know you're the only woman for me.'

To be honest, she didn't look well. Intimations of mortality. Time's wingèd chariot and all that. She wasn't ready to die yet. She imagined Phoebe giving the oration at her funeral, talking about her 'dear friend', everyone sad for five minutes. She would be a footnote for a few years and then nothing. An unsatisfactory afterlife on Alibi and ITV3. Mind you, she had, apparently, already joined the ranks of the might-be-deads. There was a woman on set the other day, Tilly had no idea who she was, a journalist probably – middle-aged, the gushy sort, wide-eyed and faux-innocent. When she was introduced to Tilly she said, 'Gosh, I thought you were dead!' Just like that. How rude.

'Don't worry, Till,' Julia said. 'I put a nasty curse on her. She'll be dead long before you.'

Julia was nice, like a normal person. More or less. Knew how to have a conversation, didn't just talk *at* you, like everyone else seemed to do. And Julia always had something interesting to say, which is more than you could say for poor Saskia who, when it came right down to it, was only interested in herself. Her photo had been in the *Mail* last week, awful rag, on the arm of a man – some rugby player – coming out of a restaurant. '*Collier* star Saskia Bligh.' Showed it to everyone. Twittering on about it. Twitter! Her phone was never out of her hand. She twittered, she said, 'Do you?' Showed Tilly on her phone. A technological step too far. Tilly didn't even know how to turn a computer on, wrong generation, of course. Twittering just seemed to be people telling other people what they were doing – getting in the shower, making coffee. Who on earth wanted to know these things?

'Tweets,' Saskia said. Well exactly. Babble and twitter. Full of sound and fury, signifying nothing. People couldn't cope with empty space any more, they had to fill it up with anything that came to hand. There was a time when people kept their thoughts to themselves. Tilly liked that time. They had a blue budgerigar when she was small. Tweety-pie. It was hard to be fond of a budgerigar. Her father accidentally stood on it. Her mother said she didn't see how you could stand on a budgerigar. Too late now to get to the bottom of what had really happened. Tilly wanted to bury it but Father put it on the fire. A pyre. She could still see its little body, the feathers flaring. She hadn't particularly liked the bird but she had felt sorry for it and gave some time over to crying for it. Shame. Tilly didn't want to be cremated. Thrown on the fire. She should write that down somewhere, make a will, make it clear. She'd had a horror of fire ever since Hull was bombed when she was a child. Although, of course, being buried alive would be no fun either.

Marjorie Collier was knitting now, waiting for Vince to phone her. The camera kept well away from the actual knitting. Tilly had no idea how to knit so she did a lot of sighing and resting of the needles on her lap. She was pleased with how convincing it looked. It was all pretence. Acting was, let's face it, just plain daft. Everything was daft these days. Everything was pretence. Nothing was real any more. Baseless fabric. And so on.

* * *

Came to with a start again and struggled into a sitting position and put the bedside light on. Clambered out of bed, shuffled into her slippers and went downstairs. Sat for a while at the table, she was sure she was looking for something but she couldn't remember what. There was a fruit bowl on the table, apples and bananas rotting quietly. Saskia never ate and Tilly forgot to. She'd offered Saskia a Polo mint yesterday and she recoiled as if Tilly was peddling heroin.

She was hungry. Fancied something delicious. Douglas used to take her for afternoon tea at the Dorchester sometimes. Lovely.

Surely something could be done about the little suffering children. All of them. Tilly would lead a crusade, the children's crusade, no, that was something different, wasn't it? Fighting the infidel. You still saw it, boy soldiers in Africa, she'd seen a programme on the telly. It used to be the Arabs who were the infidels, now it was us. She picked up an apple, the skin was wrinkled and it felt soft in her hand. Decomposing. That was what was happening to her mind. It was decomposing.

'Jesus, Tilly,' Saskia said. 'What are you doing?'

'I am baking,' Tilly announced grandly. 'In fact, I am making a cake.'

'You're covered in flour,' Saskia said. 'The kitchen's covered in flour. Every single pot and pan is out. It looks like a bomb's gone off in here.'

'Oh no, I can assure you bombs make much more mess,' Tilly said. 'I was in Hull, you know, during the war.'

'Do you know what time it is, Tilly?'

Tilly looked at the kitchen clock. 'It's three o'clock,' she said helpfully. Teatime. A nice pot of tea and a dainty slice of cake would go down a treat. Mother was a good baker, an excellent pastry hand and made lovely sponge cakes, soft as clouds. Mother despaired of Tilly in the kitchen. *You'll never get a husband if you can't cook.* Well, she'd show her. Invite her round for tea and—

'Three in the *morning*, Tilly,' Saskia said crossly. 'Three o'clock in the *morning*.'

'Ah,' Tilly murmured. 'I thought it was awfully dark.' She found that she had tears running down her demented old cheeks. It was the beginning of the end.

He fell asleep and then woke from a nightmare. In the nightmare he was being chased by a torso, the headless, limbless body of a woman, part Venus de Milo, part dressmaker's dummy. Jackson knew that really it was his sister. It was always his sister. She might be incorporeal now but she lived vividly in his dreams.

Jackson's sister had been saving up for a dummy when she died. Niamh had made a lot of her own clothes. Jackson could still remember the evening dress she had been making for herself for her firm's Christmas do. She had come to Leeds to buy the emerald-green satin material. The dress was knee-length and she had stood on the kitchen table in the shoes she planned to wear and made Jackson pin up the hem. He had circled around her, measuring from the table-top to her knee, using the smooth triangle of tailor's chalk from her sewing basket to mark the dress with little crosses.

He had experienced a strange, intimate acquaintance with both the emerald satin and his sister's legs encased in fine-denier stockings. Their mother, not one given to compliments, never having received any herself, used to comment occasionally on Niamh's lovely figure and shapely legs. Jackson's mother, their father said, had legs like bedposts. If their mother hadn't been dead for six months she would have been the one pinning up the hem. 'A girl needs her mother,' Niamh said, and because she was sad he didn't say, 'So does a boy.' And anyway she knew that.

'This will be easier when I have a dummy,' she said, twirling around, trying to see the hem. Jackson thought a dummy was something that you sucked. Or one of his brother's friends. 'No,' Niamh laughed, 'a dressmaker's dummy. You adjust it so it has your measurements.'

The dress wasn't finished when she died, the hem still tacked with big white stitches. It hung on the back of her bedroom door, flat and limp without her body to inhabit it, as if she had suddenly been made invisible. Which she had, of course. Jackson's brother, Francis, said, 'Shame she didn't finish it, she would have liked to have been buried in it.' And then he said, 'What t'fuck am I talking about, Jackson? *Shame?* What kind of a nancy word is that? Shame she's dead, more like,' and he threw the dress on the fire where it burned up so much more quickly than Jackson would have expected. Too quickly, certainly, for him to snatch it back from the flames.

Jackson had gone to view Niamh's body in the undertakers. She was wearing a shroud like an old-fashioned nightdress. It came right up to her chin so you couldn't see the marks on her neck where she'd been strangled. Nonetheless her face looked wrong, as if the corpse was pretending to be his sister and not making a very good job of it. The shroud wasn't something she would have chosen to wear. His sister liked smart, old-fashioned clothes, high heels, soft sweaters, knee-length pencil skirts.

He had had a couple of old photographs in which she didn't look like herself either, but not in the same way that her corpse had felt alien. He didn't know what had happened to the photographs. Gone in the fire, he assumed. When he lived in Cambridge, after Josie left him, his house had been destroyed by an explosion. (Again, the résumé of his life more exciting than the extended version.)

Niamh would have looked much nicer buried in that green dress. Nobody would have been able to see that it wasn't finished.

When he left home a handful of years after her death, the only thing of his sister's that Jackson still had in his possession was a small pottery wishing well that said, 'Wishing you Well from Scarborough'. Niamh had been on a day trip with a group of friends and had brought it back for him. Presents were all the more precious for being almost unheard of in his family. The British Museum had intact pots that had survived for thousands of years but not a shard of the wishing well remained now, the explosion having taken care of that too.

He lay awake, staring at the ceiling, knowing that sleep would be a long time returning. He wondered what the woman he slept with last night was doing at that moment. Perhaps she was out on the town again with her gaggle of friends, or, more probably, she was at home with the owner of the skateboard, fast asleep having sorted out packed lunches and school uniforms, preparing for another working day. Jackson felt a stab of guilt that he hadn't said goodbye, but had slipped away like a fox from a henhouse. Although what difference would it have made? Really?

From the other bed came a companionable kind of canine snoring from his new partner. Let sleeping dogs lie, he thought.

His phone buzzed and he fumbled for the light by the bed.

It was a message from Hope McMaster in tomorrow's world – *OMG, where did you get that photo?! It's me, I'm sure of it. HAVE YOU FOUND OUT SOMETHING?? WHO AM I??!!!!*

Not yet, he replied, rather tersely. *Sit tight, don't get excited.* He didn't want to be responsible for Hope McMaster going into a premature labour brought on by exclamation marks. Jackson realized, rather late in the day, that perhaps he shouldn't have drip-fed information to her, allowing her anxiety room to bloom as each new mystery revealed itself. Better to have presented the whole thing at the end, tied up with a big red satin ribbon – *Surprise, you are in fact a true descendant of the Romanovs!* (And no, this had never happened to one of Jackson's clients.) The way things were going, he would never be able to tell Hope McMaster who she was, only who she wasn't.

∽

'. . . so it's a late finish for us all and it's going to be an early start tomorrow and most of us won't know the difference because we'll be working through. I just want to bring you up to speed on where we are now. If there's some of you here who haven't met me before, I'm DI Gemma Holroyd and I'm the SIO on this case.'

Barry lolled carelessly against the back wall of the incident room and closed his eyes. Two murders in two days. Same MO. Same-ish. He had two weeks to go before he was out of this place. He didn't want to leave a mess behind. Clean pair of heels. Shut the door, last person in the building turn off the light. Goodbye to the Homicide and Major Enquiry Team.

'To recap, Kelly Anne Cross, forty-one years old, was found at approximately ten p.m. this evening by a neighbour. Rough estimate from the pathologist puts time of death somewhere between seven and nine, we'll have a more accurate time after the autopsy. There's a bit of a queue, I'm afraid, we're still processing the murder of Rachel Hardcastle whose body was found in a skip in Mabgate yesterday evening, a suspected arson in Hunslet, and a three-car pile-up on the inner ring road.

'There's no question that the lady was murdered, however. It was a vicious attack, she appears to have been punched in the head as well as having knife wounds to the chest and abdomen. No sign of any weapon on the premises. Similar but not the *same* MO as Rachel Hardcastle,' she said, with unnecessary exaggeration. Barry didn't have to open his eyes to know she was staring pointedly at him. Wouldn't give her the satisfaction of opening them.

'Rachel Hardcastle, the lady in the Mabgate skip, and Kelly Cross were both known prostitutes. Lots of prints at Kelly Cross's murder scene, lots of DNA, all being processed. I'm sure the lab will have useful information for us tomorrow.

'From the house-to-house we haven't got much yet, not a lot in the way of CCTV in that area, car registrations haven't turned up anything. Preliminary report back on the blood pattern . . .'

Barry tuned out. She was efficient, he'd give her that. Neat suit, neat hair, proper shoes, plenty of make-up, not like some of the butch lezzies you saw around. Strangely, the woman she reminded him most of was his wife. But then, all women did. Perhaps not Tracy.

He'd been planning on making Gemma Holroyd SIO on the next big case anyway, even without Tracy's prompting.

He had gone down to Kelly Cross's squalid dump of a house, sat in the incident van, second time in twenty-four hours. Barry remembered Kelly Cross's mother, couldn't recall her name, something Irish. A real piece of work, but good for a quick knee-trembler up a dark alley. Those were the days. Different days, different Barry. He sometimes wondered if he had his time over again and lived his life like a saint – would it make a difference? No drinking, no smoking, no swearing, no dishonesty or immorality, no whores. He could join a public library, take Barbara out to dinner, buy her flowers. Change nappies, heat bottles and try and come home every night in time to read Amy a bedtime story. He would even try to give Barbara a hand with the housework. Then maybe, just maybe, he would clock up so many Brownie points that the universe would give him a pass and Amy wouldn't climb into a little tin can of a two-door car with her drunken husband at the wheel and her baby in the back.

In fact, maybe it would just have been easier if he had ripped his chest open the day that his daughter was born and offered up his heart as a sacrifice on an altar somewhere. And then everything would be all right. Oh, and Carol Braithwaite. He would have to tell the truth about her as well. Just to make things right. You had to make everything right before you went.

Barry sucked in air through his mouth. Drowning in

air. He was in his last days. The empire crumbling, the barbarians at the gate. Not barbarians, just shiny smart-arses with degrees in criminology.

'Anything concrete to link the two murders?' he'd asked the Holroyd girl.

'Both women. Both dead, boss,' she said. She obviously didn't like him but then not many people did.

'Do we know if there's anything to connect your victim to the Mabgate whore?' he asked. 'Did they know each other?'

'"The Mabgate whore",' she said. 'Sounds like a character in a revenge tragedy.'

Barry knew bugger all about revenge tragedy. Never wanted to, thank you. He knew a lot about tragedy though. And revenge was coming, he could smell it on the wind. Carol Braithwaite ascending, a cloud of bone and ash, looking for justice. *Risen from the grave*, Tracy said.

'Someone is asking questions,' Linda Pallister had said on the phone. 'What should I do?'

'I'd keep my mouth shut if I were you,' Barry said. *Keep your mouth shut.* That wasn't the right answer, was it? Spill the beans, tell the truth. Silence for thirty-five years and now her name was on everyone's lips.

'. . . did she usually take punters back to her house?' Gavin Archer asked. 'Didn't she work the streets?' Archer was a DC. Lean and bespectacled, he came into work on a racing bike in the full Lycra scrotum-squeezing clobber, although he never raced, just commuted from the boxy, thin-walled house in Moortown that he shared with his pregnant wife. Another clever bugger.

'We're intending to . . .'

There'd been a lot of blood. Even watching the video in the incident van outside Barry could see that. Gemma whatshername had got everyone off the mark quickly. Inside the house there had been a photographer, two SOCOs, two forensic scientists, pathologist was ten minutes away. Two family liaison officers, looking for life antecedents. Good luck with that. Everyone in the house zipped and booted in bunny suits. All for a dead prostitute.

On the video screen Barry had watched the biologist tracing a blood pattern. When he first started in the police they used to wander all over crime scenes like they were out for a walk in the park.

'Someone didn't like her,' Gemma said, standing next to him in the incident van.

'That usually is at the root of murder,' Barry said.

'. . . so anyway if we can all be back here at seven a.m. sharp tomorrow for the briefing. Thanks, everyone.'

The incident room emptied, a stream of tired but eager people flowing past him. Barry felt ill, a heart attack walking. Needed a drink. He'd been needing a drink all day. All week. The last two years. The anniversary. You would think it would get better with time but it just got worse. Sam was still in his pushchair when he was killed, now he'd be toddling around, maybe having a stumbling game of kickabout with Barry. And his daughter, in limbo, because none of them could bear to talk about turning off the life support.

He should be coasting towards the end, clearing up paperwork, handing over to his successor, attending a valedictory bash or two. Had something been arranged? No sign of anything. Tracy had joked that there wasn't one but it was unlikely. A surprise party perhaps. He couldn't think of anything worse. Tracy's farewell piss-up had already acquired legendary status. Everyone liked Tracy, although a lot of them had liked to pretend that they didn't.

'Detective Superintendent Crawford. Did you want something?'

'Sorry, DI Hardcastle, I fell asleep there. Bedtime story too long, I guess.'

'It's Holroyd actually, boss, Gemma Holroyd. Rachel Hardcastle is the woman who was murdered on Wednesday night. The Mabgate whore,' she added sarcastically for his benefit.

His phone rang. Strickland. No surprise there then. Carol Braithwaite in her rising pulling them all out of their hidey-holes.

'Barry? How's things?' Ray Strickland said.

'Things are things,' Barry said.

'Just phoning to see if you were coming to the golf club dinner-dance tomorrow night.'

'Golf club dinner-dance,' Barry repeated, trying to

make sense of the words. A vague memory of some fifty-quid-a-head fundraiser that he'd been press-ganged into buying a ticket for. Strickland, Lomax, they never stopped, Len Lomax the worst. They couldn't hack being retired, losing their power, so they spent their time on charity boards, fundraising committees, magistrates' panels, keeping their names alive in the press and the community. They weren't doing good works, they were just denying their impotence. The nearest Barry intended to come to charity when he retired was buying a Remembrance poppy.

'Yes,' Strickland said patiently, 'dinner-dance. Are you coming?'

He couldn't sleep. Barbara, next to him in sponge rollers and greasy face, was snoring. He thought about taking some of her sleeping pills. Maybe all of them. Taking the easy way out rather than the hard way. He'd just managed to fall into an unsatisfactory doze when the phone rang. Barbara made a noise in her sleep, the low moan of a wounded animal. Bedside clock said five thirty. Wasn't going to be good news, was it?

'Another murder, boss,' Gemma Holroyd said.

'This one a working girl as well? And don't tell me you're all working girls.'

'Are we? We don't have a positive ID yet. She was found in the doorway of the Cottage Road Cinema in Headingley. Head wounds, stabbed.'

'Well, you know what they say. One's unfortunate, two's a coincidence, three's a serial killer.'

'I don't think we should jump to conclusions, boss.'

'Faster you jump to conclusions sooner you get to the end.'

'Anyway if they are related sounds more like a spree.'

'All just words, killing's killing.'

He put the phone down and lay on his back and stared at the ceiling. Leeds and dead prostitutes. Don't use the 'R' word. He turned to Barbara and patted her back. 'Want a cup of tea, love?'

He could do without a trio of dead women on his plate. If there were no women, men wouldn't kill them. That would be one solution to the problem.

Carol Braithwaite. Wondered where that kiddy was. Locked in that flat for weeks with the mother's body. Barry couldn't remember his name. Tracy had banged on about him for months. Michael. That was it. Michael Braithwaite.

1975: 10 April

The next day on the kiddies' ward. Uncomfortable place to be. Tracy touched the little hand, slack in sleep, with the back of hers. 'Michael,' she said softly.

Tracy had considered taking him a teddy bear but thought that perhaps he was too old for a soft toy. When they broke into the Lovell Park flat he had been clutching a blue-and-white police car as if his life depended on it, so she bought him a fire engine instead. Tucked it in beside him. He was hollow-eyed and hollow-cheeked but he looked peaceful in repose. They reckoned he'd been in the flat with his mother's body for nearly three weeks. He had been unable to unlock the front door. No one had seen him standing on a chair at the fifteenth-floor window, waving to attract attention. He had lived off what food there was in the house – Carol Braithwaite had been to the supermarket that afternoon, there were unpacked shopping bags in the kitchen. After that, he'd pulled packets of dry food from cupboards, drunk water from the tap. It was freezing in the flat. He'd fed the meter with coins from his mother's purse until the coins ran out.

He'd pulled a blanket over his mother to keep her warm. Tracy supposed that at first he must have slept next to her. By the time they broke in he was sleeping in a den he had made from a nest of cushions and blankets in the living room. 'Tough little bugger,' Lomax said. Perhaps he was a boy used to fending for himself. All this reported to her third-hand by Arkwright.

Linda Pallister appeared suddenly at the opposite side of the hospital bed as if she'd been lurking nearby. 'You again,' she said to Tracy by way of greeting.

'Want to get a cuppa?' Tracy said. 'In the canteen? Human being to human being?'

They drank weak, stewed tea. Tracy had picked up a large Kit Kat while Linda chose a sour-looking apple. Tea and apples didn't go together, everyone knew that.

'What's going to happen to that poor kiddy now?'

Tracy asked, snapping her Kit Kat into four fingers and already lamenting their finish before she'd even begun eating them.

'He'll be discharged, eventually, and go to a foster home,' Linda said, biting into her green apple. 'There aren't any relatives.' Big horsey teeth, would have made a good herbivore.

'What about his father?' Tracy asked and Linda Pallister raised an eyebrow and said, 'Isn't one.'

'Can I talk to someone about the kiddy?' Tracy asked.

'You are talking to someone,' Linda said. 'You're talking to me.'

'You know he witnessed his mother's murder, don't you?' *Chomp-chomp-chomp*, mechanically eating her apple. 'He told me his father killed his mother,' Tracy persisted. 'CID just dismissed it.'

'He's four years old,' Linda said. 'He doesn't know what's real and what's a fairy tale. Kids lie, it's just what they do.' There was a pause while her – rather piggy – little eyes seemed to assess Tracy. 'A man he *thinks* of as his father,' she added, tapping a folder in front of her on the table. 'Carol didn't know who his father was.'

The manila folder had a label in one corner, the name 'Carol Braithwaite' typed on it.

'She was already a client?' Tracy asked, touching the folder. Linda slammed her hand down on it as if Tracy was about to prise it open with her eyes.

'Miss Braithwaite was known to Social Services,' she said primly.

'What for?'

'I can't talk about individual clients.' She stood up abruptly, clamping the manila folder to her chest.

'You knew the kid was at risk?' Tracy said, standing up as well, aware of how much taller than Linda Pallister she was. 'Maybe if you'd visited you would have found Michael a bit sooner. Before he spent three weeks locked in a flat with his mother's corpse.'

Tracy had a sudden flashback to Linda Pallister taking the boy off her in the flat to give to the ambulance men. She held him high on one hip so that he was facing over her shoulder and his eyes locked on to Tracy's as he was being carried away. Tracy felt as if he had reached in and scooped something out of her soul. She shuddered at the memory.

'I have a very heavy caseload,' Linda Pallister said defensively. 'Every case is assessed on its individual merits. And now, if you don't mind, I have to go.'

'Look,' Tracy said, taking out a Biro, 'let me write down my phone number.' She prised the folder from Linda Pallister's grip and said, 'Not going to look inside, honestly.' She wrote 'WPC Tracy Waterhouse' on Carol Braithwaite's file and her home phone number.

'This is my phone number,' Tracy said. 'If you ring, my mum will probably answer, but just talk her down. OK?' She added the date to make it seem more official. 'Just, you know, to keep in touch.'

'Keep in touch?'

'About the kiddy. About Michael.'

'I have to go,' Linda said, snatching the manila folder back, her face as sour as her apple core.

'Yeah, I know, heavy caseload,' Tracy said.

After Linda left, Tracy returned to the children's ward. Michael was still asleep but she sat by his bed and watched him until a doctor came round, a simpering, silent nurse by his side. 'Is there a problem?' he asked, seeing Tracy's uniform – she was due on shift in half an hour.

'No, I just wondered how he was.'

'You're one of the people who found him?' Tracy didn't think of herself and Arkwright as people, she thought of them as police.

'Yes,' Tracy said. 'Me and my partner.'

The nurse took the boy's pulse, cast a dismissive glance in Tracy's direction. Wrote something on the boy's chart. 'Thank you, Margaret,' the doctor said. Well, that was a first, Tracy thought, a doctor thanking a nurse. First-name terms, a medical romance perhaps. Tracy's mother, on the afternoons that she didn't go to her bridge club, put her feet up on the sofa and read Mills and Boon novels.

'Ian Winfield,' the doctor said, 'I'm the consultant paediatrician on the ward.' Tracy thought he was going to shake her hand and have a chat about Michael's condition but instead he said, 'The boy's doing fine, but he needs to rest now. It's probably best if you leave.' Dismissed. Tracy couldn't see what harm there was in just sitting there. The nurse looked at her, ready for trouble.

* * *

As Tracy was leaving the hospital she caught sight of Linda Pallister again. So much for her heavy caseload. She was coming out of the Cemetery Tavern, deep in argument with Ray Strickland. The odd couple. He got hold of her by the elbow and pulled her close, said something angrily to her. She looked terrified. Then Ray let her go and she walked unsteadily off. No bike, Tracy noticed.

'I went to the hospital yesterday, to see the kiddy,' Tracy said to Ken Arkwright, over a pint of Tetley's bitter.

'How was he?'

'Asleep. I bumped into that social worker. Linda Pallister.'

Ken Arkwright grunted.

'Anything happening? Anyone being questioned?'

'You've got to remember,' Arkwright said, 'that the police don't have the resources for law enforcement, for old-fashioned policing. Best we can do is clean up after people's mess.' He ripped open a packet of salt and vinegar crisps as if it was a trial of strength and offered one to Tracy. She hesitated, as befitted a girl on a cottage cheese and grapefruit diet. The chip-shop smell of the salt and vinegar crisps made her nose twitch.

'Well, make up your mind,' Ken Arkwright said.

'All right. Go on then,' she said, succumbing finally and grabbing a handful.

'People are their own worst enemy,' Ken Arkwright sighed. 'What can you do?'

'I know,' Tracy said. They were in a pub on Eastgate

frequented by refugees from the HQ in Brotherton House. That was just before they moved to the new HQ at Millgarth. A fug of cigarette smoke and the ripe smell of fresh and stale beer swilled together. Double Diamond works wonders. In 2008 Carlsberg would announce the closure of Tetley's brewery and it would be 'regenerated' – restaurants, shops and apartments. 'A sparkling destination on Leeds waterfront'. Ken Arkwright would have been dead for twenty years by then and in 2010 Tracy would be having a Mud 'N' Scrub Body Cleansing Massage in the Waterfall Spa, courtesy of the vouchers that were her leaving present from the force.

'You haven't seen Strickland or Lomax?' Tracy asked through a mouthful of crisps. 'They haven't said anything more to you? About the investigation?'

'To me? Eastman's golden boys?' Arkwright said. 'No, lass.'

'Thing is, Arkwright,' Tracy said, 'the flat was locked.'

'So?'

'I didn't see a key anywhere, did you? We had a good look around, we had enough time, Lomax and Strickland took for ever getting there. Yale and a deadlock. Someone left and locked the door after them.'

'What's your point?' Arkwright said.

'It was locked from the *outside*. Don't you see, it wasn't just some random punter that she picked up. It was someone who had a *key*. Someone who locked that little boy in.'

Arkwright frowned into his pint. 'Just leave it, lass, eh? CID know what they're doing.'

'Do they?'

Tracy went back to the hospital the next day. Kiddy's bed was empty, she thought, oh no, not dead, please God. She found the nurse who had been on Ian Winfield's round with him yesterday. 'Michael Braithwaite,' Tracy said, fear wringing her insides. 'What's happened to him?'

'Who?'

Arcadia

Friday

She woke with a jerk. Something unnatural had disturbed her sleep. Not birdsong, not an alarm clock, not the first bus grumbling its way past the top of the street. Tracy shot out of bed and hurried to the landing window from where you could get a good view of the street. A street crawling with police. Two uniforms knocking on the door opposite. A couple of squad cars parked further up the street. A plainclothes she recognized, Gavin Archer. More uniforms. They were doing door-to-door in Tracy's street. Could only mean one thing, they knew she'd been at Kelly's house last night. They knew about the kid. They'd probably seen the security tapes in the Merrion Centre, seen Kelly Cross swapping the kid for cash like a street-corner drug deal.

Two uniforms coming this way.

Tracy went into mental overdrive. Made a dash for the bedroom, pulled on her old tracksuit and ran along the hall to Courtney's room. The kid woke up quickly as if she was used to having to exit houses with little warning. Tracy put her finger to her lips and whispered, 'Shush.' Something else the kid seemed to understand.

The kid jumped into action and seized the precious pink rucksack and the even more precious silver wand.

They padded quickly downstairs. Just as they reached the hallway, the doorbell rang, loud and insistent. A wave of adrenalin cascaded through Tracy's body. She snatched up her bag, pushed the kid into the red duffel coat and hustled her to the back door. Tracy fumbled with the lock, her hands shaking. When she finally got the door open she hefted Courtney under one arm – it was like trying to run with a small sheep – and made a dash for the back gate. No one in the lane. Tracy pulled open the door to the lock-up, bustled the kid into the back of the car and said, 'Buckle up.'

Tracy's heart was knocking so hard it was making her chest feel sore. She came out of the lane, turned left, drove away sedately. Passed an empty police car and a uniform on a doorstep speaking to a sleepy woman. A dog van coming the other way ignored her. Tracy made her getaway, moving through them all like a ghost.

Behind her, a grey Avensis with a pink rabbit hanging from its rear-view mirror glided stealthily away from the kerb, like a big fish. It was cut off by one of the uniforms, asking questions.

Tracy decided it would be safer on the deserted back roads. They could hang around in the vicinity of the National Trust holiday cottage she had booked. She could get the keys to the cottage at two in the afternoon. Not keys exactly, just a code for a keypad on the door that a housekeeper activated ahead of their arrival. They wouldn't have to see anyone, talk to anyone. Then they could be invisible, off the radar, like stealth fighters. She only needed a day or so.

The kid fell asleep. It was foggy on the back roads. The fog felt good, like a friend. What had she done? One minute she was buying a sausage roll in Greggs, the next she was on the run from murder and kidnapping. Not that she'd murdered Kelly Cross, she just felt as if she had. Next time she was tempted to buy a kid, Tracy thought, she would take out some kind of warranty against buyer's remorse. A twenty-four-hour test run to make sure that she hadn't picked one that came trailing clouds of gory baggage. As if. As if she was going to go and buy another kid. No chance, she was sticking to this one like glue. Thick and thin, hell and high – oh, bugger and blast – suddenly there in front of them a deer stepped delicately out of the fog and into the road, and stood there, surprised, like someone who finds herself unexpectedly on a brightly lit stage in front of an audience.

Tracy heard someone scream, thought it might be herself, wasn't sure she'd ever screamed before. She slammed on the brakes, yelled, 'Hold on!' to Courtney, remembering all the things she'd heard about people running into cows, horses, deer, kangaroos, even sheep, and not walking away alive. She prayed to the particular god who kept kidnapped kids from being killed by wildlife. Tracy closed her eyes.

There was a thud, like driving at full speed into a wall of sand. Tracy was socked in the face by an airbag. It hurt like hell. She was going to have some great bruises. She spun round to check on Courtney. No rear-side airbags, that was a good thing, kids got injured by them. Courtney wasn't hurt, didn't even look surprised. 'OK?' Tracy said. Kid gave her a thumbs-up. You had to love her.

The windscreen looked as if someone had thrown a rock into the centre of it. A starburst clock. Thank God, the deer hadn't come through the windscreen and into the car. That would have been too much.

'Stay here,' she said to Courtney and clambered out of the car. The deer was lying on the road, illuminated by the headlights. A female, a hind. It was panting, making nasty tubercular sounds. Tracy knelt down next to it and its eyes rolled wildly. There was a huge gash across its neck and blood was pumping out from some-where beneath its body. It made a frantic effort to struggle to its feet but this was a deer that was going nowhere, today or any other day. It was horrible to see an animal so wounded. Tracy felt more for the deer than she had for Kelly Cross. She had to put it out of its suffering but she could hardly whack it with a jack in front of the kid.

Courtney appeared at her side. 'Bambi,' she whispered.

'Yeah,' Tracy said. 'Bambi.' More like Bambi's mother. Disney had a lot to answer for. No intention of getting *that* DVD for the kid. Dead Disney mothers (murdered mothers, in fact) leaving their kids to face the world alone, that was a story the kid could do without. Story Tracy could do without.

To Tracy's relief, the animal grew quieter, no longer trying to lift its head. Tracy welled up. Poor bloody thing. Courtney patted her hand. The deer's eyes grew dull and it gave a great shuddering breath and lay still.

'Is he dead?' Courtney whispered.

'Yes,' Tracy said, swallowing hard. 'She. She's dead. Gone to join all her friends in deer heaven.' Sacrifices, to save the kid. Save the kid, save the world. Tracy put out a hand and stroked the deer's flank. The kid passed the wand over its body.

The Audi was as mortally wounded as the deer. 'I guess we'll have to walk,' Tracy said. 'Find a garage.' She heard the sound of another car approaching, the noise baffled by the fog. The fog didn't feel like a friend any more.

They were going to have to take their chances. Tracy just hoped the car wasn't being driven by the police. A grey car materialized out of the grey mist. An Avensis. 'Shit,' Tracy muttered as the driver climbed out of the car and approached through the gloom.

Tracy grabbed the kid by the hand and hissed, 'Run.' She could hear him shouting behind her as they crashed through the undergrowth. 'Tracy? Tracy Waterhouse? I just want to talk.'

'Yeah,' she muttered to the kid, 'that's what they all say.'

She stopped and sat on the ground, exhausted, at the foot of a big tree. 'Get our breath back,' she muttered to Courtney. Had life with Kelly Cross been so bad, compared to this? Would Kelly still be alive if Tracy hadn't bought the kid off her? The kid knelt next to her, picked up a skeletal leaf left over from autumn and tucked it into her backpack. Her priorities were different from Tracy's.

The wood seemed to enfold itself around them. Tracy thought of Sleeping Beauty. They could die here and turn into leaf mould before they were found. A crack broke the silence, startling them both, and Tracy wrapped her arms round Courtney and clung on to her. Nerves screwed tight as piano wires.

'Are there wolves in the wood?' the kid whispered.

'Not as such,' Tracy said.

She understood she was on the edge of everything now, the abyss ahead, behind the darkness, desperation the only way forward. Kid smelled of last night's shampoo, and something green and sappy. A woodland nymph.

'Come on, let's keep moving.' She hauled herself to her feet, picked up the kid. She was too small to keep running. Wasn't that what had made Tracy take notice of her in the first place? Tracy had assumed that Kelly Cross was running with the kid because she was late or impatient or just plain bad but perhaps she hadn't been running *towards* something, perhaps Kelly had also been running *away*. What if, in her own fashion, she too had been trying to save the kid? Was that why she was dead? Had she been punished for finding the kid or for losing her?

Was the Avensis driver trying to get the kid back, was

she someone's property, a paedo ring maybe? The Avensis driver looked like he might be harbouring a pervert inside his grey skin. Was he this so-called private detective, the Jackson bloke?

'Where are we going?' Courtney asked.

'Good question,' Tracy puffed. 'I've got absolutely no idea.'

The trees started to thin and there was light ahead. Go towards the light, that was what they said, wasn't it?

They crashed out of the wood. And nearly got run over.

Said he used to be a policeman. Anyone could say that.

He had woken dead on five thirty as usual. When he switched on the bedside light in his bedroom in the Best Western the first thing that Jackson saw was the dog standing next to the bed, staring intently into his face as if it had been willing him to wake. Jackson growled a greeting and the dog wagged its tail enthusiastically in response.

He drank a poor man's cup of instant coffee in the room and gave the dog its breakfast. It wolfed its food down in seconds. Jackson was beginning to see that the dog always ate as if it was starving. He understood because it was the same way he ate. First rule of life, acquired in the army, reinforced in the police – if you see food, eat it because you don't know when you'll see it again. And eat anything that's put in front of you. Jackson had no qualms where meat was concerned, he could eat his way from snout to tail without any queasiness. He suspected that the dog was equally omnivorous.

Half an hour later and he was checked out and ready to hit the road. Marilyn Nettles was going to have two unexpected visitors. One man and his dog. He'd been planning to go to Whitby anyway so, clearly, fate was talking to him. In a difficult foreign language, like Finnish, it was true, but you couldn't have everything.

He informed SatNav Jane that he was heading for the coast on the scenic route and then, like Lot before him, he left the city behind without a backward glance.

The tracking device that the room-service waiter had attached to the dog's collar was currently in the Saab's glove compartment. Jackson had considered placing it on a long-distance lorry, imagining with some satisfaction the misdirection caused by an Eddie Stobart eighteen-wheeler pulling up in Ullapool or Pwllheli, but then he might not discover who wanted to keep tabs on him. Pursuit was a two-way enterprise, quarry and hunter united in the quest, not so much a duel as a duet.

The tracking device was a nice bit of kit. Jackson had no idea they made them so small these days. It was a while since he'd had reason to purchase anything from a spyware site. He would like to buy something similar for Marlee, a gadget so tiny that she would fail to notice it because she would never (*'No way!'*) agree to carry anything that implied parental supervision or control. If he could, Jackson would have his daughter chipped, like a dog. Nathan as well, of course. He had two children, he reminded himself, it was just that one didn't seem to count quite as much as the other.

Was the dog chipped? 'Colin' hadn't looked the type to care enough about a dog to chip it but then Colin didn't look the type to own a dog that didn't exactly advertise his machismo. He was a pit bull man, right down to his St George's tattoo and his shaved head. Did the dog, in reality, belong to a wife, a mother, a child? Was someone waking up each morning and feeling a lurch of sorrow for their missing pet? *Going to put you down, should have done it the minute that bitch left,* Colin had yelled at the dog in Roundhay Park. Jackson experienced a pinch of annoyance at the woman who had escaped Colin's clutches but had left her dog behind to suffer.

What had been a light veil of mist in Leeds had grown thicker as he drove. It held the promise, although not the certainty, of a glorious day later, but in the early hours it had made driving perilous. He regretted now not having cashed in the prescription for spectacles that an optician had given him.

'Things seem a bit blurry,' he had said to the

impossibly young girl testing his eyes. He wanted to ask if she was qualified but felt oddly vulnerable in the dark as she stared into his eye with a torch, so close that he could smell the mint on her breath.

'Yes,' she said, matter-of-factly. 'The lenses in your eyes are growing harder. It happens at your age.' Some things grew harder with age, some things grew softer.

On the road less travelled all kinds of wildlife were gambling recklessly with their lives on the unforgiving tarmac. A narrow miss with a badger a few miles back had tuned his reflexes up a notch. Jackson liked to think of himself as a knight of the road. It would be a shame to tarnish his shining armour with the blood of the innocent. He flicked the switch on the light-up Virgin Mary on the dashboard. The Mother of God might not have the candle wattage of the Saab's full beam in her belly but perhaps she had a different kind of protective power. A sanctified figurehead leading him through the valley of darkness.

A sudden dip took Jackson, the Saab and the Holy Mother into a denser pocket of fog. It was like flying through a cloud and Jackson almost expected the Saab to buck with turbulence. In the cotton-wool heart of the dip he saw a flash of silver and *Split the lark* came unwonted into his brain, the little men running his memory lazily reaching, in their morning lethargy, for the nearest thing to hand. *Bulb after Bulb, in Silver rolled.* The argent blaze heralded a new kind of hazard – a woman. A woman who suddenly hurtled out from the trees at the side of the road.

For a split second Jackson thought she was a deer – a mile or two back there'd been a barely visible road sign displaying a stag that looked as if it was running for its life. The woman looked that way too. No bears and wolves any more, the only predators women ran from nowadays were men. She wasn't alone, she was dragging a child by the hand, a small one, wearing a red duffel coat. The coat was a dark flare in the fog.

Jackson absorbed all of this in the nanosecond between spotting the woman and child and slamming on the brakes in an effort to avoid making roadkill out of the pair of them. The dog, startled awake by the Saab's emergency stop, remained safely lodged in the footwell of the car and gave him an unreadable look. 'Sorry,' Jackson said.

When he got out of the car he found the woman down on all fours like a cat, gasping for breath. Jackson was sure the Saab hadn't come into contact with her. And she was a big woman, maybe not as much of a buffer as a deer but he would have noticed the dunt, surely? 'Did I hit you?' he puzzled. She shook her head and, sitting back on her heels, managed to wheeze, 'I'm out of breath, that's all.' She nodded in the direction of the child standing impassively by, and said, 'I was carrying her. She's heavier than she looks. Good brakes,' she added, glancing at the Saab, inches away from her.

'Good driver,' Jackson said.

The child's red duffel coat was open, revealing a gauzy pink dressing-up costume beneath. A fairy, an angel, a princess, they were all pretty much cut from the same cloth as far as Jackson was concerned. It was an area of retail Marlee had familiarized him with, somewhat against his will. A battered star-topped silver wand indicated 'fairy'. Was this the flash of silver he had seen in the fog? The girl was clutching the wand, two-handed like a battleaxe, as if her life depended on it. Jackson wouldn't have liked to be the one who tried to wrestle it off her, she might be small but she was a punchy-looking kid.

The rest of her ensemble was also the worse for wear. There was a rip in the skirt and bits of twig and leaf were caught in the cheap fabric. It reminded Jackson of a production of *A Midsummer Night's Dream* that Julia had taken him to see. The fairies in the play had been filthy, mud-stained creatures who looked as though they had crawled out of a bog. At fourteen, Julia had played Puck in a school production of the play. At the same age, his own daughter had aspirations to be a vampire. 'It's a phase,' Josie said. 'Well, I should hope so,' Jackson said.

He helped the woman struggle to her feet. She was wearing a tracksuit that only served to emphasize how broad in the beam she was, built like a collier, Jackson thought. She had a big, practical handbag strapped across her front.

Jackson wondered if she shouldn't be even a little wary of the fact that she was stepping into the vehicle of a complete stranger in the middle of nowhere and, for all she knew, was walking into a worse nightmare than the one she had left behind. Who was to say that the

Saab driver wasn't a murderous psycho, combing the countryside for prey?

'I used to be a policeman,' he said, for reassurance. Although, of course, that was exactly what you would say if you were hoping to trick someone into getting into a car with you. (Perhaps it was himself he was trying to reassure, perhaps it was the woman who was a psycho.)

'Yeah, me too,' she muttered and laughed a grim kind of laugh.

'Really?' he said but she ignored him. 'Is someone after you?' he asked. The woman and the child both turned instinctively to look towards the wood. Jackson tried to imagine something flying out from trees that he didn't feel up to dealing with and, short of an armoured tank (or a small wand-wielding girl), came up a blank. Instead of answering the question the woman said, 'We need a lift.'

Jackson, also not one to waste words, said, 'You'd better get in the car then.'

He adjusted the mirror to try to look at the woman in the back seat. He couldn't see her face, however, as she had twisted herself round awkwardly in order to keep watch out of the rear window of the car. It wasn't worth the effort. If anyone was behind them there would be little chance of spotting them in this fog. Or vice versa. He adjusted the mirror so that he could inspect the small girl sitting next to the woman. The girl raised her eyebrows at him, an inscrutable gesture.

Eventually, the woman turned round to face the windscreen and stared straight ahead. She had bruises blooming on her face and dried blood on her hands.

'Are you hurt?' he asked.

'No.'

'You've got blood on you.'

'It's not mine.'

'That's all right then,' Jackson said drily. Both his new passengers had the same slightly stunned look that he had seen many times on survivors. They looked like refugees from a disaster – a fire or an earthquake – people who had abandoned their home in the clothes they stood up in. Domestic abuse, he supposed. War on the home front – what else would a woman and child be running from?

Minutes passed before the woman said to him, 'My car broke down,' as if that explained the state of the pair of them. Sighing wearily, she added, more to herself than to him, 'It's been a long day.'

'It's only half seven in the morning,' Jackson puzzled.

'Exactly.'

When he glanced in the mirror again he saw that the woman had strapped the child in. The seat-belt was much too big and looked as if it might strangle her if he braked too quickly. It was a long time since he'd had a child-seat in a car. If he ever drove Nathan he had to borrow one from Julia, something which annoyed her out of all proportion, in Jackson's opinion anyway.

Although he might not have admitted it, he felt

slightly unsettled – the fog, the woods, the *Midwich Cuckoos* kid, not to mention the sense of fear the woman had brought into the car with her – it was all more like an episode of *The Twilight Zone* than a comedy by Shakespeare.

She didn't seem to care where they were heading, anywhere except where she had been seemed to be a good direction. Jackson was no longer sure it mattered which way you went, you never ended up where you expected. Every day a surprise, you caught the wrong train, the right bus. A girl opens a box and gets more than she bargained for.

'Don't you want to know where I'm going?' he asked after what seemed like an eternity of silence.

'Not particularly,' she said.

'Magical mystery tour then,' Jackson said cheerfully.

'I can't help but worry about you, son. I'm your mother, it's my job to worry.'

'I know, Mum, and don't get me wrong, I love you for it, but I'm OK, I really am.'

'Oh, all right, on you go then, but just remember, all work and no play makes Jack a dull boy.' (*They kiss.*) 'Bye, bye then, love. See you on Friday, and then we'll—'

'The line, Tilly, is actually "All work and no play makes *Vince* a dull boy." '

'Really?'

'I think it's supposed to be amusing in some way.'

'Amusing? Is it?' Tilly puzzled.

'Blame the writer, darling, not me. We're playing to a low common denominator here.'

Never underestimate the intelligence of an audience. That was what Douglas used to say and, as in so many things, he was right, of course.

'Can we run it again, Tilly, please?'

She heard someone mutter, 'Oh Christ, just leave it or she'll come out with every Tom, Dick and Harry before she gets to "Vince". If ever.'

The actor playing Vince gave Tilly a wink. She knew him quite well, knew him as a boy, he was with the Conti school, did a turn as Oliver in the West End – or was it the Artful Dodger? – but damned if she could remember his name. It was a shame that everyone thought names were so important. A rose would smell as sweet by any other. And so on.

'Do you want to get a cup of tea? You've got some time, Miss Squires.' The nice Indian girl had Tilly's call sheet, Tilly just couldn't keep her hands on it. 'Thank you . . .' Pima? Pilar? Pilau! 'Thank you, Pilau.'

'I'm sorry?'

Ooh dear, that inflection, Tilly thought. What had she said wrong now?

'Pilau? Like pilau rice. I find that quite offensive, you know, Miss Squires. Like calling someone "Poppadom". My name's *Padma*. If I didn't know how much trouble you had with names I would think you were being racist.'

'Me?' Tilly gasped. 'Never, oh, never, dear.'

In her defence (a poor defence, it was true), Tilly wanted to say, 'My baby was black' (or at any rate, half-black) but no baby existed to prove that. No baby that had grown into a strapping man. Tilly always imagined him looking rather like Lenny Henry. Phoebe came to visit her in the hospital afterwards and said, 'Well, it was for the best. Even you have to admit that, Tilly.'

'Do I?'

The nurses were all horrible to her, starchy and un-forgiving, because the baby they had sluiced away without even showing her hadn't been as white as the lilies, as white as the snow. 'It would have been a *coloured* child, Tilly,' Phoebe said in a (theatrical) whisper at her bedside. It took Tilly a second to work out what she meant. Her first thought was, like a rainbow?

'You would have had such a difficult time,' Phoebe said. 'You would have been ostracized. And the work would all have dried up. It's for the best this way.'

Of course, that was 1963, the sixties had only just got started. Tilly hadn't cared, the baby could have been purple and yellow with polka-dots and stripes and she would have loved it.

It was just chance (but then isn't everything?). Phoebe had been invited to some kind of diplomatic party and twisted Tilly's arm to come along with her. For cover, of course. Phoebe was having an affair with a Cabinet minister – married, naturally, all very hush-hush. It was anybody's guess who else she was sleeping with, she could easily have been the Christine Keeler of her day but she was too lucky to be found out. Always lucky. In life and love. And so there they were at this party and Phoebe dumped her the minute they walked in the door.

All sorts of people at the party, a famous elderly actor, camp as coffee, and a lot of beautiful young things, boys and girls. That model Phoebe knew, Kitty Gillespie, and a film star, a man, who would soon drop out of this bright, shiny world to go to India and find himself. They were all mixed in with guests from various embassies, a photographer from *Vanity Fair* was there, Phoebe, in a diamond necklace borrowed from her mother and never given back, conspicuously avoiding being photographed with her politician.

'Good evening,' a deep voice said and Tilly turned round and saw this lovely young man smiling at her. Black as the ace of spades. (Would the girl – Padma, Padma, Padma, surely if she said it enough she could remember – *Padma* think that was a racist way of describing him?)

'I don't know anyone here,' he said. 'Well, now you know me,' Tilly said. He was from Nigeria, he said, a secretary to an attaché or some such, Tilly never quite understood, but he knew how to have a proper conversation – he had been to Oxford and Sandhurst, sounded more English than Prince Philip, and he was so intrigued by everything that Tilly had to say, unlike some of Phoebe's friends who were forever looking over your shoulder to see if someone more interesting had entered the room.

Anyway one thing led to another – conversationally – and Tilly invited him round to the little Soho flat the following night, said she would cook him a meal, she had no idea how to cook anything, of course. He seemed quite lonely, homesick, well, Tilly understood that, she had felt homesick all her life, not for her own home, just the idea of a home.

Her flatmate – the ballet dancer – was on tour so they had the place to themselves. She made a spag bol, it was a difficult dish to burn but Tilly managed it. But there was some nice bread and a decent piece of Stilton and afterwards tinned peaches and ice cream and he brought a lovely bottle of French wine, so the evening wasn't an unmitigated disaster and afterwards one thing led to another – not so much conversation this time – and there she was the next morning lying naked in bed next to an equally naked black man and her first thought when she opened her eyes was *What would Mother think?* A thought that made her laugh. He was called John but he had only said his surname once, when he introduced himself, and it was something African and strange with lots of vowels (was that a racist thing to say?).

She made coffee, proper percolator coffee, and ran down to Maison Bertaux and bought pastries and they ate them in bed. Felt like a tremendous adventure, felt like a romance.

She had a rehearsal to go to and he had work, of course, mysterious diplomatic work, and they walked together to Leicester Square tube station. It was a beautiful spring morning, everything felt clean and fresh and full of promise. Tilly had stood on tiptoe and kissed him goodbye right there in the station, a white girl kissing a black man in public. Desdemona to his Othello, except he wasn't going to be twisted by jealousy and end up murdering her. No opportunity – never saw him again.

She was so tired. Usually enjoyed an egg roll at this time of the morning but didn't feel like it today. A nice reviving cup of tea, just what the doctor ordered. No sign of Padma anywhere, probably just as well.

She hobbled off to the catering truck. A bit wobbly this morning. Her hip was hurting. Ladies who lurch. The doctors had started talking about a replacement. She didn't want an op. All alone, being shipped off into the darkness. An anaesthetic like death.

He was so lost in thought as he clumped along the corridor that Barry nearly collided with a woman from the lab. Chinese, no hope of getting that name right, always referred to her as 'that Chinese woman from the lab'. Lucky he didn't call her a Chink, he supposed. She was waving a bit of paper around, asking him, 'Have you seen DI Holroyd? We've got a fingerprint back from the house in Harehills.'

'Kelly Cross? Quick work.'

'It was on file, one of our own. Ex-Superintendent Tracy Waterhouse. It's probably old. It's unlikely it's connected to the murder.'

'Yeah,' Barry agreed. 'Very unlikely. Their paths must have crossed at some point.'

Like last night maybe. Kelly Cross, tart with no heart, bashed in the head, stabbed in the chest and the abdomen. Body discovered by a fellow waste-of-space crack whore who lived on the same street. What had Tracy said the other night? *Just wondered if you'd run into Kelly Cross recently, Barry?* And now Kelly Cross was dead and Tracy's fingerprint was at the scene. And when he phoned last night she had been in the heartland of Kelly's killing fields. *Looking for someone.* Who? Kelly Cross?

He hadn't been to Tracy's new house before, hadn't been invited. She'd had a Polish builder working in there for ever and anyway she wasn't exactly the kind to throw a housewarming. The front door was locked but the back door was wide open and Barry knocked and stepped inside, saying loudly, 'Tracy? Trace? Are you at home?'

The *Marie Celeste*. The dregs of wine in a glass, an empty packet of crisps. He climbed the stairs, feeling more like an intruder than either a policeman or a friend. Bathroom was clean and tidy. Tracy's bedroom a bit less tidy, hideous wallpaper. Something a bit too intimate about being in here for Barry. Didn't like to think of Tracy getting undressed, climbing into bed, sleeping. He'd never had any of those kinds of feelings towards her. Second bedroom was full of boxes. Third bedroom was a mean-spirited one but someone had slept in the single bed. Who? Goldilocks?

There were some kiddy's toys lying on the floor. Barry picked up a little blue plastic teapot from the carpet. Amy used to have a doll's teaset. Why did Tracy have kids' things in her house? Had something bad happened to her? Tracy could look after herself. Thirty years on the force, a heifer of a woman, anyone with any sense would think twice before messing with her but something felt wrong.

He drove to the Merrion Centre to make sure she had left for her holiday. He showed his warrant to a spotty youth, he liked to cow spotty youths with his credentials. 'Looking for Tracy,' he said to the cowed spotty youth.

'Has she done something? There was a private detective here looking for her the other day.' That bloody Jackson bloke, Barry thought, poking his nose in. 'I thought maybe you'd come to pick up the tapes?' the spotty youth said.

'Tapes,' Barry said vaguely. He had learned a long time ago to avoid words like 'yes' and 'no'. They backed you into corners you couldn't get out of.

'Yeah, security tapes. You were sending someone over. That woman who was murdered last night—'

'Kelly Cross?'

'Yeah, well known to us, and you. Apparently a policeman remembered seeing her in here on Wednesday. You wanted to see the tapes, see if she was with anyone. Thought they'd send a grunt to pick them up,' he added, 'not a superintendent.'

'I am a grunt,' Barry said. 'I grunt all the time.'

There were three tapes, grainy black-and-white. He watched them back at Millgarth, took hours. Tracy flitted in and out of view occasionally, on patrol on her new beat. He'd almost dropped off to sleep when Kelly Cross finally came into view, dragging a kid behind her. Seconds later, there was Tracy again, on her heels. Tracy was yomping along as if she was about to storm a fort.

There were another two cameras outside, trained along the street in both directions. Barry picked up Kelly again on one of them. She was at a bus stop with the little kiddy standing next to her. Then Tracy hove into view again and she and Kelly Cross had a brief exchange of words. A bus arrived and Kelly suddenly disappeared inside it. Tracy was left on the pavement, holding the little girl's hand. After a few seconds the pair of them walked off, out of reach of the camera.

Kids who disappeared after their mothers were murdered. Yeah, Barry could see why Tracy would have got herself involved in something like that. But kiddies who disappeared *before* their mothers were murdered, that was a more puzzling matter. Something Barbara said to him this morning, something about meeting

Tracy in the supermarket, Tracy having a kid with her. This kid?

Barry ejected the tape, fitted it into the inside pocket of the coat that was hanging on the back of his chair. He found a clerical assistant in the corridor and said, 'Tell DI Holroyd that the tapes from the Merrion Centre have come, will you. Two of them.'

Perhaps this Jackson bloke had managed to find Tracy. Seemed unlikely that a so-called private detective could find her when Barry had failed. Still, worth a shot, he thought. Said he was staying at the Best Western, didn't he? Shrugged himself into his coat. 'Barry Crawford is leaving the building,' he said to the desk sergeant.

Outside the Slug and Lettuce on Park Row there was a big builder's skip. Barry tossed the third tape from the Merrion Centre into it.

What was it they said – discretion was the better part of valour?

1975: 12 April

'What do *you* think, Barry?'

'What?'

'What do you think, Barry?'

They'd come from Elland Road, where a good-natured match had got bumpy at the end. They'd brought the horses in. Tracy didn't think horses should be used for crowd control, it was like sending them into battle. Barry was with them, trying to avoid buying a round.

It wasn't that Tracy valued Barry's opinion particularly but no one seemed to want to talk about it. Carol Braithwaite was being swept under the carpet like a bit of rubbish. 'She was somebody's mother, somebody's daughter. We don't even know the cause of death.'

'Strangled,' Barry said.

'How come you know?' Tracy asked. Barry shrugged. 'No one seems to be doing much, case just seems to be disappearing,' Tracy said. Three days since Arkwright had put in that door in Lovell Park but it was as if it had never happened. Tiny piece in the paper by that Marilyn Nettles woman and that was it. 'It doesn't even feel as if anyone's looking,' Tracy said. 'And you,' she added, turning accusingly to Barry, 'what were you doing there anyway?'

'What are you getting at?'

Tracy thought of Lomax and Strickland in Lovell Park, both looking shifty, behaving like Special Branch, knowing more than they were saying.

'Have they spoken to you at all?' she asked Barry. He shrugged. 'You're doing a lot of shrugging, Barry.'

'Ah, the mysteries of CID,' Arkwright said. 'Ours not to reason why. It seems pretty straightforward to me. The poor lass picked up a punter, took him back to her flat and he turned out to be a wrong 'un. It happens.'

'The oldest profession,' Barry said, as if he was a man of the world. 'Ever since there've been whores there's been people killing them. They're not going to stop now.'

'And that makes it OK, does it, Barry? The whole door-locked-from-the-outside thing, what about that?'

'What's your point?' Barry said. 'You think a couple of CID blokes knocked off a prozzie and then covered it up? That's nuts.'

Sounded almost reasonable to Tracy's ears.

'You're talking through your hat, Tracy,' Barry said. 'You'd better not spread rumours like that, you'll be out on your arse quicker than you can say "Eastman".'

'They had a witness,' Tracy said. 'He was four – so what? He said to me, he told me, his father killed his mother. Shouldn't they at least be trying to find out who his father is?'

'I'm sure they are,' Barry said. 'But it's nothing to do with you.'

'Barry's right,' Arkwright said. 'It's an ongoing investigation. They're not going to come running to you every time they get a bit of information, lass.'

'Thought I'd go and see Linda Pallister, that social worker,' Tracy said to Arkwright once Barry had left.

'That hippy bird?' Arkwright said.

'She lives in a commune.'

'Filthy nutters,' Arkwright said. 'Do yourself a favour, Trace. Call off the attack poodles, eh?'

An 'urban commune', according to Linda. Fancy term for what was really just a squat, a dilapidated old house in Headingley that was due for demolition. The residents kept chickens in the back garden. Muddy parsnips and leeks grew stunted and misshapen where once there had been a small parterre.

Tracy had just come off shift and was still in uniform. 'Pig,' she heard one of the blokes who lived in the house mutter as she passed him in the hallway. Someone else made a grunting noise. Tracy felt like arresting them, marching them out of there in handcuffs. Wouldn't have needed much of an excuse, the sweet sickly stink of marijuana drifted from the living room.

Linda, mother hen, queen bee, was wearing sensible hiker's sandals beneath her long patchwork cotton skirt. Her droopy hair was pulled back in a ponytail so you could see the whole of her disgustingly healthy face. She was part of some wholefood cooperative, ate brown rice and grew 'sprouts', not the type that came from Brussels, and made 'cultures' for stuff like yoghurt and bread. Linda was attending an evening class in beekeeping. All these facts conveyed righteously over a cup of tea that she reluctantly offered. They sat in the kitchen, within the circle of warmth coming from a big, ancient Aga.

The tea was horrible, not proper tea. 'Rooibos,' Linda said. Rubbish more like, Tracy thought. The tea was in big, clumsy mugs that 'someone we know' had made. 'We bartered eggs for mugs,' Linda said smugly. 'One day,' she added earnestly, 'there'll be no money.' Well, turned out she was right about that.

Like Tracy, Linda Pallister was still on probation. Unlike Tracy, she had a kid, having got knocked up in the middle of whatever worthy degree it was that she had done, social admin, politics, sociology. She spent the rest of her degree hauling the kiddy around on the back of her bike to nurseries and child-minders.

The boy was wandering around the kitchen half-naked, his rubbery little penis bouncing about. Tracy felt shocked.

'Jacob,' Linda said. He peed on the floor right in front of Tracy and Linda didn't seem bothered. 'Children should be free to do what they want,' she said. 'We shouldn't impose our rigid, artificial structures on them. He's very happy,' she added as if Tracy had said something that indicated otherwise.

Linda mopped up Jacob's pee and, without washing her hands, cut slices from a brown cake that she'd made. 'Banana bread?' she offered Tracy. Tracy politely declined. 'Watching my figure,' she said. 'Someone has to.'

'What do you want?' Linda said. 'You didn't come here to talk about self-sufficiency and poultry.'

'No, I didn't. I just wondered how Michael was doing.'

'Michael?' Linda said vaguely, suddenly very pre-occupied with wiping Jacob's nose.

'The Braithwaite kiddy,' Tracy said. 'Is he with foster parents now, because he's not in the hospital?'

'He's in a different hospital now.'

'Where? Why?'

Linda stared at the unpalatable-looking piece of banana bread on her plate and said, "Fraid I can't say. Against policy.'

'So no chance I could go and visit him?'

'Why would you want to do that?' Linda asked.

'To see how he's doing.' Because I held him in my arms and it broke my heart, Tracy thought, but she wasn't about to show any weakness to Linda Pallister.

'I told you, he's fine,' Linda said, suddenly as snappy as a crocodile. When Linda found God a few years later her personality would improve a lot. One of the few arguments Tracy could muster in favour of Christianity.

'I don't see how he can be "fine",' Tracy protested. 'He was locked in a flat with the rotting corpse of his mother for nearly three weeks.'

'Well, "fine" is perhaps the wrong word,' Linda conceded. 'But he's getting all the help he needs. You should just leave it alone.' She pulled her own kiddy close and put a protective arm around him and said again, 'Just leave it alone.'

'So I definitely can't visit him?' Tracy persisted.

'No,' Linda sighed. 'No visitors. It's a directive from above.'

For a mad second Tracy thought Linda Pallister meant heaven.

It was ridiculous but Tracy had half formed the notion that if no one wanted Michael Braithwaite she could foster or even adopt him herself. Of course, Tracy knew nothing about children and she was still living at home. She could just imagine the look on her mother's face if she brought home a neglected, traumatized little boy.

'He'll be adopted by someone who will love him,'

Linda Pallister said. 'He'll forget what happened to him, he's too young to remember. Children are very resilient.'

Tracy asked Len Lomax herself, didn't intend to but she bumped into him the next day. He was coming out of Brotherton House as she was going in.

'Sir, do you mind me asking what's happening in the Carol Braithwaite murder case?'

'What's happening?'

'Any suspects?'

'Not as yet.'

'You haven't found the key?'

'Key?' He flinched. He definitely flinched. 'What key?'

'The key to Carol Braithwaite's flat. It was locked from the outside.'

'I think you might have made a mistake there, WPC Waterhouse. Fancy yourself as a detective now, do you?'

He stalked off righteously, climbed into a red Vauxhall Victor that Tracy recognized from somewhere. She tried to get a look at the driver, caught a glimpse of a razor-sharp bob and a beaky nose that liked to poke itself where it shouldn't. Why was Len Lomax getting into a car with Marilyn Nettles? And why had he flinched when she asked about the key?

'He knew about that key,' she said to Barry.

'That's crap,' Barry said. Barry got nervy every time she mentioned Carol Braithwaite's name, why was that? ('Because you never stop fucking mentioning her, that's why.') He drained his pint in one go and said, 'Got to be off, got a date. That Barbara's agreed to go to the pictures with me. *Monty Python and the Holy Grail* at the Tower.'

'Monty Python? Oh, very romantic, Barry,' Tracy said.

Took Tracy years to get out of uniform and into CID. You had to wonder, was it because she was a woman, or because she was a woman who asked the wrong questions? Or the right questions. Barry's star, on the other hand, rose quickly. It wasn't long before he was drinking pals with Lomax, Strickland, Marshall, even Eastman, a scrum of beer-swilling, fag-smoking blokes. Thick as thieves, all of them. The good old days.

She was like a terrier with the scent of a rabbit in its nose. Wouldn't let it go.

'And what's her name?' Ray Strickland said, frowning into his pint.

'Tracy Waterhouse. She's all right, Tracy,' Barry said hastily, 'but she just keeps going on about how the kiddy said his father did it. Won't let it drop.'

A week later, Len Lomax took Barry to one side and told him that they'd lifted a bloke in Chapeltown who confessed to being Carol Braithwaite's killer. 'Said he was the boy's father,' Lomax said.

'So, he's been arrested, there'll be a trial?' Barry said and Lomax said, 'Unfortunately not, bloke got into a fight in Armley while he was on remand, someone stuck him with a knife.'

'Dead?'

'Yeah, dead. In the light of everything, the kiddy, what happened to him, the whole thing will probably be dropped.'

It was only much later that Barry wondered if what Lomax had told him was true. He could just have made it up. Barry never asked questions, always took what Lomax and Strickland said as gospel. God knows why.

'Let your lady friend know,' Lomax said.

'My lady friend?' Barry puzzled. He had had one not entirely successful date with Barbara. Turned out she didn't like Monty Python. (*But they're just idiots, what's funny about that?*) Morecambe and Wise was more her thing.

'Your WPC,' Lomax said.

'Tracy? OK.' Barry wondered when he had become Strickland and Lomax's dogsbody.

'Remember, Crawford, discretion's the better part of valour.' Barry had no idea what he was talking about.

The lights of a petrol station loomed out of the fog and the woman said, 'Can we have a pit-stop, please?' Jackson pulled the Saab on to the forecourt and she led the kid by the hand to the toilets round the back.

'Just be a sec,' she said. The kid looked back over her shoulder at Jackson. She was gazing at him as if she was wondering whether he was about to leg it and leave them in the lurch. She hadn't said a word so far. Jackson wondered if she was mute, or perhaps just traumatized. He gave her his reassuring Queen Mother wave and she semaphored slowly back with her silver wand.

He supposed it might be a good idea to stock up on supplies. The garage wasn't big but it still managed to sell everything from bunches of flowers and bags of smokeless fuel to foodstuffs and top-shelf magazines. Eight o'clock in the morning and the place was deserted, just one young, very bored girl at the counter, watched over by a couple of CCTV monitors that allowed her to keep an eye on the pumps. She was chewing on a piece of her long, stringy hair, as if it were liquorice. The girl was small and slim and Jackson wondered if she should be out here all on her own. It would be too easy to over-power her and force her to open the till, or worse.

Once inside he had trouble deciding what to buy. He supposed he should get something for his new acquaintances, the kid had a little backpack but it seemed doubtful it was filled with rations. He bought bottled water, milk and juice, a couple of pasties, apples, a bunch of bananas, a packet of nuts, chocolate, some dog treats and, lastly, a plastic cup of black coffee to take away. The shop was bigger inside than it was outside.

Back in the Saab Jackson waited. He sipped his coffee. Hot and wet and that was about all. It tasted vaguely of rust. He opened the packet of nuts and threw a handful in his mouth. He heard a train somewhere, muffled by the fog, and wondered where it was going. A cow bellowed nearby, low and moody, like a foghorn. It was at times like this that he felt like taking up smoking again. He waited some more. He wondered if he should go and see if the pair of them were OK. Perhaps there had been some kind of emotional breakdown in the toilets.

He watched as the girl in the garage came out from her sanctum and started hauling the buckets of flowers and bags of smokeless fuel out front. Whatever they were paying her, he thought, it didn't seem like enough. She paused on the threshold, clutching a plastic bucket of flowers that were already tired inside their cellophane shrouds, the same kind of weedy-looking bouquets that were propped against trees or stuck through wire fencing to indicate where some unfortunate cyclist or pedestrian had been knocked off the planet. A rotting pile had been left at the site of the train crash. Someone had shown him a photograph later. The bouquets had been placed at the bridge above the track. Kitsch-looking soft toys and teddy bears too.

'Twas just this time, last year, I died. Two years to be accurate. For some reason Schrödinger's cat popped into his mind. 'Both alive and dead at the same time,' Julia said. That had been Jackson after the train crash. 'Neither one thing nor t'other,' his brother would have said.

The girl from the garage cast a suspicious glance in Jackson's direction but then her attention was drawn away from him as a black Land Cruiser suddenly appeared out of the fog, slowing to a stop on the other side of the forecourt. It waited with the engine running, looking vaguely menacing, like a pent-up bull waiting to go into the ring. Before Jackson could form much of a thought about it (such as what a stupid, badass kind of vehicle, who do they think they are, warlords, gangsters?), a man – a cross-bred species, half rugby fullback, half silverback gorilla – climbed out of the passenger side and also made his way round the back.

The driver then climbed out of the Land Cruiser and started to approach the Saab. Brothers-in-arms. Both men had the doughy faces of people reared on a diet of fat and potatoes and were dressed in leather jackets that had last been fashionable some time in the seventies, unless you lived in Albania where they had never become démodé and possibly never would.

Before he reached the Saab the woman reappeared, screaming her head off at Jackson. She lumbered across the forecourt like a charging rhino, carrying the girl under one arm while with her free hand she was struggling to remove the bag that was strapped across her front. The silverback gorilla was on her heels but not for long because she managed to pull the bag over her head and, holding it by the strap at arm's length, in one surprisingly graceful movement – more ballet than hammer throw, the kid under her arm forming a kind of ballast – she twirled round and socked the guy following her full in the face with the bag. He went down like lead. Jackson flinched inwardly and wondered what a woman would carry in a handbag that could do that kind of damage. An anvil? Thatcher would have liked a handbag like that.

The driver of the Land Cruiser changed trajectory and started heading towards the woman. Jackson was halfway out of the car, intending to head him off, but the woman yelled and gestured at him to get back in the Saab. He did, surprised at his own obedience to her barking parade-ground tones.

The girl from the garage, ignorant of the ruckus that was developing, stepped out uncertainly on to the fore-court, holding a bucket of tulips. Unfortunately the driver of the Land Cruiser, running towards the Saab as if he was heading for the try-line, failed to swerve in time and sent the girl flying across the concrete, tulips spilling everywhere. It put the driver off his stride long enough for the woman to fling the kid in the back seat of the Saab and lunge in after her, bellowing at Jackson, 'Drive, drive! Just fucking drive, will you?'

Again, obedient to orders.

In the rear-view mirror he could see the girl still sprawled motionless on the ground. She would be lucky if something wasn't broken. Like her head, for example. He could make out the shape of the guy who had been handbagged, still out cold on the ground, but then everything behind them was swallowed by the fog. He cast a glance over his shoulder and saw that the woman had pulled the kid down on to the floor of the car and was snailed protectively over her body. Did she think they had guns? When there were guns around, Jackson preferred being inside a vehicle that was armoured and official rather than a thin-skinned family saloon, manufactured in a neutral country.

Domestic abuse didn't quite seem to fit the bill any more.

'Who were those goons?'
   'I haven't got the faintest idea,' she said.
   'They seemed to be after you.'
   'Looked like it,' she said.

Jackson was still on adrenalin overload but the other occupants of the car appeared imperturbable. In the footwell, the dog remained determinedly asleep. Jackson was pretty sure it was pretending. How long before it regretted its choice of new pack leader? The kid also had a pretty good poker face on her and his Amazonian hitchhiker was raking through her bag as if finding a lipstick or a tissue was more interesting than contemplating the carnage in their wake. They had made an attempt to clean themselves up a bit in the garage toilets. He noticed that the woman no longer had blood on her hands. Jackson felt there might be a metaphor hiding in there somewhere.

He thought of the guy she had smacked with her handbag, laid out cold on the concrete. *Frailty, thy name is woman!*

'What have you *got* in that bag?' he asked. Me and the cat, he thought, helplessly curious.

She removed a big black Maglite and displayed it for his appreciation in the rear-view mirror. It looked like old police issue. They weighed a ton, no wonder the guy hadn't bounced back up again. She was taking no prisoners, that was for sure. She replaced the Maglite and returned to delving in the bag, finally coming up with a mobile phone. Jackson assumed that she was going to phone in the incident at the garage.

'Are you phoning the police?' he said.

'Yeah,' she said and promptly rolled down the window and threw the phone out of it. He turned round and looked at her.

'What?' she said.

'What do you think you're doing?' she asked when Jackson took his own phone out of his pocket. Another chippy woman, Jackson thought with a sigh. Chippy women wherever he went. Chippy mothers who begat chippy daughters and so the circle of chippiness was unbroken.

'Phoning 999.'

'Why?'

'The girl in the garage,' he said, with exaggerated forbearance. 'An innocent bystander,' he added, thinking of the tulips, the primary-coloured spearheads scattered across the forecourt.

'Innocent bystander?' the woman said. 'What innocent bystander? Is anyone really innocent?'

'Kids? Dogs?' Jackson offered. 'Me?'

She snorted derisively in the way that a woman married to him ten years might have done.

'I get it, you don't want to involve the police,' he said. 'Do you want to tell me what's going on?'

'Not particularly,' she said. 'And anyway, is anyone

really a *bystander*?' she mused as if they were in the middle of a philosophical debate. 'You could argue that we're all bystanders.'

'It's not a case of semantics,' Jackson said. 'We've just left that girl and I would say, yes, "innocent" and "bystander" pretty much cover her role in the proceedings.'

'Semantics,' she murmured. 'Big word for this time of day.'

Your average upstanding citizen tended to phone for the emergency services in these circumstances. Fugitive, criminal, woman with a lethal handbag, what was her story? Jackson sighed. 'Seeing as I appear to be helping you escape from something that seems pretty dodgy, to say the least, can I take it on trust that you're on the side of good?'

'Good?'

'As in the opposite of bad.'

'Because I'm a woman? A woman with a child? Doesn't always follow.'

The child in question was now asleep. The silver wand, no longer really fit for purpose, had finally slipped from her slack fingers. He hoped this wasn't a routine kind of day for her. 'No,' he said. 'Because you said you were police.'

'Again, doesn't always follow,' she said with a shrug.

'I'm still going to phone it in.' He half expected her to knock him out with the Maglite but at that moment the kid woke up and said, 'I'm hungry.'

*   *   *

'Got any bananas in there?'

'It just so happens,' he said, producing a bunch from the plastic carrier bag on the passenger seat. Like a magician. Or a fool. He was a cocky so-and-so. Was he really ex-police? He seemed a bit on the wimpy side, the sort that liked to rescue damsels in distress but not if it involved too much hardship. He was quite attractive, she'd give him that, but that was possibly the last thing on Tracy's mind. Dodging and weaving to escape mysterious men who were chasing you could do that to a woman. Being a woman could do that to a woman. He had a silly little dog, you had to wonder what attracted a man to an animal that size.

'I don't even know your name,' he said.

'No you don't,' Tracy agreed.

'Banana? Apple? Dog treat?' he offered. The girl took an apple. 'Would Mummy like something?' Jackson said, looking at Tracy in the rear-view mirror.

'She's not my mummy,' the kid said, matter-of-factly. Little kick to Tracy's heart.

'The things kids say,' she said, returning his gaze in the mirror. 'Keep your eyes on the road,' she said. 'You don't want to have an accident. You've got a fairy on board.'

Who were those guys back at the garage? A pair of leather-jacketed thugs working in tandem, but for who and why? The first one had banged open the door of the toilets while the kid was washing her hands. He opened his mouth to say something but before he could spit anything out Tracy kneed him hard where it hurt the most. And ran. Someone wanted that kid back, didn't they? And it wasn't Kelly Cross, she didn't want anything any more. Would never want anything ever again.

The Saab driver dialled 999 while driving, phoned it in anonymously, reporting an 'incident', made it sound serious. He came across as a professional rather than – his pet obsession, it seemed – an 'innocent bystander'. 'Send an ambulance,' he said authoritatively.

'Using a mobile phone while driving,' Tracy said when Jackson finished the call. 'That's a crime right there.'

'Arrest me,' he said.

Her own phone had been like a beacon, flashing her identity out to anyone who might be looking for her. Anyone could find you if you had a mobile. A woman on the run with a kidnapped kid shouldn't be advertising herself. She had thrown the phone out of the car window. They were outlaws now.

They were on roads that weren't familiar to her, places that meant nothing – Beckhole, Egton Grange, Goathland – but then signs began to appear for the coast. Tracy didn't really want to go to the coast, she wanted to get to the holiday cottage. She could see that there was an argument to be made for staying with this man. Without him she was a lone woman on the run with a kid who didn't belong to her. Together they were a family. Or something that resembled a family to anyone looking for them. Tracy contemplated sticking with him a bit longer, dismissed the idea. She reached over and tapped him on the shoulder. 'Pit-stop again, I'm afraid,' she said ruefully.

He drew to a halt. They were in the middle of nowhere. Tracy liked the middle of nowhere better than the middle of somewhere.

'That dog could probably do with getting out as well,' she reminded him. 'Stretch its legs, powder its nose.'

'Yeah,' he said, 'you're probably right.'

They all climbed out of the car. Tracy moved a short distance away to a discreet little limestone outcrop hillock. 'I'm not needing,' Courtney whispered to her.

'Good,' Tracy said, watching the dog bounding off into the heather, the man following it. All Tracy needed was for him to be further away from the car than she was. And to be slower to react. And on the whole to be more stupid. Turned out he was all of those things. She seized the kid's hand and said, 'Come on, quickly. Get back into the car.'

The fog was their friend again. Before the Saab driver knew what was happening Courtney had scrambled into the back seat and buckled herself in. You had to hand it to the kid, she was pretty good at the old fast exit. Tracy got in the driving seat and turned the ignition. Within seconds they were half a mile further down the road than Jackson Brodie.

His phone was on the passenger seat. Tracy slowed down and threw it out of the car on to the verge.

A hundred yards further along the road Courtney said, 'He left his bag.'

Tracy stopped this time and hauled the rucksack over to the front seat, opened her door and threw it out.

'Good riddance to bad rubbish,' she said.

∽

Barry went into the Best Western, his warrant card blazing a trail ahead of him. The woman behind the desk was taken aback by his bullish entrance. She was wearing full air-hostess make-up, a suit that was a size too small for her and had her hair pinned up in a style so complicated it had surely needed a couple of Victorian ladies' maids to arrange it that morning. On the lapel of the jacket was a badge that said Concierge, as if it might be her name. Barry remembered when hotel concierges were all unscrupulous middle-aged blokes who were on the take left, right and centre.

'Well, I thought he was a bit strange?'

'Strange? How?' Barry asked. Barry didn't think there was anything left in the world that would seem strange to him these days. She was an Aussie. They were everywhere.

'Bit, I don't know, paranoid? He always looked as if he was sneaking around. One time I thought he had something concealed in his jacket and he always carried his bag with him, a rucksack. You think "terrorist" these days, don't you? He definitely seemed a bit dodgy. What did he do?'

'I don't know yet,' Barry said. 'If I could just get a look at his room?'

There was nothing in the hotel room. The Jackson bloke had checked out early this morning and the chambermaid who had cleaned had done a good job. Barry couldn't see any helpful clues as to who he really was – no pubic hairs curled up in the corner of the bathroom or a big greasy thumbprint on the underside of the toilet seat. He had left nothing behind, apparently, apart from a generous tip for the maid. Shame he hadn't left a note pinned to the wall explaining what exactly he was up to.

Barry took a miniature of vodka from the minibar and sat on the single bed and drank it down in one. He felt tired all the time. He put his head in his hands and stared at the carpet, noticed something the chambermaid had missed – a hair. It didn't look human. He tweezered it up with his fingers and examined it closely. Looked like a dog hair.

This Jackson bloke had come searching for the truth about Carol Braithwaite, hadn't he? Linda, Tracy, Barry. Bit players, walk-on extras in the drama of Carol Braithwaite's death. Maybe it was time the main players stepped up to the stage. End of days now. Barry was going down in flames, he might as well take a few more down with him.

What he would really have liked to do right now was to lie down on the bed and have a snooze but he heaved himself up and drank down another miniature vodka. Then he filled up the two small bottles with water and replaced them in the minibar.

He couldn't go on. He didn't have it in him. The reckoning was coming. For Barry. For everyone.

'Thanks, love,' he said, returning the plastic room key. 'Tie me kangaroo down, sport, eh?'

The dog sat by his side as they both stared at the retreating Saab. 'I don't believe it,' Jackson said. He felt as if he had lost an old faithful friend. 'I *liked* that car,' he said.

The car started to slow down and Jackson said, 'Come on, she must have changed her mind,' and sprinted after it. The Saab stopped long enough for his phone to be thrown on to the verge before moving off again, Jackson and the dog in pursuit. The car goaded him by stopping once more and ejecting Jackson's rucksack. He ran after it again and just before he reached the Saab it set off again. He retrieved his phone and his bag and waited to see if anything else was going to be bailed out of the car but this time the Saab accelerated away. 'The fairer sex,' Jackson said to the dog. ('Fairer in what way exactly?' he had once asked Julia. 'In love and war,' she said.)

In the rear window of the car Jackson could see the

silver wand moving from side to side, like a metronome. The kid's farewell.

They were in the middle of nowhere. Phone a friend? Did he have any? Julia perhaps. Not much she could do. Ask the audience? He turned to the dog. A dumb creature. He found the packet of dog treats in his pocket, all he had salvaged from his shop at the garage. They were little biscuits in the shape of tiny bones. They looked surprisingly appetizing but he resisted and tossed one to the dog.

A taxi firm seemed like a sensible option but the phone, although it seemed to have survived its ousting, showed there was no signal up here. Nothing for it but to set off and walk. The dog, naturally, was happier with this plan than Jackson.

They hoofed it for a good half-hour before they encountered any sign of civilization. The dog heard the approaching car before Jackson did. Jackson caught hold of its collar and towed it over to the verge where they waited for the vehicle to appear out of the fog. Memories of the Land Cruiser made Jackson consider throwing himself in the nearest ditch but there was no ditch and he could see now that it wasn't the Land Cruiser that was advancing towards them along the deserted road, it was an Avensis, a grey one.

Jackson put out his hand to flag it down. 'Stand and deliver,' he murmured to the dog.

The Avensis stopped and the nearside window rolled

down. 'Hello there, fancy seeing you here,' the driver said.

Jackson peered at his face, regretting again not having bought those spectacles. Did he know him?

The Avensis driver opened the passenger door and said, 'There's a hell in hello, isn't that what they say? Give you a lift, squire?'

It was the room-service waiter who had left the tracking device. Jackson looked to the dog for confirmation but the dog had already hopped niftily into its now customary position in the footwell.

Reluctantly, Jackson climbed in after it.

A small pink furry rabbit hung droopily from the rear-view mirror. If it came to a contest between dreck car accessories Jackson was confident that his own little mascot, the light-up Virgin Mary wobbling on the dashboard, attached by a sucker and bearing an AA battery in her holy insides, would win hands down against a pink furry rabbit.

'Whitby, is it, guv?' the Avensis driver said, tipping an imaginary chauffeur's hat.

'Please.' Well, this took weird to a new level.

'Nice mutt,' the Avensis driver said.

'Yeah,' Jackson said. 'I think you said that last night when you put a tracking device on him. Why do you want to follow me?'

'Maybe I'm following the dog.' He restarted the Avensis's engine and said, 'Right, squire, here we go. First we take Manhattan, eh?'

'Who *are* you?'

'Straight in there with the difficult questions. Who am I?' his new friend repeated thoughtfully. 'Who am I? Of course, you might ask – who are any of us?'

'It wasn't really a philosophical question,' Jackson said.

'Name, rank and number?'

'Just a name would do.' Close up Jackson could see that the man looked slightly moth-eaten. He had the ashen skin of a smoker and on cue he retrieved a packet of cigarettes from the glove compartment. 'Want one?'

'No thanks.' Just accept you've entered into an alternative reality, Jackson counselled himself. It probably happened round about the time he reached Leeds. 'Is this something to do with Linda Pallister?' he hazarded.

'Who?'

'Or Hope McMaster?'

'Ah, *Hope springs eternal in the human breast: / Man never is, but always to be blest.* Pope. Wrote some good stuff. Know him?'

'Not personally,' Jackson said.

'What you doing all the way out here then?'

'Well . . .' Jackson said, defeated by the complexity of the story before he even started it. He settled for the simple version. 'Someone stole my car.'

The fog had finally begun to lift, streaks of pale gold gleaming through the thinning wisps.

'Looks like it's going to be a nice day,' the Avensis driver said.

* * *

'First to see the sea,' was always the call when they went to the seaside. Jackson, Josie and Marlee. It seemed a long time ago now that they had been a tight little family threesome. The winner (always Marlee even if she had to have the sea pointed out to her) merited three chocolate buttons. Josie rationed sweets as if there was a war on.

And no sign of the sea at all today, the coast still entombed in fog. A 'sea fret', they said in Yorkshire. In Scotland, the far, far north, Ultima Thule, Louise would have said 'haar'. They were separated by a common language and an invisible border crossing. Did she ever think about him?

By the time they crested a final hill the fog had begun to roll back and Whitby started to reveal itself in all its dramatically Gothic glory – the abbey, the harbour, West Cliff, the higgledy-piggledy fishermen's houses.

'You can see why Count Dracula landed here, can't you?' the driver of the Avensis said.

'Dracula isn't real,' Jackson pointed out. 'He's a fictional character.'

The driver shrugged and said, 'Fact, fiction, what's the difference?'

'Well . . .' Jackson said. But before he could embark on a convincing proof (such as *Do you want to feel the difference between a fictional punch and a real one?*) they began their descent into town and the Avensis driver said, 'Drop you at the police station, shall I?'

'The police station?'

'Report the theft of your motor.'

'Yeah, of course, good idea,' Jackson said. So strange had been the advent of the Avensis that it had managed to push the whole escapade with the woman and child to the back of his mind. It felt like he was in an episode of *The Prisoner*, any moment a giant ball of bubblegum would come bouncing along the road and swallow him up and demonstrate that there was indeed only a thin line separating fact and fiction.

They had slowed to a crawl, the Avensis driver peering around, a stranger in town.

'Do you know where the police station is?' Jackson asked.

The Avensis driver tapped the SatNav on his dashboard. 'No, but she does.' Jackson felt a possessive pang. In his mind Jane was a one-man woman.

The Avensis pulled into the police station car park on Spring Hill. Jackson got out of the car, as did the Avensis driver. 'Stretch my legs a bit,' he said. This turned out to be a form of exercise that involved leaning against the side of his car and lighting up another cigarette.

'Believe it or not, squire,' the driver said, 'but I think we're both on the same side, both working towards the same end, just coming at it from different starting points.'

'The same end?'

'Lawks, is that the time?' the driver said, making a great show of looking at his wristwatch. (Lawks? Who said lawks any more? Well, apart from Julia, of course.) 'Have to go, got to see a dog about a man.'

Short of tying him up, blindfolding him and playing non-stop heavy metal in his ears, Jackson couldn't think of a way of getting the other man to identify himself or his mission. Jackson was surprised, therefore, when the driver stuck out his hand and said, 'The name's Bond, James Bond. Nah, mate, joking. It's Jackson.'

'I'm sorry?' Jackson said.

'Brian Jackson.' He searched in his pockets and finally came up with a thin card – *Brian Jackson – Private Investigations*. 'Two hundred quid an hour, plus expenses.' Before Jackson could say anything, and there was quite a lot he wanted to say, Brian Jackson had climbed back in the car. He rolled down the window and said, 'Sayonara. Be seeing you around,' and drove off.

'Two hundred quid an hour,' Jackson said to the dog. 'I'm undercharging.'

'Plus expenses,' the dog said. In a parallel universe obviously, the one where dogs communicate and men are dumb creatures. In this reality, the dog simply waited silently for its next orders.

He tied the dog up outside and entered the police station. The desk sergeant was on the phone and held up a finger to Jackson indicating he would be with him in a moment. The finger then pointed at a functional chair against the wall. Jackson admired a man who could communicate so much in so few words. No words at all in fact, just a digit.

The desk sergeant finished his phone call and made a

beckoning gesture to Jackson with his admirably articulate finger.

'Can I help you with something, sir?' he asked when Jackson approached the desk.

Jackson hesitated. It was theft pure and simple. His car had been taken without his permission. The woman had not only stolen the Saab but she was on the run with her kid, being chased by two pretty nasty men. That was quite a list of possible police matters. '*She's not my mummy.*' The girl's words came back to him. Surely he didn't have to add kidnapping to that list? Kids were always saying things like that. A couple of months ago Marlee had screamed at him, 'You're not my real father!'

'Sir?'

If he reported the Saab as stolen, the police would be after a woman who was in a bad place but claimed to be on the side of good. And Jackson's instincts tended towards the renegade.

On the other hand . . .

She had taken his *car*.

He thought of the kid, solemnly waving her wand. He thought of the woman using her body as a shield for the kid to stop a possible bullet. He sensed the balance was tipping in the woman's favour.

Still.

His car.

'Sir?'

'It's nothing,' Jackson said. 'A mistake. Sorry to bother you.' Of course, there was one person who could find his car for him. The person whose tracking device was in the glove compartment. But then he'd be employing Brian Jackson at *Two hundred quid an hour, plus expenses*, to do a job he should be able to do himself. Male pride couldn't countenance that.

'Business before pleasure,' he said to the dog. A small map that he had picked up from a Tourist Information office near the harbour led Jackson to his destination – a cottage that was hiding down a narrow passage, in a yard. The address that Jackson was looking for, courtesy of 192.com, was the end-stop, shouldering all the weight of three other cottages that lurched dramatically, due to some ancient subsidence.

When Marilyn Nettles finally shuffled to the door, Jackson held up one of his business cards to prove his credentials. He caught a whiff of an old-fashioned scent – lavender and gin. The beginnings of a dowager's hump and a mouth that looked as if it had spent a lifetime clamped around a cigarette. She took the card from him as if it might be smeared with something infectious and, peering at it, said dismissively, '*Private Investigator*, that could mean anything.'

'Well, what it means,' Jackson said helpfully, 'is that I'm investigating something private. Carol Braithwaite,' he added.

Marilyn Nettles gave a grunt of recognition at the name and said, 'Well, come in, come in,' suddenly impatient, even though she had been keeping him on the doorstep before.

Jackson had to duck to get through the door. The

place was tiny, the front door opening directly into what an estate agent would have called 'a living-kitchen'. An open stairway led up to the next storey. The house was simply one room stacked on top of another. Walking across the floor he felt its incline, like a funhouse. There was a wash of nicotine over the walls.

'Sit down,' she said, indicating a two-seater sofa, one half of which was occupied by what Jackson first took to be a cushion, then a piece of feline taxidermy and just as the question *Why would you stuff a cat?* passed through his brain the object itself turned into a real cat. At the sight of Jackson the animal rose from the sofa and stretched extravagantly, arching its back like a caterpillar. It was a strangely threatening gesture, a fighter warming up for the ring. It unsheathed its claws and flexed them, digging them deep into the fabric of the sofa. Jackson was glad he had left the dog tied to a railing in the yard outside.

As if reading his mind, Marilyn Nettles said, 'Have you been with a dog?' in much the same tone of voice a jealous wife would have used to ask him if he had been with another woman. 'He hates dogs, can smell them at a hundred paces.' Jackson sat down gingerly next to the cat, which had now settled grumpily back into its impersonation of a cushion. Jackson wondered if it suffered from the effects of passive smoking.

A little carriage-clock on the mantelpiece struck a tinny-sounding hour and Marilyn Nettles flinched like a woman who had just realized how long it was since she'd had a drink.

'Coffee, Mr Jackson?'

'It's Brodie, actually. Jackson Brodie.'

'Hmm,' she said as if that seemed unlikely and wavered her way to the back of the room where some basic and pretty elderly appliances lined one wall. She flicked the switch on an electric kettle and spooned instant coffee into mugs before adding a slug of gin to one of them, which explained her unexpected hospitality, Jackson supposed.

The place was shabby, cat fur and dust floating on sunbeams. Nothing had been papered or painted, or indeed washed, for a long time. Something uncomfortably hard behind the cushion at his back turned out to be an empty bottle of Beefeater. There were clothes draped on the sofa. Jackson didn't like to look too closely in case they proved to be Marilyn Nettles's undergarments. He got the impression that she slept, ate and worked in this one room.

An old Olivetti Lettera sat on a table by the window, surrounded by piles of paper. Jackson got up from the sofa and investigated the manuscript. He started to read the unfinished page in the typewriter –

Little did petite blonde Debbie Mathers realize that the handsome debonair man she had married was really a monster in disguise who would use their apparently idyllic honeymoon as an opportunity to murder his new bride in order to collect on the insurance policy that he—

'Mr Jackson?'

'Sorry,' Jackson said, flinching. He hadn't heard Marilyn Nettles's approaching tread on the biscuit-crumbed carpet. 'Couldn't help taking a peek at your latest oeuvre. It's "Brodie", by the way.'

'It's crap,' she said flatly, nodding her head at the Olivetti. 'But it pays the bills.'

She nodded in the direction of a bookcase where a series of books displayed their titles on their spines – *The Poisoned Postwoman*, *The Faithless Fiancé*. Red Blood Press were the publishers, their logo a drawing of a fountain pen dripping with blood. Marilyn Nettles removed a book from the line-up and handed it to Jackson. *The Slaughtered Seamstress* was the title, raised and embossed in a metallic red on a lurid cover that depicted a half-naked, bug-eyed woman in the foreground, her mouth open in a scream as she tried to escape from a shadowy male figure who was wielding a huge knife. On the back page there was a soft-focus photograph of 'Stephanie Dawson' that looked as if it had been taken decades ago. There had been a lot of cigarettes and alcohol on the road between that photograph and the woman who stood before Jackson now.

'*The Butchered Bride*. They call it "True Noir",' Marilyn Nettles said. 'Basically they're books for people who can't read.' She contemplated the screaming woman on the jacket. 'Women in jeopardy,' she said, handing Jackson a mug of coffee. 'Very popular. You have to wonder.'

'You do,' he agreed. The mug looked as if it was some

time since it had made the acquaintance of any washing-up liquid. Oiled by her alcohol-infused Nescafé, Marilyn Nettles seemed more inclined to talk, albeit reluctantly. She lit a cigarette without offering one to Jackson and said, 'So what do you want?'

'What can you tell me about Carol Braithwaite?'

'Not a lot. Not much more than was in that original newspaper report. Why? What's your interest in her?'

'I'm working on behalf of a client,' Jackson said. 'Someone who I think may have some connection to Carol Braithwaite.'

'Who?'

'That's confidential information, I'm afraid.'

'You're not a sodding priest. We're not talking secrets of the confessional.'

Jackson pressed on. 'There was your piece in the newspaper and then the whole case seems to disappear. Did you interview anyone at the time, did you find out anything about Carol Braithwaite?'

She stared quizzically at the tip of her cigarette as if it was going to provide the answers. 'So many questions and such a long time ago,' she murmured.

'But you must remember,' Jackson said.

'Must I?'

'Have you ever heard the names Linda Pallister or Tracy Waterhouse? A social worker and a policewoman, in 1975? Ring a bell?' A little flicker of something in Marilyn Nettles's eyes. 'Hope McMaster? Dr Ian Winfield? Kitty Winfield?' Jackson persisted.

'For heaven's sake, all these names,' she said irritably.

'I knew next to nothing. I was *encouraged* not to know anything, as you might say. I was warned off.'

'Warned off?'

'Yes, warned off. I didn't believe that they were idle threats either. No more articles, don't report the inquest, forget it happened.'

'So someone threatened you?' Jackson said. 'Who?'

'Oh, names, names,' Marilyn Nettles said dismissively. 'Everyone always wanting to name names. It doesn't matter now. Most of us are dead anyway, even the ones that are alive.' She seemed to drift off to some place in her head. She came back after a while and tapped the manuscript on the table in front of her. 'I went down to London, wanted to make it big on the broadsheets, but it never really happened. Ended up back here, covering local stories for the *Whitby Gazette* and writing this stuff to keep my head above water.'

'Well,' Jackson said, 'none of us end up where we expect to.'

'I don't know why the woman can't be left dead and buried, I don't know why everyone's so intent on digging her up.'

'Everyone?'

'There was a man here earlier. He said he was a private detective as well. The pair of you look like brush salesmen if you ask me.'

'Did he give you a card?'

Marilyn Nettles rooted around amongst the pages of *The Butchered Bride*, and handed over the cheap card. 'Brian Jackson,' Jackson sighed. They had obviously been dogging each other's footsteps all week. He had been driving away from Whitby when he offered Jackson a lift. His had been the name, hadn't it, that was written in Linda Pallister's diary for the morning of Jackson's original appointment with her. Jackson had read the name 'B. Jackson' and thought Linda Pallister might have been confused. Was it Brian Jackson's questions that had spooked Linda Pallister into disappearing?

Marilyn Nettles sighed, seemed to gather herself and continued, 'And anyway a lot of what happened had to be kept out of the public domain, had to be censored "to protect the innocent", as they say. Restraining orders all over the place. I was allowed to write hardly anything about Carol Braithwaite and nothing whatsoever about the child.'

'The child?' Jackson said, almost leaping off the dusty sofa with eagerness. This had to be Hope McMaster, surely? 'You didn't say anything about a child.'

'You didn't ask. He was called Michael,' Marilyn Nettles said. 'A boy, four years old.'

Jackson sagged back on to the sofa, deflated by disappointment. 'Carol Braithwaite had a son?'

'Yes. They said they were protecting him from the press, from public curiosity. It was a sensationalist kind of story.'

'Why?'

'Well, he was locked inside the flat with the body of his dead mother. They estimated it was about three weeks. But you know, he witnessed a murder . . . and then he disappeared.'

'Do you think someone killed him?'

'As good as. He disappeared into the system, wretched life in care, et cetera,' she said wearily. 'I'm growing tired of this interrogation, I have work to do,' Marilyn Nettles said. 'It's time you went.' She stood up suddenly and swayed a little and hung on to the table for support and Jackson jumped up from the sofa, intending to shore her up if necessary. In doing so he dislodged the manuscript on her desk, sending the pages of *The Butchered Bride* fluttering like disembodied birds on to the floor. The cat, startled awake, narrowed its mean marble eyes and went from nought to sixty in two seconds, hissing and spitting at Jackson.

Exit Jackson stage right, pursued by a cat.

Escaped by a whisker. He threw the dog a dog treat, casting the tiny bone high in the air. The dog jumped and caught it neatly.

Perhaps, after all, then, the girl in the photograph was not Hope McMaster. But it did rather beg the question, if this Brian Jackson bloke was mining the same mysterious seam as Jackson himself – Linda Pallister, Marilyn Nettles, Tracy Waterhouse – then what – or who – was *he* looking for?

As soon as he pulled up outside Linda Pallister's house

Barry could sense the lace curtains twitching all around. Nosy neighbours, a policeman's best friend. Barry climbed out of the car and tried the doorbell but it didn't look like a house where anyone was home. The curtains were closed and it had an abandoned air. He banged loudly on the door and shouted 'Linda!' through the letterbox.

A Hyacinth Bucket type, one-woman Neighbourhood Watch, popped up out of nowhere as if she'd been crouched behind the privet ready to spring.

'Janice Potter,' she said. 'I live next door. Can I help you?'

'I don't know,' Barry said. 'Have you got a runner for the three thirty at Lingfield Park?' He flourished his warrant card and said, 'I'm looking for Mrs Pallister, Linda Pallister?'

'Someone else was looking for her yesterday. He said he was a private detective.'

'Can you tell me when you last saw Linda?' Barry asked.

'Last night,' she said promptly. 'Just after *Collier* finished. She was getting into a car. She didn't come back.'

'What kind of car?' Who needed CCTV, Barry thought, when you had twitchers?

'A four-door saloon,' she said. 'Grey.'

'All cars are grey at night,' Barry said.

This Jackson bloke was the ruddy Scarlet Pimpernel, here there and everywhere, always one step ahead of

Barry. And everywhere he went, women were disappearing.

'OK,' Barry said to himself as he climbed back in the car. He talked to his car quite a lot these days. It didn't talk back, didn't have any expectations of him. 'Let's say, for argument's sake, this Jackson character is investigating on behalf of Carol Braithwaite's kid, all grown up now, what – in his late thirties?' All that 'finding out more about myself' shit that people went in for these days. Not Barry, Barry would happily know less about himself. 'And so, on Michael Braithwaite's behalf, he contacts Linda Pallister.' *Someone's asking questions*, she'd said to him when she phoned him on Wednesday. 'And the same bloke, this Jackson, was looking for Tracy for the same reason – Carol Braithwaite. But then both Linda and Tracy disappear. That can't be good, can it?'

Michael Braithwaite had woken his mother from her endless sleep. And now she was rising, a dust storm, looking for justice, looking for vengeance. A revenge tragedy.

Jackson and the dog strolled along the pier, a pair of flâneurs by the sea. Jackson could feel the warmth of the sun on his scalp. He had been to Whitby as a boy. He didn't know where the money had come from for a holiday, there was never money for decent clothes and food, let alone for ice creams or pantomimes, certainly not holidays. Jackson must have been five or six when they came here, half his sister's age and still young enough to be her pet. Francis, their brother, was already a teenager slouching moodily around the arcades in the evening. There was no photographic proof of their furlough as none of them had ever owned a camera. The rich had always commissioned portraits of themselves but the poor moved invisibly through history.

Jackson couldn't explain this primitive past to his daughter, let alone his son, born into a science-fiction future where every breathing second of his life was being digitally recorded, usually by Mr Metrosexual, Jonathan Carr. (Julia was being unusually shifty, even for her, about Jonathan. Was it over between them?)

He could remember very little about their family holiday here in that faraway time, only impressionistic memories of sounds and smells. They had stayed in a guest house where a gong was rung at dinnertime and meals were served that were astonishingly different from the potato and bread-laden fare of home and even now his most vivid memory of the holiday was of a stewed chicken dish and a lemon pudding, both of which had prompted his mother to sniff and say, 'Huh, very fancy', as if the food were a criticism of her rather than something to be enjoyed.

There had been milk and arrowroot biscuits for the children in the evening – unheard-of luxuries at home, where a vicious rub on the face with a flannel by his mother had been the only herald of bedtime.

He suddenly recalled something long ago tucked away in a forgotten corner by the little men running his brain. His mother had bought him a set of paper sand-castle flags – in his mind's eye he could still see a red lion on a yellow background. And his father wearing his cheap suit to sit on the beach, his trouser legs rolled up to reveal his pale, hairy, Scottish shins. It had been a poor sort of childhood, in every way. Belonged in a museum.

Not one as interesting as the RNLI museum on the prom where recorded tales of heroism and disaster brought an uncomfortable lump to Jackson's throat. *We have to go out, but we don't have to come back*, the motto of the US Coastguard, the watchword of all rescuers. Sacrifice, like stoicism, not a fashionable word. Jackson stuffed a twenty-pound note into the miniature lifeboat collecting-box at the door.

He carried on, passing shops that sold shells, shops devoted to vampires (no getting away from them), to jet, to scented candles the smell of which made him retch, and endless cheap and nasty souvenirs. He crossed the swing bridge to the old town and visited the Captain Cook Memorial Museum to pay homage to the great navigator himself.

Afterwards, he bought some fudge in Justin's Fudge Shop and noticed a house on Henrietta Street that was for sale, but he saw that the whole street was subsiding and the kipper smokehouse at the end was atmospheric in all the wrong ways.

The place was heaving with visitors. May Bank

Holiday weekend, used to be Whitsuntide, when did that change? He ran up the 199 steps to the abbey and was pleased at how fit he still was. Everywhere people were puffing and panting their way up the steps. He had never seen so many fat people in one place at the same time. He wondered what a visitor from the past would make of it. It used to be the poor who were thin and the rich who were fat, now it seemed to be the other way round.

He left the dog in the porch when he went into St Mary's Church. He took a seat in a box pew marked in old lettering, *For Strangers Only*. It seemed appropriate. These days he was always the stranger in town. He contemplated the interior of the church, fashioned long ago by shipwrights. The only other people there were a young – very young – Goth couple, black clothes, black lipstick and piercings everywhere, who were messing about in the pews. The boy said something to the girl and she sniggered. Vampire freaks.

He sat for a while on a bench in the graveyard of St Mary's. The headstones all leaned like trees in the wind, the names on them erased by the salted air. '*Safe in their Alabaster Chambers*,' he murmured to the dog. The dog cocked its head inquisitively as if it were making an effort to understand what he was saying. Seagulls were squabbling yobbishly overhead. The sun winked on the sea like diamonds. Jackson was long enough in the tooth to know that it was over when you started reaching for clichés. He stood up and said out loud, 'Time to go,' to the dead beneath his feet, but the meek members of the resurrection made no effort to stir themselves and only the dog obeyed his call.

He walked back down into town on the cobbled donkey road rather than the 199 steps, finishing off Justin's fudge as he went.

'Come on,' he said to the dog. 'I'll race you.'

He hit the beach running. Jackson couldn't remember when he had last run on a beach.

When they reached Sandsend the dog investigated the rock pools, finding a small dead squid like a deflated condom that it worried for a while until it disintegrated. A large brackish piece of seaweed kept it entertained for several minutes more. Jackson sat on a rock and contemplated the horizon. What was out there? Holland? Germany? The edge of the world? Why had someone tried to bury Carol Braithwaite's murder? And how was it relevant, if at all, to Hope McMaster? And other questions that he didn't know the answer to, in fact, the more questions he asked, the more they multiplied. It had started with one, *I wondered if you could find out some information about my biological parents?* and had exploded exponentially from there.

He spent some time drilling his new recruit on the beach – *sit, stay, heel, come*. The dog was pretty good. At *sit* its haunches dropped as if its back legs had been taken from beneath it. When Jackson said *stay* and walked away the dog might as well have been glued to the sand, its whole body quivering with the effort of not hurtling after Jackson. And when Jackson found a stick of driftwood and held it above the dog's head, the dog not only stood on its hind legs but even walked a few steps. What next? Talking?

An elderly man in the company of an equally elderly Labrador ambled by. The man tipped his cap in Jackson's direction and said, 'Th'should be in circus, lad.' Jackson wasn't sure whether he was referring to the dog or himself. Or both. Jackson and the Amazing Talking Dog.

The dog and Jackson played at throw and fetch for a while and then, unfortunately, the dog blithely deposited one of its antisocial brown wreaths on the sand and a guilty Jackson had to use the driftwood stick as a makeshift shovel to bury it, the plastic bags having been stolen along with his car.

It seemed a good moment for two naughty boys to turn around and run away.

He bought fish and chips – northern soul food – and sat on a bench on the pier while watching the tide come in. He shared his fish supper with the dog, wafting pieces of fish in the air to cool them down before handing them on, just as he had once done for Marlee. The tide had turned, the sea crawling up the beach now. Further along, the waves had more power and Jackson watched as they *voomphed* against the stanchions of the pier.

It was growing dark and the dark brought the cold with it, the warmth of the afternoon now an unlikely memory. The wind skating off the North Sea was an icy blade that cut through to the bone, so he threw the fish and chip paper in the bin and headed for the bed and breakfast he had booked over the phone last night. Twenty-five pounds a night for 'Complimentary toiletries, hospitality tray and a full Yorkshire breakfast'. Jackson wondered what made it a Yorkshire breakfast as opposed to any other kind.

'Bella Vista' – what else. It was in the middle of a street of similar houses, five storeys from basement to attic. Most of Bella Vista's neighbours were also guest houses – Dolphin, Marine View, The Haven. Jackson wondered if any of these guest houses had been around in his childhood, if perhaps it was the hallway of Marine View or The Haven where a copper gong had been beaten to announce dinnertime, perhaps was still being beaten.

Bella Vista seemed a misnomer, there was no sign of the sea at all. Perhaps if you stood on a chair at an attic window. NO DOGS, NO SMOKING, NO GROUPS, a sign announced on one of the pillars at the door. In smaller cursive script underneath were the words *Mrs B. Reid, Proprietress*.

'It's late,' Mrs Reid said, by way of greeting. Jackson checked his watch, it was eight o'clock. Was that late?

'Better than never,' he said affably. He wondered if Bella Vista got many returning guests. Mrs Reid was a hardened blonde, a woman of a certain age, the only kind that Jackson seemed to meet these days. She led him into a big square hall where a table displayed a pile of leaflets about local tourist attractions and an honesty box for the phone in the shape of a small, old-fashioned red telephone box. Opening off the hall were a guest lounge and a breakfast room, their function announced by little china plaques affixed to the doors.

In the breakfast room he could see tables set for the morning with small pots of jams and marmalade, tiny tablets of foil-wrapped butter. It was strange, this miniaturization of everything, every expense spared. Jackson thought that if he was running a guest house (a big leap of imagination required) he would be generous with his portions – big bowls of jam, a dish with a fat yellow block of butter, giant pots of coffee.

He was led up three flights of stairs to an attic room at the back where servants would once have been crammed like sardines in a tin.

The 'hospitality tray' sat on the chest of drawers – an electric kettle, a small stainless-steel teapot, sachets of tea, coffee and sugar, tiny tubs of UHTmilk, a cellophane packet containing two oatmeal biscuits, everything again parcelled out into the smallest quantities. The room also harboured an assortment of completely unnecessary clutter – crocheted mats, little dishes of pot pourri and a troop of ringletted, porcelain-faced dolls sitting to attention on top of the wardrobe. In the small, cast-iron fireplace there was a vase of dried flowers, which, as far as Jackson was concerned, were simply dead flowers by another name. Jackson wondered if there was a Mr Reid. The house felt as if it had long ago been released from the sober, restraining hand of a man. Divorcee or widow? Widow, Jackson guessed, she had the look of someone who had successfully out-survived a sparring partner. Some women were destined for widowhood, marriage was just the obstacle in their way.

On the outside of the bedroom door there was a plaque that said *Valerie*. On the way up, Jackson noticed that other bedrooms also had names – *Eleanor*, *Lucy*, *Anna*, *Charlotte*. They seemed like the names the dolls would have. Jackson wondered how you decided on a name for a room. Or a doll. Or a child, for that matter. The naming of dogs seemed even more perplexing.

Mrs Reid looked around the room doubtfully. It was pretty obvious that Jackson wasn't the kind of person who belonged in a room like this. She was probably thinking about amending her notice: NO DOGS, NO SMOKING, NO GROUPS, NO SCRUFFY MEN IN BLACK COMBATS AND BOOTS WITH NO APPARENT REASON TO BE HERE. The air in *Valerie* smelled cloying and chemical, as if the room had just been vigorously sprayed with air freshener.

'Business or pleasure, Mr Brodie?'

'I'm sorry?'

'Are you here on business or pleasure?'

Jackson thought about the answer a little longer than seemed necessary to either of them. 'Bit of both really,' he said finally. A soft whine came from his bag.

'Thank you,' Jackson said to Mrs Reid and closed the door.

He pulled up the sash window to let some real air into the room and discovered that there was a fixed metal fire escape outside the window. Jackson liked the idea that he could make a quick getaway from *Valerie* if necessary.

An uncharacteristically brief email from Hope McMaster pinged its way through the ether to him. *Anything?* she asked. *Nothing*, he replied. *I thought I'd found you but you turned out to be a boy called Michael.*

Always looking, the sheepdog returning the lost lambs. In London he'd met a guy called Mitch, South African, tough Boer type, politics somewhere to the right of Thatcher, if that was possible, but with his heart bang, slam in the centre of his being. Jackson didn't know the whole story, just that a long time ago Mitch had had a small son who was abducted and of whom not a scrap was ever found. Now, many times divorced and not short of a bob or two, he ran an investigative outfit that looked for missing kids worldwide. It didn't advertise itself. Hundreds of kids around the world disappeared every day, here one moment, gone the next. Some of the people they left behind found their way to Mitch.

Mitch had a dossier, a huge file, depressing in its size, full of runaways and abductions of all kinds. He knew more about some of the kids in that dossier than Interpol. All those photographs broke Jackson's heart. Holiday snaps, birthdays and Christmases, all the highlights of family life. Jackson found photographs unsettling enough at the best of times. There was a lie at the heart of the camera, it implied the past was tangible when the very opposite was true.

Jackson himself always made sure that in the course

of taking snaps of Marlee there was, every year, one good, clear head-and-shoulders shot, facing the camera. That was usually the one that if he showed it to Josie she would say, 'That's a great likeness,' and he never told her that it was in case their daughter went missing. Children changed by the day, if you stared at them long enough you could see them grow. When he was on the force he had seen too many poor portraits (holidays, birthdays, Christmases) over the years ('She doesn't really look like that now'). This was what happened to you when you were a policeman, even on a sunny day in a *bateau-mouche* on the Seine or on a picnic in a Cornish cove, death was ever present, and you were staring at it down a lens. *Et in Arcadia ego*. And, of course, he knew the statistics, 99 per cent of abducted children dead within twenty-four hours. Going on half of them dead within the first hour. No photograph, however good, was going to help with that.

A child who is lost was the worst thing in the world. The ones who came back from the dead, the Nataschas, the Jaycee Lees, were the decimal-point percentage of the statistic, offering futile hope.

Mitch's dossier charted height, eye colour, hair colour. Distinguishing marks, left arm broken at age five, small scar on left knee, birthmark the shape of Africa on forearm, little finger broken, two teeth missing, allergies, illnesses, missing appendices and adenoids and tonsils, X-rays, a scar like a crescent moon, DNA. Desperate little signs. Those missing kids were never coming back, that was the truth. All of them dead or ruined by now.

There were other kinds of missing kids, of course. The ones that stayed below the radar. Parental abductions. The black ops. Of course it was better to have your kid taken away by a disgruntled possessive ex than for the same disgruntled possessive ex to stick the kids in the car and run an exhaust into it or stab them in their hearts while they slept over on an access visit, but that didn't mean that you could just ignore custody orders and run off to somewhere without extradition. Or somewhere that didn't care. Or somewhere that thought it was OK to take a kid away from its mother. Someone had to bring them back, might as well be Jackson. Better than being a real mercenary, all those private security firms in Iraq he'd been approached by, or running security for diamond mines in Sierra Leone, frontier living where you took your life in your hands every time you stepped out of the door.

He had looked for kids in Japan, Singapore, Dubai. Munich. It was surprising. Jennifer, the girl in Munich, had a brother who had been taken to live with relatives somewhere else. Jackson didn't know if anyone had ever found him. Neither kid had ever been away from their mother before their Egyptian father took them on a court-arranged holiday. He lived and worked in Germany, he simply changed the girl's name, enrolled her in school, said her mother was dead. By the time the girl learned enough German to explain her situation to someone she'd probably have forgotten her mother. Kids forget easily, it's a protection thing. Jackson caught up with them a lot quicker than the slow wheels of

German bureaucracy were likely to. Six hours after he and Steve took her from that gingerbread house she was back home in Tring with her mother. Mother and child reunion.

Something was nagging at him but he didn't know what. From his wallet, Jackson took the photo that he had stolen in Linda Pallister's office. A little girl on a beach. One good head-and-shoulders shot. In his heart Jackson felt sure that it was Hope McMaster. He sighed and put the photograph away again.

It was barely half past nine when Jackson took to his bed. It was a single bed, and the dog had already claimed a considerable part of it. When Jackson climbed between the thin sheets, the dog stirred, raised its head and looked at him blankly, like a sleepwalker, and then settled down again. Jackson lay in bed for a long time beneath the unblinking watch of the dead-eyed dolls.

He found the invitation to the golf club dinner-dance at the back of a drawer in his office. Barry sneered at the command to 'Dress to impress – black tie.' There was, the invitation promised, a live band until midnight, followed by a seventies disco, a raffle with 'fantastic prizes' – a mini-break for two to the Isle of Wight '(including ferry crossings)', a signed DVD boxed set of *Gavin and Stacey*, not to mention a 'full-sized cricket bat signed by the Yorkshire CCTV First XI'. It was the kind of do Barbara used to like – an excuse to get dolled up in some horrendous outfit and brag to other women about Amy's 'A' Levels, her college certificate, her engagement, her baby. Not much to boast about now.

'Dress to impress, it says, Barry,' Len Lomax laughed when he caught sight of him. Unlike Barry, he was in a tux, smoking a cigar, expansive, polished. He was a big bloke who hadn't shrunk with age yet, looked in much better shape than Barry. How old was he – seventy, seventy-two? Pensioners didn't behave like pensioners any more, they all thought they were ruddy Sean Connery.

'I can get you a plate of something if you like?' Ray Strickland's wife offered. Margaret. Scots. Barbara said she had some kind of women's cancer but she looked the same as ever, all gristle, no meat. Soft on the outside, hard on the inside. Barbara had never liked Margaret Strickland – that didn't say much though, there were a lot of people Barbara didn't like, Barry included. 'I'm sure the kitchen has food left,' Margaret said. There was a menu propped up on the table, *Agneau rôti et purée de pommes de terre.*

'That's roast lamb and mashed potatoes to thee and me,' Ray Strickland said. Strickland didn't look in quite as good nick as Len Lomax but he still had that same nervous power running through him. Barry always used to think that you never quite knew which way he was going to go, nice or nasty. Just a little bit unstable. Barry wished he could go back, wished his younger self had had the nerve to tell Strickland and Lomax to bugger off and leave him alone.

'Or some dessert?' Margaret offered. 'There's tiramisu.'

The great and good had all finished their tiramisu, judging by the smears of what looked like shit on their plates.

'I'm not hungry,' Barry said. 'Thanks all the same.'

'We never see you here, Barry,' Margaret Strickland said.

'That's because I don't play golf,' Barry said.

'You drink though,' Lomax said, pouring him a glass of whisky. The band was tuning up and Alma, Len's wife, said, 'Will you have a dance, Barry?' She'd aged badly, too many holidays in cheap foreign sunshine. Over seventy and still in stilettos and full slap. They made Alma and Barbara and then they broke the mould. Thank God.

Ray Strickland made a little gesture with his head, indicating that he wanted Barry to go outside with him. Barry patted Alma on the shoulder and said, 'Maybe later, pet.' When hell froze. He followed Ray Strickland outside. The cool night air felt like medicine.

'Thought we might not get a chance to have a chat at Rex's funeral tomorrow,' Strickland said.

'Oh aye?' Barry said.

'I don't know how to put this exactly,' Strickland said.

He looked down at his polished shoes and frowned.

'Someone's nosing around asking questions about Carol Braithwaite?' Barry offered helpfully.

'Yes,' Strickland said, relief all over his face.

'Do you want me to do something about it?' Barry asked.

'Could you?' Ray Strickland asked uncertainly.

'Oh yeah,' Barry said. 'I can do something.'

As he climbed wearily back into his car, Barry wondered if the great and the good would be raising a glass to Rex Marshall before the night was over. Maybe before the 'seventies disco' started.

They'd all been there at that New Year do in the Metropole, Eastman in his pomp, Rex Marshall, Len and Alma Lomax, Ray Strickland and his odd little wife, Margaret, the Winfields.

Ian Winfield might still be alive. Barry didn't know if anyone had heard from the Winfields after they decamped to New Zealand. He hadn't thought about the Winfields in a long time. Kitty Winfield. Ian Winfield. He found himself falling down a long black tunnel and came out in the past. *Can I get you anything, Constable? Barry, isn't it?*

Carol Braithwaite rising. Rising, rising.

1975: 21 March

Barry lit up a fag. He was sitting in his car outside the Winfields' house. Very nice house. Barry couldn't even imagine what it would be like to live in a house like this, to live in Harrogate, the capital of northern posh. He should bring Barbara to Harrogate. If he could ever pluck up the courage to ask her out. He was going to ask her to go to the flicks with him. Barbara was very sophisticated compared to most of the girls he knew, always immaculately turned out. 'She'll spend all your money, a girl like that,' his mother said.

He had no idea what Strickland was playing at. Rambling on about how his car was in the garage for its MOT so he didn't have any wheels, could Barry pick him up? Barry didn't see what was stopping him getting a taxi. Barry was off duty, just sat down to a big fry-up his mother had cooked for him. Wished Ray Strickland didn't have his home phone number. 'Not a squad car,' Strickland said.

Strickland was waiting outside the flats in Lovell Park when Barry drew up in his old Ford Cortina. The Mark 2. A car Barry still remembered with affection over thirty years later.

Strickland was carrying a kiddy, asleep, wrapped in a blanket in his arms. He looked shaky, really shaky. He seemed to be in some kind of stupor. Alcohol, Barry assumed. Everyone knew that Strickland couldn't hold his drink. Barry opened the back door of the Cortina for him. 'Boss?' he said, hoping for an explanation.

'Just drive, Crawford,' he said wearily, 'Harrogate, the

Winfields.' Barry knew who the Winfield couple were. She was glamorous, used to be a model. Barry would give her one any time.

Strickland roused himself as they turned into the Winfields' street. 'It's good of you to do this,' he said as they came to a stop outside the house. 'I'd really appreciate it if you kept this between the two of us.'

'Your secret's safe with me, boss,' Barry said. No idea what the secret was, mind you.

'This isn't what it looks like,' Strickland said to Barry as he climbed out of the car, kiddy still asleep in his arms. Again, Barry had no idea what it looked like. Barry watched him walk up the path, ring the doorbell.

He waited ten, fifteen minutes. The front door opened and Ian Winfield came out. Barry rolled down the Cortina's window and Winfield said, 'Can I get you any-thing, Constable? Barry, isn't it?' Smooth bedside manner.

Barry wondered what kind of thing was on offer. 'No, thanks,' he said.

'Detective Constable Strickland will be out in a minute,' Winfield said in the soothing tone you would use to a restless child.

Five minutes later and Strickland was back in the car, even shakier than before. 'Take me home, Crawford,' he said. 'My wife'll be wondering where I am.'

That was three weeks before they discovered Carol Braithwaite's body in Lovell Park. They said she'd been lying dead for three weeks. Even Barry could do the maths. Strickland had killed her and taken the kiddy.

⁓

(*Marjorie Collier's living room/Int/Night*)

Marjorie Collier
Who are you? What are you doing here?

First Thug
We're looking for Vincent, where is he?

Marjorie Collier
I don't know, I don't know where he is.

Second Thug
Do you think we're stupid, love?

Marjorie Collier
You can't just barge in here like this. Get out!

First Thug
Not until we see Vince, sweetheart.
I suggest you get your blue-eyed boy
on the blower right now and tell him
his old mum's going to be taking a trip
down the boneyard if he doesn't get
back here double-quick.

Marjorie Collier
I will do no such thing.
I didn't fight Hitler just to give in
to schoolyard bullies like you.

(*She looks around, spots the poker by the fireside.*)

First Thug (to Second Thug)
Game old bird, isn't she?

Second Thug (to First Thug)
Stupid old bag, more like.
(to Marjorie) Don't try and be a heroine, love.

Marjorie Collier (making a grab for the poker)
You don't frighten me.

(*They struggle. First Thug hits Marjorie and throws her to the floor. She hits her head on the fender.*)

Not with a bang but a whimper. Director had handed her the script personally, features arranged sympathetically. A notice of execution. Poor old Marjorie Collier was coming to a sticky end. Sticky toffee pudding end.

'Watch out, Till,' Julia said as he approached. 'It looks like he's bringing you your invitation to board the death ship.'

'Well, this is it, Tilly darling,' the director said. 'The end.'

*   *   *

Now it was Saskia who was treating her like an invalid. She had brought her up a mug of warm milk with honey in it and a plate of digestives, along with her own pashmina which she tucked around Tilly's shoulders.

'It's a bit of a shock, isn't it?' she said. 'I know when I was killed in that awful car crash in *Hollyoaks* – my boyfriend was a psycho stalker who was planning on planting a bomb in the church at my funeral – remember that, who could forget? When I first read the script it gave me the real heebie-jeebies, but I was nominated for best actress in a soap, so it all turned out OK in the end. You'll see, everything will be fine. And anyway, you could do with a good rest, couldn't you? Not the RIP sort, obviously, just put your feet up for a bit, watch some daytime telly, treat yourself to a visit to a spa.'

Thank goodness Saskia finally ran out of steam and, making a vague gesture towards Tilly propped up on pillows, said, 'Well, night then.'

'Night,' Tilly said, relieved to be able to remove her wig at last.

Saskia couldn't hide her happiness at the thought of Tilly leaving, she'd already had a guarantee from the production staff that she would never have to share digs with anyone again, although there were rumours that she would be leaving soon anyway. Apparently she was 'off to LA' to try her luck. 'Little fish, big pond,' Julia said. 'She'll drown.'

'Well, not *drown*, I hope,' Tilly said. 'Just splash about helplessly for a bit.'

Of course, Saskia was so cheerful because her boyfriend was arriving tomorrow night. Not the rugby player, apparently he was yesterday's news (literally). The new one was 'a civilian', which was confusing because he was actually in the army, a lieutenant in the Coldstream Guards.

'Don't you love a man in uniform?' Saskia said to Tilly.

The closest Tilly had ever got to a man in uniform was in a production of *HMS Pinafore*, she'd had rather a nice singing voice in her early days. Funny, she'd forgotten all about that production. Wondered if she could still hit the notes. Saskia's lieutenant was called Rupert and apparently he came from a very traditional background. This seemed to make Saskia quite anxious. 'Well, naturally,' Julia said. 'Saskia's a complete cokehead. She'll never be able to hold it together. She'll go for lunch at his ma and pa's country pile and put on her Tara Palmer-Tomkinson accent and a twinset and pearls and then they'll catch her snorting dope off their posh loo seat or one of their posh loo seats because I'm sure they have more than one.' Tilly had trouble following Julia sometimes. She didn't know if it was her poor shrinking brain, or just Julia.

She sighed and put her specs back on and returned to reading the script. What did they mean when they said Marjorie Collier 'fought Hitler'? She was supposed to be sixty-eight – not exactly old unless you were a pre-pubescent script editor only interested in bringing in a younger audience. Joanna Lumley was in her mid-sixties, for heaven's sake, no one expected her to wear carpet slippers and knit in front of the fire. Tilly had met her at a charity do. 'Come with me,' Phoebe had said, 'I need you there.' Phoebe was rickety, she'd had her knees replaced, her hips replaced, she'd even had her thumb joints replaced. They were talking about her shoulders next. Tilly had no idea they could replace shoulders. Shame they couldn't replace her heart. Still, Joanna Lumley was very nice, although the seafood canapés had given Tilly a gippy tummy for days. Funny word, 'gippy', came from 'Egyptian', didn't it, was it racist? Better be careful not to say it in front of Paddy what's-her-name.

(Close-up on Marjorie's face.)
   (Whispers.) Vince. My boy. *(She dies.)*

Honestly, what a lot of rot. She'd have to stretch out her death scene as long as possible. She wasn't going that quickly. Put some real feeling into it so that a few tears would be shed at her passing.

She thought she'd better get on with running her lines but she had hardly got past the first one before she fell asleep. Some time later Saskia must have come in and removed her specs and turned off the light because when she woke up in the middle of the night, after the usual hectic dreams, it was dark and she couldn't see anything. A little rehearsal for the real thing.

Four o'clock in the morning, if the old clock radio on the bedside table was correct. The dead time. Something had woken him, but he didn't know what. The dog was awake as well.

Jackson slipped out of bed and padded across the dark room to the little attic window. He looked down into the deserted yard below and, beyond, into a narrow lane that ran behind the yard. Not much of a *bella vista*. Someone was lurking in the lane, a bulky figure dressed in the clothes of darkness. The creature detached itself from the shadows and slouched off down the street, too far away for Jackson to get a clear view of its features.

Common sense dictated that he should leave it alone. Leave it alone and climb back into a warm bed and go for a harmless adventure in the Land of Nod, rather than throwing on his clothes and climbing out of the window on to the fire escape in order to participate in a nightmare in the land of the living.

'*Allez oup!*' he said to the dog. The dog cocked its head to one side and gave him a quizzical look. Jackson demonstrated by climbing back in through the window and then climbing back out again. After a second's hesitation, in which Jackson felt he was being assessed for trustworthiness, it jumped neatly out on to the fire escape and, shepherded by Jackson, scrabbled down the metal steps.

Jackson unlatched the yard gate with exaggerated delicacy. He didn't want to incur the wrath of his hostess for the night by waking her from her beauty sleep. She needed all she could get.

When he stepped into the lane it was deserted. He thought of his mutinous hitchhiker and her handy Maglite-in-a-bag combo and wished he had something similar on his person. His Swiss Army knife was the nearest thing he had to a weapon and that was in his rucksack in his room.

He walked the length of the lane and came out on to another street of houses identical to Bella Vista. The dog stuck cautiously to his side, apparently not enjoying their escapade.

A figure sprang up ahead. Ill met by moonlight. One of the Land Cruiser guys. By their jackets shall ye know them. The hairs on Jackson's scruff rose and he spun round to see what was behind him. Yep, they came as a pair, leather jackets, leather gloves, big leather boots, Jackson the filling in the cow sandwich. The one behind flexed his knuckles, an action that reminded Jackson of Marilyn Nettles's cat trying to put the frighteners on him.

The dog's hackles rose and it growled, a surprisingly threatening sound coming from something so small. Yeah, Jackson thought, come on then, take me on, me and my tiny dog, we're ready for you. He positioned himself on the pavement so that he could see both of the Land Cruiser guys at once. Tweedledum and Tweedledee.

'We were just coming up to see you,' one of them said. 'Nice room, is it? Oh, I do like to be beside the seaside.' He sounded disconcertingly like Jackson's brother, same rough accent, same cynical undertone. Jackson's own accent had been sanded down over the years and he wondered sometimes if he would have recognized his younger self if he heard him now.

'Who *are* you?' Jackson said. 'And what do you want? Have you come here just to beat me up – for no discernible reason that I can see – or what?'

'The what. We came for the what bit,' the other one said. 'But we'll probably do the beating-up bit as well.' Jokers, always the worst types.

'Gentlemen, I think we're at cross-purposes here,' Jackson said. 'You're looking for that woman, the one you were after at the garage. I don't know where she is.'

'Do you think we're stupid?' the one who sounded like his brother said.

'Well . . .'

'It's you we're after.'

'Me? What did I do?'

'You've been sticking your nose in where it doesn't belong,' Tweedledee said. 'Asking questions all over the place.'

'Someone's got a message for you,' Tweedledum said.

'What, you're a greeting cards firm now?' Jackson said. Some people might think that when the odds seem stacked against you it's a good idea to simply walk away rather than poke the enemy in the face with a big stick. Jackson got his big stick out and poked. 'Don't tell me, you're a strippergram,' he said to Tweedledum, who bent his knees, ready for battle. Tweedledee did his knuckle-flexing thing again. Cry havoc, Jackson thought.

Tweedledum suddenly launched himself at Jackson, barrelling into him at full tilt, knocking him like a top, and before he could even respond to this sudden joust, Tweedledee punched him hard on the side of his head. Jackson reeled round but at least he managed to land a punch on Tweedledum's nose. 'Touché,' he managed to say before Tweedledee started pummelling him in the stomach.

Jackson found himself on the ground, all he could hear was the dog barking furiously. He wanted to tell it to stop before it got hurt, these guys probably wouldn't think twice about kicking it into touch.

Then the one who sounded like his dead brother spoke, startlingly close to his ear. 'The message, you southern smart-arse, is to leave Carol Braithwaite alone. And if you don't, then this is just going to keep on happening.' Jackson wanted to protest, worse than being punched to the ground was the idea that the confrères of his native county couldn't recognize him as one of their own. Unfortunately, before he could say anything one of those confrères kicked him in the head and darkness fell for a second time that night for Jackson.

❧

Toowit-toowoo. Not really. It was more like *kewick . . . oo-oo*. A female calling, a male answering. Very territorial birds, owls. Tracy only knew that because there was a book about British birds on the bookshelf. 'Holiday cottage' was a bit of a misnomer, the place was huge, she seemed to have overlooked that when she was booking it. 'Designed by Burges' it said, as was the church a couple of hundred yards away. Victorian Gothic. The house was in the middle of a medieval deer park. Extraordinary.

If they were to stay here for the full week they would be rattling around like two peas in an enormous pod. As it was, they were camping out for one night in the living room. Tracy didn't want to get stuck up in the bedrooms, didn't want to be batting blokes down staircases with her Maglite. Ground floor, quick escape out the back. The Saab was tucked away safely out of sight behind the house. No one would be looking for it here.

When they first arrived, earlier this afternoon, they had walked down a hill from the house to the manmade lake. There was a café overlooking the water and they sat outside and ate ice creams. They saved the ends of the cornets and fed them to a greedy goose. Tracy had had a Ladybird book called *The Greedy Goose* when she was a kid herself. Anyone looking at them would think that they were normal people on a day out. Mother and daughter. Imogen and Lucy.

When they finished their ice creams they walked through the water gardens, all the way to Fountains Abbey. Eighteenth-century landscaping, cascades and lakes and follies, nothing wrong with improving on nature in Tracy's opinion. Gangs of tadpoles congregated at the edges of ponds, here and there the flicker of a little fish. Tracy thought about Harry Reynolds's koi. Big expensive fish. Tracy couldn't imagine buying a fish if you weren't going to eat it.

Kid was a good walker, one foot in front of the other kind of walker. Utilitarian. When they got to Fountains itself there was some kind of medieval fair taking place. Or 'fayre' probably. Re-enactors in costume – cooking over an open fire, showing people how to weave with flax, shoot an arrow into a target. A whole hog roasting.

They left before the dancing started. 'Always know when to make an exit,' Tracy said.

They ate a makeshift supper of beans and cheese on toast and then they went walkabout again, wandering around in the balmy evening air. Kind of place made you want to use words like 'balmy'. Twilight, the witching hour. May, the magic month. All the visitors had gone home for the day and they had the whole place to themselves, just Tracy and the kid, the deer and the trees. None of the usual bestial sounds of the country, the lowing and bleating and crowing that ultimately signified the abattoir and slaughter. Here it was just birdsong, grass growing and being eaten, trees inching towards the clouds.

There were hundreds of deer in the park. Lots of baby deer. 'Bambis,' Courtney said. Alive, thank God, all of them. Tracy wondered if they could tell that she had recently slaughtered one of their own. She was seriously considering becoming a vegetarian.

These deer were almost tame. If you got too close they just raised their noses, gave a little twitch of the tail, moved off a few yards and went back to hoovering up the grass. Kid looked astonished, other than a rabid dog she'd probably never seen an animal close up. Tracy would have to add farms and zoos to the list of things that she needed to be introduced to.

And then, miraculously, as the day finally headed towards the dusk, a white stag, a young one, appeared out of the twilight, out of some medieval past. Not a re-enactor but the real thing. A white hart. It stood stock still and stared at Tracy. You would never get a man who looked as handsome. It knew it owned the place, it was her superior in every way. A prince among men.

Bloody hell, she thought, this was special. It had to be a good sign. Didn't it?

The place was full of ancient trees, oaks that must have been alive in Shakespeare's time. Three hundred years growing, three hundred years living, three hundred years dying. That's what it said in another book from the cottage bookshelf. She was reading her way through the night. Coal on the fire, Courtney asleep, wrapped in a blanket on one of the enormous sofas. Tracy had her feet up on the other one. She was keeping a vigil, Maglite to hand, learning all about oak forests, deer parks, medieval abbeys. It was one way to get an education – stay awake all night in case any mad bastards happened to stop by to say hello.

First the Avensis driver, then the leather-jackets, Tracy had never had so many men after her in her life. Shame their intentions were all so dishonourable. Not to mention the 'private detective' looking for her to ask about Carol Braithwaite. Who the hell were they all? Had they been sent to retrieve the kid or exact vengeance on Tracy for taking her? Both, probably. Was one of them responsible for Kelly Cross's death? Probably. Could Courtney be so valuable that someone would go to so much effort?

There was a phone in the house and she decided to give Barry a call, see if he knew anything about who killed Kelly Cross, see if he knew anything about anything. He sounded even more morose than usual. He must have been drinking.

'Barry? You know this private detective that's been asking questions? Is he driving a grey Avensis?'

'Dunno.'

'And he was asking about Carol Braithwaite?'

'Asking all sorts of questions about all sorts of people apparently. You, Linda, the Winfields. He's like some bloody virus that's got in the system.'

'Back up,' Tracy said. 'The Winfields? The bloke who was a doctor, married to that model?'

'They adopted a kiddy not long after Carol Braithwaite's murder, then they emigrated sharpish to New Zealand.'

'Oh my God,' Tracy murmured. That was why Michael disappeared, the Winfields took him. She remembered

Ian Winfield from her visit to the hospital, how protective he'd been of Michael.

'I've said too much,' Barry said.

'You haven't said enough.'

'It's all going to come out eventually.'

'What's going to come out, Barry? What's going on?'

Barry sighed heavily. The sigh was followed by a long silence.

'Still there, Barry?'

'Haven't gone anywhere. Tracy? I've seen you on tape with Kelly Cross, at the Merrion Centre.'

'Shit.'

'Yeah, shit. Exactly. And they found your fingerprint in Kelly's house. What's going on?'

'I didn't kill her.'

'I never thought you did,' Barry said.

'I bought the kid off her,' Tracy said.

'Shit.'

Dark outside. The darkest dark she'd ever known. If she went outside and walked down the short path to the gate, which she did every hour or so to make a perimeter check, Tracy could sense the vastness of the black sky, a scattering of stars, disappearing as the mist fell again. Tracy imagined that out there somewhere in the darkness she could hear the deer breathing.

1975: July

Tracy had finally managed to dispense with the awkward burden of her virginity. She'd started to take driving lessons, fed up with waiting to get on the police driving course. Her instructor was a one-man business, Dennis, separated from his wife, in his forties.

After the first lesson he suggested to Tracy that they go for a drink and he took her to a place off the Harrogate Road and bought her a brandy and Babycham without asking her what she would like. It was 'a lady's tipple' apparently. Wondered what Arkwright would say if she told him that, next time he plonked a pint glass of Theakston's in front of her. Same thing after the next lesson ('You've got a good sense of where you are on the road, Tracy'). After the third lesson ('You've got to watch that speedometer, Tracy'), they drove up beyond Heptonstall and they did it in the back of his car on a forestry trail somewhere. He wasn't what you'd call a catch, but then Tracy wasn't looking to keep him.

'Where've you been?' her mother said when Tracy came back from her tryst. Her antennae were twitching, they could have used Dorothy Waterhouse in the war. Wouldn't have needed to bother with Bletchley Park. 'You look different,' she said accusingly.

'I am different,' Tracy said boldly. 'I'm a woman.'

She was grateful to Dennis for the matter-of-fact nature of the act but he was more grateful to her for being twenty and 'well upholstered' so it was a reasonably well-balanced exchange. She cancelled her next lesson, told him she was emigrating. Signed up with

BSM and passed her test after eight lessons. It seemed an unfriendly thing to do but it was no more than he expected. He phoned the house once afterwards and, Sod's Law, her mother answered. 'Someone by the name of Dennis called for you,' she reported when Tracy came in from work. 'He wanted to know where your disembarkation port was. I told him not to be filthy.'

Things continued to look up for Tracy. Not long after she passed her driving test she signed the rental lease on a place of her own. *She's Leaving Home.* She had left behind the single bed in her parents' house where, apart from their annual evacuation to Bridlington, she had slept every night since coming home from the private maternity hospital that her parents thought would give their baby (hopefully a boy) a better start in life than an NHS ward. The maternity hospital was so underheated that Dorothy Waterhouse came home with chilblains and the infant Tracy with croup. Still, they had mixed with a better class of mother and baby and that was the important thing.

Tracy's new home was a boxy little bedsit with an Ascot water heater and filthy carpets. A two-bar electric heater that smelled dangerous and a hot-water bottle to embrace at night as she huddled in her sofa-bed. The bedsit was unfurnished and Tracy had bought everything second-hand, keeping stuff in her father's shed until she'd accumulated enough goods and chattels for the bachelorette life. When she got the key Arkwright and Barry helped her move it all in. When they finished they had tea and biscuits, sitting on the sofa-bed. 'You won't be here long, love,' Arkwright said. 'Some bloke'll come along soon and snap you up.' He patted the sofa-bed as if this would be the location of a future marriage proposal.

Barry smirked and choked on his Blue Riband.

'Something, lad?' Arkwright said.

'Nothing,' Barry said.

Having a place of her own raised many questions for Tracy that she never really grappled with successfully. For example, should she buy four dinner plates or two? There was a stall on the market that sold Wedgwood seconds. It was a stupid question, she only needed one plate, she dined alone every night. Findus Crispy Frozen Pancakes, Vesta curries, Smash potato. The nearest she got to cooking was frying up a batch of potato scallops.

She had imagined a future of domesticity, of inviting people from work round for 'a bite to eat' and turning out a fish pie or a plate of spaghetti, bottle of cheap plonk and a block of Wall's Cornish ice cream afterwards and everyone saying, *Tracy's OK, you know*. Never happened, of course. It wasn't that kind of life. Not those kind of people.

Coming out of the station, not long after the move, Tracy nearly jumped out of her skin when Marilyn Nettles stepped out of nowhere in front of her. There was definitely something of the night about the woman.

'Can we have a word?' she said. If she was looking for a story she'd come to the wrong person. 'Maybe we can grab a coffee somewhere? I'm not looking for information,' she added. 'The opposite, in fact. *I* wanted to tell *you* something.'

They drank sickly, milky coffees in a steamy café. It was drizzling outside, miserable summer rain. Not for the first time and certainly not for the last, Tracy wondered what it would be like to live somewhere different. Marilyn Nettles took a pack of cigarettes from her handbag and said to Tracy, 'Do you want a cancer stick?'

'No thanks. No – wait, go on then.'

'So?' Tracy said, drawing on the fag. She might lose some weight if she took up smoking. She stirred the foam on her coffee round and round. 'What is it you want to tell me?'

'The boy,' Marilyn Nettles said.

Tracy stopped stirring. 'What boy?'

'The Braithwaite boy. Michael. Do you know where he is?'

'He's in foster care. Unless you know something different.'

'I do. He was sent to an orphanage. Nuns.' Marilyn Nettles shivered. 'I hate nuns.'

'An orphanage?' Tracy said. She had imagined Michael Braithwaite with experienced foster parents, the solid church-going type who'd seen hundreds of distressed kids pass through their hands, people who knew how to heal and comfort. But an orphanage? The very word sounded melancholic. Abandoned.

'His name has been changed. There's a restraining order in place,' Marilyn Nettles said. 'All kind of legalese. To protect him, supposedly. I've been warned off. From on high.'

Tracy heard Linda Pallister's voice in her head, *No visitors. It's a directive from above.*

'He witnessed a murder,' Marilyn Nettles said, dropping her voice to a whisper. 'And then he disappears. Pouf! Just like that. I would call that suspicious. I would say that perhaps someone *made* him disappear.'

Barry had told Tracy that Len Lomax had told him 'in confidence' that 'someone', someone who claimed to be Michael's father, had confessed to the murder and had promptly died in custody. It wasn't something she could tell Marilyn Nettles, she'd be all over it like a rash and before she knew it Tracy would be reading about it in the papers. 'Why are you telling me this?' she asked.

Marilyn Nettles shook her head as if trying to dislodge an insect from her hair. 'I've said too much already.' She glanced nervously round the café. 'I just wanted to tell someone. It's not that I'm big on little kids but you have to feel sorry for that one. What chance does he have?'

'Which orphanage did they send him to?'

'Doesn't matter, he's been moved around.' She got up abruptly and left a handful of coins on the table. 'For the coffee,' she said, as if Tracy might have thought the money was for something else.

Tracy paid for the coffee and checked her watch. She groaned inwardly, perhaps outwardly too. She had a party to go to.

Tracy's parents were taking a leap into the unknown, attempting something that had never been attempted before in the Waterhouse household. They were throwing a party. The bungalow in Bramley was humming with tension.

Only a few years off retirement her father had been given 'a significant promotion' and, quite aberrantly, her parents had decided to celebrate in public. The invitation list was problematic as her parents had no friends as such, only acquaintances and neighbours and a few work colleagues of her father. Somehow or other they managed to scrape together a quorum.

The next dilemma was how to phrase the handwritten invitations in a way that would ensure that people left promptly at the end. *Drinks and snacks, 6.00 pm to 8.00 pm* was the wording finally decided on. 'The guests', her mother said, as if they were a dangerous breed of animal. Tracy was press-ganged into making an appearance. Her mother said, 'You can invite a couple of friends if you like.' ''S'all right,' Tracy said. 'I'll come on my own.'

She arrived early and speared toothpicks, charged with pineapple and cubed cheese, into the pale green skull of a cabbage. When the guests arrived Tracy wandered around like a waitress with platters of vol-au-vents her mother had spent all afternoon stuffing with prawns or shredded chicken. There weren't enough to go round and when they ran out her mother hissed, 'Get the cheese straws from the kitchen. Hurry!' As if she was asking for weapons reinforcements.

Dorothy Waterhouse had hoped that they would be able to hold the whole thing outside, on the newly laid concrete slabs of the patio. Tracy's mother lived in fear that their previously orderly acquaintances would be transformed into a rowdy crowd under the influence of Tracy's father's rum punch, the main ingredient of which was not rum but orange squash.

To her mother's disgust it had rained of course and everyone was crushed, elbows like chicken wings, into the newly extended (but not enough) living room. The banality of the occasion was depressing (*The builders didn't try and rip you off then? . . . In my day you stood still when a hearse passed you . . . Someone said number 21 had been sold to a Paki family.*) Tracy filched a handful of cheese straws and escaped to the bathroom. Sent up a little prayer of thanks that she didn't live here any more.

She put the toilet lid down and had a seat, munching her way through the cheese straws while she watched the rain streaming down the raindrop glass of the bathroom window. Wondered about that, raindrops on raindrop glass, seemed an excess of water in an already wet town. Heard the hollow word 'orphanage' in her brain. She could have given that kiddy a home. She should have taken him from that hospital bed, run away with him, given him the love he needed.

Tracy sighed and crammed the last bit of cheese straw

into her mouth, brushed the flakes off her clothes and washed her hands. She had a sudden image of the cold, poky bathroom in the Lovell Park flat. There had been make-up scattered messily on a shelf. A plastic submarine lay beached in the grubby bathtub. Were Carol's last thoughts for her son? She must have been afraid that he'd be killed as well. *What chance does he have?* Marilyn Nettles said.

In the kitchen her mother was unmoulding a temperamental charlotte russe. 'Have to go out, Mum,' Tracy shouted down the hallway. She unhooked her lightweight summer mac from the hallstand and accelerated out of the house, her mother's faint cries of protest following her down the garden path.

She traipsed through the rain, visiting every orphanage and care home in the book. None of them had heard of Michael Braithwaite, but, of course not, his name had been changed, according to Marilyn Nettles. She tried describing him, *Little boy, four years old, mother murdered,* but everywhere she went heads were shaken, doors were closed. Warrant card didn't seem to help at all, positively hindered, in fact. It was ten o'clock at night when she finally got back to her own flat, soaked through to the bone. The party would be long over now, her mother would already have hoovered up every last crumb.

Linda Pallister had a Hillman Imp now, it seemed.

Couldn't drive it though because Tracy was standing in the road in front of it.

'Tell me where he is, Linda. Tell me what he's called.'

Linda rolled down the car window and said, 'Go away, leave me alone or I'll call the police.'

'I am the police,' Tracy said. 'This uniform isn't fancy-dress.'

Should have thumped her one. Should have pulled her fingernails out one by one until she told. But that was then.

Sacrifice

Saturday

The next thing he knew was best described as nothing. Jackson was in the pitch dark, he was paralysed and the air around him was as noxious as the netherworld. He had already died once in his life but it hadn't resembled this at all. The first time round, after the train crash, it had been the classic white corridor scenario, complete with his dead sister and a sense of euphoria. He had gone, briefly, to a heaven, a heaven which had almost undoubtedly manifested itself as a result of oxygen deprivation to his brain. This time round he had apparently taken the staircase that went down the other way.

He drifted off, came to again, and realized that he wasn't in fact paralysed but was trussed, not so much a turkey as an Egyptian mummy. His ankles were tightly bound, his hands were tied behind his back and his mouth was taped up. To begin with it was painful, then it was excruciatingly painful and then after a time the pain was replaced with a numbness which was worse, somehow. His head hurt but no more than you would expect if you had been kicked and punched in it, that is to say, a lot. He would be lucky to escape without brain damage.

Perhaps he would be lucky to escape at all. He wriggled, awkwardly, like a particularly incompetent worm, until his head butted up against a hard surface. Slowly, he manoeuvred his way round what turned out to be a disturbingly claustrophobic space, not much bigger than a coffin. An oddly shaped sarcophagus filled with something stinking.

In the course of his squirming it eventually dawned on Jackson that he was sharing air with food refuse, an aroma of chop suey and the indefatigable scent of chips and fried fish. He was entombed in some kind of large, commercial waste bin along with the collective leftovers of several fat-based local restaurants. *I heard a Fly buzz – when I died.* That would be because there really was a fly in here with him, buzzing irritably with the knowledge that it, too, couldn't get out.

There was a certain relief in the realization. At least he hadn't gone mad, nor had he gone to hell or turned into a giant worm. He had simply been knocked on the head by a couple of hulking thugs and dumped in a garbage bin.

The relief didn't last long. He couldn't shout for help, he couldn't move – writhing didn't really count – and had no way of escaping. And where was the dog, it didn't seem to be in here with him. Was it lying hurt or maimed somewhere? Dog in jeopardy.

Then something worse happened. Much worse. The heavy engine sound of an industrial vehicle. The snarling of slow gears, hydraulic arms rising and falling, the careless clattering and comradely exchanges that all signalled the arrival of an early morning bin lorry. He struggled furiously, trying to rock the bin, but to no avail at all. He tried kicking with his bound feet but could barely make an impact. Nothing more than a low, desperate moan escaped beyond the barrier of tape across his mouth.

There were other bins parked nearby, he heard them being wheeled away towards the lorry, heard them being lifted, emptied, returned. Two of them. His was about to be the third. He heard one binman say to another, 'Did you see *Top Gear* last night?' and the other one replying, 'No, the wife watches *Collier*. I need to get Sky Plus. *Collier*'s crap.'

Jackson could hear them, clear as a bell. He was inches away from them but incapable of attracting their attention. He had survived the Gulf, he had survived Northern Ireland and a devastating train crash and he was going to die like trash (exactly like trash, in fact), by being crushed to death in a bin lorry.

The wheelie-bin was suddenly jolted and he found himself being bumped and rumbled along towards his nemesis. Jackson in jeopardy.

This was it then.

The end.

Jackson caught the sound of a dog barking. Not just barking, yapping furiously, the kind of noise that drove people crazy if there was no let-up to it. There was no let-up. On and on, the dog barked. Yap, yap, yap. There was something familiar about it.

'What is it?' he heard one of the binmen say. 'What are you trying to tell me, eh?'

'What's that you say, Skippy?' another said, in a bad Australian accent. 'Someone's in trouble, d'you say?'

'Me!' Jackson roared silently.

Someone laughed and said, 'Skippy's a kangaroo, not a dog. It should be Lassie.'

'This one's a Laddie by the looks of him.'

He was going to die while all around him people were discussing the gender of a dog?

Daylight suddenly. So sharp it dazzled him. And fresh sea air. Light and air, all a man needed when you got right down to basics. And a faithful friend who wasn't going to let you go to the great boneyard in the sky without kicking up a hell of a fuss.

'Leave no man behind, eh?' Jackson said to the dog as he staggered back to Bella Vista.

Tilly made herself an early morning cup of tea. The nice weather had broken and the rain was lashing against the little window of the kitchen. The clocks said ten past five and although Tilly could no longer feel entirely certain about what that meant, she was pretty sure it was the morning because she could hear Saskia snoring behind her bedroom door. Saskia denied that she snored, she was always muttering about the noise that Tilly made, 'Gosh, Tilly, you were like an express train in a tunnel last night,' or (overheard saying to Padma – there, Padma, remembered her name, no problem) 'I can't stand it, I'm getting no sleep, you know, it's like sharing a house with a giant hog.' Padma saying, 'Have you tried earplugs, Miss Bligh?'

Cap'n Bligh, yes, sir. Or rather, 'no, sir', Tilly supposed, given the mutiny. Did you call a naval captain 'sir'? Or 'captain'? *HMS Pinafore* not much help with that. Would Saskia's Guards lieutenant know? Military was military after all. What was his name? Saskia was the lieutenant's woman. Tilly had a small part in that film, a servant of some kind. Lyme Regis, lovely place, *the young people were all wild to see Lyme*. Her favourite Austen. *Persuasion*. Her brain was like lace, delicate and full of holes. Or a christening shawl. White wool on black skin. Coddling.

Rupert, that was his name! Like Rupert Bear. She used to love getting those annuals at Christmas. Rupert and his friends. Bill the Badger, Ping-Pong the Pekinese (was that racist in some way?). Couldn't remember the others. One Boxing Day she had done something that angered Father – who knew what, so many little things made him angry – and he had taken her new *Rupert* annual and torn the pages out one by one. Oh, dear God, would someone put a stop to all this. The memories, the words. Too many of them.

The lieutenant was arriving tonight, wasn't he? That would explain the shepherd's pie that was sitting mysteriously in the middle of the kitchen table.

The rain sounded as if someone was throwing buckets of water against the window. There was a grumble of thunder, like a sound effect. *On a ship at sea: a tempestuous noise of thunder and lightning heard.* She had played Miranda in an open-air production. Home Counties somewhere, couldn't remember much about it, her heart hadn't been in it the way it should have been because she was in love with Douglas. She'd been stuck in the wilds of Berkshire or Buckinghamshire, some Home Counties shire anyway, while Douglas was in London directing a play. He was fifteen years older than Tilly. She was only twenty, it was a lovely role – such sweet innocence – she hadn't realized at the time that she would never play it again. She was Prospero now, poor old Tilly, breaking her staff, about to give it all up. The revels were ending. Sticky toffee pudding ending.

Of course, *that* was the summer that Phoebe stole Douglas. He was directing her in *Major Barbara*, you see. She was the youngest actress ever to play the role on the London stage. *The brightest new star of her generation,* critics said. The springboard for her glittering career. Tilly had never understood why Douglas hadn't cast her in the role, she was just as good an actress as Phoebe, certainly no worse. Too late to ask him now. After that Phoebe got all the juicy roles, of course, Cleopatra, Duchess of Malfi, Nora Helmer.

When Tilly looked again she saw that it wasn't raining, wasn't wet outside at all. The rain was *inside* her head? A tempest in her brain. *O, I have suffered / With those that I saw suffer.*

The shepherd's pie on the table was defrosting beneath its suffocating cling-film. Miniature green trees of broccoli were all chopped and washed in a colander. Tonight's dinner on the table at six in the morning. Of course, the lieutenant in the Guards was arriving tonight. Saskia was doing her domestic act. She hadn't actually made the shepherd's pie, nice man in catering had done it for her. 'Make it look authentic,' Saskia had told him, 'home-made. As if I'm a good cook, but not cordon bleu.' Silly girl.

In a café with Douglas. Near the British Museum. He bought her a rum baba, her favourite, and then put his hand over hers and said, 'Sorry, Matilda dearest' – that was how he spoke, he had been brought up on matinee idols. His mother had been a Bluebell Girl before she had him. (And here was Tilly in Bluebell Cottage. Funny that.) No father in the picture for Douglas, his mother was the racy sort, that kind of background was bound to turn a boy's head. Inhaled greasepaint with his first breath. Made her terribly sad to think of Douglas as a little baby, he had been so racked at the end, nothing more than a skeleton. Aids, of course. Took off a lot of those poor boys. Tilly's baby had been a boy. Sluiced away. Black. Black as night. *She hangs upon the cheek of night / As a rich jewel in an Ethiop's ear.* First time she played Juliet was at school. An all-girls school, her Romeo was a girl called Eileen. Wonder what happened to Eileen. Could be dead.

* * *

There was a shepherd's pie sitting on the table. It seemed strange. She should pop it in the oven. Vince and his boyfriend were coming round tonight, 'to cheer her up'. They said they would bring food – had they already brought it? Were they already here? Where? Her brain was doing that swimmy thing again, like a television gone wrong. Maybe she was having little strokes, one after the other, that would explain how the weather had got inside her.

They had made shepherd's pie in 'housecraft' at school. Housecraft classes taught you all the things you would need to run a house, be a good wife—

'Jesus fucking Christ, Tilly! What are you doing? You're cooking the fucking shepherd's pie, it's fucking six o'clock in the morning. You stupid fucking senile bitch!'

Tilly flapped her hands helplessly in the air. She wanted to say, 'Don't shout at me,' she did so hate being shouted at, made her shrink inside. The great maw of Father's mouth, the smell of dead fish he carried on his skin. She couldn't say anything, the words wouldn't come out properly. *Ar-aw-oo-ar-ay-ee-ar-aw-oo-ar-ay-ee-ar-aw-oo-ar-ay-ee-ar*.

❧

They breakfasted on toast and Marmite, sitting at an oak refectory table made by Robert Thompson, the

Mouseman. Tracy had read a leaflet and pointed out the Mouseman's signature to Courtney, the little carved mouse climbing up the table leg. A set of ten matching chairs ringed the table. Courtney crawled around on hands and knees and counted all the mice on the chair legs.

Imagine a life too where you ate your breakfast every morning sitting at an oak table, in a Victorian Gothic house, looking out of a window at a herd of deer. The wand rested next to the Marmite jar. Broken now, Courtney had retained the top half with the star, more like a hatchet than a wand. When she finished her toast Courtney hauled out the faithful pink backpack and arranged her swag on the Mouseman table. After three days of witnessing this ritual Tracy thought she knew the catalogue by heart but every time Courtney seemed to have added something new. The current inventory was:

the tarnished silver thimble
the Chinese coin with a hole in the middle
the purse with a smiling monkey's face on it
the snow globe containing a crude model of the
  Houses of Parliament
the shell like a cream horn
the shell shaped like a coolie hat
the pine cone
Dorothy Waterhouse's engagement ring
the filigree leaf from the wood
a few links from a cheap gold chain

The gold chain was new. Kid was a magpie. She had an obsession with finding, collecting, arranging. She was self-contained. Did it foretell a scientist patiently collating data, an artist absorbed by creation, or was there something autistic about it?

Tracy cleared the plates away, took them through to the kitchen that was next to the dining room. A minute or two later she heard a noise coming from the other room. It was so unexpected that it took her a moment or two to understand that the sound was that of Courtney singing. 'Twinkle, Twinkle, Little Star'. The first verse. Tracy peered into the room. Courtney sang the first verse again (Who knew the second verse? No one). On the word 'star' she closed her fists and then opened them and made starfish hands. A damaged child that could still sing could be rescued, couldn't she? Could be taken to pantomimes and circuses, zoos and petting farms and Disneyland. Wasn't going to end up hanging around Sweet Street West looking for business. Chevaunne. She could have been rescued once. They could all have been rescued, all the Chevaunnes, all the Michael Braithwaites, all the starved and beaten and neglected. If there'd been enough people to rescue them.

'I'm sorry,' she said to Courtney. 'But we have to leave this nice place.'

She phoned Harry Reynolds. She could hear the sound of ice cubes tinkling in a glass. Seemed early for alcohol. Maybe it was his morning orange juice. She imagined him standing by the phone in his expensive house, wearing his expensive slippers, looking at his expensive fish. The ice made her think of diamonds. Diamonds and cockroaches. The end of the world. He answered cautiously. 'Yes?'

'I'm coming in,' she said. She sounded like a Cold War spy.

Long straight drive took you to the gates, took you to the road to Ripon. Kicked out of paradise, heading east of Eden, driving a stolen car. In possession of a stolen child.

Before they reached the gates, a car appeared coming from the opposite direction. Grey, nondescript, it travelled slowly towards them. Something about its dismal aura made Tracy's heart sink. The driver flashed his lights and raised a hand like a traffic cop. The Avensis.

Tracy had met her nemesis, she felt it in her bones. She was going to have to find out what he wanted sooner or later, she supposed.

The Avensis drew level with the Saab and the driver gave Tracy a little salute, like an old-fashioned AA man, and rolled down his window. Tracy rolled down hers.

'What?' she said, forgoing pleasantries.

'Tracy, mind if I call you that?' he said. Very chummy. Who the hell was he? 'I've been looking for you,' he said.

'I'm very popular at the moment,' Tracy said. 'Particularly with men, or morons as they're sometimes called. Why are you following me?'

'Depends on your perspective, doesn't it? Some might say that *you're* following *me*.'

'That's bullshit.'

He laughed and said, 'You're a wag, Tracy.'

'A wag?' Tracy puzzled. Where did this joker come from, out of a box on a shelf somewhere marked *Essex geezer, circa 1943*? He proceeded to get out of his car and walk round the front of the Saab. Tracy considered running him over. Like a deer, leaving his carcase on the road for the tourists to find. No CCTV here. Or was there? The National Trust probably had cameras camouflaged in bird boxes. He had reached the passenger side of the Saab before Tracy could decide whether or not to flatten him. He opened the car door and she reached for the Maglite.

'No need for that,' he said pleasantly. 'I'm not the person you should be worried about.' He sat in the passenger seat and sighed as if he'd just settled into a warm bath. 'Name's Brian Jackson, by the way.' He took a thin card from his pocket and handed it to her. *Private Investigations* it said, and a mobile phone number. You could get cards like that from machines in railway stations. *There's been a bloke down the station looking for you*, Barry said. *Says his name's Jackson something or other. Claims to be a private detective.*

'It's lovely here, isn't it?' he said conversationally. 'It's as if time has stood still. Have you had an opportunity to visit the abbey? It's a World Heritage site, you know.'

She stared at him until he put his hands in the air and said, 'Just making conversation. I've been looking for you all week. I found everyone else but you've been elusive.'

'Everyone else?'

'Every time I catch up with you, you shoot off. You nearly gave me a heart attack when you whacked into that deer. Could have been nasty. Was for the deer, obviously.'

'That was *you* chasing me?'

'Following, not chasing,' he said in a hurt voice. 'I don't know why you ran off into the wood like that.' He opened the glove compartment and rustled around inside and then came up with some kind of small electronic gadget. 'I'd never have found you without this,' he said. 'Tracking device.' He held it up for her inspection. 'I had it on your friend, wanted to make sure I could keep up with him. We're both after the same thing, bit of a tag-team thing going on. Nice coincidence, although I always say that a coincidence is just an explanation waiting to happen.'

'What are you talking about?'

'Very handy the way it led me to you. Your friend's very cross about his car, by the way.'

'No friend of mine,' Tracy said.

'He could be.'

A sense of defeat fell on her, a leaden cloak. What was the point? She couldn't run, she couldn't hide, there was always going to be someone looking for them. Someone sticking tracker devices on them. Satellites up in the stratosphere turned on their every move. Cameras aimed in their direction. Eyes in the sky and

camera drones playing I-Spy – someone beginning with
'T'. The Pentagon and the Kremlin probably had an eye on
them too. Aliens had them in an invisible tractor beam.
No escape, no way out. Wondered if she could just lay her
head down on the steering wheel and go to sleep and
when she woke up everything would be different. Maybe
the forest would grow around them, a cage of thorns and
briars. Should have thought about that before, got the kid
to prick her finger on a spinning wheel and they'd be safe.
Asleep but safe, like Amy Crawford.

The man was still rifling through the glove compartment. This time he came up with what looked like a
black-and-white humbug. 'Everton mint,' he said.
'Haven't seen one of those in a long time.' He took out
a handkerchief and cleaned the mint up a little and then
handed it to Courtney, who received it with the solemn
devotion of one accepting a communion wafer.

The sweet was a cartoon bulge in the kid's cheek.
Tracy imagined her swallowing it, choking on it. 'Chew
on that,' she warned, 'don't suck it.' She turned to Brian
Jackson, still grubbing through the glove compartment,
and said, 'What are you looking for?'

'Nothing, just wondered what he had in here. Can't
help but be curious, he's like – what's the fancy term,
alter ego, yeah, this geezer's like my alter ego.'

'What are you talking about?'

'*Looking good here, all the best, N*.' he read out from an old
postcard that he found. 'Nice place, Cheltenham,' he said.
'Ever been there?' He flicked through the CDs. 'Country
music,' he said. 'Good lord, who'd have thought it.'

'You're here about the kid,' Tracy said.

'Yeah,' he said. 'Bang to rights. I'm here about the kid. Not this one though, as interesting as I find her.' He turned round and stared at Courtney. She stared back.

'Don't bother,' Tracy said. 'She won't look away first. What do you mean, you're not interested in her?' Her spirits rose. She felt incredibly chuffed. 'You mean you haven't come to get her back?'

'Nah. I'm here about a different kid.'

'Different kid?' Tracy said.

'Not a kid any more. Used to be a kid.'

'We all used to be kids.'

'Not me.'

A group of fawns sauntered across the road in front of the car. 'Look,' Courtney said.

'I see them, pet,' Tracy said, keeping her eyes on Brian Jackson.

'Why don't we all hop in my car, Tracy?' Brian Jackson said. 'A lot safer for you than this one. This one's been reported stolen. Mine's not stolen – thief's honour. I'll give you a lift to wherever you're going – Leeds, is it? And we can have a little chat along the way.'

'Not until you tell me what this is about.' She suddenly felt incredibly irritated, the leaden cloak of defeat, now no more than a poor metaphor, dropped from her shoulders. Tracy had her mojo back. 'I am very busy at the moment and I do not have time for your mucking me about, so start talking.'

'OK, OK,' he said. 'Keep you hair on.' Courtney made

a noise indicating surprise and Tracy said, 'Not literally,' to her, without turning round.

'I'm waiting,' Tracy said.

'Michael Braithwaite,' he said. 'Name mean anything to you?'

'Michael Braithwaite?'

'Yeah, thought it might. I've got a couple of questions. Need to fill in some blanks. You're a key witness, as you might say. What do you reckon – shall we get going?'

'You said that you weren't the person I should be worried about,' Tracy said. 'Who *is* the person I should be worried about?'

He sat in the dining room of Bella Vista and ate his 'full Yorkshire breakfast' as if the only thing that had happened to him between closing his eyes last night and opening them again this morning had been an untroubled sleep in *Valerie*'s flowery bower.

The baffled (one might say traumatized) binmen had wanted to phone emergency services but somehow or other Jackson had managed to persuade them that he had ended up in the bin as a result of a dangerous prank on the part of his friends. 'A joke that went wrong.'

'Some joke,' one of them said.

They had had to tilt the bin to free him and he had

rolled out with the rubbish, like a legless bug. One of them produced a Stanley knife and cut the duct tape that was binding his ankles and wrists. It took some time for his limbs to come back to life but he managed to rip off the duct tape gag himself and to stumble off down the road, aware of the dubious glances at his back. He passed a shop window full of clocks. All the hands of the clocks were stretched out vertically. Six o'clock. He thought he had been in the bin for hours but it was less than two. Not a wheelie-bin but a Tardis.

The dog scampered by his side all the way back to Bella Vista in a state of near-delirium. At the site of the train crash two years ago Jackson's life had been saved by a girl administering CPR. Now he had been saved by the loyalty of a dog. The less innocent he was, the more innocent his saviours became. There was some kind of exchange at work in the universe that he didn't understand.

They had re-entered *Valerie* the same way that they had left, via the fire escape. The smell of bacon was already seeping under the door, fighting with the scent of air freshener trapped in the soft furnishings.

He squeezed himself into *Valerie*'s small ensuite bathroom and had the best shower of his life, despite the postage-stamp size of the towel and the wafer of soap that soon melted into nothing. A near-death experience proved to be just the thing to work up a man's appetite and once he was presentable again he left the dog – immediately forlorn at this ungrateful desertion – and exited *Valerie* in the conventional way to investigate Mrs Reid's 'full Yorkshire breakfast'.

Nothing discernibly Yorkshire about the breakfast at all. Jackson didn't know what he'd expected – Yorkshire pudding, a symbolic white rose cut into the toast perhaps – but instead there was the usual fry-up consisting of flabby slices of bacon, a pale, glassy egg, mushrooms like slugs and a sausage that inevitably reminded him of a dog turd. Worst of all was the (predictable) disappointment afforded by the coffee, which was weak and acidic and left Jackson feeling slightly queasy.

Only one other table in the dining room was occupied, by a middle-aged couple. Apart from the occasional inaudible remark of the 'pass-the-salt' kind the twosome breakfasted in a glum silence, bordering on the hostile.

The lack of marital conversation gave Jackson peace to digest the night's events. The 'message' in the early hours – *Leave Carol Braithwaite alone*. What did that mean – that he had got too close to an inconvenient truth? Yet he didn't feel as if he had found out anything at all about Carol Braithwaite's death. Quite the opposite. Who was warning him off and why? Was it because of something Marilyn Nettles had told him yesterday, something she had said? Or perhaps something she *hadn't* said? She had been economical with her answers.

Something had been nagging away at him as he fell asleep last night, before his encounter with

Tweedledum and Tweedledee. He had been thinking about Jennifer, the girl he and Steve had snatched in Munich, trying to remember the name of her brother and then – it came to Jackson suddenly – he hadn't asked Marilyn Nettles the right question. It was such a simple question as well.

The breakfasts were being served by a young girl. She looked familiar and it was only when she refilled his cup, caffeine was caffeine, after all, no matter how bad, that he recognized her as the female half of the Goth couple in St Mary's Church yesterday. Now her hair was pulled back in a ponytail and she was devoid of make-up. All her piercings, or at least the ones that were visible, had been removed. A truculent teenager rather than a wannabe vampire.

'Lovely morning,' Jackson said conversationally to her and was rewarded with a surly look.

'If you're not being made to work,' she said.

'Are you?' he said. 'Being made to?' She didn't look as if she could be made to do anything.

'White slave trade.'

It seemed unlikely. In Whitby.

She shambled out of the dining room, carelessly dripping coffee from the pot as she went. He heard the door to the kitchen being pushed open aggressively and the sound of something crashing and breaking. Mrs Reid's militant response was countered by the girl's voice whining, 'Oh, *Mum!*' in exactly the same mardy tone that Marlee adopted nowadays.

The girl barged out of the kitchen again and stomped up the stairs.

'You just can't get the staff these days, can you?' Jackson said cheerfully to his gloomy fellow break-fasters, neither of whom felt it necessary to come back with witty repartee, or indeed any repartee at all.

He rewarded the dog with the turd-like sausage, purloined from the Yorkshire breakfast, only regretting that everything that went in one end had to come out at the other.

Jackson stripped the bed, bundled up the sheets and left them on the mattress. On top of the sheets he placed twenty-five pounds in payment for the night. No tip, as there had been no discernible service worth rewarding. Easy money for Mrs Reid. He could have checked out in the normal way, of course, it just felt better like this. Saved a lot of unnecessary talking.

'Won't be long,' he said to the dog, tying it to a railing in Marilyn Nettles's yard.

There was no sign of life in her cottage. He was surprised, she hardly seemed the type to be an early riser. The house had the same abandoned feeling as Linda Pallister's. Where on earth were all these women disappearing to? Was there a black hole somewhere that was sucking in middle-aged women – Tracy Waterhouse, Linda Pallister and now Marilyn Nettles. And all somehow connected to Hope McMaster.

Or was it some kind of conspiracy – Brian Jackson,

Tracy Waterhouse, Marilyn Nettles, Linda Pallister – the whole lot of them involved in it. Jackson didn't know what 'it' was, but that was the point, wasn't it? That was what solving something was about, it was hunting the 'it' down, pinning its arms above its head and making it spill the beans. It was like being in a game, a game where you didn't know the rules or the identity of the other players and where you were unsure of the goal. Was he a pawn or a player? Was he becoming paranoid? (*Becoming?* he heard Julia say.)

He got down on his hands and knees and peered through the cat- flap. Dead air. 'You'll never fit through there,' a voice said.

Marilyn Nettles shuffled into the yard, laden with Somerfield plastic bags. Jackson heard the clink of glass on glass. Not a black hole then, nor a woman in jeopardy, just a raddled old alcoholic out doing her daily shop.

'What is it now?' she asked.

'How many children did Carol Braithwaite have?'

They left Whitby. On a bus.

Jackson sat on the top deck and admired the scenery. The dog lay at his feet. They were going back to Leeds. The place it all started. The place it would all end, if Jackson had anything to do with it. In Scarborough they exchanged the bus for a train. Jackson didn't like trains. He still had flashbacks to the crash, unpleasant sensory hallucinations – the smell of burning oil and electrical fires, the screech of metal on metal. He hadn't been back on a train since.

A woman had lost control of her car, the car had gone over the bridge, fallen on the track, derailed the train. Fifteen people dead. The woman had a brain tumour that had caused a seizure. One small cluster of rogue cells personal to the owner, that was all it took to kill and maim *en masse*. For want of a nail.

Jackson really didn't like trains.

He had eaten breakfast at home. Barry hadn't done that for a while, usually downed a quick cup of coffee and left for Millgarth. Barbara used to fret when he did that, *you need a breakfast inside you, everyone knows it's the most important meal,* yackety-yak. Not any more.

'I fancy bacon and eggs,' he said.

When she set it down in front of him he said, 'Aren't you going to have any?' and she said, 'Not hungry,' but she sat opposite him and had her usual breakfast of Valium and tea. She was dressed in a smart two-piece, her hair teased and backcombed.

'Thanks, love,' he said when he'd wiped the plate clean with a piece of bread. He stood up and drained his coffee down and then said, 'Well, I'll be off then.'

'He gets out today,' she said in an emotionless voice.

'I know,' he said. He attempted to kiss Barbara goodbye, something else he hadn't done for a long time, but she successfully feinted the move and instead he ended up patting her on the shoulder. 'Bye then,' he said.

It was two years since Barbara had invited Amy and Ivan to dinner, spent all day making complicated Delia recipes and then Barry had spent all evening telling Ivan what a waster he was. He was losing his business, going to be declared a bankrupt, the man who had promised to protect and support his daughter.

'Barry? How's it going?' he said when Barry opened the front door to them. He hated the way Ivan called him 'Barry', as if they were mates down the pub, as if they were equals. 'You can't expect him to call you Mr Crawford,' Barbara said. 'He's your son-in-law, for heaven's sake.' In fact, Barry thought, he would have preferred it if Ivan called him Superintendent.

'A little aperitif?' Barbara said when she'd taken their coats and they'd parked Sam in the cot upstairs. Barbara had bought duplicates of everything – cot, car seat, high chair, buggy – for their own house, imagining a lifetime of babysitting.

'Lovely, Barbara,' Ivan said, rubbing his hands, 'I'll have a white wine.' Barry knew he made him nervous but he didn't care. Before Barbara had even got as far as taking the Chardonnay out of the fridge Barry had started muttering sarcastic comments under his breath. 'Dad. Don't,' Amy said, touching his arm.

Ivan looked apprehensively at Amy over Delia's chocolate ricotta cheesecake. He had the look of a man about to jump off a cliff. Cleared his throat, said, 'We were wondering, Barry – Amy and I – about a loan, ten thousand pounds, to help get us back on our feet?'

Barry wanted to belt him one right there at the table. 'I've worked hard all my life,' he said, all patriarchal bluster, 'and you want me to hand over my money to you because you're a useless tosser. Why not just cut out the middle man and piss it straight down the drain?'

Amy jumping up from the table, 'I'm not staying to hear my husband insulted, Dad,' running up the stairs to get Sam out of his cot.

Before Barry knew it she was outside, strapping his grandson into his car seat. 'Honestly, Dad, sometimes you are such a shit.'

Barbara standing on the doorstep, face set in concrete, staring after the car. 'He's over the limit,' she said. 'He shouldn't be behind the wheel of a car. This is all your fault, Barry. As usual.'

He would have given his daughter anything and he had baulked at a measly ten-thousand-quid loan. He could have said yes, they could have opened a bottle of something fizzy to celebrate and eaten the chocolate ricotta cheesecake. Barbara could have said, 'Oh, you can't drive like that, the beds are all made up, you'd better stay over,' and Barry could have gone upstairs and kissed his sleeping grandson goodnight. Didn't happen like that, did it?

When he walked into Millgarth he nearly fell over Chloe Pallister, as agitated as a disturbed anthill. 'My mum's gone missing,' she said.

'Missing?' Barry said.

'Since Wednesday night. I went round to her house, no sign of her, she hasn't been into work, no one's seen her.'

Barry remembered how Amy had tossed her bouquet, aimed it directly at her best friend, but Chloe managed to fall over her own orange-satin feet and a more competitive girl caught the flowers.

'Did you notice if anything was missing?' he asked.

'Her passport.'

'Her passport,' he said. 'Well, if her passport's missing she's most likely run away.'

'Run away? My mother?'

It did sound unlikely, Linda wasn't the kind to run away, still he persisted with this easy explanation. 'Given up this crap life and gone to live on a beach in Greece,' he said. 'At this moment she's probably sitting in a taverna somewhere, making eyes at a waiter, hoping for a bit of Shirley Valentine.'

'Not my mum,' Chloe said stoutly.

'Well, we can all surprise ourselves sometimes, pet,' he said. His head felt woolly. Didn't have the energy for this. Had things to do. Take no prisoners, leave no bodies. Led Chloe Pallister into an interview room and said someone would come and take a statement. Left her there and forgot to tell anyone.

Gemma Holroyd put her head round the door to his office and said, 'Fyi, boss, the lab matched the DNA at Kelly Cross's murder scene to what they found on the

Mabgate whore.' *Fyi*, Barry thought, how he hated words like that. Not even a word. 'What about this third one?' he asked. 'The Cottage Road Cinema one.'

'Results aren't back yet.'

He went to his office, sat at his desk, turned his computer on and began to write his last testament.

Just dotting the i's and crossing the t's when there was a knock on the door. It opened before he had time to say, 'Come in.'

'You,' Barry said. 'I'd like to know what your game is. What do you want exactly?'

'The truth?' Jackson Brodie said.

'Superintendent. Come in.'

Harry Reynolds held the door open, a tea towel in his hand, the picture of contented domesticity.

The greenhouse heat of his house hit you as you walked through the door. And the aroma of coffee, overlaid by the smell of apples and sugar. 'Making an apple pie for Sunday lunch tomorrow,' Harry Reynolds said. 'What happened to your face?' he asked Tracy.

'Got into a fight with an airbag.'

Glancing down at Courtney, a tattered and torn fairy, he said, 'Hello, poppet, you look a bit the worse for wear as well. Magic not working too well? Your "mummy" will have to buy you a new wand, won't you, Mummy?' he said, raising a sarcastic eyebrow at Tracy. Then in a different tone of voice he said to her, 'You can't travel looking the way you do, "hedge" and "backwards" come to mind. You and the ugly duckling need some decent clothes. You don't want to attract attention.' She could imagine, only too easily, what it would be like to get on the wrong side of Harry Reynolds. Frightening. Tracy was way beyond being frightened.

Ugly duckling, how dare he. Should have decked him, right there in his overstuffed, overheated living room. Stuck him in his expensive koi pond, let Harry Reynolds swim with the fishes. Instead she said, 'Yeah, thanks for the advice, Harry. Unfortunately I had to leave my Louis Vuitton luggage behind and all my Gucci gowns were in it.'

'Are you in trouble, Superintendent? More than before? If that's humanly possible. I don't want trouble at my door, make sure you keep it away from me.'

'Is that a threat?'

'Just friendly advice.' He looked at the ugly sunburst clock on the wall and said, 'Susan'll be here soon with Brett and Ashley. They're popping in on their way to Alton Towers.' Stated as a fact, meant as a warning. No offer of scones this time. Strictly business. 'And I've got a funeral to go to,' he added.

He took a large, stout manila envelope from his sixties G Plan sideboard. 'Everything's here. New passports, birth certificates. An address in Ilkley – no point in pretending you're not from Yorkshire, open your mouth and you'll betray yourself – utility bills to that address, you'll be able to set up a new bank account wherever it is you're going. France is it? You should go somewhere that doesn't extradite. New national insurance number as well, and as a little extra, you've got a profile on Facebook and you'll be pleased to hear that you have seventeen friends already. Welcome to the brave new world, Imogen Brown.'

Tracy handed over an envelope bursting with notes. 'Expensive business,' she said. Second envelope this week, this one containing a lot more money than the first. She had definitely joined the cash economy.

'You're not in a position to bargain, Superintendent.' 'Just saying.'

'Did you instruct your solicitor to get a move on with the sale of your house?'

'Yes.'

He sighed the sigh of a put-upon entrepreneur. 'It takes bloody weeks to buy or sell a house, all those searches and surveys. Ridiculous amount of bureaucracy. A man's money and his word should be enough. And don't get me started on the money-laundering regulations. Gone are the good old days when you could just go out and buy a nice little piece of real estate with the cash in your pocket.'

'Yeah, those good old days,' Tracy said. 'Everybody misses them. Especially the criminals.'

'You're in no position to throw stones, Super-intendent. Anyway, don't worry, I can get it pushed through. Expedited is the word, I believe. Nice word. Stay in touch with your solicitor. Solicitor sells the house to me, I'll take my finder's fee, as it were, and put the rest into the new bank account you're going to set up.'

'I threw my phone away.'

'Wise move. They can find you anywhere these days if you've got a phone. Hang on,' he said and disappeared out of the room. Tracy could hear him moving about upstairs. Courtney had her face glued to the patio doors, watching the fish pond. Tracy caught sight of a big blue-and-white-marbled fish gliding by like a cruising submarine.

Harry Reynolds came back in the room with a carrier bag of clothes. 'Some stuff in here of Ashley's and my wife's. She was a big woman, they should fit. I should have cleared her things out before now, given them to charity or whatever. Susan's always on to me. Doesn't like seeing her mum's things around the house when she comes.' He drooped, suddenly an old man without a wife. He noticed Courtney's grubby face-print on the glass of the patio doors and absent-mindedly took out a handkerchief and polished the imprint away.

'Here,' he said, putting his hand into the bag of clothes and coming out with a couple of mobile phones that he handed over to Tracy, saying, 'Throw them away when you've used them once. They're pre-paid.'

'Of course they are,' Tracy said. An old age pensioner with a wardrobe full of burner phones, what was there to be surprised at in that?

The doorbell rang and Harry Reynolds hurried off to answer it.

'That'll be Brett and Ashley then,' Tracy said, raising an eyebrow at Courtney. She raised an eyebrow back, an enigmatic response.

Harry Reynolds's grandchildren rushed into the house and were brought up short by the sight of Courtney, a scruffy cuckoo usurping their place in the nest. They were dressed in mufti, Brett in a Leeds United football strip, Ashley in jeans and a pink velour *High School Musical* hoodie. Courtney stared open-mouthed at this unattainable vision of pre-pubescent chic.

Their mother blustered into the room behind them and said, 'What's all this then?'

'Nothing, Susan,' Harry Reynolds said, placatory, slightly cowed. 'An old friend, passing by. Dropped in.'

Tracy wondered if Harry Reynolds's daughter knew what kind of 'old friends' her father used to have, or did she think all this – the roast beef, the school fees, the koi – was the just rewards for clean living and hard work? 'Don't worry, we're just going,' Tracy said.

'I'll escort you to the door, shall I?' Harry said, sounding like a policeman.

The Avensis was parked outside. Brian Jackson was leaning against the bonnet, smoking. He raised a cigarette in mute greeting when he saw them.

'Who's this?' Harry Reynolds muttered to Tracy when he saw him.

'Nobody,' Tracy said.

'Well, have a nice life, Superintendent,' Harry Reynolds said.

'Try my best,' Tracy said.

⁓

1975: 21 March

A toddler! Darling little thing, in her pyjamas, fast asleep, wrapped in a dirty old blanket. Had there been an accident of some kind? Ray Strickland was white, he looked as if he'd just witnessed something dreadful.

'Come in, it's freezing out there,' Ian said. He led Ray into the living room, sat him down, poured him a huge tumbler of whisky. Ray's hand was shaking so much that he couldn't get it to his lips.

'What happened, Strickland?' Ian asked. He was kneeling beside him, checking the girl to see if she was injured in some way. Kitty felt a rush of pride in her husband's expertise. 'Who is she, Ray?' Ian asked but Ray just shook his head.

'Is she all right?' Ray asked and Ian nodded and said, 'As far as I can make out.' Kitty took the little girl from Ray and wrapped her up in a clean blanket. 'There, snug as a bug in a rug,' she said, holding her in her arms. The girl didn't stir. The solid weight of the child felt so lovely. Imagine if she was yours to keep, to hold like this every day. *Kitty Winfield brushed her sleeping daughter's hair from her face.*

'Will you take her?' Ray said.

'Take her?' Kitty echoed. 'For the night?'

'For good.'

'Mine? To keep? For ever?' Kitty said.

'Ours,' Ian said.

A couple of weeks later, over a nice candlelit dinner at home, Ian poured her a glass of wine and said, 'I've been offered a job in New Zealand, I thought it best if I take it.'

'Oh God, yes, darling,' Kitty said. 'That's perfect. We can leave everything behind, start again where no one knows anything about us. You are clever.'

∽

A plague upon this howling! The wild waters roaring in her head. Tilly had run out of Bluebell Cottage, abuse from Saskia echoing in her ears, got into her car and driven off. She wanted to go home. She needed a train, trains were in stations, the station was in Leeds. Something horrible had happened to Tilly in Leeds but for the life of her she couldn't remember what it was exactly. Something to do with a child. A child, a poor, poor child. A little black thing in the snow. Her little black baby.

When she had kissed her lovely Nigerian man at Leicester Square tube station, he said to her, 'Shall I call for you tonight, perhaps you'd like to go to the cinema, perhaps some supper afterwards?'

'That would be wonderful,' Tilly said.

'I'll call for you,' he said. 'About seven.'

She spent the whole day thinking about him, wondering what to wear, how to do her hair. She was absolutely useless in rehearsal but she didn't care, her heart was skipping. She got home at six, got ready in a terrific rush and then stood at the window looking down at the street, waiting for a glimpse of her handsome new man.

Was still standing there at eight, at nine. At ten she knew he wasn't coming. Understood he would never come.

It was only much later that she learned that he had got lost. He had never written down her address, thought he could easily find his way back to her flat but once he was in Soho he realized he had mistaken her street. He had wandered up and down and all around the houses, looking for some familiar landmark, some reminder of where he had been the night before. He had even tried doors and got short shrift because of his colour, except from some of the ladies who had cards above their doorbells. Nearly midnight when he gave up and went home.

The next day he tried to track her down again. He had done the rounds of the theatres asking about her and in one someone directed him to Phoebe, about to go into a matinee performance of *Pygmalion*. He recognized her from the party at the embassy. She told him that yes, she knew Tilly, in fact Tilly was her best friend and had told her all about the previous night's 'tryst', and 'I am afraid I am the bearer of bad news,' she said, her hand sincerely on her heart, or where her heart would have been if she had had one. Phoebe went on to inform him that Tilly had realized, in the cold light of day, that she did not want to see him again. It had been a mistake, she had been carried away. 'You understand?' Phoebe said. He did. 'So sorry,' Phoebe said, 'that's the beginners' call, I must go.'

'I was looking out for your interests,' Phoebe said, sitting by her bedside in hospital after she had lost the baby. 'Sometimes you can be rather foolish.' *Silly Tilly.* 'It would only have ended in disaster, Tilly.'

It had already ended in disaster.

When she felt stronger she paid a visit to the Nigerian embassy, she had to apologize to him, explain about her treacherous friend. There was a man on reception but what could she say to him? 'You have someone called John who works here?' The man on reception looked at her with something like contempt, rather like the nurses on the maternity ward, and said, 'We have several people working here with that name. I would have to know his surname.'

What could she do? *O, the cry did knock / Against my very heart!* She trudged home in the rain, defeated. Perhaps both of them gave up too easily. She had always thought that of Princess Margaret and Captain Townsend. Duty over love. What nonsense. Love should always come first. It wasn't as if Princess Margaret had been *necessary* to the country in any way. Quite the opposite.

Perhaps she wouldn't have lost her baby if she hadn't lost his father. Perhaps it was the stress she was under. She had started to buy things, mittens and bootees. She kept one of the little mittens for years, at the bottom of her bag, until it disintegrated. Silly really.

It was hair-raising on Leeds station, so many people rushing backwards and forwards, their faces grim, everyone running for trains, impatient with each other, with themselves. Jolting and jostling. No manners!

The cloud-capped towers, the gorgeous palaces. It was all make-believe, wasn't it? Reality itself was nothing. Words, everything was made out of words, once you lost the words you lost the world. The howling tempest all around her. At sea in a high wind. The men on the trawlers, their bodies spiralling through the cold icy waters, after their brave little ships were torpedoed. Down, down, down, to the seabed. *Those are pearls that were his eyes*. Treasure in the deep.

She had that funny feeling of darkness again, of the curtain of Northern Lights before her eyes. She was on a ship ploughing through the dark waters. All about her was desperation. The spars breaking, the mainmast cracking, the sails hanging in rags. The figurehead of the ship was a naked baby howling in the wind. There were babies everywhere, hanging on to the rigging for dear life, clinging to the sides of the ship as it began to sink into the icy, oily sea. Tilly must save them, she must save them all, but she can't, she is going down with the ship. *Mercy on us! We split, we split!*

And then suddenly there she was, like a ray of light, a port in a storm – the little 'Twinkle, Twinkle' girl. On the station platform. Her wings crushed, a poor little butterfly, a bedraggled fairy, flitting amongst the crowd ahead on the walkway above the platforms. Tilly had been given a second opportunity to save her. Someone should do something. Tilly should do something. Be bold, Tilly! Be a bold girl!

Courtney. The name came unbidden. (*Would you just shut the fuck up, Courtney, you're getting on my tits!*) 'Courtney,' Tilly whispered, her voice suddenly hoarse. The girl turned her head and looked at her. 'Courtney,' Tilly repeated more confidently this time. She smiled and held out her hand. Courtney walked towards her, put her little hand in Tilly's old one as if she were obeying invisible instructions. Tilly remembered her dream, the feel of the velvety rabbit's paw in her hand as they flew. 'Come with me, darling,' Tilly said.

☙

Tracy was clad in Harry Reynolds's dead wife's clothes. Marks & Spencer trousers with an elasticated waist and a tunic top decorated with a jungle design that would have allowed her to step into the rainforest and become invisible. No rainforests in Leeds. Courtney, trundling along beside her, had got the better end of the deal, but only just – sporting Ashley's cast-off denim pedal-pushers and a Peppa Pig top. On top of them she insisted on wearing the rags of her fairy dress. So much for Harry Reynolds's idea of 'decent clothes', they looked like homeless people, but that was OK, no one was interested in homeless people.

There was an announcement about a 'through train', telling people to stand back from the edge of the platform. The platform was swarming – Bank Holiday weekend, Tracy supposed – and she hung on to Courtney's hand as if the kid was about to be carried off to Kansas. Tracy had once attended an incident where someone had been pushed off a crowded platform beneath a train. Bloke who did it – ordinary bloke, looked a bit like Les Dennis – said he couldn't help himself. The more he told himself not to shove the bloke standing in front of him, the more he felt impelled to do it. Seemed to think that was a reason, didn't even plead temporary insanity. Caught on camera, got life, would be out in five years. 'Keep back from the edge,' Tracy said to Courtney.

No idea how it happened. There was a surge in the crowd – maybe they thought that the train was pulling into the station, not pushing its way through, but one second she had hold of the kid, the next she'd slipped from her grasp. Panic clenched Tracy's chest as she spun round looking for Courtney and came up almost jaw to jaw with Len Lomax.

It was years since she'd last seen him. Three-piece silk suit, black funeral tie, specs that belonged on a younger man. He must be pushing seventy if he was a day but he looked good on it considering he'd spent the best part of his life smoking and drinking and who knew what else.

'Tracy, long time no see,' he said as if they were at a garden party.

'Not now, boss,' she said, scanning the crowded platform for the kid. Over fifteen years since he'd been her boss but the subordination came naturally.

She spotted Courtney further along the platform, being led away by an old woman. Kid would probably go with anyone. A dog would have more sense. An old woman was a safe pair of hands, wasn't she? Old women found kids and took them to Lost Property and pressed a sixpence into their hand. (This had happened to an infant Tracy once on York station. She had rather hoped the old woman in question would take her home.) Unless they were evil witches, of course, in which case they took the kid home and fattened it up before putting it in the oven.

She lost sight of the old woman in the crush, started to hyperventilate. Keep calm. Stay in control. Saw the old woman again and began shoving her way through the crowd but something was tugging at her arm, pulling her back. Not something, someone. Len Lomax again. What was he playing at? He reached out and grabbed hold of her upper arm and she felt the surprising strength of his grip on her bicep. He wouldn't let go, he was an anchor, dragging her away from the kid, saying, 'You're a hard woman to get hold of, Tracy. You and I need to have a little chat.' *Who is the person I should be worried about?* she'd asked Brian Jackson. 'Strickland and his sidekick Lomax,' he said. Funny but Tracy had always thought of Strickland as Lomax's sidekick rather than the other way round. 'They're trying to keep the lid on the past,' Brian Jackson said. 'But the truth will always out.'

'Fuck off and let go of me.' She tried to twist away but Lomax was holding on hard. 'Sorry, boss,' she said and kneed him in the groin.

'Bitch!' she heard him shout as she dashed off. She had got within breathing distance of the kid when one of the Land Cruiser blokes from the garage suddenly stepped in front of her like a wall. She started to put two and two together, it was a sum that had been a long time coming. The leather-jacket thugs were Lomax's men. Ex-cons whose path had crossed with his at some point. 'Key witness,' Brian Jackson said to her on the drive from Fountains to Leeds. 'You were there when they broke down that door.' Witness to nothing, she was the last person who was key.

Tracy didn't break stride, just punched the Land Cruiser bloke hard in the face and steamed on towards the kid. She caught sight of the other hulking leather-jacket – no surprise there – weaving his way through the throng towards her. Wolves every-where, closing in. This one was expecting her to dodge out of his reach but instead Taurean Tracy charged straight at him and rammed the hulk out of the way.

The crowd shrank back from her, nothing like a mad cow on the rampage to clear a space. Courtney spotted Tracy and let go of the old woman's hand and ran towards her. Tracy snatched her up and clutched her tightly in her arms. Save the kid, save the world. Kid was the world. The world, the whole world and nothing but the world. 'Can't breathe,' Courtney murmured.

'Sorry,' Tracy said, loosening her grip, looking round for the escalator. No way out, too many people. And here was bloody Len Lomax again, what was wrong with the stupid old bastard? He was spitting mad, he never did like to be thwarted, especially by a woman. 'I want to fucking talk to you, OK?' he said.

He darted forward and tried to seize the kid, started pulling her away from Tracy. Courtney, clamped on to Tracy like a baby koala, screamed her head off and started bashing him with her wand. Like hitting an elephant with a stalk of grass.

The old woman, wig askew, made a sudden, unexpected lunge at Lomax, more like falling than lunging, and grasped him round the waist. Lomax twisted round so that he was face to face in the old woman's embrace and for a second they looked like a pair of grappling pensioners at a particularly fraught tea-dance.

The old woman had sent Len Lomax off balance and the two of them wobbled perilously as he tried to regain equilibrium. There was another, more urgent platform announcement about the through train and a rush of air and noise signalling its approach. There was a collective gasp of horror from those members of the crowd who were close enough to the bumbling old waltzers to see the imminent danger in their dance. People started to yell and shout and a couple of blokes leaped forward and tried, and failed, to pull them back.

There was a quantum second of silence, counting for nothing in one dimension and stretching to infinity in another. In the balance between triumph and disaster Tracy sensed the inevitability of the outcome.

Sound returned with a vengeance as the train roared into the station and Tracy watched in disbelief as Len Lomax and the old biddy, still clasped in each other's arms, both lost their footing and toppled over the edge into the engine's unforgiving path. Tracy slapped her hand over the kid's eyes but it was all over in a second. The noise of the train's shrieking brakes outdid the screams and cries from the people on the platform. It was no longer a through train, it was a stopping one now.

Turning away, Tracy caught a glimpse of the leather-jackets, resuscitated like a pair of cartoon villains, scrambling away up the escalator. The puppet-master was gone, no need for the puppets to hang around.

'I can't see,' Courtney said.

'Sorry,' Tracy said, removing her hand from the kid's eyes.

A pair of railway police were sprinting down the other escalator and into the pandemonium on the platform. Two platforms over, another train was standing patiently. 'Come on,' Tracy said to the kid. The guard was already blowing the whistle to signal that the doors were about to shut. They stepped on to the train just before its jaws hissed and closed.

They walked to the far end of the train, took their seats sedately, like any passengers. All the kid had left of the wand was the silver star. She put it in the backpack.

Tracy found an old freckled banana nestling next to the Maglite in the bottom of her bag. Kid gave the thumbs-up. Made starfish hands out the window.

For a hallucinogenic moment Tracy thought she saw the Saab driver standing next to Brian Jackson on the platform.

Goodbye to Leeds. Good riddance to bad rubbish, Tracy thought. She was never coming back. She was finished with the past. She was an astronaut who'd travelled too far. No return to earth for Tracy. She wasn't Tracy any more anyway. She was Imogen Brown. She had seventeen friends on Facebook and cash in the bank. And she had the kid to look after. Sleep, eat, protect. Repeat.

Poor old Tilly with her shaky knees and her dicky hip dancing her last waltz in the arms of a man. A brief encounter on a railway platform. *Nothing lasts really. Neither happiness nor despair. Not even life lasts very long.*

She'd played Laura Jesson once, a pretty dreadful repertory production – the Wolsey in Ipswich, or maybe it was the Theatre Royal in Windsor. It didn't matter now. At the time she was too young to understand the notion of sacrifice, of what love demanded of a person.

A bad man who wanted to hurt the 'Twinkle, Twinkle' child. For a second she thought she saw her father in his face.

And then she was rolling, rolling through the air and she thought it will be all right, it's not far to fall to the tracks, but then the train got in the way. Silly Tilly.

Our little life is rounded with a sleep. She thought her wig might have fallen off. You didn't want to be un-dignified at the end. *If only it was somebody else's story and not mine.* Coiling down into the cold water, the big silver fish shoaling around her, escorting her, protecting her, as she sank slowly down on to the seabed. Be not afeard. Her bones already coral. Her eyes as blind as pearls. The rest is silence.

A Wounded Deer – leaps highest. Crossing on the glassed-in bridge over the tracks, he saw the whole drama play out. He recognized the bizarre cast of players – Vince Collier's mother, the woman who had stolen his Saab, the little girl, Tweedledum and Tweedledee – in this strange impromptu performance. The only new actor was the old man who fell beneath the train with Vince Collier's mother. From up here it looked as if she might have pushed him. What was the title of that Mary Gauthier song? 'Mercy Now'?

Jackson really didn't like trains. He really didn't.

He should go down, take charge, do something, help someone. He scooped up the dog, it was only too easy to imagine it being trampled underfoot in this mêlée, and scooted down the escalator and got stuck in the clamour jamming up the platform. He caught sight of his thieving hitchhiker, little girl in tow. She was getting on to another train, leaving more chaos in her wake. He ran towards them but the train was already leaving the platform. He caught sight of the little girl, waving good-bye to him, making hands like stars, until she was out of sight.

An arresting hand on his shoulder made him jump. Brian Jackson. The false Jackson, as he had begun to think of him. Somehow Jackson – the real Jackson – wasn't surprised.

'She's a slippery fish, that Tracy Waterhouse.'

'Say again?' Jackson said, wheels spinning in his brain. 'That was Tracy Waterhouse?'

'Call yourself a detective.'

'I don't understand,' Jackson said. He didn't know why he didn't just get that sentence tattooed on his fore-head.

'I think we're both after the same thing,' Brian Jackson said. 'It's just that we've been coming at it from different starting points.' Police and paramedics had begun to arrive on the scene now. 'What a mess,' Brian Jackson said. 'Let's go.'

Jackson hesitated. Shouldn't he be helping, at the very least giving a statement about what he'd seen?

'Innocent bystanders,' Brian Jackson said, encouraging him in the direction of the escalator, like a sheepdog rounding up an obstinate ewe. 'Come on, I've got someone you'd like to meet. Someone who'd like to meet you.'

'Who?'

'My client. A man called Michael Braithwaite. We'd both like to know who it is that *you're* working for.'

'You're phoning me,' she said.

'I am,' Jackson agreed.

'You're not emailing or texting,' Hope McMaster said. 'You're speaking. You've got news. What's happened?' All exclamation marks suppressed beneath the breathless weight of expectation. Hope in the balance.

'Well,' Jackson said cautiously, 'it goes like this. Good, bad, good. OK?'

'OK.'

'First of all, the good news is that I've found out who your real mother is. The bad news is that she was a prostitute who was murdered by your father.'

'OK,' Hope said. 'I'll digest that later. And the other good news?'

'You have a brother.'

Hope McMaster. Michael Braithwaite. The two sides of a jigsaw. A perfect fit.

Hope McMaster was Nicola Braithwaite, Michael's sister.

('Why didn't you say that?' Jackson had asked Marilyn Nettles this morning.

'You didn't ask,' she said.)

Nicola Braithwaite, two years old. There had been no gagging orders about her, no injunctions, no need to 'protect' her because she didn't exist. She didn't go to school, she'd never been to the doctor's, Carol Braithwaite had avoided health visitors and district nurses. She moved house all the time. Neighbours hadn't even noticed her.

'Disappeared,' according to Marilyn Nettles. 'She wasn't in the flat when they broke down the door, so they didn't know about her. Well, of course, some people knew about her . . . I had to dig deep to find out, but I never told anyone. Did she have a good life?'

'Yes,' Jackson said. 'I suppose she did.'

'Oh, it's such a lovely story,' Julia said, tears in her eyes.

'Well, only the ending's lovely,' Jackson said, 'not the story itself.'

'A child who is found,' Julia said. 'Isn't that the best thing in the world?'

'What was left in the box,' Jackson said.

⁓

1975: 21 March

She'd been in one of her moods when he arrived at the flat in Lovell Park. You never knew which way it would go, sometimes she was as high as a kite, other times she was sunk in self-pity and low spirits. It was so quick that sometimes you could see it happening, see her face changing. It didn't help that tonight she'd been drinking – she was a mean drunk – and waved a bottle of cheap wine in his face as a greeting when he came in the door.

'Kiddies are asleep,' she said.

Only Michael was in bed – presumably, because there was no sign of him. Nicola was on the couch where she must have fallen asleep. Her face and hands were grubby, her pyjamas unwashed. What hope did the kid have?

'I brought the money round.' He handed her a five-pound note. Like a punter. He hadn't slept with her for two years but some mistakes you paid for all your life. She didn't know who the boy's father was. No doubt about the girl though, she said. The girl could have been fathered by anyone, he said, but he knew in his heart she was his. And if he denied it she'd go to his wife. She was always threatening.

'We have to talk,' she said, lighting up a cigarette.

'Do we?' he said.

The photographs were fanned out on her cheap glass coffee table. 'Look at that,' she said, pointing at a photograph of all four of them together, 'like a real family.'

'Not really,' he said. She'd hauled a youth working in

a chip shop outside and asked him to take the picture 'of us all together'.

She had been nagging since Christmas about wanting a day out and they'd ended up in Scarborough in a gale force wind. The place was deserted. At least it meant that the chances of him seeing anyone he knew would be nil.

She'd run down to the sea and taken her shoes and tights off and left them lying on the sand. Her tights looked as if a snake had shed its skin. She ran into the water and danced around in the waves. 'Jesus Christ, it's fucking freezing!' she yelled at him. 'Come on in, the water's lovely.'

'Don't be ridiculous,' he said.

'Coward! Your daddy's a cowardy custard!' she said to the boy when she ran back on to the beach.

'Don't call me that,' he said irritably, 'I'm not his father.' He had taken the boy to one side and said, 'Don't call me Daddy. Or Dad. Don't. OK? I'm not your father. I don't know who your father is. If your mother doesn't then why the fuck should I?'

She had been unpredictable, embarrassing to be out with in public, he had realized. 'Larger than life, me,' she said, but it was more than that. He thought that perhaps she had some kind of mental illness.

She'd brought a camera with her, a cheap second-hand thing, and insisted on taking photographs all the time. He'd tried to avoid her snapping him but had finally agreed to one to shut her up.

'Let's see if we can find somewhere that's open for ice

creams.' It was early March, out of season and freezing, nobody ate ice cream by the sea in winter. 'Or chips!' she said, getting excited. 'Let's all have chips!'

He was holding the girl in his arms, trying to protect her from the wind. 'Come on, I'll race you!' she shouted at the boy but he was intent on digging a sandcastle in the wet, muddy sand. Carol ran off towards the pier. The wind seemed to bowl her along. He wished it would take her away altogether.

'Like a real family,' she said, running her hands over the photos, squinting at them through her cigarette smoke. She had begun to talk about them being 'a proper family', hinting that he could leave his wife. She was completely deluded.

It seemed to go on from there. She said she would go round and see his wife and take the kids with her and shame him on his own doorstep. He said, 'Be quiet, you'll wake the whole neighbourhood.' She began to hit him, flailing at him with her fists. He hit her back hard, an open-handed slap to the face, he thought that would be enough to stop her but instead she became hysterical, screaming her head off. She had her claws out and the next thing he knew he was chasing her into the bedroom and had his hands round her throat. And if he was honest it felt good. Just to shut her up for once. To stop her.

It was over in seconds. She was such a force of nature that he hadn't expected she would suddenly go limp like that. He knelt down and felt for a pulse and didn't believe it when he couldn't find one. He hadn't meant to *kill* her. He glanced up and saw the boy standing in the hallway, staring at him, but all he could think of was getting out of that place. He ran down the stairs, couldn't wait for the lift, got into his car, drove into town and sat in a pub where he downed a double malt. His hands were shaking. His whole life in ruins before him. He would lose his job, his marriage, his reputation.

He stayed there drinking. It took a lot to get him drunk. He lost count of the time.

'One more for the road, detective?' the barman said and he said, 'No,' and went to the Gents and threw up.

There was a phone box round the corner and he found refuge in its cold white light. He phoned the only person he could think of who might get him out of this mess, he phoned Eastman. 'Sir?' he said. 'It's Len Lomax here. I've got myself into a spot of bother.' He didn't mention the boy.

Ray handed him the photos the next day and said, 'We're even. Don't ask for another favour ever, OK, Len?'

'She was definitely dead, was she?' Len asked. He had spent the rest of the night tossing and turning next to Alma, imagining Carol Braithwaite coming to, pointing an accusing finger at him.

'Yes,' Ray said. 'She was dead.' He looked disgusted. 'I took the girl to the Winfields. They're not going to question anything, trust me.' Ray didn't mention the boy because he didn't know about him.

The Winfields had been Eastman's idea. 'I'll get

Strickland to take the kiddy round,' he said. 'You're in no shape to do anything. Get yourself home to Alma. Do you have keys? To her flat?'

The next day Eastman invited Len for a game of golf. 'You're not a bad man, Len,' he said, practising his swing. 'A bad thing happened to you, that doesn't mean that your life should be destroyed, not on account of one dead whore. And that kiddy of yours has gone to a wonderful home, think of everything she'll have.' Len still didn't mention the boy.

He expected Carol to be found. That's what happened, people died, other people found them. Then time went on and nothing happened. It began to seem unreal, it began to seem as if it had never happened at all. He'd had a cousin, Janet, still had her but nobody in the family talked about her much any more. Aged fourteen she gave birth in her bedroom at home. Nobody even knew she was pregnant, everybody just thought she was getting a bit fat. When her mother asked her why she hadn't said anything, Janet said she'd hoped that if she ignored it, it would all just go away. That was how Len felt. He never thought about whether the boy was alive or dead, never really thought about the boy at all.

'What are you brooding on?' Alma asked.

'Nothing,' he said, gave her some flim-flam about stress at work.

When they got the call it was a shock, like a body blow, like some bugger running into him on the rugby field.

'Woman's body discovered in the Lovell Park flats, uniforms in attendance.' Still no one mentioned the boy. Len wondered if he really had disappeared. Melted into thin air.

'Jesus,' Strickland said. 'This is going to be difficult. Her body's been there for weeks.'

Eastman caught them before they got in the car. 'Now then, steady, lads, steady,' he said. 'Keep your heads.'

Len finally mentioned the boy.

'You daft bastard,' Eastman said. 'You should have said something, I could have helped you clear up the mess a lot sooner.'

It never struck him that the boy might still be alive. He'd expected they would have two bodies on their hands. Couldn't believe it when he saw the boy in that WPC's arms.

The boy was a witness, of course. Eastman 'had a word' with the social worker. Neither Len nor Ray knew what he said. Threatened her with losing her own kiddy probably. He was a good man to have on your side but a very bad one to have against you. Ray followed up for him, caught her coming from the hospital and took her for a drink in the Cemetery Tavern. 'She's sound,' he reported back to Len. 'She's terrified. Eastman said the Drug Squad would "find" hard drugs in her place.'

Eastman got a gagging order 'to protect the boy', his name was changed and he was put into a Catholic orphanage. Len never heard anything more about him. The Winfields got new papers for Nicola, that bad bastard Harry Reynolds organized it, and then they buggered off to New Zealand. New Zealand might as well have been Jupiter or Mars as far as Len was concerned. It had all been a nightmare, he told himself, a terrible nightmare. A hole that opened up in front of his feet and then closed over again.

Eastman phoned him, gave him his instructions. Pick up the girl from the Lovell Park flats, lock up behind you. Eastman gave him a set of keys. 'Forget about what you see inside.' He told Ray to take the girl to the Winfields. 'We're doing the right thing here, Ray,' Eastman said. 'It might not be the letter of the law, but it's a moral imperative. Giving the kiddy a good home instead of her ending up who knows where. I phoned Ian Winfield, he knows what to expect but he'll pretend to be surprised. For the wife's sake, you know, she can get a bit overwrought.'

When they arrived at the Lovell Park flats three weeks later, Ray said to Len, 'I can't go in there again, Len. I can't face what we're going to find in there.' They had argued before they had gone up in the lift. 'Band of brothers,' Len said, thumping him on the shoulder, more aggression than affection. 'All for one, one for all.' Eastman's motto.

Len had *known*. He had known about that kiddy in the flat and left him there.

'I thought he'd be found,' Len said. 'And then, I don't know, it just became unreal.' Attempted murder as far as Ray was concerned. He threw up his breakfast when he saw the state of the kid. If he had known he would never in a million years have left that kiddy behind in that place.

Ray had paid a visit to Carol Braithwaite at New Year. He'd been drunk, missing sex with Anthea, unwilling to go back to Margaret, sober and schoolmarmish in her cotton nightdresses. So he had gone to see Lomax's whore. Never done that before, never been with a prostitute. 'An uncomplicated fuck,' he imagined Len saying.

Carol Braithwaite opened the door to him and said flatly, 'I'm not doing business tonight, go and look somewhere else.' She looked tired, old before her time. She was holding a little girl in her arms. It seemed wrong that women like her got to be mothers just by opening their legs to any man and his own wife couldn't get a baby to save her life. He didn't know at the time that the kiddy was Len's. No sign of the boy.

'Fuck off, why don't you?' Carol said.

He'd sent Barry Crawford home by then, of course. No hope of getting a taxi in the early hours of 1975. He'd walked all the way home, tail between his legs, and slipped into bed next to Margaret. Told her he loved her.

The worst thing wasn't what happened to the boy, nor was it the fact that Len murdered Carol Braithwaite or that Eastman helped cover it up. The worst thing was that when Ray whisked the little girl away – stole her, really – and he was sitting in the back of Crawford's Cortina he realized they were driving past his own house. There was a light on downstairs, Margaret waiting up for him probably, sitting there knitting, listening to the radio. She preferred the radio to the TV. He could have pulled into his own driveway, rung his own doorbell and given the best gift possible to his own wife. But he hadn't done that, he'd given that little girl to Kitty Winfield instead. And the boy. He could have saved that little boy, brought him up as his own. Two chances, both lost.

Barry thought he would puke when he went into that flat. He hadn't thought of anyone actually being *dead* in there, he just thought Strickland had taken the kid. But when he heard about the little boy, he realized that he had been left behind that night. Imagined what his own mother would have to say about that. She loved kiddies, couldn't wait for Barry to get wed and become a father. Eastman had called him. Told him to help clean up the mess. Didn't say who had made the mess but it was pretty obvious to Barry that it was Ray Strickland.

She was sleeping peacefully. He watched the rise and fall of her chest. She was never going to wake up, never going to be Amy again. She would have hated to be here like this, would have begged Barry to put an end to it. The last thing you would ever wish for your child turned out to be the one thing you had to do. He took the pillow from beneath her head and held it over her face. 'I love you, pet,' Barry said. He tried to think of something else to say, something bigger and more important but there wasn't anything, he'd said the only thing that mattered. He thought that she might struggle but she didn't. The only difference when he took the pillow away was that her chest no longer rose and fell.

He felt empty of everything now. It was a good feeling. He checked his watch. Twelve o'clock. Ivan was getting out of Armley Jail at one. He'd better get a move on. Barry felt the heft of the gun in his pocket. He liked the feel of it, it put him in control. A Baikal. Gangland gun of choice. Modified in Lithuania, here you pay twenty times what you would for them there, apparently. He'd never actually seen one before. This one was courtesy of Harry Reynolds. All these old blokes who wouldn't give up their thrones. Strickland, Lomax, Harry Reynolds.

He'd picked it up on his way over. Found Harry Reynolds fumbling with a black tie. 'Arthritis in the thumbs,' he said. 'What do they say – old age doesn't come by itself.' The house smelled of apple pie. Harry gave him the Baikal and Barry gave him an envelope. 'Get that to Tracy, will you?' he said.

'You could have given it to her yourself if you'd been here earlier. She's in the wind now.'

'Good. How much do I owe you for the gun?'

'Treat it as a gift, Superintendent Crawford. A thank-you for the neglect you've shown me over the years.'

* * *

He left Amy's room and didn't look back. How could you look back? You couldn't. One to the head, one to the heart. Bang bang.

'Ivan,' he said. Ivan stared at him, deer in the headlights, for a moment Barry thought he was going to turn round and run away. Or thump on the door of the prison and beg the wardens to let him back in.

'Barry,' Ivan said.

There you go again, Barry thought, calling him Barry. He felt the gun in his pocket. Barry took his hand out of his pocket, stuck it out in front of him. Slowly and hesitantly, Ivan took the hand. Shook it.

'I'm sorry,' Barry said. 'I was harsh. My daughter loved you, I should have thought about that more.'

'You're apologizing?' Ivan said uncertainly.

'That flash-drive you lost? Barbara found it down the back of the sofa after you and Amy had been round for lunch one Sunday. She had no idea what it was, of course, doesn't know the first thing about computers. I knew it was yours, stuck it in a vase on the mantelpiece. I just thought . . . I don't know what I thought, suppose that I'd mess you about. I didn't know it had all your clients' details on it, that it was important.

'Barbara didn't tell me what happened,' he continued, 'I just thought the business had gone down. She didn't tell me why, thought I'd think you were even more of an incompetent pillock than I already did. Mind you, you *are* an incompetent pillock,' Barry added. He wasn't a man for unqualified grovelling. 'But,' he said, 'you didn't deserve what happened.'

'None of us did,' Ivan said.

Barry got back in the car and drove away. Not interested in a dialogue. He didn't tell Ivan that Amy had gone for good. Ivan could start again. Barry couldn't. But first he had a funeral to attend.

Rex Marshall's funeral was in the crematorium. The place was stuffed to the gunnels with the great and the good come to say goodbye to him. The coffin was the centrepiece, his gleaming police medals laid out on top of it. Wreaths and bouquets all lined up at the entrance to the chapel. Barry caught the scent of freesias, turned him funny for a second. He could see Ray Strickland standing at a lectern giving the eulogy – '. . . a senior policeman who never lost the common touch, a man of the people . . .' *Blah, blah, blah*. The usual shit. Ray hesitated when he caught sight of Barry standing in the doorway.

Overweight men in expensive suits, underweight women in the kind of clothes Barbara would like to be able to afford, they all turned to look at what had made Ray stop mid-sentence. Barry caught sight of Harry Reynolds in the back row. Paying his respects. Making a point of not looking at Barry as he barged into the chapel and, marching up to the coffin, rapped on it hard with his knuckles. 'Knock, knock,' he said, 'is there anybody there?' A murmur of distress rose up from the people closest to the coffin.

'Just checking,' Barry said to a stout woman who was clutching a photocopied programme for the service. He grinned at her and she shrank from him in horror. He wrestled the programme from her hands. Order of events. It was cheap and flimsy, like something an amateur theatrical company would produce. On the cover there was a photograph of Rex Marshall in his prime. Barry tapped the photograph and said conversationally to the stout woman, 'He was a right bastard. But then takes one to know one, that's what they say, eh?'

All around him the great and the good began to protest, but in a muted way as no one likes to openly challenge someone who is clearly deranged. Out of the corner of his eye, Barry saw Harry Reynolds slink out of the chapel. No sign of Len Lomax anywhere. Barry was surprised he hadn't been rugby-tackled by now but he carried on up the aisle, unimpeded. The grieving widow flinched as he approached and the – ridiculously young – vicar twitched as if he was considering confronting him. Barry grunted, 'Don't even think about it, lad.'

He reached the lectern and Ray, all conciliatory, hail fellow, well met, said, 'Come on, Barry, be sensible. Take a pew and show some respect.' Barry cocked his head to one side as if he might be weighing this up as an option but then he turned and looked out over the sea of the great and good and cleared his throat as if he was the toastmaster about to tell the assembled company to raise their glasses. He said, 'Raymond James Strickland, I am arresting you for the murder of Carol Anne

Braithwaite, the reckless endangerment of the life of Michael Braithwaite and the abduction of Nicola Jane Braithwaite. You do not have to say anything, but it may harm your defence if you do not mention, when questioned, something which you later rely on in court. Anything you do say may be given in evidence.'

Ray didn't even move, just stood there. Barry had half expected him to concertina down to the floor in shock, but he stayed where he was, eyes wide. 'It wasn't me,' he said.

Barry laughed. 'They all say that. You should know that, Ray.'

Barry hadn't thought much beyond this point. He had his handcuffs with him though – never without – and he slapped one cuff on Ray and the other on the brass rail that bordered the front of the lectern. Then he took his phone from his pocket and rang the station and asked for a couple of uniforms.

Everyone in the crematorium seemed to have lost their appetite for death. Barry watched as a couple of women in designer black picked their way from the chapel like gazelle that had suddenly found they had strayed into the lions' enclosure. Then they all began to melt away. All the great and the good.

The vicar hovered like a nervous waiter and asked Barry if he could get him anything. 'No, lad,' Barry said, 'but thanks for asking.'

'Last men standing,' Barry said to Ray.

'Thirty-five years ago, Barry,' Ray said. 'It's history, water under the bridge.'

'I don't understand,' a soft voice said. Margaret, Ray's wife. If he'd been in a kind mood Barry would have said, 'Get your husband to explain,' but he wasn't in a kind mood, and so he said, 'Your husband fathered a child on a prostitute called Carol Braithwaite and after he had murdered Carol Braithwaite he took that child – his daughter – and gave her away to your bosom friend, Kitty Winfield.' The truth was going to come out anyway, might as well be Barry who told it. *Speaking truth to power.* That was what the Quakers said, he'd had to arrest a few in the eighties, peaceniks, yakking on about 'direct action' and Cruise missiles. For people who worshipped in silence they seemed to talk a lot.

'Ray?' Margaret said.

'It wasn't me,' Ray said again, this time to Margaret. 'It really wasn't.' He turned back to Barry and said, 'You only saw half the story, Barry.'

'Tell it to the judge, Ray.'

A lone uniformed constable arrived, could have been Barry thirty-five years ago. You'd do anything a superior officer told you to. Turn a blind eye? Yes, boss. Keep your mouth shut. Yes, boss. Three bags full, boss. A dogsbody.

'Boss?'

'Take this gentleman into custody, officer. He's been charged with murder. I'm not coming. When you get to the station, go to my office. There's a letter on my desk. I want you to give it to DI Gemma Holroyd and she'll take it from there.'

'Yes, sir.'

'Good lad.'

*   *   *

He drove to the moors above Ilkley, all the way to Upper Barden Reservoir. There wasn't a soul around. The sky marbled with clouds, all tinged with opal. Like a painting, lovely. Barry imagined Carol Braithwaite rising. The Assumption. Carol Braithwaite hand in hand with Amy. Carol and Amy, one to the head, one to the heart.

Pair of buzzards circled overhead, waiting for him.

1975: October

Wilma McCann's body was found on the eve of Halloween on a typical foggy Leeds morning on the Prince Philip Playing Fields in Chapeltown. Two head wounds, fifteen stab wounds. Convictions for drunkenness, disorderly conduct and theft. Her four children left alone in a filthy house. Another good-time girl.

Wilma McCann's was just one of several sordid deaths, nothing to write home about, yet three months later 137 police officers had clocked up 53,000 hours, taken 538 statements and accumulated 3,300 index card references. All leading to nothing. Everyone still gloriously innocent of the fact that it was Sutcliffe's first official kill. There wouldn't be another one until January of the following year. Carol Braithwaite, on the other hand, seemed to clock up hardly any police hours at all.

Tracy took no part in the investigation into Wilma McCann's murder. She was still in uniform, another working girl, walking the streets.

'It's different anyway,' Barry said. 'Your woman—'

'My woman?'

'The Braithwaite woman was killed in her own home. Strangled, not hit on the head and stabbed.'

'You're talking like you're in CID already, Barry. All that brown-nosing paying off, is it?'

'Piss off.'

Leeds, Manchester, Huddersfield, Bradford. Emily Jackson in January of the following year. The roll-call went on and on. Not just prostitutes any more, any woman would do. The last two in 1980. In the wrong place at the right time. Marilyn Moore's photofit early on was one of the best they had. The Jason King beard, the mean little eyes. Over five million vehicles logged. He was the devil and he couldn't be caught.

The past was a dark place, a man's world. There was a time when the male officers escorted the WPCs and the female office staff across to the car park. She heard one of the blokes say, 'I wouldn't worry about Tracy Waterhouse. Pity t'Ripper if he tackles her.'

No chance of Carol Braithwaite being remembered once Sutcliffe's reign of terror was in full swing. Carol Braithwaite pretty much fitted the victim profile. But they didn't really do victim profiles in those days. Tracy would wonder for years to come if Carol Braithwaite hadn't been one of Sutcliffe's first.

Tracy ended 1975 in style by buying a five-year-old

Datsun Sunny. At the end of the year Kirkgate Market burned down and she used her warrant card to get past the safety barriers and have a better look at the conflagration. It seemed a good way to say goodbye to the year, everything going up in flames.

1977 was a busy year for the Ripper. Barry moved on and up, made plainclothes in 1980. Tracy had a new boyfriend. A twenty-eight-year-old sharp-suited, degree-toting medical instruments salesman. Not a great degree that he toted, just a third in 'business management' from a new concrete university, but a degree more than Tracy was in possession of.

He had taken her as far afield as Durham and Flamborough Head in the lime-green Ford Capri that he drove like a maniacal test pilot. Tracy never squashed herself awkwardly into the passenger seat without thinking that she might die before journey's end. That was part of the attraction of it, probably.

They drank in beer gardens throughout the north-east, Timothy Taylor's Landlord, with Wood's Old Navy rum chasers, for him, pints of snakebite for Tracy. Then they would go back to his flat and eat Indian takeaways and he would light up a big spliff and say, 'Are you going to handcuff me, officer?' Same 'joke' every time. Tracy never partook, preferred her mind to be altered by alcohol, not drugs. The sex was quite good, although she only had Dennis the driving instructor as a comparison, but that must have been what kept her because the bloke was, let's face it, a complete wanker. When he dumped her for a more streamlined model, she phoned him in anonymously to the Drug Squad. Never heard if anything came of it. He died in a car smash in 1985, wrapped his TVR coupé round a disobliging tree.

Lime-green Capri – same car as the Ripper was driving in '75. She should have phoned him in for that as well. Tracy had never seriously considered him for it. He was too self-obsessed to be bothered to kill anyone. Still, she notched up her first broken heart. She was, slowly but surely, passing the landmarks of life.

Linda Pallister hooked up with some bloke from the Labour Party and moved to a house near Roundhay, a traditional between-the-wars semi, not Linda's style at all. She gave birth to Chloe in the same year that Barry's Amy was born. In lieu of a christening, Barry and Barbara threw 'a little party' to welcome the baby. Sausage rolls, pork pie, cake made by Barbara's mother and a crate of Asti Spumante. Tracy wasn't invited.

Linda Pallister threw a party for her new baby as well. Tracy not invited to that one either. No pork pie for Linda. Rumour had it that she dished up the baby's placenta. Raw or cooked? Tracy wondered.

Ray Strickland was never promoted above the rank of DCI. Said he was happy with that, didn't want to spend his time driving a desk. Lomax, on the other hand, went to the top of the tree, took all the laurels going.

Life went on. Before Tracy knew it she had clocked up thirty years and was getting pissed at her own leaving do.

Treasure

June

'And you saw it happen? You saw poor old Tilly go under the train? What on earth were you doing there?'

'It had nothing to do with me,' Jackson said.

'The inquest ruled it was an accident,' Julia said. 'Which I was glad about because I really don't think Tilly was the suicidal type. She was in the early stages of dementia though, poor old thing, so I suppose you don't know what was going through her mind, do you? I went to the funeral, in St Paul's in Covent Garden. It was a lovely service actually, lots of people saying nice things about dear old Till. Her friend Dame Phoebe March gave the eulogy, chewed up the scenery, of course, but it was good, really moving – all sorts of anecdotes about Tilly when she was young.'

You just had to wind Julia up and let her go.

Jackson was picking her up from the set of *Collier* and giving her a lift to the airport. She had a couple of weeks off. Her pathologist character, Beatrice Butler, was spending the time in a coma after being attacked by the crazed relative of a – oh, as if Jackson cared.

Julia was amusing herself with the dog, crouching

down and running her hand along its spine, like a masseuse. 'Roll over and die for queen and country,' she commanded and the dog spun over on to its back with its legs in the air.

To look at it, anyone would think the dog had a crush on Julia. Julia herself, of course, was in love with every dog on the planet. Unfortunately every dog on the planet made her sneeze.

'This used to be a woman's dog,' Julia said.

'Well, he's a man's dog now,' Jackson said defiantly.

He was in the middle of fitting the booster seat that he had finally bought for Nathan. ('About time,' Julia said.) Jackson had managed to rescue a grateful Saab – mysteriously denuded of the light-up Virgin Mary – from a police pound just before it was sent to auction, thanks to Brian Jackson's tracker. It had been found abandoned in the grounds of Fountains Abbey, a location that baffled Jackson. It was as if Jane had known where he wanted to go and had tried to make her way there ahead of him. 'That's ludicrous,' Julia said.

Nathan was following him around, telling him about dinosaurs, barely stumbling over the names, 'Velociraptor, Avaceratops, Diplodocus.' Jackson wasn't sure if his son knew they were extinct, didn't want to ask him in case he spoiled some kind of mystery, like Santa Claus and the Tooth Fairy. Jackson didn't know that four-year-old boys could pronounce words like 'Avaceratops'. He could barely remember Marlee at that age, her current sullen incarnation had begun to dominate earlier, sunnier versions of his daughter. Of course, there were a lot of things he didn't know about four-year-old boys. He thought of his son as a baby and it was disturbing to see how far along the road to manhood he had already walked. One day that boy would outrun him, overtake him in the relay race of existence. And so it would go on and on until the sun cooled, or the meteor hit, or that bloody great volcano beneath Yellowstone grumbled its way back into life.

'Well, everything dies,' Julia said, absorbed in scratching the dog's belly and staving off a sneeze. 'That's the way it goes. *Omnia mors aequat*. The great leveller.'

'From darkness we come and to darkness shall we return,' Jackson said. Darkly.

'I think it's dust, not darkness,' Julia said. 'And I choose to think that we come from the light and return to the light.'

'What a glass-half-full kind of person you are.'

'One of us has to be,' Julia said. 'Or the glass would be entirely empty.' *One of us*, as if they were a couple. Yet she was going to Italy on holiday, 'with a friend'.

'Who?' Jackson asked and she shrugged and said, 'Just a friend.'

'Could you be any vaguer?'

This despite the fact that Jackson had suggested to her that perhaps the three of them might take a holiday together during her time off. A step towards reconciliation, perhaps towards reunion.

'Like a family holiday?' she said and Jackson thought about it and said, 'Yes, I suppose that is what I mean.'

Julia wrinkled her nose and said, 'No, sweetie, I don't think so.'

He was surprised at how disappointed he felt. But then women were full of surprises. Every one of them, every which way, every day.

'Where is Jonathan anyway?' he asked.

Julia put up a hand as if stopping traffic, as if stopping an enormous towering truck. 'I'm not speaking about Jonathan. OK?'

'Happy never to mention his name again, I'm sure.'

'That poor boy,' she said, putting her arms protectively around her own boy. Their boy.

'Michael?'

'He went through so much.'

'He's OK now.'

'In the same way that you and I are?' Julia said. 'After what happened to us when we were children?'

'Yeah. That way.'

Michael Braithwaite was on his way to New Zealand even as they were speaking. A brother and sister reunion. He was a nice bloke, top-to-toe denim, over-weight, unhealthy, cheerful. He liked nothing more than a barbecue with his wife and kids next to his swimming pool. He'd made a fortune in scrap. Some people lived their life against all the odds.

'You and me too, sweetie,' Julia said, patting him on the hand.

Linda Pallister had returned to Leeds and was set to appear before a tribunal and be made to answer for her actions. ('Ah, the whirligig of time,' Julia said.) She had helped a four-year-old witness to disappear. Put him in a care home in Roundhay run by nuns, changed his name. And never mentioned his sister to anyone. Told the nuns he was a liar, lied all the time, about having a sister, about his dad killing his mum. When Michael was eighteen he was handed his birth certificate and found out his name, but Linda Pallister never came forward and told him the truth about his mother, or his sister. 'She was coerced,' Michael Braithwaite said, 'her own kid threatened.'

'Not an excuse,' the two Jacksons said in unison. Brian Jackson, Michael Braithwaite and Jackson were eating lunch in the bistro in 42 The Calls. Jackson, still shaken by the scene on Leeds station, drank a double malt instead of lunch.

Michael Braithwaite's memories faded until the slate was wiped clean, but he realized there was an emptiness that would destroy him eventually. 'Therapy in rehab,' he shrugged. 'My name is Michael Braithwaite and I'm an alcoholic, all that stuff.' Guiltily, Jackson put his whisky down. 'Decided to go looking,' Michael Braithwaite said.

'And found me,' Brian Jackson said, beaming. 'Twenty years in the Met behind me. Give me a task and I'm like a dog with a bone.' Jackson had begun to think of Brian Jackson as his doppelgänger – God knows why – but now he could see that really he was his polar opposite. 'Made an appointment with Linda Pallister, tracked her down,' Brian Jackson said. 'Dog, bone, et cetera. She spilled the beans, most of them anyway, seemed keen to get it off her chest. Changed her mind, took fright, of course.'

Brian Jackson's phone rang – the opening bars of Beethoven's Fifth, Da-da-da-*daa*. Sounded naff on a phone. He didn't answer it. 'In constant demand,' he said to Jackson.

Linda Pallister had not been squirrelled away by Brian Jackson. She had, despite her daughter Chloe's protestations, simply run away. 'Bolted,' Brian Jackson said, 'to avoid facing the music.' She had caught an easyJet flight to Malaga and hidden herself away like a desperado in a cheap apartment block on the Costa del Sol.

'It's all quite banal really, isn't it?' Julia said. 'People frightened of losing their jobs, their reputations, their marriages. You feel that tragedy should be more *operatic* somehow.'

Jackson's knee-jerk reaction was to disagree with her but when he thought about it he suspected Julia might be right. His own sister, as beautiful as she was, more beautiful than was possible in his memory, wanted nothing more than the most ordinary of lives and what she got was the most ordinary of murders. A random act of violence. A girl who opened the wrong box. As far as her killer was concerned, Niamh could probably have been anyone – the girl before her, the girl after her. Better to go up in flames at the stake, or jump from a mountain ledge, be torn apart by wolves, rather than have your fate placed in the hands of some wanker waiting at a bus stop.

'The Ambassador loves having his tummy tickled,' Julia said.

Jackson was definitely going to give the dog a different name. He wondered what Louise, back in Edinburgh, had called the puppy he had given her. She probably hadn't even kept it.

'Where are you going now?' Julia asked him when he said goodbye to her at security in Manchester airport.

'Journey's end,' he said.

'In lovers meeting?'

'I doubt it.'

He was still looking for a new home, he had to lay his head down somewhere every night. He supposed he was still looking for his thieving wife as well, but his enthusiasm for the hunt had cooled. He suspected he might have done with travelling for now. He held Nathan, the boy, in his arms, and kissed him goodbye. And there it was.

To his surprise, to his alarm – the fierce churning of the heart, the unbreakable, sacrificial bond. Love. He knew who he was, he was this boy's father.

It just went to show, you never knew what you were going to feel until you felt it. It was terrifying, although Julia would have said 'wonderful', being the full half of the glass.

'Stop putting words in my mouth,' Julia said.

In the security control room at the Merrion Centre, Grant had his feet up, reading the paper instead of watching the screens. Leslie could see the headline in the paper, 'Leeds prostitute murders – man held for questioning' and then something about 'a new Ripper'.

'It never stops,' Leslie said.

'Slappers, what do you expect?' Grant said, reaching for a packet of Monster Munch.

'I expect people to behave better.'

'You'll be waiting a long time. What've you got there?' Grant asked.

'A purse.' Someone had handed it in, found it in the car park. The purse was bulky, stuffed with all kinds of things, credit cards, store cards, little cards with dental and hair appointments, some of them well out of date. Notes of the 'Remember to' variety that the owner must have written to herself. *Miss Matilda Squires*. Leslie remembered her, how upset she'd been. She found a note tucked into the back of the purse with a name and address on it. 'My address,' it said helpfully, just in case someone wanted to steal her identity or turn up on her doorstep and rob her at knifepoint. 'Matilda Squires,' Leslie said. 'Isn't that the name of the actress who fell under the train?'

'Dunno,' Grant said. He turned the page and gawped openly at the good-as-naked Page 3 girl on offer. Leslie missed Tracy. She didn't allow sleazy newspapers and snack food. Leslie wondered why she had never come back from holiday.

'Maybe she's dead,' Grant said, quite animated by the

idea. She wasn't dead. She had sent Leslie a postcard, a picture of the London Eye, and on the back Tracy had written, 'Won't be coming back, it was nice knowing you, have a good life, best wishes, Tracy.' She didn't tell Grant. The message wasn't for him.

Leslie was decamping as well. She hadn't told anyone but her flight to Canada left in a couple of days. She had taken her cue from Tracy, she was simply going to disappear. She'd get a job for the summer, go to the lake with her parents and her brother and her dog and then after that she'd get started on her good life. Leave this place far behind.

❧

The best room in the house. The 'Sleeping Beauty suite'. It was meant for a bigger family, of course, but big and best was what Tracy wanted for the kid. She had been lucky to get the suite, only managed it because the hotel had a last-minute cancellation. Tracy's old friends, the world and his wife, or in this case Europe and his *Frau*, all seemed to be taking their holidays in Disneyland Paris at the same time.

She had expected there would be only parents with children in the park but there were all sorts of permutations – groups of young guys, gangs of giggling girls, old couples and honeymooners. Tracy couldn't imagine why you would want to spend a romantic break in the centre of the dark beating heart of capitalism.

There was even the occasional lone male. 'Beware,' Tracy murmured to the kid.

It was surprising how easy it was to step out of one life and into another. They had spent a couple of weeks lost in London, where no one knew who you were or cared. They'd tested out their new identities on doctors and dentists and opticians. Kid had had her ears syringed, eyes tested, wore specs now. Added to her allure. Tracy, or rather Imogen Brown, had opened a new bank account and Harry Reynolds had transferred funds into it, all nicely laundered with a credible history. She was surprised, she hadn't actually expected him to come through with the money, thought he would simply sell her house on and pocket the profit.

When they passed through passport control at St Pancras Tracy had expected there to be questions, expected to be scrutinized suspiciously. Expected an expressionless official to take them to one side and say, 'Would you just come this way, madam?' but they boarded the Eurostar train with ease and in no time at all they were in the Magic Kingdom.

The kid had her priorities. In the hotel shop Tracy bought her a new fairy outfit – Tinker Bell's green attire. The matching wand had a butterfly hovering on the top. Half the kids in the hotel were dressed up, dozens of fairies and Peter Pans, the occasional pirate. You couldn't walk along a hotel corridor without bumping into an adult re-enactor pretending to be Goofy or Mary Poppins. It was surreal and vaguely alarming. The kid accepted it as normal.

'Mirror, mirror on the wall,' Tracy said when they returned to the hotel suite, 'who's the fairest fairy of them all?'

'Me,' Courtney said when she saw her reflection. Little hands making stars, 'Twinkle, Twinkle'.

'You look lovely,' Tracy said.

'I do,' Courtney agreed.

They walked down Main Street towards the hallowed walls of Sleeping Beauty's castle. *Le Château de la Belle au Bois Dormant*. 'That's French,' Tracy said to Courtney. Everything was in French, because unlike other countries the French refused to compromise on that. What were those planning meetings like? All those Disney executives, the Mouse's men, sitting down to coffee and croissants around a table with French officials insisting that there would be no translation (*Non*) and the Americans trying to imagineer that.

Tracy wondered if Disneyland Paris was technically American soil and if she could throw herself on the mercy of Mickey and ask for asylum. They could move to the States, somewhere quiet, away from the public eye, Oregon, New Mexico, a small town in the Midwest, somewhere no one would look for them.

All the bright shiny places. Long way from the starlight and the firelight. Long, long way. They queued. And then they queued again. And then after they had queued they queued some more. They queued to see Sleeping Beauty's castle, they queued to see Snow White's cottage, both, frankly, rather disappointing. They queued to fly with Peter Pan into Neverland, which they both liked. They queued to ride around in the Mad Hatter's teacups and on Dumbo's back. They queued for the Voyages of Pinocchio which was rubbish and for Pirates of the Caribbean which was good and, they both agreed, just a little bit scary. They stood for an eternity corralled between railings in a queue that was like a fat snake, waiting to be loaded on to boats on a shallow artificial waterway before being carried away on the current, borne helplessly into the terrifying animatronic vision of 'It's A Small World'. When they finally escaped back into the big world they spent another lifetime in the pythonesque grip of a queue in order to ride on the Disneyland Railroad.

Kid was a heroic queuer.

They stood on Main Street and watched the parade go by and ate ice cream. By the end of the day Courtney had that stunned look again, the one abused kids wore. Tracy expected that if she looked in a mirror she would see the same look on her face as well. The music from 'It's A Small World' was lodged in Tracy's brain. She wasn't sure she'd ever be able to get rid of it.

'And we can do it all again tomorrow,' she said, as they staggered into the hotel through the back entrance.

This was what you did if you had a terminal illness,

wasn't it? You packed the days, took the helicopter flight over the Victoria Falls, the boat down the Nile, the train to Venice, the elevator to the top of the Empire State Building, You went on safari in Africa and played the slots in Vegas because you were suddenly greedy for the world you were about to lose. Or you just rode round in giant teacups taking endless photos of a kid giving you the thumbs-up. Wondering how long it could last.

When they returned to their Sleeping Beauty suite an envelope with the Disneyland logo and *Mme Imogen Brown* written on it had been pushed under the door. Tracy thought it would be information about activities in the park but inside the envelope was another one, one word, 'Tracy', handwritten on it. She'd been found. Her hand trembled as she opened the envelope. Another envelope. This was ridiculous. Again, her name written on it, a hand she recognized as Barry's. It was like Chinese whispers, was she just going to keep on opening envelopes that grew smaller and smaller until what, a final message? *Gotcha!* or *The treasure here is you?* When she turned over the third envelope she found a message written on the flap. A message from Harry Reynolds. Perhaps she shouldn't be surprised he'd been able to find her.

Tracy – Barry asked me to send you this. I owe him a couple of favours. Don't know if you heard but Barry's dead. Killed his daughter and then topped himself. Left a fucking mess behind. Len Lomax went under a train and Ray Strickland's

*being done for a prozzie murder decades ago. Thought you'd
like to know – yours, Harry.*

Turn your back for a minute and the world shifted on
its axis. There was a PS from Harry – *Took the money you
owed round to the Pole like you asked me.*

She put a cartoon on the TV for the kid and read
Barry's letter, finally found out the truth about Michael
Braithwaite. He had a sister. Tracy's heart dropped ten
floors. First thing the kiddy had said to her. *Where's my
sister?*

'What was your favourite thing?' Tracy asked Courtney
as they queued to go into the restaurant.

'My dress,' she said without hesitation.

The waiter led them to a table by the window where
they had an excellent view of Sleeping Beauty's illuminated castle. They toasted each other with wine and
Coca-Cola. Tracy drank a modest half-bottle of red
although she could have drunk a vineyard. She thought
of the kid, sitting next to her while they flew to
Neverland. The feeling of cherishing someone small
and helpless. Made her think of Michael Braithwaite, all
those years when nobody cared what happened to him.
A Lost Boy. She was grateful to Barry for providing her
with the happy ending. Poor old Barry, never
got to have his retirement do after all. She raised a silent
toast to him.

Mickey did the rounds of the tables. As did Goofy
and Pluto. The kid liked Pluto best. Thumbs-up all

round. Tracy took photo after photo. Terminal illness.

After dinner Courtney got dressed in her new Minnie pyjamas, bought in the hotel shop, and they ordered hot chocolate on room service, watched a DVD in bed. Disney obviously.

Kid had her chattels laid out on the bed:

the tarnished silver thimble
the Chinese coin with a hole in the middle
the purse with a smiling monkey's face on it
the snow globe containing a crude plastic model of
    the Houses of Parliament
the shell like a cream horn
the shell shaped like a coolie hat
the pine cone
Dorothy Waterhouse's sapphire engagement ring
the filigree leaf from the wood
the links from a cheap gold chain
the light-up Virgin Mary from the Saab
the silver star from the old wand

Another couple of years of this and they would need a truck to carry the kid's cargo around. *Another couple of years.* Tracy couldn't imagine she would be able to hang on to that future because although this was the beginning of something it felt like the end. Always had. Always would.

From now on Tracy would forever be looking over her shoulder, waiting for the knock on the door. Cameras had tracked them everywhere, if somebody was looking for them they would find them. Harry Reynolds had. And if the bad didn't get them then the good ones probably would.

When she bought the kid she made a covenant with the devil. She could have someone to love but it would cost her everything. She thought of the Little Mermaid, every step torture, a pain like the piercing of sharp swords. Just to be human, to love.

Kid dipped her wand in Tracy's direction. Granting a wish or casting a spell, hard to tell which. Courtney had knitted herself into Tracy's soul. What would happen if she was ripped away?

This was love. It didn't come free, you paid in pain. Your own. But then nobody ever said love was easy. Well, they did, but they were idiots.

Her phone rang. New phone, new name, new number. No one had the number. Perhaps it was her service provider with a courtesy call. Perhaps it was another mysterious caller, or even the same one. Or something more sinister. She switched the phone off, watched the DVD instead. Tinker Bell was looking for lost treasure. Wasn't everyone?

1975: 22 March

When he woke he immediately reached beneath the pillow for his favourite car, a blue-and-white panda police car. With the car clutched in one hand he climbed out of the bed he shared with his sister. They slept top-to-tail, squeezed in. 'Like sardines,' his mother said. His sister wasn't in the bed. He thought she must have gone through to their mother's bed some time in the night.

He was a monkey, his mother said. *Full of beans.* Sometimes his mother laughed and squeezed him and said he was *tiny*. He was four. Other times, when she was cross, she said, *For fuck's sake you're a big boy now, Michael, why don't you behave like one?* Sometimes she danced around the kitchen with him, he stood on the tops of her feet and she whirled him round and round, laughing and laughing, until he shouted at her to stop. Other times she told him to get out of her sight and stay out of it. He never knew how it was going to be.

He was hungry and went into the kitchen to get some cornflakes. There was nowhere to sit in the kitchen and he carried his bowl carefully through to the living room. He ate his cornflakes before he went to look for his mother. She was lying on the bedroom floor. He tried to wake her up. He switched the kettle on and made her a cup of tea the way he had watched her do. He spilled a lot of it and forgot to put milk and sugar in it. She said she had to start the day with a cup of tea and a fag. He went and looked for her fags. Put the cup of tea and the cigarettes next to her head but she still didn't wake up. Tried to put a cigarette in her mouth.

'Mummy?' he said and shook her. When she wouldn't wake up he lay down beside her and tried to cuddle her (*Who's my lovely boy, give us a cuddle then*). After a while he got bored, scrambled up off the floor and went looking for his other cars.

Later when she still hadn't got up he dragged a chair to the front door and tried to unlock it. He'd done it before but there was no key in the lock this time and it wouldn't open.

That night he got a blanket from his bed and lay down to sleep on the floor next to his mother. He did that for another two or three nights but after that he knew he couldn't. His mother had begun to smell funny. He closed the door of her bedroom and didn't look in there again.

He dragged the chair over to the window and every so often stood on it and tried to attract someone's attention down below, banging on the glass and waving, but no one ever saw him. The people looked like ants. He stopped trying after a while.

He had looked everywhere in the flat for his sister, worried that she was playing hide-and-seek and had got trapped in a cupboard or under a bed, but he couldn't find her anywhere. Kept shouting, *Nicky*? Or sometimes *Nicola! Come here!* The way his mother did when she was cross. His sister was funny, always doing silly things. His mother said, *Oh, you're so serious, Michael, you're going to be a serious old man. Your sister's going to be like me, Nicky knows how to have fun.* He missed his sister more than he missed his mother. Someone would come soon, he thought. But nobody did.

9 April

The sound of the doorbell ringing woke him up. Someone was banging on the door, saying they were police. Daddy was a policeman. He didn't like being called Daddy. He stumbled into the hallway and saw that the letterbox was open. He could see a mouth, the mouth was moving, saying something.

It's OK, it's OK, everything's OK now. Is Mummy there? Or your daddy? We're going to help you. It's OK.

The big policewoman was holding him tightly. *Where's my sister?* he whispered and she whispered back, *What, pet?* and the other woman, the one he would come to know as Linda, said, 'He doesn't have a sister, he's delirious.' Then she took him away in an ambulance. When they were in the ambulance he asked her again, 'Where's my sister?' and she said, 'Shush, you don't have a sister, Michael. You have to stop talking about her.' So he did. He locked her away where you lock away everything that's precious and he didn't bring her out again for over thirty years.

Fountains. At last.

There were deer and ancient trees and the long shadows of a midsummer evening. The trees were in full new leaf, the alchemy of green into gold. The sweet birds were singing. Julia would have loved it here.

He'd arrived after the gates were closed and had to find another, slightly less legal way in.

The deer were quiet, not startled at all by a man and a dog. The dog was on a lead. They walked past a big house and a church, both 'designed by Burges', whoever he was. Jackson may have been a trespasser but he was a well-informed trespasser. The place was better without people. Most things were, in Jackson's opinion. 'Just you and me,' he said to the dog.

The abbey itself didn't disappoint, although Jackson still preferred the more homely remains of Jervaulx. He let the dog off the lead and walked up to the High Ride, the path that ran along the top of the valley that sheltered Fountains. He stopped at Anne Boleyn's Seat to contemplate the glorious vista of lawns and water that led to the ruins of the abbey in the distance. No sign of any headless women. Twilight. In Scotland, where Louise was, it would be the gloaming.

He walked back down again and wandered amongst the ruins. The dog ran off, chasing like a cheetah after a rabbit. Jackson sat on the low stones of an old wall. He thought it might be part of the cloister but when he peered at the signage he saw that it was part of the latrines. Probably time he cashed in that prescription for spectacles.

'*This is my letter to the World*,' he said to the dog when it returned, rabbit-less, '*That never wrote to Me*.' The dog cocked its head. 'I don't know what it means either,' Jackson said. 'I think that's the whole point of poetry.'

Just for a second, he thought he saw his sister, dressed in white, running and laughing, the petals falling from her hair. But that was poetry too. Or a certain slant of light.

Because all this time, in all these places, standing in the bare ruined choirs and the echoing engine sheds or sitting in the tearooms and the Golden Fleece pubs, his sister was there in the shadows, laughing and shaking blossom off her clothes, out of her hair, like a bride, a shower of petals like thumbprints on the dark veil of her hair.

She was locked in the echo-chamber of his heart as the queen of the May, a holy virgin. ('For ever,' Julia said fiercely, thumping her chest and then keeping her arm folded across it like a warrior giving allegiance. 'Dead to the world but alive in your heart.' The eternal paradox of the missing.) She had gone before him and he was never going to catch her. He could live with that, he decided. It wasn't as if he had a choice.

'On the road again,' Jackson said, getting into the Saab. 'Miles to go, and so on.'

His compliant co-pilot in the footwell gave an encouraging little yap. Jane awaited instruction.

There was still something nagging at him. Not Michael and Hope, not Jennifer, the little girl in Munich – it was thinking about her missing brother that had finally prompted him into asking Marilyn Nettles the right question.

It was something else. A scar, a sign, a birthmark the

shape of Africa. Something he had seen recently. He supposed the small men in his brain would locate it eventually.

He was about to start the engine when his phone rang. *Louise*, the screen informed him. Jackson hesitated, imagining what might happen if he didn't answer it.

And what would happen if he did.

'Hope' is the thing with feathers –
That perches in the soul –
And sings the tune without the words –
And never stops – at all –

And sweetest – in the Gale – is heard –
And sore must be the storm
That could abash the little Bird
That kept so many warm –

I've heard it in the chillest land –
And on the strangest Sea –
Yet, never, in Extremity,
It asked a crumb – of Me.

Emily Dickinson

LIFE AFTER LIFE
Kate Atkinson

'If you wish to be moved and astonished, read it'
Hilary Mantel

*What if you had the chance to live your life again and again,
until you finally got it right?*

During a snowstorm in England in 1910, a baby is born
and dies before she can take her first breath.

During a snowstorm in England in 1910, the same baby
is born and lives to tell the tale.

What if there were second chances? And third chances?
In fact an infinite number of chances to live your life? Would
you eventually be able to save the world from its own inevitable
destiny? And would you even want to?

'Truly brilliant'
The Times

'Her most ambitious and most gripping work'
Guardian

'A dizzying and dazzling tour de force'
Daily Mail

'Deliriously inventive . . . magnificently tender and humane'
Observer